I0778285

Joseph Thomson

Mungo Park and the Niger

Outlook

Joseph Thomson

Mungo Park and the Niger

1. Auflage | ISBN: 978-3-73263-003-5

Erscheinungsort: Frankfurt am Main, Deutschland

Erscheinungsjahr: 2018

Outlook Verlag GmbH, Frankfurt.

Reproduction of the original.

The World's Great Explorers and Explorations.

Edited by J. Scott Keltie, Librarian, Royal Geographical Society; H. J. Mackinder, M.A., Reader in Geography at the University of Oxford; and E. G. Ravenstein, F.R.G.S.

MUNGO PARK AND THE NIGER.

MUNGO PARK.

MUNGO PARK AND THE NIGER.

BY
JOSEPH THOMSON,
AUTHOR OF "THROUGH MASAI LAND," ETC.

NEW YORK
DODD, MEAD & COMPANY
PUBLISHERS

EDITORIAL PREFACE.

The story of the world's exploration is always attractive. We naturally take a keen interest in the personality of the men who have dared to force their way into the unknown, and so unveiled to us the face of mother earth. The interest in the work of exploration has been particularly strong and widespread in recent years, and it is believed that a series of volumes dealing with the great explorers and explorations of the past is likely to prove welcome to a wide circle of readers. Without a knowledge of what has been accomplished, the results of the unprecedented exploring activity of the present cannot be understood. It is hoped, therefore, that the present series will supply a real want. With one or two exceptions, each volume will deal mainly with one leading explorer, bringing out prominently the man's personality, telling the story of his life, and showing in full detail what he did for the exploration of the world. When it may be necessary to depart somewhat from the general plan, it will always be kept in view that the series is essentially a popular one. When complete the series will form a Biographical History of Geographical Discovery.

The Editors congratulate themselves on having been able to secure the co-operation of men well known as the highest authorities in their own departments; their names are too familiar to the public to require introduction. Each writer is of course entirely responsible for his own work.

THE EDITORS.

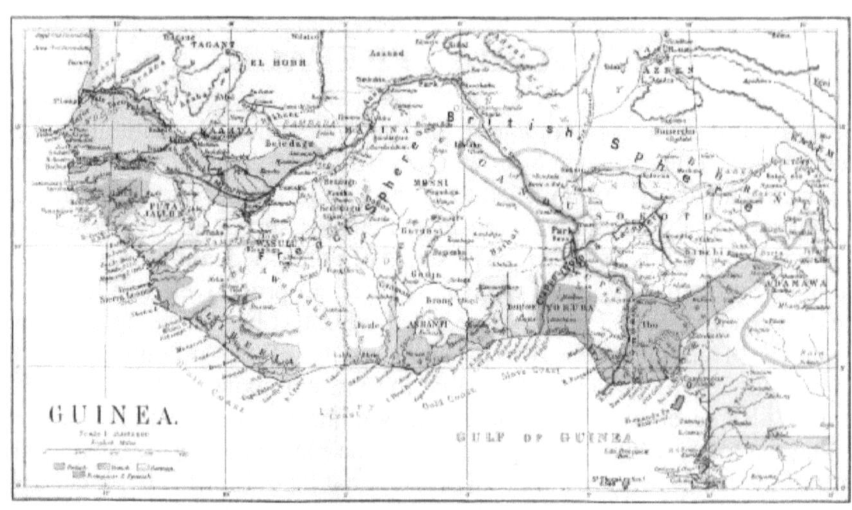

GUINEA.
TAGANT
EL HODH
KAARTA
FUTA JALLON
WASSULU
LIBERIA
MOSSI
ASHANTI
YORUBA
SOKOTO
ADAMAWA
AZBEN
British Sphere
GULF OF GUINEA
Grain Coast
Ivory Coast
Gold Coast
Slave Coast

MUNGO PARK AND THE NIGER.

CHAPTER I.
THE FIRST GLIMMERING OF LIGHT.

To find the first allusion to the River Niger we have to go back to the very dawn of history.

Many centuries before the Christian era the spirit of geographical inquiry was abroad. There were then, as in later times, ardent minds whose eager curiosity would not let them rest content with a knowledge of their own countries. Then, as in the Middle Ages, kings and emperors thirsted for political aggrandisement, merchants for new sources of wealth, and enterprising spirits for opportunities to do deeds of high emprise which would send their names down to posterity.

Phœnicia, Greece, Carthage, Rome, had each its bold navigators and travellers, whose explorations can be more or less credibly gleaned from the mass of fable and misrepresentation which time and ignorance have gathered round them.

Even in those early days—twenty or more centuries ago—Africa was the chief centre of attraction to such as longed to extend their possessions or their knowledge of the earth's surface. Already the mystery of the Nile and Inner Africa beyond the Great Desert had asserted its fascination over men's minds. The Mediterranean nations vied with each other in sending expedition after expedition to explore the coast-line, and if possible circumnavigate the continent. Of these some ventured by way of the Straits of Gibraltar—the Pillars of Hercules, as they were then called—while others tried the Red Sea and the eastern coast. What these ancient mariners actually accomplished has been for centuries a matter of keen dispute, with but small clearing up of the obscure horizon. It is not therefore for us to enter into the debatable land, and happily the questions involved lie outside our province. Sufficient for our purpose is it to know that very extensive voyages were undertaken along both the east and west coasts of Africa. Among the most noteworthy and credible of these is the expedition sent by Necho, King of Egypt, with Phœnician navigators, which is said to have accomplished the circumnavigation of the continent; and the Carthaginian expedition of Hanno, which undoubtedly explored the western coast for a very considerable distance towards the equator.

But the enterprise of the Mediterranean nations was not confined only to the coast-line. The commercial spirit of Carthage and the warlike genius of Rome alike led them to seek the interior.

In this direction, however, each was fated to be as effectually checked as their sailors had been by sea. The burning heat, the wide stretches of barren sand, the waterless wastes, and the savage nomads which they had to encounter, were as terrible to face as the huge waves and frightful storms of the Atlantic. To the natural terrors of this desert region, forsaken of the gods, their imagination added every conceivable monstrosity, so that he indeed was a bold man who ventured from the gay and pleasant confines of the northern lands into the awful horrors of the Sahara.

Yet men there must have been, whether warriors, merchants, or simple explorers, we know not, who crossed the dreaded desert zone, and reached the more fertile countries of the negroes which lay beyond. In the pages of Herodotus and Strabo, of Pliny and of Ptolemy, amid all the mythological absurdities and ridiculous stories with which they abound, we find not only ample evidence of such successful adventure, but a wonderfully just estimate of the physical conditions which characterised the region lying between the Mediterranean and the Sudan. They describe first a zone of sharply contrasted fertility and barrenness, of green oasis and repellent desert, scantily inhabited by wild, roving tribes. Next comes a more terrible region lying further to the south—a land of desolation and death, swept by the wild sirocco and sandstorm, burnt by fierce relentless suns, unrefreshed by sparkling earth- born springs, unmoistened by the heaven-sent rain or by the gentle dew of night. Beyond lies a third region—the land of the negroes—made fertile by spring and stream, by marsh and lake.

More remarkable still is the fact that in each of the writers mentioned we find clear indications of a knowledge of a great river running through Negroland.

With minds on the search for a solution of the Nile problems—its origin, its course, and the mystery of its annual overflow—and from the likelihood that some of their informants had actually seen this river when it ran in an easterly direction, the opinion generally adopted by the ancients was that the river of the negroes was the Nile itself.

Of the various sources of information upon which the classical writers depended for their descriptions of these savage lands we know but little. One there is, however, which stands out with wonderful clearness and prominence and a general air of credibility—the expedition of the Nasamones as related by Herodotus.

The Nasamones—five young men of distinction, doubtless without suitable outlets for their ambitions and energies at home—set out from their native country to the south-west of Egypt, bent on the exploration of the heart of Africa.

Travelling partly south and partly west, they crossed the semi-inhabited, semi-sterile zone. Arrived at the confines of the great desert, they collected provisions and supplied themselves with water, and bold in heart "to seek, to conquer, or to die," plunged into the terrible unknown. For many weary days they pursued their quest with unabated courage and perseverance. At length they emerged from the region of desolation and death, and found themselves in a fertile country inhabited by pigmies, having abundance of fruit trees, and watered by vast lakes and marshes. Furthermore, they found a large river flowing from west to east.

Whether these enterprising young African explorers had reached the neighbourhood of Lake Chad, as we might be disposed to believe, or the Niger in the vicinity of the great bend of the main stream, it would be waste of time to ask. Let us be satisfied with knowing that at this very early period of the world's history, many centuries before the Christian era, the Central or Western Sudan of our days was reached, and the fact established that through it ran a great river.

In this way the exploration of Central Africa was inaugurated—the first uncertain glimmer of light thrown upon its dark surface; and the River Niger revealed to the world to be a theme of discussion to arm-chair geographers, and a goal to be aimed at by the more adventurous spirits who would realise their thoughts in deeds rather than on paper.

CHAPTER II.
MORE LIGHT: THE ARAB PERIOD.

For many centuries but little was added to the knowledge of Africa acquired by the early classical writers. Carthage fell from its high estate, and on its ruins Rome, with boundless ambition and seemingly boundless powers of attainment, built for itself a new and equally magnificent African Empire. But where man could not stay the advancing tide, Nature set bounds to the force of Roman arms, and at the borders of the desert mutely said, "Thus far shalt thou go, and no further."

The Roman power rose to the zenith of its glory, and still the desert remained uncrossed; it dwindled towards its fall, and then its days of geographical conquest were over. In Northern Africa, as elsewhere, the mythological gave place to the Christian era, and the influence of the new religion spread apparently to the remotest desert tribes. It was not, however, fated to be permanent. In the seventh century a new prophet had risen in the Sacred East, and the seeds of a mighty revolution were germinating in the deserts of Arabia. The boundaries of its parent country soon proved too small for the astonishing vitalities and ardent missionary enterprise of the new faith—the faith of Islam. Bursting out, it pushed with incredible rapidity along the north of Africa, overwhelming Paganism and Christianity alike in its irresistible course, till reaching the Atlantic it turned to north and south in search of new fields to conquer for God. The natural difficulties which had stopped the southern progress of the Carthaginians and the Romans formed no barrier to a people born in a desert. In the plateau lands of the Berber tribes the Arabs were at home. Winged with a fiery enthusiasm which nothing could withstand, and inspired by a hope of heaven which nothing could shake, they swept from district to district, from tribe to tribe, everywhere carrying the blazing torch of Islam, everywhere striking fire from the roving people with whom they came in contact, till from every Saharan oasis there was heard the common cry, "There is no God but the one God." In the new conflagration Christian symbols and Pagan idols alike disappeared in one fell holocaust.

To a race so educated and nurtured, so steeped in fiery ardour and unquenchable faith, and so imbued with the paramount importance of their mission—provided, moreover, as regards the practical part of their work, with the drought-enduring camel, hitherto unknown in Africa—the so-called impassable desert was no barrier to the performance of the task divinely set them. Only for him who turned back did hell yawn. For him who went forward it might be death, but it was death with Paradise gained.

In this spirit the terrors of the Sahara were faced, and faced only to be conquered; and ere the ninth century gave place to the tenth, the land of the negroes was reached, and the forces of Islam set themselves in array against those of heathendom. For the first time the Niger basin was now brought into direct relation with Northern Africa. The actual time when this was accomplished is still a matter of some doubt, though the statement is quoted by Barth that within less than a hundred years of the commencement of the Mohammedan era, schools and mosques were established in the negro kingdom of Ghana or Ghanata, to the west of Timbuktu. More incontestable is the statement of the Arab writer, Ebn Khaldun (A.D. 1380), that trading relations existed about 280 A.H. or 893 A.D. between the Upper Niger and Northern Africa. When these were first established we are not informed.

The vital forces which had found no barrier in the fierce nomads and physical difficulties of the Sahara, and had carried the disciples of Mohammed to the borders of the Sudan, met a check to their sweeping progress where one would have least expected it. Half the secret of the success of Islam had been that principle in the creed which was calculated to attract and inflame the ardent imaginations and easily excited temperaments of the Berber tribes of the north. With these Mohammedanism required but little aid from fire and sword for the spread of its tenets. It had but to be preached to be believed, making every hearer not only a convert but a missionary aflame with enthusiasm for the cause of God and Mohammed. Such, however, was not the case when Islam came face to face with the undeveloped lethargic minds of the barbarous blacks of the Sudan. The intellect of the negro had to be prepared for the reception of the new spiritual doctrines.

For a time a hard and fast line existed between Islam and Heathendom more or less closely coinciding with that drawn between Berber and Negro, Sahara and Sudan.

Only for a time, however. Though the new religious force could sweep on no longer in an irresistible, all-embracing tide, it was not to be prevented from gradually working its way into the sodden mass of Paganism. Along the whole line of opposing forces from Senegambia to Lake Chad, Mohammedan missionaries penetrated, not with fire and sword and all the horrors of brute force, but armed with the spiritual weapons of faith, hope, and ardent enthusiasm. Under their fostering care schools and mosques arose, around which converts gathered in ever-increasing numbers, until at length every region had its leavening germs, and awaited but the proper moment and the inspired leader to raise the watchword of Islam, and once more sweep onward with all the accumulated force of the dammed back torrent.

Within a short time of each other two such leaders appeared at opposite points of the Niger basin. In the west, near the great bend of the Niger, a king of Songhay embraced Islam about the year 1000, while near the close of the same century a king of Bornu followed his example.[1]

From those dates a new and more promising era commenced for the Central and Western Sudan. Under the fostering care and impulse of the new religion these backward regions commenced an upward progress. A new and powerful bond drew the scattered congeries of tribes together and welded them into powerful communities. Their moral and spiritual well-being increased by leaps and bounds, and their political and social life took an altogether higher level. The arts and industries of the North speedily became established among them, and with them came the love of decent dress, of cleanliness, of more orderly conduct. Whatever might be said of Mohammedanism in its final influence, there could be no question but that it had the amount of good in it necessary to raise a barbarous people to a higher level of civilisation. There was an adaptability and a simplicity about it well suited to the comprehension of untutored minds, and in that lay the secret of a success such as has never since been even distantly approached by any other propagandist religion in Africa.

To the rulers of Songhay and Bornu the watchword of Islam, "There is no God but the one God," soon became a war-cry destined to be irresistible in its magic influence. Armed with the new spiritual force these hitherto barbarous kingdoms rose to extraordinary heights of power. Songhay gradually spread its influence over all the upper reaches of the Niger till it had absorbed the old kingdoms of Ghanata, to the north of the Niger, and Melli, to the south. With the political influences of Songhay went the religious forces at its back. At times there were checks to its military power, but only when the religious enthusiasm and missionary ardour of its rulers temporarily sank and were outstripped by the greater zeal of neighbouring princes. With these exceptions, the history of Songhay was that of general progress, political, social, and commercial. The kingdom reached the zenith of its power at the beginning of the sixteenth century under a powerful negro king named Hadj Mohammed Askia, whose rule extended from the centre of the present empire of Sokoto to the borders of the Atlantic, a distance from east to west of 1500 miles, and from Mosi in the south as far as the oasis of Tawat in the north, *i.e.*, something over 1000 miles.[2]

Askia was no mere warrior anxious for his own aggrandisement. As was the case with all the great Sudanese rulers of those early days, he was noted for his ardent faith as well as for his love of justice and clemency, so that, as his historian, Ahmed Baba of Timbuktu, wrote of him, "God made use of his services in order to save the true believers (in Negroland) from their sufferings and calamities." He built mosques and schools, and did everything in his power to encourage learning; and not unmindful of the material prosperity of his people, encouraged merchants from all parts of the Sudan, the Sahara, and North Africa. Thus not only was he loved and revered by his subjects, but his fame extended to the most distant countries.

Unhappily the magnificent empire thus founded had not the elements of stability. There was too much of the one man power, with no firm governmental foundations apart from the ruler. In consequence, the history of Songhay was one of varying fortunes. Old kingdoms such as Melli temporarily regained their independence, distant provinces were continually breaking loose, and there were constant wars of succession and military revolts. But though often scotched it was never killed, till an altogether new enemy appeared in the person of Mulai Hamed, Sultan of Morocco, before whose musketeers it was doomed to become extinct as an independent kingdom. This happened in 1591, in the reign of Askia Ishak. Ahmed Baba, the native historian, who lived at the time, and was himself not only a material sufferer, but a prisoner carried off to Morocco, said of this terrible disaster: "Thus this Mahalla (or expedition) at that period found in Sudan (Songhay) one of those countries of the earth which are most favoured with comfort, plenty, peace, and prosperity everywhere; such was the working of the government of the Emir el Mumenin, Askia el Hadj Mohammed ben Abu Bakr, in consequence of his justice and the power of his royal command, which took full and peremptory effect, not only in his capital (Gogo), but in all the districts of his whole empire, from the province of Dendi to the frontier of Morocco, and from the territory of Bennendugu (to the south of Jinni) as far as Zeghaza and Tawat. But in a moment all was changed, and peaceful repose was succeeded by a constant state of fear, comfort and security by troubles and suffering; ruin and misfortune took the place of prosperity, and people began everywhere to fight against each other, and property and life became exposed to constant danger; and this ruin began, spread, increased, and at length prevailed throughout the whole region."[3] If it be remembered that this was written in Arabic by a Niger native at the end of the sixteenth or beginning of the seventeenth centuries about a negro sultan ruling over a kingdom partly negro and partly Berber, the wonder of it cannot but strike the thoughtful mind.

But in the Niger basin Songhay was not the only centre of marvellous political and social development under the influence of Mohammedanism. Bornu was in every sense its rival. We have already seen that towards the close of the eleventh century the king of Bornu (Dunama ben Humé) had embraced Islam. The result of the union of material power with spiritual inspiration was soon made manifest, for before Ben Humé died he had founded a vigorous empire whose influence was felt as far as Egypt. It was not, however, till the middle of the thirteenth century that Bornu rose to its greatest power and the zenith of its glory under the able rule of one Dibalami Dunama Selmami. At that time Bornu, or, as it was sometimes called, Kameni (?), which was then the seat of government, extended from the Nile to the Niger, and from Mabina (Adamawa?) in the south to Wadan in the north, according to Imam Ahmed (1571-1603), the native historian of Bornu, as Ahmed Baba had been that of Songhay. But Dunama did not only increase the material power of Bornu. Like Askia of Songhay, he encouraged religion, so that "the true faith in his time was largely disseminated," according to Ebn Said (1282), an Arab writer.

After Dunama's death troublesome times fell upon the empire, and a long period of civil wars and disastrous expeditions followed. Brighter times came back with the ascent of Ali (1472) to the throne, and once more Bornu regained its former grandeur. It is clear that Ali's kingdom extended far to the west of the Niger, and became known to the Portuguese, who as far back as 1489 show Bernu or Bornu on their maps.

Under the two succeeding reigns of Edris and Mohammed, Bornu still further added to its importance, and had relations with the northern sultans of Tripoli.

The most remarkable, however, of all the Bornu rulers seems to have been Edris Alawoma (1571-1603), who had the advantage of having a contemporary biographer in the person of Imam Ahmed. This prince seems not only to have been an enterprising and able warrior, but was distinguished alike for mildness and justice, and for far-seeing statesmanship. Under him the empire grew to enormous proportions, and included almost the whole of the Central and much of the Western Sudan. At the same time the country became more prosperous, the wealth of the towns increased, and the Mohammedan religion and education spread widely and rapidly.

Happily Bornu was established on a more stable basis than Songhay. It had more cohesion in its various elements, and was less dependent on the warlike character of its rulers to keep it from falling to pieces. Its princes also seem to have been of a better and more liberal-minded stock. We even gather from the native chronicles that they were "learned, liberal towards the Ilama, prodigal dispensers of alms, friends of science and religion, gracious and compassionate towards the poor." Hence it was that while Songhay and other states rose and fell, Bornu retained its position and independence. In the beginning of this century it experienced a temporary eclipse before the conquering arms of the Fillani in their mission of religious regeneration, but only to emerge again as vigorous as ever, though now restricted in its political influence to Bornu proper and the immediate neighbourhood of Lake Chad.

But while Songhay and Bornu were for centuries working out their remarkable political, religious, social, and commercial development, they were, as we have already pointed out, by no means shut off from intercourse with the outside world. The thirst for the slaves of Bornu and for the gold of Melli and the Upper Niger was almost as potent a force with the later generations of Arabs as was religious zeal among their ancestors. For the one as for the other all the terrors of the desert route were braved, and constant communication kept up with the Sudan. At first Egypt seems to have been the first point of departure of the Sudanese caravan, one route passing westward to Songhay and the region of the Upper Niger, while another diverged from it, and passed south to the Chad basin. In later times Egypt gave place to Tripoli as the starting-point, though practically the same routes were utilised to reach the same goals. At an early period also the most dangerous part of the whole Sahara, that region, namely, lying between the Upper Niger and Morocco, was traversed by indefatigable Moorish traders for the sake of its slaves and gold. The terminus of their route was at first considerably to the west of Timbuktu, at a place called Biru or Walata, where, indeed, nearly all the western trans-Saharan traffic converged in the earlier days of commercial intercourse.

Towards the end of the eleventh century Timbuktu was founded as a trading station by the Tuaregs of the Sahara, but it was not until it fell into the hands of a powerful king of Melli some two centuries later that it became a place of some importance. At once it developed into an international market of the first rank, where merchants from Egypt, Tripoli, Morocco, the Saharan oases, and the Sudan met to exchange their various articles of barter.

At no time was Timbuktu the capital of a great kingdom. Its greatness solely depended upon its trade, and its convenience as a collecting and dispersing centre. That it should have become so well known above all the places of the Sudan is easily understood if it be remembered that it was the goal for which all the merchants of Northern Africa aimed. Politically, Timbuktu was thus raised to a position of undue importance, though commercially, as the merchant capital, it could not be overrated.

With the rise of the Songhay power Timbuktu became subject to that kingdom. With the fall of the former it assumed a measure of political importance as the centre of Moorish power, till on the division from Morocco it resumed its old status as nothing more nor less than a trading centre, a position it has retained to this day.

Among a people of such commercial activity and enterprise as the Arabs of Morocco, Tripoli, and Egypt, naturally there were not awanting numbers of students eager to collect and collate information regarding the inland countries to which their merchants travelled. Among the host of historians and geographers who supply us with interesting facts, we may mention El Bekri, El Edrisi (1153), Ebn Said (1282), Ebn Khaldun (1382), and Makrizi (1400).

But the Arabs had their explorers as well as their writers. Among these two stand out with marked prominence, viz., Ebn Batuta (1353), and Leo Africanus (1528). Ebn Batuta, who seems to have been devoured with a thirst for travel, and had visited almost all the countries of the then known world, commenced his Central African explorations from Morocco, and crossed the desert to Walata, the frontier province of Melli, situated not far from the Niger. From Walata he crossed the Niger to the capital of the kingdom, and thence by land proceeded to Timbuktu. From Kabara, the "port" of Timbuktu, he sailed down the Niger to Gogo, the capital of Songhay, and thence turned northward again across the desert by way of the oasis of Tawat to Morocco.

The travels of Leo Africanus were even more extensive, for he travelled over the whole of the Central and Western Sudan. Considering that he wrote an account of his travels from memory many years after, the events recorded, and the accuracy and amount of varied information he gives regarding the countries he visited, are astonishing. He describes not only the kingdoms of Melli, Songhay, and Bornu, but also the countries that lie between, Gober, Katsena, Kano, and Agades, of all of which he has something important to say. Even when he seems to draw most upon our credulity he is generally quite correct, as for instance when he describes the people of one district kindling fires at night under their bedsteads to keep themselves warm. To the truth of this statement the writer of these lines can testify from personal observation, the precaution being adopted, however, not to ward off external cold, but that of ague, a disease to which many places on the Niger are subject at certain times of the year.

It is not our intention to enter into the vexed question of what the Arab writers and travellers knew regarding the course and final destination of the Niger. Those of them who travelled did not do so as geographers, and though they noted accurately enough what they did see, they troubled themselves very little with what they did not see, and held aloof from inquiries of a purely speculative character. M'Queen[4] has made it clear, however, that many of them were aware that the Nile and the Niger were distinct, and that the general tendency of Arab opinion was to make the latter river fall into the Atlantic.

Much of the confusion as to what the Arabs did know or believe arose largely from the ignorance of European geographers in confounding the western kingdom of Ghana with the central one of Kano, and of the town of Kugha, near the Upper Niger, with that of Kuka in Bornu. With the new light thrown upon the history and geography of the Niger basin, we can now see that the Arab writers had a wonderfully accurate conception of the political and physical characteristics of the region in question. To them is due not only the honour of having raised the veil which shrouded the Sudan, and spread the seeds of civilisation, which have flourished so remarkably, but also of disseminating a knowledge of that region among western nations—a knowledge destined, as we shall see, to be caught up and carried to great ends with European vigour and scientific accuracy.

CHAPTER III.
OPENING UP THE WAY TO THE NIGER.

With Leo Africanus the Arab period in the history of African exploration practically closed. Even in that traveller's day the incurable diseases so characteristic of the Mohammedan states of our time were rapidly developing. Learning and the arts were no longer encouraged. Liberality of thought and missionary enterprise were replaced by Fanaticism, hatred of the stranger, and isolation from all outside genial influences. A blight was falling over everything that had made the Arab name great and glorious in the world's history.

Happily for the cause of progress, while the Crescent thus waned and lost its lustre in the rising mephitic fogs, the Cross was ever gathering to itself new glories, and proving the herald and morning-star of a brighter and greater era. Under its inspiring influences the western nations were emerging from the gloom and ignorance in which they had been enshrouded, and were feeling the throbs of new heroic impulses.

Among the Christian nations thus awakening Portugal was taking the lead. Facing the Atlantic, it was ever looking over the wild waste of waters, picturing the possible beyond on the blank expanse, and rearing a hardy race of navigators all unconscious of the great mission that was yet to be theirs. Southward, too, their thoughts were ever turning, following their soldiers as they fought against the Moors and planted their most Christian flag along the entire coast-line of Morocco. Echoes there were which came to them of the vast wealth of Inner Africa, of the power of Prester John and the riches of far Cathay, till the imaginations of kings, soldiers, merchants, and priests were alike inflamed with a desire to share them. With it all the vaguest ideas were current as to the extent of the African continent. The northern coast-line was well enough known, but at the beginning of the fifteenth century no one had ventured southward beyond the western termination of the Atlas Mountains, and how much further south the land extended no one pretended to know. This ignorance, however, did not last through the century.

Under its energetic and far-seeing kings, John and Immanuel, Portugal set itself to penetrate behind the veil and attain the honour and the more substantial rewards secured, as was believed, to those who should first reach the sources of the gold supply of Inner Africa, the capital of Prester John, or the countries of the Far East.

Extensive voyages were then unthought of. Sailing was very much a matter of feeling one's way along the shore. Hence it was not by any one extensive voyage, but by many successive expeditions, that the shore-line of Africa was gradually mapped out. In this way greater courage, confidence, experience, and skill were gained with each successful addition to the limits of the known, and a spirit of emulation was aroused which irresistibly carried the new knight errants of commerce and science further and further south in search of the promised land.

In 1433 Cape Bojador was reached by Gilianez, and the Island of Arguin by Nuno Tristan ten years later. So far deserts and burning suns, a repellent coast-line and a meagre population of wild nomads, were what they found— no news of Prester John, no evidence of the vast riches they had taught themselves to expect. But nothing was allowed to damp their eager spirit or quash their sanguine expectations.

In 1446 Fernandez passed Cape Verd, and in the following year the fertile region of Senegambia was reached by Lancelot.

It now seemed as if the bold adventurers were to have their reward. They had at last arrived at a fertile region abounding in gold and ivory, and, better still, they began to hear of a great kingdom named Melli, not then absorbed in the rapidly rising empire of Songhay. This, they thought, must be the country of Prester John.

These important discoveries, and all the glowing hopes they developed, gave a new impetus to the course of Portuguese discovery. With renewed enterprise and persistence adventurous navigators pursued the path of exploration. By 1471 they had reached the Gold Coast, and before the close of the century the Cape had been rounded, and, under the leadership of Almeida and Albuquerque, some of their magnificent dreams of wealth and power realised in the foundation of their Indian Empire.

But though the Portuguese had thus revealed to the world the Senegal and the Gambia, and apparently thrown open a door to the kingdom of the Niger basin, nothing came of it. From the writings of De Barros we gather that embassies from the King of Portugal were despatched to the rulers of Melli and Mosi, and even, it is said, to that of Songhay. Of these missions, however, nothing more has come down to us. They added seemingly nothing to our knowledge of the interior. Factories were established along the coast, and even some distance up the rivers Senegal and Gambia, but the thirst for gold and slaves evidently swamped all other considerations with the agents in charge, for not an iota of information do we gather from them—or at least none is now on record—of the geography of the far interior.

The magnificent enterprise of Portugal in the fields of maritime discovery was destined to be of the most transient character. Evil days speedily came upon it, and between Philip II. of Spain on land and the Dutch at sea, it seemed for a time as if it would lose its place among the independent nations of Europe.

From the time of its conquest by Spain its course was backward, and its history became a record of shrinking empire and gradual loss of all spirit that tends to national greatness and progress. As far as we are concerned the work of the Portuguese ended with the exploration of the Senegambian Coast, the discovery of the rivers Senegal and Gambia—then thought to be branches of the Niger—and the revelation to Europe of the future route to the Niger and Timbuktu.

The work of exploration so well begun, so magnificently carried on, though so disastrously closed, began now to fall into other hands. Contemporaneously with the dwindling of the Portuguese into the background the English came to the front. It was then the Elizabethan period, that era of glorious memory, the dawn of Greater Britain. Bold mariners, like the world has never seen, sprang up on all sides, and made England the mistress of the seas. A spirit of commercial enterprise and adventurous daring was developed which nothing could dismay, nothing withstand. Before the close of that eventful period Drake had led his countrymen to the rich spoil of the Spanish Main, Raleigh had laid the foundation of English rule in North America, Baffin and Hudson had cleared the way for Arctic exploration, and Davis had not only started the series of heroic expeditions connected with the North- west Passage, but had led English ships to the Indian Seas.

With these, however, we have nothing to do. Of more importance is it to us to note that Hawkins had made his first voyage to the West African Coast, and inaugurated that horrid traffic in human flesh and blood which has left such an indelible stain on British commerce.

But it was not only the slave trade which drew the attention of English merchants to Africa. To them as to the Portuguese the Niger and Timbuktu were words to conjure with. Both were believed to be veritable mines of wealth. To the imagination of the time the one was pictured as flowing over golden sands, the other as almost paved with the precious metal. It was believed that the Senegal and the Gambia constituted the Niger mouths, and accordingly that to ascend either river would bring the traveller direct to the source of so much wealth. To accomplish this now became the dream of nations, so that it may well be said that the Niger and its fancied treasures were the magnet which drew men on to the exploration of the interior of the Dark Continent.

It had been the mission of Portugal to draw a girdle round Africa; it was now to be the *rôle* of Britain to take up the work and penetrate inland with more lasting results than had followed Portuguese embassies and missionary and commercial enterprises.

The year 1618 saw the commencement of this noble work. A company was formed to explore the Gambia, with the object of reaching the rich region of the Niger.

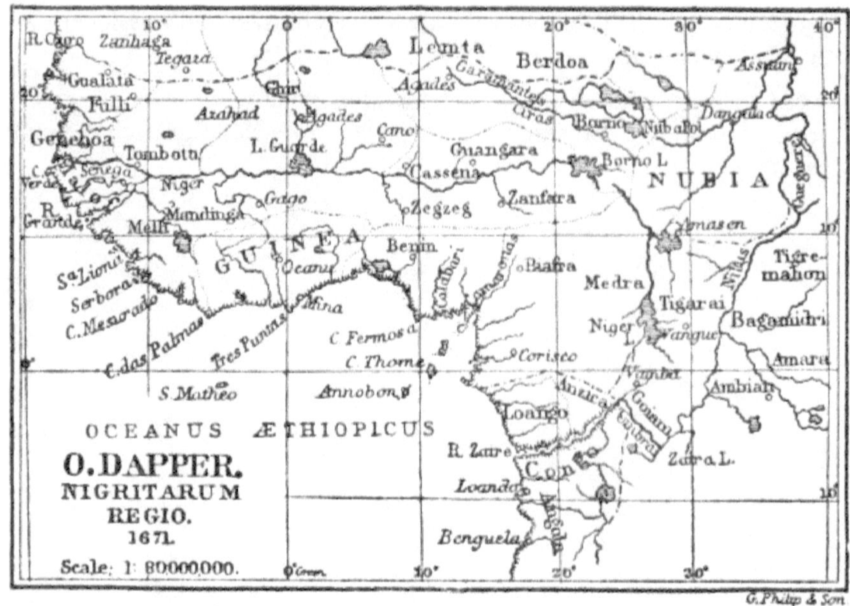

The honour of being Britain's pioneer in African exploration fell to the lot of one Richard Thompson, described as being a man of spirit and enterprise. He left England in the *Catherine*, of 120 tons, with a cargo worth nearly £2000, and reached the Gambia towards the end of the year. Here he found the Portuguese still in power, ruling the nations with grinding tyranny, though rapidly sinking into the commercial and national apathy which has made them a byword in the nineteenth century.

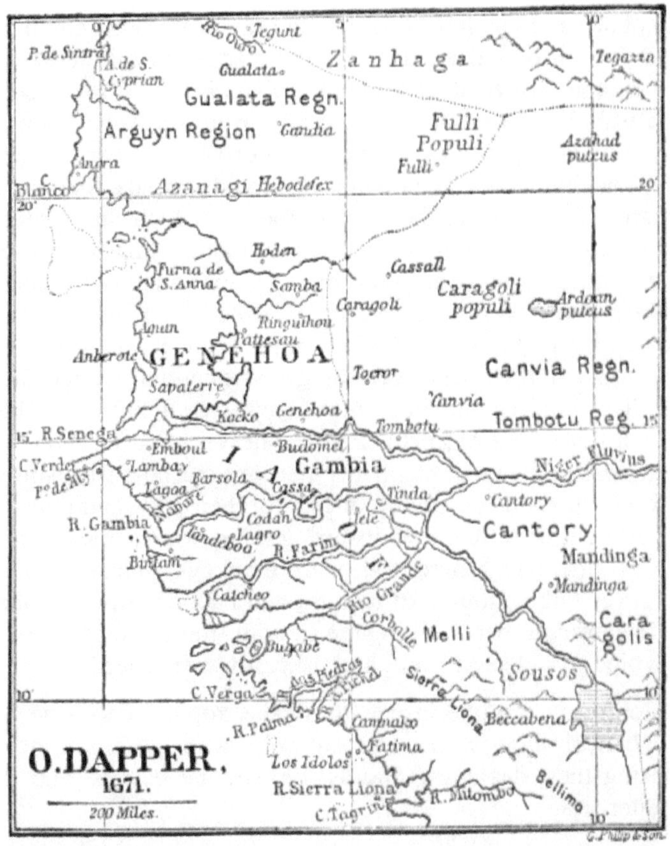

Thompson's enterprise, like so many which succeeded it, was doomed to suffer sad disaster. First the Portuguese fell upon and massacred a large part of the crew while its captain was exploring up the river. Undismayed he stuck to his post, and demanded reinforcements and supplies. His employers were of like metal to himself, and promptly sent another vessel to his assistance. The climate proved as formidable an enemy as the Portuguese, and most of the crew of the new ship succumbed to the deadly miasma.

Still another vessel was fitted out, its owners undaunted by loss of men and goods, and sanguine as ever of the glorious prize to be achieved.

This time one Richard Jobson took command. He arrived in the Gambia in 1620, only to hear of a new calamity and a new and even more paralysing source of danger—Thompson's men had mutinied and murdered him. Portuguese hostility, a deadly climate, and mutiny in the camp were all arrayed against the hoped for advance into the country. But those old mariners were made of stern unyielding stuff, which only death itself could break, and undismayed Jobson defied all dangers and started on his quest. With each succeeding mile new difficulties beset the gallant band. No pilots could be got to show the way. For a time this proved no serious obstacle. Soon, however, the current grew stronger, and threatened to drive them back. They were in hourly peril from hidden rocks, and falls and rapids raised a foaming barrier to further progress. Sand-banks there were, too, on which they grounded, and crocodiles had to be braved in getting clear of them, while sea-horses snorted angrily and threatened to swamp the boats. Unprovided with the mosquito-nets of modern times, their days of overpowering fatigue under a melting sun were followed by nights of maddening torture under the stings of myriad mosquitoes and sandflies. But everything was new and wonderful to them. They were like children bursting into a new world full of undreamed of marvels, a veritable land of enchantment. The voracious crocodiles and the monstrous hippos in the river, elephants in troops crashing irresistibly through the dense forest, leopards watching cat-like for their prey, and lions disturbing the silence of night with their awe-inspiring roars, were some of the elements of this new wonderland. There, too, were monkeys among the trees—their gambols a never failing source of delight; and baboons trooping through the underbush in enormous herds, filling the air with strange outcries, except when "one great voice would exalt itself, and the rest were hushed."

Not less astonishing was the insect life of the tropic forest—the fireflies in myriad numbers flashing with iridescent colours in the gloom of night, the crickets raising their deafening chorus, the strange beetles, and the many-coloured butterflies.

How marvellous, too, must the tropic foliage have appeared to the explorers, fresh as they were from England. The immense grasses, the almost impenetrable undergrowth, the beauties of the palm tribe, the majesty of the silk-cotton tree. Last, not least, how passing strange the appearance of the natives, their comparative absence of dress, their simple habits and rudimentary ideas about all things under heaven. The modern traveller, *blasé* with the rich heritage of a hundred predecessors, cannot but envy the sensations of such an one as Jobson on seeing for the first time all the marvels, beauties, and novelties of Africa.

But while we vainly try to realise the feelings inspired in the mind of this pioneer, we are not oblivious of the terrible earnestness and determination, the indomitable courage and dogged perseverance of the man. The very devil himself has no terrors for Jobson. Hearing certain remarkable sounds, and being told by the natives that it is the voice of the devil, the intrepid sailor seizes his gun and rushes forth to do battle with his Satanic Majesty, who, on our hero's appearance, changes his terrible roars into notes of terror, and shows himself as a huge negro grovelling in the dust in an agony of fear.

On the 26th January 1621, Jobson had reached a place called Tenda, where he heard of a city four months' journey into the interior, the roofs of which were covered with gold. Unhappily, however much his appetite might be whetted by such wonderful stories, it had to remain unsatisfied. The dry season soon began to tell upon the volume of water in the river, making advance daily more difficult, till within a few days of a town called Tombaconda, some 300 miles from the sea, he was compelled to desist from further attempts, although he believed that Tombaconda was Timbuktu itself, in reality distant about 1000 miles. On the 10th February he commenced his return, hoping to go back and complete his work with the rising of the waters, a project he however never executed.

Quarrels broke out between the merchants on the river and the Company, and the enterprise for the time being collapsed.

It was not till nearly a century later that a new attempt was made to prosecute the task of reaching the Niger and the wealth of Inner Africa. In 1720, the Duke of Chandos, acting as chairman of the African Company, instigated a new expedition by way of the Gambia to the land of promise.

This time the enterprise was placed under the leadership of one Captain Bartholomew Stibbs, who left England in 1723, and arrived in the Gambia in October of that year. His experiences were identical with those of Jobson, though he did not reach the latter's highest point. Between them, however, it was made quite clear that the Gambia had no connection with the Niger, and as little with the Senegal.

With Stibbs ended the English commercial attempts to open up the way to the interior of Africa.

The addition to our knowledge of its geography amounted to the exploration of the navigable part of the Gambia, and the determination of the fact that it had no connection with the Niger.

The French meanwhile were doing for the Senegal what the British were accomplishing in the sister river. Six years after Thompson had entered the latter, the French had established themselves at the mouth of the Senegal and founded the town of St. Louis. Their first exploring trip was made in 1637, when they penetrated some distance along the navigable part of the river.

More important, however, was the expedition in 1697 of one Sieur Brue, director-general of the French African Company, which achieved considerable success. This expedition was backed up by a second voyage up the river two years later, when the fort of St. Joseph was founded, and trade opened with merchants from Timbuktu.

Sieur Brue's experiences were in every respect similar to those of Jobson and Stibbs on the Gambia, though commercially more fortunate, inasmuch as he had to do with more advanced races, and contrived to reach the frontiers of a rich gold-bearing district (Bambuk) on the one hand, and of an equally profitable gum region on the other.

He also heard much of the Niger and Timbuktu, and seemingly satisfied himself that the Senegal had no connection with the famous river of the interior, and that the latter flowed east, not west, as it was the tendency of his day to believe, since we find the French maps of the eighteenth century showing the Niger flowing towards the interior and an uncertain bourne.

CHAPTER IV.
PREPARING FOR PARK: THE AFRICAN ASSOCIATION.

The latter part of the eighteenth century marks the commencement of the modern period of African exploration. So far all African enterprises had been instigated by governments for national aggrandisement, or by merchants with commercial objects in view. Early Portuguese discovery was a type of the one; the British expedition to the Gambia an example of the other. But now the time had come when, dissociated from both, African exploration was to start forth on a new line of unselfish research, and accomplish what governments and commercial communities had failed in doing.

To the African Association belongs the honour of inaugurating this new and more glorious era. Lord Rawdon, afterwards Marquis of Hastings, Sir Joseph Banks, the Bishop of Landaff, Mr. Beaufoy, and Mr. Stuart, were the first managers of this Association, whose objects were the promotion of discovery in Africa, and the spread of information, commercial, political, and scientific, regarding the still sadly unknown continent.

At first the Association devoted their attention to Northern Africa, and in a short time were instrumental in gathering together much reliable and valuable information as to the Mohammedan states of that region.

Their inquiries, however, were not to be bounded by the Sahara any more than the first onrush of the Mohammedan torrent.

The routes of the large caravans to the Sudan were made a subject of investigation, and the Arab writers laid under contribution to satisfy the demand for more light.

To the Niger especially their inquiries were turned, in the hope of solving the mystery of its true position and its course. Where did it commence and where did it end? was the double problem which puzzled the eighteenth century geographers more even than the question of the source of the Nile.

Not content with inquiries which only landed them in perplexities and endless discussion, they resolved to send out explorers. To such they offered no monetary inducements, no hope of tangible reward. The honour and glory of discovery were to be their prize: the Association at the same time undertaking, for their part, to defray the traveller's expenses.

The inducements offered were quite sufficient. Admirably qualified men presented themselves in greater numbers than were needed, so that the chief difficulty of the Association was to choose rather than to seek.

The first of the heroic band of African pioneers was Ledyard, already a traveller of the most varied experience. His mission was to cross the African Continent from the Nile to the Atlantic. At the threshold of his enterprise he perished of fever in 1788.

Mr. Lucas was the next to take up the work. His qualifications were an intimate knowledge of Moorish life and language, gathered first as a slave in Morocco, then as British Vice-Consul to that empire. The work marked out for him was to start from Tripoli and cross the Sahara to the Sudan. In this he failed. A revolt of Arab tribes barred the way, and Mr. Lucas abandoned the enterprise, bringing back with him only additional particulars regarding the interior, which he had gathered from native merchants.

More successful in the earlier part of a succeeding expedition was Horneman (1789), who undoubtedly crossed the desert, but crossed it only to disappear for ever.

Clearly Africa was a hard nut to crack, and dangerous to whomsoever should essay it.

Foiled in their attempts to reach the goal of their desires from the north, the African Association next turned to West Africa for a possible opening to the interior. Once more the Gambia was chosen as the most direct and feasible route.

In Major Houghton they seemed to have got the right man for the work. As Consul at Morocco he had gained an acquaintance with the Moors and their language, and at Goree, then in British hands, he had come in contact with the West African negro, and learned the conditions of life and travel obtaining in the Gambia region.

The new attempt was made in 1791. Unlike Jobson and Stibbs, the adventurous explorer did not proceed by boat and with a large European party, but by land, single-handed, and attended by the most modest of retinues. At first all went well; no difficulties or troubles retarded his progress. Generally following the course of the river he safely reached Medina, the capital of Wuli, and was hospitably received by the king of the place. Less kind were the elements. A fire which reduced the town to ashes deprived him of much of his goods. From Medina Houghton's route diverged from the Gambia, passing west to the Falemé, a southern tributary of the Senegal, and frontier line of the gold-bearing region of Bambuk. Here also he was received with hospitality, and was sent on his way through Bambuk rejoicing. Not to rejoice long, however. The last communication received from him contained these graphic lines: "Major Houghton's compliments to Dr. Laidley; is in good health, on his way to Timbuktu; robbed of all his goods by Fenda Bukar's son." No despair in these words, whatever calamities might have befallen the writer; no halting in the resolution to achieve his object—only the one unhesitating determination to go forward. But it was to go forward to die. In spite of Fenda Bukar's son he seems still to have possessed sufficient means to rouse the unscrupulous cupidity of some Moors. Lured on by these wretches he was led into the desert, where he was stripped of everything and left to a horrible death.

It would seem that the disastrous ending of these various expeditions had thrown a damper upon the eagerness of volunteers to continue the work, for we now find the African Association offering the inducement of a liberal recompense to whomsoever would take up the task broken off by Houghton's death.

Little wonder if qualified men hesitated to offer themselves. African fevers had a terror then which they no longer possess. The continent was practically unknown, and to the imagination, with no facts to act as correctives, everything wore a terrible aspect. Cannibalism, general bloodthirstiness and ferocity, a love of plunder, and all manner of horrible practices, were associated with the name of negro. Death by thirst or starvation was thought likely to be the lot of those who escaped the miasma of the land or the murderous spear of the native. Brave indeed would be the man who should face such an accumulation of vaguely discerned and mightily exaggerated horrors.

Nevertheless the African Association had not long to wait. At this crisis in their affairs the man for the work was forthcoming, one destined to crown their hopes with a triumphant success, to inaugurate a more brilliant future for African travel, and give it such an impetus as would carry it on to a glorious issue. This was Mungo Park.

CHAPTER V.
MUNGO PARK.

To continue our narrative of exploration we must now leave the sweltering suns and miasmatic atmosphere of Western Africa for the temperate climate and bracing breezy hillsides of southern Scotland—turning from the river dear to the geographer to the stream loved of the poet—from the Niger to the Yarrow.

The man whose mission it was to break through the isolating barriers reared by savagery and a deadly climate between the land of the negro and all outside humanising influences, must needs have an heroic cradle, and come of an heroic race. His must be the nurture of the Spartan, physically equipping him to battle with hardship and privation—his the education and upbringing which tend to all forms of noble discontent and deeds of high emprise.

Such a cradle and such a race were Ettrickdale and its peasantry. Theirs was the life of honest toil and constant self-restraint, and theirs the direct and indirect education which in the right man develops romantic instincts, and weds to a perfervid imagination stern religious convictions, intense practicality, and prosaic tenacity of purpose. Theirs were the surroundings fitted alike to mould the poet or the hero—him who should sing of the chivalry of the past, or him who should be of the chivalry of the present, in whatever field is scope for praiseworthy ambition and highest aspiration— clear-sighted vision and undaunted courage, dogged persistence and untiring perseverance, fortitude under reverses, and physical powers to endure privation.

This, then, was the heritage which Ettrickdale had to offer to her sons; and this, as one of them, the heritage of Mungo Park, the first of the knight errantry of Africa.

BIRTHPLACE OF MUNGO PARK.

Of the early life of him who was destined to partially unveil the face of Africa we know but little, though that little is sufficiently significant and satisfactory.

Mungo Park was born on the 10th September 1771 in the cottage of Foulshiels, some four and a half miles from Selkirk. Foulshiels stands in the very centre of the loveliest scenery of the glen of Yarrow, facing on the opposite side of the valley the stately tower of Newark. Eastward it commands a view over the woods and groves and "birchen bowers" of the widening dale to where it merges in the valley of the Ettrick near Selkirk. Westward it fronts a magnificent panorama of hill and dale, through which curves the Yarrow in broken gleaming reaches, from the wild romantic scenery of its loch and mountain sources. To front and rear rise stately hills, their bases separated and washed by the rushing streams, their lower slopes clad with oak and fir, their upper with grass and heather, over which the winds sweep unopposed.

But if the surroundings of Park's birthplace were grand, the cottage, of which the ruins still exist, was humble in the extreme. It was neither better nor worse than might be tenanted by shepherds of the present day in out-of-the-way places, being built substantially of whinstone and lime, and containing at the most three apartments. The building presents not a trace of ornament, not a relieving cornice, thus fitly expressing the character of its occupants, their extreme practicality, their plain honest soundness and indifference to all external graces. From such a cottage sprang a Burns, and later on a Carlyle.

Mungo was the seventh child of a family of thirteen, of whom, however, only eight reached the age of maturity. By unremitting care and hard work his father had raised himself to the position of a small farmer—how small his cottage sufficiently shows. In him, however, we have undoubtedly one of that type of Scottish fathers who will pinch his own body and double the slavery of his life in order that his children may receive a better education than he himself had, and that their minds at least may not be starved and stunted. As Park's first biographer puts it, writing in 1816, "The attention of the Scottish farmers and peasantry to the early instruction of their children is strongly exemplified in the history of Park's family. The diffusion of knowledge among the natives of that part of the kingdom and their general intelligence must be admitted by every unprejudiced observer; nor is there any country in which the effects of education are so conspicuous in promoting industry and good conduct, and in producing useful and respectable men of the inferior and middle classes admirably fitted for all the important offices of common life."

It would seem that there was no school near enough to Foulshiels for the Park children in the earlier years of their life to be able to attend, since we find a resident teacher engaged to impart the necessary rudiments of education.

With maturer years Mungo was transferred to the Selkirk Grammar School, to which he probably walked each morning.

From this time we begin to get glimpses of his peculiar personality and character. It does not appear that he showed any special talent while at school, though constant in his attendance, and studious in application. We gather that he was dreamy and reserved, a great reader, a lover of poetry, and passionately fond of the quaint lore and simple minstrelsy so markedly associated with the border counties of Scotland.

His, clearly, was not the temperament which would receive its guiding impulses from the routine work of school or the precepts and instruction of schoolmasters. Such conventional influences would never have led him to Africa. His inspirations were derived from the ballads that were sung and the tales that were told by every country fireside. For him the rushing Yarrow, Newark's ruined towers, the spreading field, the swelling hillside, and the mountain top were teachers, each with a tale to tell of bold adventure or of deadly strife.

The whole country was redolent with the romance of the half-forgotten past, with a hundred memories dear to a patriotic heart. In all around him there was something to throw a glamour over his young eager mind, something to fire his imagination and arouse eager longings to be up and doing deeds undefined, yet ever great and noble. From the stately castle, which now looked down on him in melancholy ruined majesty, brave knights of bygone days had ridden forth to fight for king and country or for love. Their day was past, but might not he in other guise emerge from his lowly cottage, and with other weapons win his golden spurs.

In what way all these vague ambitions and this spiritual fermentation was to end there was but small indication. It is given only to the few to realise in after life the romantic dreams of their youth.

At first it seems Mungo was destined by his father for the ministry, but he himself preferred medicine, to which choice no objection appears to have been made.

To acquire the rudiments of his medical education, when fifteen years of age he was placed, as was the custom of the time, as apprentice to Dr. Thomas Anderson, a surgeon in Selkirk, a gentleman whose descendants still practise the healing art in the same town. For three years he remained with the Doctor, not only acquiring a knowledge of medicine, but still further grounding himself in the classics and other branches of education at the Grammar School.

Further than this we know nothing of his life in the Anderson family, though that his time was agreeably spent we may deduce from the fact that, as we shall see later on, he some years after married Dr. Anderson's eldest daughter.

In the year 1789 Park left Selkirk for the University of Edinburgh to complete his medical studies. Three successive sessions seems to have been all that was necessary to qualify in these days.

We are told that he was an ardent student, and distinguished among his fellows. Botany was his favourite subject, this fact being doubtless largely due to the inspiring influence of his brother-in-law, Mr. James Dickson, who from being a gardener had raised himself by his own exertions to be no common botanist and the author of some valuable and important works.

It was while still a medical student that Park came more directly in contact with Dickson, and with him he went a botanical tour in the Highlands.

Dickson did more for his young brother-in-law than inspire him with a love of botany. He was on a footing of considerable intimacy with Sir Joseph Banks, one of the chief managers of the African Association, and when Park left the University he introduced him to his influential friend, and so brought him in contact with the influences which were to make Mungo Park the first of famous African travellers.

But the time was not yet. Park had still to prepare himself practically for his great mission by widening his experience of life and travel—had still to get further bitten with the fever of unrest. Hence in 1792 we find him sailing not to Africa, but to the East, as surgeon in the East India Company's service.

At this point he supplies us with an admirable and characteristic glimpse of himself in a letter addressed to his teacher in surgery and future father-in-law, Dr. Anderson of Selkirk. The letter is dated London, 23rd January 1793, and the following is an interesting portion:—

"I have now got upon the first step of the stair of ambition. Here's a figure of it. (A pen and ink sketch is here given of a flight of steps with a man on the lowest.) It very nearly resembles one of Gordon's traps which he uses in the library. Now, if I should run up the stair, you see the consequence. I must either be mortified by seeing I can get no further, or, by taking an airy step, knock my brains out against the large folio of some succeeding author. May I use my little advantage in height to enable me to perform the office of a watchman to the rest of mankind, and call to them, 'Take care, sirs! Don't look too high, or you'll break your legs on that stool. Open your eyes; you are going straight for the fire.'

"Passed at Surgeons' Hall! Associate of the Linnean Society! I walked three or four times backwards and forwards through the hall, and had actually begun to count the panes of glass in the large window, when the bell rang, and the beadle roared out, 'Mr. Park!' Macbeth's start when he beheld the dagger was a mere jest compared to mine....

"I have purchased Stewart's Philosophy to amuse me at sea. As you are in Edinburgh, you will write to me what people say of its religious character. You told me in Sandy's (his brother Alexander presumably, who was at the time following the medical course he himself had just completed) letter that you would write me next week. I have too much to say, and therefore must speak by halves.

"The melancholy, who complain of the shortness of human life, and the voluptuous, who think the present only their own, strive to fill up every moment with sensual enjoyment; but the man whose soul has been enlightened by his Creator, and enabled, though dimly, to discern the wonders of salvation, will look upon the joys and afflictions of this life as equally the tokens of Divine love. He will walk through the world as one travelling to a better country, looking forward with wonder to the author and finisher of his faith....

"*P.S.*—I sail in about a month."

I have now got upon the first step of the stair of ambition here's a figure of it it very nearly resembles one of Gordons traps which he uses in the library. now if I should run up the stair you see the consequence I must either be mortified by seeing I can get no farther or by taking an airy step knock my brains out against the large folio of some succeeding author—

EXTRACT OF LETTER FROM MUNGO PARK TO DR. ANDERSON.

It was in this buoyant mood of the young conqueror-to-be that Park looked forth upon the field of enterprise opened up to him, and with Stewart's Philosophy to amuse him, and his deeply rooted religious convictions to sustain him, left England for the Indies.

As showing the force of these convictions, we may quote another letter, written to Dr. Anderson when on the point of departure:—

"I have now reached that height that I can behold the tumults of nations with indifference, confident that the reins of events are in our Father's hands. May you and I (not like the stubborn mule, but like the weaning child) obey His hand, that after all the troubles of this dark world in which we are truly strangers, we may, through the wonders of atonement, reach a far greater and exceeding weight of glory. I wish you may be able to look upon the day of your departure with the same resignation that I do on mine. My hope is now approaching to a certainty. If I be deceived, may God alone put me right, for I would rather die in the delusion than wake to all the joys of earth. May the Holy Spirit dwell for ever in your heart, my dear friend, and if I never see my native land again, may I rather see the green sod on your grave than see you anything but a Christian."

Nothing noteworthy marked this voyage to Sumatra, but his stay there was by no means wasted time, since it afforded him an excellent opportunity of indulging his scientific tastes, not as the collector merely, but also and chiefly as the accurate observer.

A paper in the Linnean Transactions on eight new fishes from Sumatra is sufficient evidence both of his industry and of his scientific attainments.

Park returned to England after a year's absence, and was now ripe for the work in store for him. It nowhere appears that so far he had even once thought of Africa as a possible field for his ambition and energies. His natural temperament, however, had been a fertile soil for the romantic ideas which his early environment had planted. His medical education had further fitted him for the work of exploration, besides bringing him more sympathetically in contact with his botanical brother-in-law, who again was to bring him within the sphere of influence of Sir Joseph Banks, and through him of the African Association. Following these various determining influences came the first taste of travel, the wider experience, and the knowledge of the good and evil of the wanderer's life. All that remained wanting was the golden opportunity to prove in action his potential capacity for heroic service in the fields of geographical research.

The return of Park from his first voyage was the turning point in his career. At the moment there was a crisis in the affairs of the African Association. Everything they had attempted had ended disastrously, and news had just reached them of the sad death of Major Houghton. Should the task now be given up, or was it to be resumed with renewed zeal and ardour? There could be but one answer. The work begun must be continued. Surely in the end it must be crowned with success. Meantime, who was to take it up?

While the Association was thus inquiring for the man fitted to entrust with their perilous venture, Park was still undecided as to what course in life he was to pursue. With Sir Joseph Banks as a link between, there could not fail to be a speedy understanding and a mutual settlement of the questions at issue for both. The projects of the Association speedily came to Park's ears. Here was the very work he wanted, promising opportunities to indulge in his love of travel and natural history far transcending his wildest dreams. A splendid prospect of a great work accomplished and glory won, of difficulties surmounted and fame achieved, opened up before him. Before such a chance there could be no irresolution, no doubting, no fears. His course was clear, and at once he volunteered his services, which were, on the part of the Company, as promptly and eagerly accepted as they had been offered.

Mungo Park was then twenty-four years of age.

CHAPTER VI.
AT THE THRESHOLD.

On the 22nd of May 1795, Mungo Park left England on board the *Endeavour*, an African trader. On the 21st of the following month he landed at the mouth of the river Gambia.

Bathurst, the present seat of government for the Gambia basin, was not then in existence, with its present busy European community and thriving native population, its imposing public buildings and well laid out streets. The native town of Jillifri on the north bank, and a little way up the river, was the first place of call in the early trading days of the Gambia merchants.

From Jillifri the *Endeavour* ascended the river to Jonkakonda.

The view which opened up before Park as he proceeded was neither attractive nor promising. The river flowed seaward deep and muddy, its banks covered with impenetrable forests of mangrove, forming when the tide was out a horrible expanse of swamp. The air was thick with a sickening haze, charged with the poisonous exhalations from the fœtid mud engendered by heat and moisture. Here and there only, a group of cocoa-nuts, or an isolated bombyx (silk-cotton tree) relieved the dreary monotony, and gave a momentary pleasure to the eye.

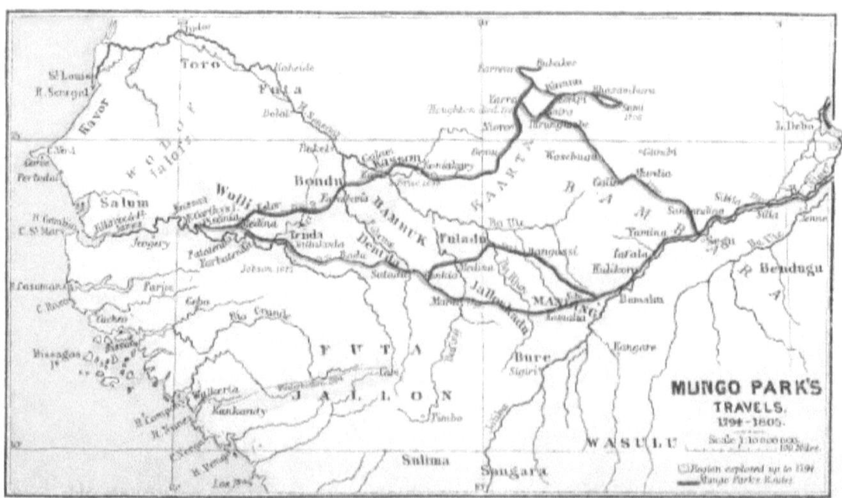

Behind the mangrove swamps the country spread out in a level plain, "very generally covered with woods, and presenting a tiresome and gloomy uniformity to the eye; but although nature has denied to the inhabitants the beauties of romantic landscapes, she has bestowed on them with a liberal hand the more important blessings of fertility and abundance."

At Jonkakonda, which seems to have been one of the chief trading stations on the river, Park left the *Endeavour*, and proceeded to the factory of Pisania, a few miles further on.

In Dr. Laidley, the agent in charge, for whom he brought letters, Park found not only a generous host, but also a thoroughly competent adviser, and for several succeeding months the merchant's house and wide experience were alike at his disposal.

The objects to be attained by his expedition were—To reach the river Niger by such route as might be found most convenient; to ascertain its origin, course, and if possible its termination; to visit the chief towns in its neighbourhood, but more particularly Timbuktu and those of the Haussa country.

Park's ardent enthusiasm was ever tempered with the caution and prudent practical character of his race. Like an old campaigner he set about learning what was ahead of him, and otherwise preparing for his difficult and dangerous task. The Mandingo language had to be acquired, that he might come into more sympathetic touch with the natives, and be more independent of interpreters, ever a source of profound danger, and often the greatest obstacle to the advance of the explorer into unknown countries. In addition inquiries had to be made regarding routes, the dangers to be avoided, and the general condition of travel in these parts. Without such information it was clear to him that he would be as a blind man walking in a country beset with a thousand pitfalls.

But while thus preparing for his task, Park was not oblivious to what was more immediately around. We get glimpses of him making natural history collections by day, and taking astronomical observations by night. In particular he occupied himself in getting up the details of the trade of the Gambia. Since the time when Stibbs had ascended the river in the vain hope of reaching the Niger, a considerable change had come over the commerce of the region. The fancied wealth of Timbuktu had not been tapped, but the commodities of the countries within reach of the river had proved no inconsiderable source of profit. In the year 1730 we find one factory alone consisting of a governor, deputy-governor, and two other principal officers; eight factors (hence the word factory) or trading agents, thirteen writers, twenty inferior attendants and tradesmen, a company of soldiers, and thirty- two negro servants, not to speak of the crews of various sloops, shallops, and boats. From that date, however, competition set in, till at the end of the century the gross value of British exports had fallen to £20,000.

It is worthy of note that even in Park's time the chief article of export is slaves. Accustomed as we are in these days to denounce in the strongest terms this vile traffic, and to brand as the most degraded and brutal of their race those who engage in it, it is difficult to realise that less than a century ago we ourselves were the chief traffickers in human flesh and blood. How little this horrible trade touched the conscience of the individual or of the country at large is sufficiently shown by Park's own narrative. We seek there in vain for a word of condemnation, or the indication of a consciousness that there was any iniquity in it. Not, be it noted, for lack of knowledge of the attendant cruelties or even through lack of pity for the victims. On the contrary, he describes "the poor wretches while waiting shipment kept constantly fettered two and two together, and employed in the labours of the field; and, I am sorry to add, very scantily fed, as well as harshly treated."

Later on he accompanied a slave caravan on its way to the coast. With simple naturalness he tells the whole story of the horrors of the route, describing the fetters and chains, the frightful marches, with heavy loads, under a sweltering sun, and with starvation rations; the whip mercilessly applied to the weary to stimulate them to further exertions, and the knife placed to the throat of the hopelessly exhausted, at once to rid them of pain and their drivers of a burden —"an operation I did not wish to see, and therefore marched on."

He is quite aware that all these horrors are perpetrated that a European market may be supplied. He knows also what has preceded the slave path, and yet, incredible as it may seem, not one indignant protest is drawn from him, not one appeal to Christian Europe, not even a word of commendation of the work already inaugurated for its suppression. Quite the opposite, in fact, on which point let Park speak for himself. "How far it (slavery) is maintained and supported by the slave traffic, which for two hundred years the nations of Europe have carried on with the natives of the coast, it is neither within my province nor in my power to explain. If my sentiments should be required concerning the effect which a discontinuance of that commerce would produce on the manners of the natives, I should have no hesitation in observing that in the present unenlightened state of their minds my opinion is, the effect would neither be so extensive or beneficial as many wise and worthy persons fondly expect."

The wonder of the thing is intensified, to our mind, when we reflect on the deep religious nature of Park, his genuine kind-heartedness, his noble ambitions, and his appreciation of all that is sweet in human nature. The story is pregnant with meaning as to the influence of our environment in opening or shutting our eyes to what is going on around us.

But while Britain was then awakening to a sense of its guilt, and preparing to purge itself of the unholy traffic, we find from Park's notes that a new trade, destined to have almost as terrible consequences, was already established. Europe, he tells us, took from the Gambia chiefly slaves, and gave in return spirits and ammunition. For over two hundred years the unfortunate natives of Africa had been treated as wild creatures, the lawful prey and spoil of the higher races. The mother was tempted to sell her child, and the chief his subjects. Village fought against village, and tribe against tribe, that American plantations might be tilled. As wild beasts and things accursed the negroes were shot down in myriads, in myriads they perished on the road, in myriads were transported to a life of shame and misery. And now, when a new order of things was about to be instituted, there had commenced another hundred years of disgraceful commerce to complete the work of brutalising the West Coast negro, of blighting all elevating impulses, and suppressing all habits of industry, transforming him into what he is to-day—the most villainous, treacherous, and vicious being to be found in all Africa.

Thanks to the slave trade in past centuries, and the gin traffic in the present, our West Coast Settlements, instead of being bright jewels in the imperial crown of Britain, are at this day little better than standing monuments to her disgrace. Happily the closing years of this century are showing signs of an awakened public conscience. Governments, companies, and private merchants alike are taking a higher view of their responsibilities to barbarous races, and before another half century has come and gone we may hope to see the vile monster badly scotched if not killed.

But while we gather from Park that in his day the slave trade was carried on by British merchants without a qualm of conscience, and that already gunpowder and gin formed the staple articles of barter for human flesh and blood, it is hardly less noteworthy that Islam was steadily making its beneficent influence felt throughout the whole land. He tells us that the inhabitants were divided into two great classes—the *Sonakies* or spirit drinkers, and the *Bushreens* or Mohammedans: the former, pagans sinking deeper and deeper in the scale of humanity under the degrading influence of European intercourse and commerce; the latter ever rising upward, adopting decent dress and decent behaviour, building mosques and establishing schools, and specially attempting to stem the flood of vile spirits poured into the country by Christian merchants.

We have in a previous chapter alluded to the mighty revolution produced by Islam in the Central Sudan. Here we are only at the missionary outposts. Further inland, as we follow the footsteps of Park, we shall see more and more of the good work Mohammedanism had accomplished in Central Africa.

Meanwhile it was not all study and observation with the young explorer. He had to go through a seasoning process of an unpleasant nature. Having on one occasion imprudently exposed himself to the night dew, he caught a fever, and while recovering had a second attack, which kept him a prisoner for some additional weeks.

Thanks to the care of Dr. Laidley no evil consequences followed, while "his company and conversation beguiled the tedious hours during that gloomy season (the rains): when suffocating heats oppress by day, and when the night is spent by the terrified traveller in listening to the croaking of frogs, of which the numbers are beyond imagination, the shrill cry of the jackal, and the deep howling of the hyena—a dismal concert interrupted only by the roar of such tremendous thunder as no person can form a conception of but those who have heard it."

CHAPTER VII.
FROM THE GAMBIA TO THE SENEGAL.

The time had at last arrived for Park to start on his great undertaking.

In the beginning of October the Gambia had attained its greatest height, or fifteen feet above the high-water mark of the tide, and then had begun to subside rapidly, so that by the beginning of November the river had sunk to its normal level. This was the time to travel. The natives had reaped their crops, and food was cheap and plentiful. The rains were over, the land well drained and dried, the atmosphere less moist and oppressive—all of which circumstances combined to make travelling more agreeable and infinitely more healthy.

At first Park had hoped to accompany a native caravan going into the interior, but abandoned the idea on finding that he would have to wait an indefinite period for such an escort. He therefore determined to depend on his own resources rather than lose another good travelling season.

On the 2nd December 1795 he was ready for the road. Accustomed as we are to read of the huge caravans, the quantities of goods, stores, ammunition, and instruments required by exploring expeditions to the heart of Africa in these degenerate days, we cannot but be surprised at the modest retinue and scanty *impedimenta* which Park thought necessary for his great task. His sole attendants were a negro servant named Johnson, who had been to Jamaica as a slave, but being freed had returned to his native country; and Demba, a slave boy belonging to Dr. Laidley, who, besides Mandingo, spoke the language of one of the inland tribes.

As beasts of burden Park had a small but hardy and spirited horse for himself, and two donkeys for his servants. As baggage he had provisions for two days; a small assortment of beads, amber, and tobacco for the purchase of fresh supplies as needed; a few changes of linen and other necessary articles of dress; an umbrella, a pocket sextant, a magnetic compass, and a thermometer. For defensive purposes he was provided with two fowling-pieces, two pairs of pistols, and some other small weapons. Thus attended, thus provided, and thus armed, Mungo Park started for the Heart of Africa—an uncertain bourne only to be reached through deadly perils and frightful miseries and hardships. How splendidly equipped he must have been with the real necessaries of the hero— unflinching determination, ardent enthusiasm, Homeric resolve, and absolute self-reliance. Thus provided with moral weapons and stimulants he could rise superior to every difficulty and danger, and emerge from the unequal struggle uncrushed, undefeated, bearing with him not all, but much of the prize for which he had staked life itself.

Besides Johnson and Demba, Park had the advantage of the company of a Mohammedan on his way to Bambarra, two slatees or slave-merchants going to Bondou, and a blacksmith returning home to Kasson.

For the first two marches Dr. Laidley and two other Europeans accompanied him on his way, feeling as if they were performing the last offices for the dead, for they never expected to see him again.

On the 3rd of December he took leave of these kind friends, and turned his face inland towards the east and the Unknown. As he rode slowly into the woods, after breaking the last link which connected him with Europe and civilisation, and took the road so lately traversed by Major Houghton, he could not but recall that to the latter it had been a road to death. Before him rose up pictures of repellent waterless deserts, of trackless jungles, gloomy primeval forests, and miasmatic marshes which had to be penetrated before his eyes would rest upon the river Niger. Only too clearly he saw the dangers from man and beast which had to be faced before he could ever hope to get once more in touch with European civilisation. "Thoughts like these necessarily cast a gloom over the mind, and I rode musingly along for about three miles, when I was awakened from my reverie by a body of people who came running up and stopped my asses." And with his reflections thus broken by one of the innumerable annoyances of African travel, they were not again resumed.

For the first few marches there was little to note either in incidents of travel or in aspects of man and nature. The scenery was pleasant, though but slightly varied—gentle wooded acclivities everywhere, alternating with cultivated interspaces surrounding towns and villages. The inhabitants were Mandingoes, untroubled by the trammels of clothes, Pagans for the most part, and confirmed spirit drinkers; the rest Mohammedans, respectable in character, decent in dress and behaviour, lovers of education and religion, haters of strong drink.

By both divisions of the community Park was hospitably received, and treated to such simple fare and lodging as they themselves possessed. With daily practice the fatigues of the way became less harassing, while a keen appetite, and the knowledge that absolutely nothing else was to be had, made otherwise coarse food seem palatable. Gradually a new standard of comfort was formed on a scale proportionate to present possibilities, so that at length positive enjoyment could be got out of both food and lodging which previously would have been deemed repulsive and miserable.

From the district of Walli Park entered that of Wuli. At Medina, the capital of the latter, he was received kindly by the king, who strongly dissuaded him from proceeding further east into countries where the white man was unknown, and where the fate of Houghton might be his. But Park was not to be discouraged, seeing which the king provided him with a guide to take him on his way.

From Medina the route diverged from the Gambia, and passed E.N.E. towards the Senegal. For some days nothing special characterised the march. Everywhere, however, the explorer gets interesting glimpses of the life and ways of the natives, of their genius for story-telling and their forensic skill, or of their love of wrestling, an art in which they are such adepts that he "thinks that few Europeans would have been able to cope with the conqueror."

At one place he finds that the men have a curious way of administering disciplinary punishment to troublesome wives.

Evidently in the huge feminine establishments of the Mandingo husband the ordinary human hand is unable to keep the women in due subjection and order. The unfortunate husband with trouble in the house, and afraid to tackle the offender or offenders in the ordinary manner, has recourse to underhand ways. In every village a masquerading dress is kept for the use of Mumbo Jumbo, a mysterious person whose business it is to seek out and punish wayward wives. When a husband finds matters becoming too hot for him in his household, he secretly possesses himself of this dress and disappears into the woods. At nightfall frightful noises are heard near the town—the signal that Mumbo Jumbo is abroad. Terror falls upon every mutinous and erring member of the frail yet troublesome sex, for no one knows on whom the rod shall descend. None, however, dare to disobey the summons, for now they have to deal with the devil himself, backed up by all the male powers of the village. For the men the occasion is a joyous one—though not so for the women. All hurry to the meeting-place to take part in the proceedings, and unite in the active assertion of marital authority. But the victim is not immediately pounced upon. The terrors and uncertainties of conscious backsliders must be endured for hours, cloaked beneath a well-simulated air of innocence and careless gaiety. The time is spent in songs and dances, as if to celebrate the coming detection of the rebel and the triumph of order and the principle of masculine rule. About midnight the witch-like revelry ceases, and a frost of uneasy silence falls upon the female throng. Who is to be the victim? The next moment the question is practically answered, as one of the number is seized, stripped naked, tied to a post, and severely scourged amid the applause of the crowd, loudest among whom are the ninety and nine other women, each of whom a moment before had thought herself a possible sufferer.

A similar spirit is not unknown in our own country and times.

On the 11th December Mungo Park, without mishap or discouragement, had reached Kujar, the frontier town of Wuli, to the east.

Between Wuli and Bondou, the next country, there lay a waterless wilderness, two days' march in extent. The guide from the King of Wuli had here to return, and his place was taken by three elephant hunters.

At Kujar, Park found himself examined with an increased curiosity and reverence, indicating a much less degree of familiarity with the white man.

On the 12th the party started for the passage of the wilderness, minus one of the guides, who had absconded with the money he had received in advance. Before proceeding far the two remaining guides insisted on stopping till they had ensured a safe journey by preparing a charm which would divert all danger from them. The charm was simple enough, and consisted in muttering a few sentences over a stone, which was afterwards spat upon and thrown in the direction of travel—a process repeated three times.

At midday the little party of travellers reached a tree, called by the natives *Neema Faba*, which was hung all over with offerings of rags and scraps of cloth to propitiate the evil spirit of the place. This practice prevails throughout the length and breadth of savage Africa, though Park appears to have mistaken its meaning, and thinking it due to the desire of travellers to indicate that water was near, followed their example by hanging on one of the boughs a handsome piece of cloth. At the neighbouring pool, where they had proposed to camp, signs of a recently extinguished fire made them suspicious of the vicinity of robbers, and they therefore pushed ahead to the next well, which they did not reach till eight in the evening.

For the first time the dangers and difficulties of his journey were brought vividly home to Park when after a hard day's work he and his party had to lie out in the open, on the bare ground, surrounded by their animals, and had to keep strict watch and ward for possible attack. With daylight they filled their water-skins and calabashes and set out for Falika, the western frontier town of Bondou, which they reached before midday.

In Bondou, Park found new aspects of nature and other races of men.

For fertility the land was unsurpassed. Lying on the parting ridge between the Gambia and the Senegal, it was better drained than the country left behind, a fact evidenced by the appearance of the mimosa. Towards the east it rose into ranges of hills.

Far different, too, were the Fulah inhabitants. A tawny complexion, small, well-shaped features, and soft, silky hair, distinguished them at a glance from the negro races around them. Among them Mohammedanism was the prevailing religion, though not by any means exercised intolerantly, "for the system of Mahomet is made to extend itself by means abundantly more efficacious. By establishing schools in the different towns, where many of the Pagan as well as Mohammedan children are taught to read the Koran, and instructed in the tenets of the Prophet, the Mohammedan priests fix a bias on the mind and form the character of their young disciples which no accidents of life can ever afterwards remove or alter." Of which latter fact let our Christian missionaries take note, and if possible learn a lesson therefrom.

This remarkable race did not originally belong to Bondou. Further south they were in even greater force, though scattered in more or less independent communities from Lake Chad to the Atlantic, a fact destined, after Park's time, to have the most important bearing upon the history of the whole of the Western and Central Sudan.

Everywhere Park found the Fulahs remarkable for their industry, and no less successful in agriculture than in pastoral pursuits, which seem to have been their original speciality. In their hands Bondou developed a degree of wealth unknown in neighbouring states. Its prosperity, however, was also in great measure due to its being on the chief highway of the commerce from the interior to the coast, considerable duties being levied on all merchandise passing through it.

At Falika, Park secured the services of an officer of the King of Bondou as guide as far as Fatticonda, the capital.

On resuming their journey a violent quarrel broke out between two of Park's companions, which would probably have ended in bloodshed, but for the interference of the white man, and his determined threat that he would shoot down the first who again drew sword—an ultimatum which had the desired effect. The rest of the march was accomplished in sullen silence, till a good supper terminated all heart-burnings, and animosities were forgotten under the influence of the diverting stories and sweet harmonies of an itinerant musician.

On the 15th the party crossed the Nereko, a considerable branch of the Gambia, and stayed for the night at Kurkarany, a walled town provided with a mosque. Four days later they crossed a dry stony height covered with mimosas, and entered the basin of the Senegal.

They were now more within the sphere of influence of French traders, who, as Park soon saw, had succeeded with characteristic genius in suiting the taste of the ladies of the country. These he found dressed in a thin French gauze, admirably adapted for the hot climate, and rendered dear to its wearers by the manner in which it displayed and heightened their charms. Their manners proved to be as irresistible as their dress, so that Park found it impossible to withstand their appeals for amber, beads, and other bits of showy finery. Having despoiled him of all he had, these "sturdy beggars" tore his cloak, cut the buttons from his servant's clothes, and were proceeding to other outrages, when finding this more than his gallantry could stand, he mounted his horse and fled, leaving them disconsolate, but with abundant souvenirs.

Next day the Falemé, a turbulent tributary of the Senegal, was reached. The natives were actively engaged fishing, and the country around was covered with large and beautiful fields of millet.

It was not without apprehension that Park on the 21st December entered Fatticonda, the capital of Bondou. His predecessor Houghton had here been plundered and badly used, and he had every reason to fear a similar fate. But the situation was not to be evaded, so he braced himself up as best he might to face whatever was in store for him.

On entering the town, he and his party took up their station at the Palaver House or Bentang, as is the fashion of strangers, who thus make known their necessities, and mutely appeal for a night's lodging. They had not long to wait before a respectable slatee invited them to his house.

An hour afterwards a messenger came to conduct the traveller to the king. Finding himself led out of the town, Park began to fear a trap, but was reassured on being shown the king sitting under a tree, and hearing that such was his way of giving a private audience. The stranger's statement that he was no trader, and that he only travelled from motives of curiosity, was received with incredulity.

In the evening Park proceeded to make a more formal call. First, however, he concealed some of his goods in the roof of the hut, and donned his best coat, hoping thus to save them from the possible plundering he might be subjected to.

The king's quarters were found to be converted into a species of citadel by a high mud wall, having a number of inner courts, each court containing several huts. After threading a series of intricate passages guarded by armed sentinels, the king, Almami, was at last reached. Again he showed himself but half satisfied with the white man's explanations of the object of his visit. The idea of travelling merely to gratify curiosity was too new to his experience. It seemed the fancy of a madman. The presents offered put him in good humour, however, in particular the gift of a large umbrella.

As Park was about to take his leave, Almami stopped him, and commenced a eulogium of the generosity and immense wealth of the white men. From the general he came down to the particular, and had much that was flattering to say of his guest for the time being—a praise soon directed pointedly to the traveller's handsome coat and shining buttons, until at length it became clear to its owner that it was not only admired but coveted. There was nothing for it but to take the coat off and lay it at the feet of the wily monarch, who did his best to console the giver by declaring that henceforth the garment should be his state dress for all great occasions.

For once Park's caution had overreached its object.

Next morning the traveller visited by request the wives of Almami. He found himself surrounded by a dozen young and handsome women, decorated with gold and amber, who clamoured for physic and beads, and to have some blood taken from them. They rallied him upon the whiteness of his skin, which they said was due to his having been dipped in milk when an infant; and on the prominence of his nose, which they declared had been pinched into that shape by his mother. Park was equal to the occasion. He had compliments for all of them. The glossy jet of their skin and the contours of their *retroussé* noses, the bright glitter of their eyes and brilliant whiteness of their teeth were alike praised. This delicate flattery, with the addition of some bloodletting and a quantity of drastic medicine, was irresistible; and, though Park does not say so, undoubtedly the good impression he left behind among the ladies contributed materially to his immunity from the fate of his predecessor. Not only was he not plundered, but his baggage was not even searched. Still better, Almami on parting gave him five drachms of gold.

On the 23rd the traveller resumed his journey in the best of spirits after his unexpectedly good reception. At mid-day a halt was called for rest and refreshment, by way of preparation for the passage of the dangerous district lying between Bondou and the next country, Kajaaga, which it would be necessary to traverse under cover of night.

As soon as the people of the village were asleep, the donkeys were reloaded, and as silently as possible, so as not to disturb the villagers, the party passed out into the wilderness. The moon was shining brightly, illumining their way. The air was perfectly still, raising neither sigh nor rustle from leaf or bough. The deep solitudes of the forest were undisturbed save by the solemn impressive howling of wild beasts, and shrieks and hoots of night-birds which mingled discordantly with the deafening musical uproar of myriad insects, and the clutter of innumerable frogs. Except in whispers, not a word was uttered. Every one was on the alert, at times guiding the animals, more often peering ahead, or to right and left, on the lookout for possible robbers.

Happily no human enemies appeared, though many were the alarms, as from time to time an unusual sound, or the vaguely descried figure of a prowling hyena, made each man seize his gun with a firmer grasp. Towards morning a village was reached where the little party were enabled to rest themselves and their animals before entering in the afternoon the country of Kajaaga.

CHAPTER VIII.
ACROSS THE SENEGAL BASIN.

The further Park proceeded east the drier and purer became the climate, and the more interesting the landscape. In Kajaaga, lying between the Falemé and the Senegal, he found a country everywhere interspersed with a pleasing variety of hills and valleys, to which the serpentine windings of the Senegal descending from the rocky heights gave both picturesqueness and beauty. The inhabitants, unlike the Fulahs, were jet black in complexion, resembling in this respect the Joloffs nearer the coast.

The people of Kajaaga are known as Serawulies, and are noted for their keen trading propensities—at this time chiefly directed towards supplying slaves to the British factories on the Gambia.

On the 24th December Park entered Joag, the western frontier town, and was there hospitably received by the chief man of the place, officially known as Dooty or Duté. The town was surrounded by a high mud wall, as was also every individual private establishment. Though the headman and the principal inhabitants were Mohammedans, it appeared that the great mass of the people were still Pagans, as was sufficiently shown by the nature of their wild night revelries—"the ladies in their dances vying with each other in displaying the most voluptuous movements imaginable."

Park's trials were now about to commence. During the night a number of horsemen arrived, and after talking with the host, took up their quarters in the Palaver House beside the traveller himself. Thinking the latter was asleep, one of them attempted to steal his gun, but finding he could not effect his purpose undiscovered, he desisted from the attempt. This, however, was but a foretaste of coming trouble. It was easy to see that Johnson was growing very uneasy at the aspect of affairs; not without cause either, as very soon became evident. Two of Park's companions, who had been at a dance in a neighbouring village, came in with the news that a party of the king's horsemen had been heard inquiring if the white man had passed, and on being told that he was at Joag, had immediately galloped off in that direction.

Even while they were speaking the horsemen arrived, and next moment Park found himself surrounded by some twenty soldiers, each carrying a musket. Resistance was useless; he could only wait in much anxiety to hear his fate.

At length, after a brief interval, a member of the party, who was loaded with an enormous number of charms to ward off all forms of evil, opened their business in a long harangue. The white man, they said, had violated the laws of the country by entering it without paying the customary duties, and had accordingly forfeited everything he possessed. The soldiers had orders to take him to the king by force if necessary.

Conceive the position Park was now in. Utter ruin stared him in the face, and the collapse of all his cherished schemes. To fight was out of the question. All he could do was to try to gain a little time to think matters out, and seek the advice of his companions and host. They were unanimous in declaring that it would be disastrous to him to accompany the horsemen. A long argument with the spokesman ensued, by dint of which, and the present of Almami's five drachms of gold, the messenger became somewhat mollified.

They demanded, however, to be shown the baggage, from which they helped themselves to whatever they happened to fancy; and having thus despoiled their victim of half his goods, they left him to his gloomy reflections and an indifferent supper after a day of fast.

Thus reduced in his already scanty resources, and his power to travel correspondingly limited, Park found but Job's comforters in his companions. One and all they urged him to turn back from his hopeless task. Johnson, especially, laughed at the very idea of proceeding further, miserably provided as they were. But the spirit of the leader rose superior to his misfortunes, and he never for a moment admitted the idea of retreat. While strength remained there could be no flinching from his task. Yet his thoughts were gloomy enough that night as he sat reviewing his situation through the hours of darkness by the side of a smouldering fire. Morning brought no improvement to his position. The scanty supper was followed by no breakfast.

What few articles still remained dared not be produced, lest they too should be plundered. It was resolved, therefore, to pass the day without food, trusting to Providence for a stray meal sooner or later.

As the day wore on the pangs of hunger began to make themselves felt. To allay this in some measure the unfortunate travellers chewed straws, a make-believe yielding as scant comfort as it did sustenance. But Park's faith in God was not belied. Towards evening an old female slave passed by with a basket on her head, and struck by his woe-begone, famished look, she asked him if he had had his dinner. Thinking she spoke in jest, he did not reply. Not so his boy Demba, who volubly, and with the eloquence of suffering, told the story of their misfortunes and their needs. In a moment the old woman had her basket on the ground, and a plentiful supply of ground-nuts was placed in their hands, the donor thereafter marching away without waiting for a word of thanks.

Further good fortune was now in store for them. It happened that Demba Sego Jalla, the Mandingo king of Kasson further east, had sent his nephew to the King of Kajaaga to try to arrange some disputes which were threatening to lead to war. The embassy, however, had met with no success. Returning homeward, the king's nephew had heard of there being a white man at Joag who was desirous of visiting Kasson, and curiosity brought him to see the stranger. On hearing Park's story, the young noble offered him his protection all the way—an offer that was eagerly and gratefully accepted.

Thus guided and protected, Park set out for Kasson on the 27th. Some distance on the way Johnson, in spite of his life in Jamaica and his seven years' residence in England, showed that he still was saturated with the superstitious ideas of his youth by producing a white chicken and tying it by the leg to a particular tree as an offering to the spirits of the woods. The same belief in nature spirits has already been alluded to in a previous chapter. Anthropologists tell us that it must at one time have been universal, and evidences of it are found not only in the charming legends of the Greeks, with their nymphs of meadow, grove, and spring, and dryads growing with the oaks and pines, but also in our own Anglo-Saxon words.

In the evening the party safely arrived at Sami, on the banks of the Senegal. Park describes the sister river to the Gambia as being at this point a beautiful but shallow stream, flowing slowly over a bed of sand and gravel. The banks are high and covered with verdure, and are backed by an open cultivated country, the distant hills of Felow and Bambuk adding an additional beauty to the landscape. A few miles below Sami was the former French trading station of St. Joseph, founded by Sieur Brue, but abandoned in the time of Park. Next morning the party proceeded a little further up the river to Kayi, where they crossed with no small difficulty and danger, the animals being swum over, and the baggage conveyed in a miserable canoe.

While Park was crossing by the same means the canoe was capsized by an injudicious movement on the part of his protector, but being near the bank, no harm came of it, and a second attempt landed him safely in the country of Kasson.

The young noble, having once brought the white traveller into his own country, soon showed that no generous motives had prompted his assistance. Unhesitatingly he demanded a handsome present. Park, seeing that it was useless either to upbraid or to complain, with a heavy heart made the necessary selection from his scanty stock of goods, and presented the offering forthwith.

On the evening of the 29th the party reached Tisi, where Park was lodged with his protector's father, Tiggity Sego, the head man of the place. Next morning a slave having run away, the use of Park's horse was asked for the chase, to which he "readily consented, and in about an hour they all returned with the slave, who was severely flogged, and afterwards put in irons."

Park was detained for several days at Tisi, while his horse was further used by his host on a more extended mission. During his enforced detention our traveller had an opportunity of seeing a somewhat more drastic method of propagating Islam than any he had yet witnessed. An embassy of ten persons arrived from the King of Futa Larra, a country to the west of Bondou, and announced to the assembled inhabitants that unless all the people of Kasson embraced the Mohammedan religion, and evinced their conversion by saying solemn public prayers, he, the King of Futa Larra, would certainly join his arms to those of Kajaaga.

Such a coalition would have been disastrous to Kasson, and without a moment's hesitation the conversion was agreed to. Accordingly, one and all did as was desired, offering up solemn prayers in token that they were no longer Pagans, but followers of Mohammed.

It was not till the 8th of January 1796 that Demba Sego, the young noble, returned with the traveller's horse, whereupon Park, impatient at the delay, declared that he could spend no more time at Tisi, and must proceed to the capital. He was informed he could not do so until he had paid the customary trading duties. Some amber and tobacco were offered, but they were laid aside as totally inadequate for a present to a man of Tiggity Sego's importance. Once more Park had to submit to seeing his baggage ransacked. One-half he had already lost at Joag, and now half of what remained had to be similarly sacrificed to satisfy the rapacity of his tormentors.

Thus despoiled, Park was permitted to depart next morning. His course, which so far had been E.N.E., was now E.S.E. In the afternoon the party arrived at the village of Jumbo, the birthplace of the blacksmith who had faithfully accompanied Park from Pisania. The entire population turned out to welcome back their townsman with dance and songs. The poor fellow's meeting with his blind mother was most touching. Unable to see him, she stretched out her arms to welcome him, and after eagerly satisfying herself by touch of face and hands that it was indeed her son who had returned, she gave wild expression to her delight. From which Park concludes, "that whatever differences there are between the Negro and the European in the conformation of the nose and the colour of the skin, there is none in the genuine sympathies and characteristic feelings of our common nature."

This affectionate welcome over, the villagers had time to turn their attention to the white man. At first they looked or affected to look upon him as a being dropped from the clouds, the women and children shrinking from him half in fear, half in awe. On being assured by their countryman that he was a good-tempered and inoffensive creature, they gradually laid aside their misgivings, and began to feel the texture of his clothes, and assure themselves that he was indeed cast in much the same mould as themselves. Still his slightest movement was sufficient to arouse their tremors and make them scamper off like a flock of sheep which had valorously marched up to view a sleeping dog.

Next day Park continued his journey to a place called Sulu, where he had an order from Dr. Laidley on a slatee for the value of five slaves. Hardly had he been hospitably received by Dr. Laidley's client, when messengers arrived from Kuniakary with orders that he should proceed at once to the king. Thither accordingly he journeyed, arriving late in the evening.

The rule of "like master, like man" did not hold good in relation to the King of Kasson and such of his subordinates as Park so far had come in contact with. His reception by one whose "success in war and the mildness of his behaviour in times of peace had much endeared him to his subjects," was an agreeable variation to the hard fate which had lately dogged his footsteps. The king was not only satisfied with his visitor's story and his poor present, but promised him every assistance in his power. He warned him, however, that the road to Bambarra was for the time being rendered extremely dangerous, if not altogether impassable, by the outbreak of war between that state and the adjoining one of Kaarta. In the hope of the arrival of more reassuring news Park waited four days, staying the while with the Sulu slatee, from whom he received gold dust to the value of three slaves. This transaction coming to the ears of the king, Park was compelled to add considerably to the value of his former present.

The country around Sulu presented an enchanting prospect of simple rural plenty, while the scenery surpassed in richness and variety any Park had yet seen. The density of the population was illustrated by the fact that the King of Kasson could raise within sound of his great war drum an army of four thousand fighting men. The one drawback to the amenities of the place was the numerous bands of wolves and hyenas which nightly attacked the cattle, and were only to be driven off by organised parties of men with fires and torches.

From Sulu, Park proceeded S.E. up the rocky valley of the Kriko, meeting everywhere swarms of people leaving the expected seat of war in Kaarta.

On the 8th he left the charming valley of the Kriko, and travelled over a rough stony country to the ridge of hills which forms the boundary-line between Kasson and Kaarta. Thence his way lay down a stony precipitous path into the dried-up bed of a stream, whose overarching trees afforded to the wayfarer a grateful shade. Emerging from this romantic glen, the party found itself on the level sandy plains of Kaarta, having the hilly ranges of Fuludu on their right.

On the third day from Sulu, Park witnessed a new method of consulting the Oracle as to the fate in store for them on the road. To his great alarm, their guide, who was a Mohammedan in name and a Pagan at heart, came to an abrupt standstill in a dark lonely part of a wood. Taking a hollow piece of bamboo he whistled very loud three times. Thereafter he dismounted, laid his spear across the pathway, and again whistled thrice. For a short time he listened as if for an answer, and receiving none, told Park that now they might proceed, for the way was clear of danger.

Next day the superstitious ideas cherished by the natives were further illustrated. Park had wandered some distance from his party, when, just as he reached the brow of a slight eminence, a couple of negro horsemen galloped from the bushes. Immediately on seeing each other Park and the negroes alike came to an abrupt stop, each equally filled with alarm. The white man was the first to regain his presence of mind, and concluding that advance was his safer course, he moved towards them. This was too much for the terrified natives, who thought they saw in the strange figure before them some terrible spirit. One of them, with a wild look of horror, turned and fled; the other, paralysed beyond action, could only cover his eyes and mutter his prayers. In this position he would have remained stationary, but for the instinct of his horse, which led him to follow his companion.

On the afternoon of the 12th, Park and his party entered the capital of Kaarta. On announcing their arrival to the king, a messenger was sent to convey them to a hut and protect them from the inquisitive crowd. In carrying out the latter part of his commission the messenger signally failed, and for the rest of the afternoon our explorer remained on exhibition, the hut being filled and emptied thirteen times by an admiring and curious mob.

In the evening his majesty gave Park an audience, seated on a clay divan raised a couple of feet above the floor, and covered with a leopard's skin, the sign of authority. The way to the throne lay through a long lane formed by a huge crowd of fighting men on the one side, and of women and children on the other.

The reception of the stranger was highly encouraging. He was told, however, that he had chosen a most inopportune time to attempt to pass into Bambarra, and he was advised to return to Kasson, and there await the end of the war just commencing. That, however, meant the loss of the dry season, and Park dreaded the thought of spending the rainy season in the interior. "These considerations, and the aversion I felt at the idea of returning without having made a greater progress in discovery, made me determined to go forward."

Hearing this determination, the king showed his kindly intentions by pointing out that there was another—though a more dangerous and circuitous route—to Bambarra, namely, that by way of Ludamar, an Arab district to the north-west of Kaarta. At the same time he promised to give the white man guides for this route as far as Jarra, his frontier town. With this offer Park only too gladly closed.

Before the audience ended a horseman arrived in foaming haste to announce that the Bambarra army had left Fuludu for Kaarta.

Next morning, after Park had sent his horse-pistols and holsters as a present to his royal host, a large escort was provided to protect and lead him on his way to Ludamar.

CHAPTER IX.
TO LUDAMAR.

It must have been with no pleasant sensations that Park turned aside from his direct route E.S.E. to the Niger, and proceeded north instead to Ludamar. In addition to the increased distance, there were the hundredfold greater dangers to be encountered. Houghton had preceded him over the same road, with what results his successor only too well knew. And yet, as matters turned out, it was perhaps as well that he elected to try his fate by the more circuitous route. Before many days were over Kaarta was desolated by the Bambarra army, which only retired laden with spoil on finding that the last refuge of the king could neither be stormed nor reduced by starvation. The trouble of the Kaartans did not end with the war with Bambarra, for they fell out with the people of Kasson, and before the year was ended had to face a coalition of various enemies.

On the 13th February Park started for Ludamar. His escort of over two hundred horsemen seems to have been of little use, for in the evening the hut in which his luggage was deposited was entered, and some of his rapidly diminishing stores stolen. Next day he came upon some negroes gathering the fruit of the *Rhamnus lotus*, which being converted into a species of bread, forms no inconsiderable addition to the food of the natives of Kaarta and Ludamar. This shrub, Park does not doubt, is the lotus mentioned by Pliny as the food of the Libyan Lotophagi.

The increased dangers of the new route were amply illustrated as Ludamar was approached. Bands of marauding Moors were taking advantage of the unsettled state of the country to carry off cattle with impunity. At one town Park saw five Moors calmly select sixteen of the finest oxen of a herd, and in the presence of five hundred negroes drive them away without even a show of resistance. One young man who had been out in the fields, and had shown more courage, had been shot, and was brought in dying. His mother, frantic with grief, filled the air with her shrill shrieks and lamentations, clapping her hands the while. "He never told a lie" was the astonishing encomium passed upon him, a phenomenal occurrence in a continent where lying is a virtue, and the art is raised to its utmost perfection. On being assured that all hope of saving the boy's life was gone, some good Mohammedans did their best to ensure him—though hitherto a Pagan—a place in Paradise, by getting him to repeat the sacred formula of Islam, in which pious effort they happily were successful.

On the 17th, Park, in company with numbers of people flying from the terrors of war, travelled during the night, to escape the more immediate danger of Moorish robbers. After resting during the early morning, they resumed their journey at daybreak. Two hours later they passed Simbing, from which Houghton had despatched the graphic letter, already quoted, telling of his destitute condition, but unalterable intention of proceeding to Timbuktu. At noon, Jarra, the southern frontier town of Ludamar, was reached. It was from this place that Park's predecessor was decoyed into the desert by Moors, and after being stripped, was left either to die of starvation or be murdered by passing ruffians, a point never satisfactorily cleared up, though Park was shown the spot where he breathed his last.

At Jarra, Park was hospitably received by a Gambia slatee, who had borrowed goods from Dr. Laidley to the value of six slaves, for which debt Park was provided with an order. The debt was acknowledged, but the merchant pleaded inability to pay more than two slaves.

Our traveller had now entered a more inhospitable region. Ludamar was found to be inhabited by negroes, an Arab race largely intermixed with negro blood forming the rulers and possessing the worst characteristics of both sides of descent.

Park and his attendants were not long in experiencing the brutal and inhospitable character of this degraded hybrid people.

Difficulties had met them at every step of their journey, and now nothing but new terrors loomed up before them. So great did these seem, and so overbearing and threatening was the attitude of the Moors, that Park's servants declared they would rather lose everything they possessed than proceed further. Not only were they liable to robbery and ill-usage, but not improbable to slavery also. These facts were so patent that, though unwavering in his own determination to push on, Park could not bring himself to force his men to follow him. Accordingly he made arrangements for parting with them. Among other things, he prepared duplicates of his papers to put into the hands of Johnson. Meanwhile a messenger had been sent to Ali, chief of the country, to ask permission to pass through his country to Bambarra. The request was accompanied by a present of fine garments of cotton cloth which Park purchased from the slatee in exchange for his fowling-piece. Fourteen days elapsed before an answer was returned, and then he was told to follow Ali's messenger to Gumba.

On preparing to depart, hopeful as ever that yet he should live to see the Niger, he was further cheered by the fidelity of his boy Demba, who seeing his master was not to be dissuaded from his determination to proceed, resolved not to desert him, whatever might be the result. It then came out that

Johnson, whose residence among Europeans had only served to corrupt him, had treacherously tried to seduce Demba to return with him and leave the white man to his fate.

To diminish the inducements to plunder, Park, before starting, left as many of his personal effects behind him as he could spare. For two days the little party toiled over a sandy country. On the third day they reached Dina, a large town built of stone and clay. The reception Park here met with at the hands of the natives was atrocious. Every opprobrious epithet which their vocabulary could supply was hurled at him. Not content with words, they proceeded to spit upon and otherwise heap ignominy upon the stranger, ending by tearing open his bundles and helping themselves to whatever they had a mind. For the victim of these outrages there was nothing but patience and resignation, with which virtues, indeed, he seems to have been amply endowed. He might be robbed of his material resources, but his spiritual stores remained untouched. With him, while there was life there was hope.

Not so with his servants. They had no magnet to draw them on, no higher impulse than monetary reward. Further forward they would not go. So be it! Their retreat was excusable, but *Onward* must be their master's watchword so long as any pencil of light glimmered through a loophole—*Onward* as long as limbs and strength and hope held out.

Not daring to face another day of insult and plunder, nor yet a night of gloomy reflection, Park gathered together such valuables as he could carry, left the village under cover of darkness, and with magnificent resolution started alone on his forlorn hope of reaching the Niger.

As the huts disappeared behind him, the moon shone out bright and clear in the heavens, filling the night with its mellow beauty, both literally and figuratively lighting up the dark path before him.

From all sides came the roar of wild beasts, adding to the terrors of the situation. Undismayed, however, and still unwavering, he plodded onward through the night. He had not proceeded far when a clear halloo stopped his resolute footsteps. The accents sounded familiar, and in a few moments more he was joined by his faithful servant Demba. Park then found that the boy had made up his mind to stand by him, though Ali's messenger returned to his master.

The little party of two now continued their journey, travelling steadily on over a sandy country covered with asclepias. At midday they reached a few huts, but were prevented from drawing water from the village well by the appearance of a lion. They therefore had to endure the pangs of thirst with patience till the evening, when they entered a town occupied by Fulahs. Park now seemed to have touched the bottom of his misfortunes. For several days he proceeded unmolested through Ludamar, each new day, each mile nearer his goal, filling his sanguine mind with brighter and fresher hopes.

On the 5th March he reached Dalli. The villagers, hearing that a white man had arrived, deserted the revelries attendant on a feast, and hastened to see the phenomenal stranger. Not pell-mell, however, like the rude mob of Dina, but in a decorous procession, and headed by flute-players, as if they felt themselves honoured by the visit. Round Park's hut they continued to dance and sing till midnight, during which time he had to keep himself continuously on exhibition to satisfy their simple and kindly if somewhat overwhelming curiosity.

Next day Park moved on to a village to the east of Dalli to escape the crowd which usually assembled there in the evening. Again his reception was most hospitable. The head man considered himself highly distinguished by having such a guest in his house, and showed it practically by killing two fine sheep to feast him and his own friends.

Park was now only two days from Gumba, the first town of Bambarra. He had but to reach that place to be safe from the thieving and brutal half-caste Moors, whose rule of the unhappy negroes was but another name for rapine and plunder. His hopes were high that now the success of his mission was almost assured. In fancy he saw himself already on the bank of the Niger, which he had come so far and suffered so much to see. His imagination revelled in a thousand delightful scenes in his future progress.

Thus buoyed up with glowing thoughts, he abandoned himself with unrestrained gaiety to the harmless festivities organised by his negro host, whose manners were in striking contrast to his experience of those of the Ludamar Moors.

But just when his golden dream was at its brightest, it was shattered by a rude awakening. Messengers arrived from Ali with orders to convey the white man either peaceably or by force to his camp at Benaun. Park was struck dumb with painful emotions, though slightly relieved on hearing that the sole cause of his being taken back was the curiosity of Fatima, Ali's favourite wife. That lady's desire to see a white man being satisfied, the chief promised that he should be conveyed safely on his way to Bambarra.

There was no gainsaying Ali's orders, and argument was of no avail. Once more Park must fall back on his patience and his hope. Now practically prisoners, he and his faithful boy Demba were carried back to Dina, where his reception had already been so brutal. Here he was brought before one of Ali's sons, who soon gave him a taste of the dangers and indignities in store for him. Barely was he seated when a gun was handed to him, and he was told to repair the lock and dye the stock blue. Knowing nothing of such matters, Park could only declare his ignorance. He was then ordered to produce his knives and scissors, and hand them over to the young tyrant. On Demba attempting to explain that they had no such articles, their tormentor sprang up in a fury, seized a musket, and was about to blow out the poor boy's brains, when the bystanders interfered and saved his life.

After this unpleasant incident master and man beat a hasty retreat from the hut, and it is little to be wondered at that the latter tried to escape altogether.

Next day the prisoners were conveyed to Benaun, the headquarters of the paramount chief of Ludamar, under a terrible sun, and over burning sands. They travelled all day with almost no water, the pangs of thirst being slightly alleviated by the use of gum, which keeps the mouth moist and allays the pain in the throat. In the evening they arrived at their destination, a temporary camp, consisting of a great number of dirty-looking tents scattered without order, among which were large herds of camels, cattle, and goats. At the outskirts of the camp, Park, by much entreaty, procured a little water.

The arrival of the white traveller was the signal for a great commotion. Women hastened from their domestic avocations and forsook their waterpots at the well. The men mounted their horses—every one came running or galloping helter-skelter, amid wild screaming and shouting. In a ferocious mob they surrounded the unhappy cause of their excitement, pouncing upon him like a pack of hyenas, tugging and pulling his clothes, threatening him with all sorts of penalties if he would not acknowledge the One God and His Prophet. In this sad plight, half dead with the pangs of thirst and the fatigues of a desert march, he was hustled and pulled towards the chief's tent. When at last he found himself in the presence of the great man, a single glance at his face was sufficient to dispel the last hope of better treatment. Ali was an old man, with an Arab cast of countenance, on whose every lineament were marked sullenness and cruelty. While he passively examined the unfortunate man before him, the women of his household were more actively engaged inspecting the dress of the victim and searching his pockets. They affected to doubt that he was a man at all, and counted his fingers and toes to assure themselves that he was indeed like themselves. Not content even with that, they must needs have a peep at his white skin, and pushed aside his garments in order to effect their purpose.

When the excitement was at its height, the sacred call to prayers resounded through the camp, but before the people fell upon their knees before the One God All Compassionate and Merciful, with bent body and face pressed in the dust to acknowledge His Omnipotence, they had a new indignity to put upon the helpless stranger. Showing him a wild hog, they bade him kill and eat it. This he wisely refused. The hog was then let loose in the belief that it would at once attack the white man, but instead it rushed at his tormentors. The sport thus missing its mark, the Moors proceeded to their devotions, and Park was conveyed to the door of the tent of Ali's chief slave, where after much entreaty he was supplied with a little boiled corn with salt and water, and then left to pass the night on a mat, exposed to cold and the dews, and still worse, to the insults and ribald mirth of the mob which swarmed about him.

CHAPTER X.
CAPTIVITY IN LUDAMAR.

The treatment which Park now experienced in the camp of Ali was brutal and barbarous beyond description.

In the eyes of the degenerate Arabs of Ludamar he was an object detestable both to God and man—a Christian and a spy. Everything, therefore, that savage ingenuity could invent to insult and torture him was heaped upon him with fiendish glee and eagerness.

On the morning after his arrival he was confined in a small square flat-roofed hut built of corn stalks, which happily admitted the breeze and excluded the sun. The hog was tied to the hut as a suitable companion to the hated Christian.

From morning till night the unhappy prisoner had to place himself on exhibition, and incessantly demonstrate the whiteness of his skin, the number of his toes, and the method of adjusting his dress—for all which torment he was repaid with curses. In common with the hog, he was made the sport of men, women, and children alike. Not even at night was he left to himself, being continually disturbed by his guards bent on satisfying themselves that he was safe in the hut, or by thieves seeking what they could carry away. To these tortures of mind and body was added the uncertainty of what might be before him. A council of elders had considered his case, and he was variously told that death, the loss of the right hand, or the putting out of his eyes, was the fate reserved for him.

To add to the miseries of his condition, he had to suffer the hardships attendant on the observance of Rhamadan, the month of fasting, during which the faithful are not permitted to eat or drink between sunrise and sunset. This fast from meat and drink, bad enough at any time in a scorching climate, was rendered doubly painful to the unhappy traveller by the extreme scantiness of the supply doled out to him once in the twenty-four hours at midnight. Then, too, it was the hottest time of the year, and so scorching at times were the winds from the desert, that it was impossible to hold the hand in a draught without pain. Sandstorms, too, now and again filled the air to the point of suffocation, while the heavens overhead were as brass, and the sands under foot as the floor of an oven.

Under these distressing conditions Park's only *rôle* was to comply with every command, and patiently endure every insult, compatible with appearing as useless as possible to the tyrants, so that they might not be tempted to detain him for the value of his services.

Day after day thus passed, each one more miserable than the preceding, but Park's iron frame and indomitable spirit stood it all. Where his savage gaolers failed, however, the fears and doubts for his future progress and the ultimate success of his mission threatened to succeed. The excessive heat and scarcity of water in the wilderness made escape in the hot season out of the question, while the hardships and dangers of travel to be faced in the wet season appeared scarcely less appalling.

The blackness of the outlook began to cloud even his sanguine temperament, and the heart sickness of hope deferred frequently manifested itself in fits of melancholy and despondency. With the lowering of his mental tone came also the bodily reaction, and a smart fever was the result.

Even then he obtained no alleviation of his sufferings. His distress was a matter of sport to the Arabs, till life became a burden to him. He trembled at times lest the peevishness, irritability, and enfeebled power of self-command accompanying the disease should cause him to overleap the bounds of prudence, and in the height of an outburst of passion commit some act of resentment which would lead to his death—death, and with his work unfinished.

On one of these occasions he left his hut and walked to some shady trees at a short distance from the camp, where he lay down in the hope of obtaining a little solitude. He was discovered by Ali's son and a band of horsemen, who ordered him to get up and follow them back to camp. Park begged to be allowed to stay a few hours. For answer one of the horsemen drew his pistol, and presenting it at Park's head, pulled the trigger. Happily it did not go off. Once more the brute essayed his weapon with the same result. None of his companions made the least attempt to stop him. Helpless, Park could but sit awaiting his doom, what indeed would have been a happy release from his miseries, only that as yet the task he had set himself was unaccomplished. With renewed precautions the pistol was presented a third time, when the hapless victim, who so far had not spoken, begged his would-be murderer to desist, promising at the same time to return with him to the camp.

Before Ali his position was no better. With fiendish malignity the latter played with his prisoner as a cat does with a mouse, opening and shutting the pan of his pistol and watching the while the effect on the demeanour of the white man before him. Getting but small amusement out of his resolute and indifferent mien, he sent him off at last with the threat that the next time he was found wandering outside the camp he would be shot forthwith.

"One whole month had now elapsed since I was led into captivity, during which time each returning day brought me fresh distresses. I watched the lingering course of the sun with anxiety, and blessed his waning beams as they shed a yellow lustre along the sandy floor of my hut, for it was then that my oppressors left me, and allowed me to pass the sultry night in solitude and reflection."

With habit and time Park began to be inured to his situation. Hunger and thirst were more easy to bear than at first, and the people getting accustomed to his presence, were not quite so troublesome. To beguile the time he made inquiries regarding the route to Timbuktu and the Haussa countries, and even got some of his tormentors to teach him the letters of the Arabic alphabet.

About the middle of April Ali proceeded north to bring back his chief wife Fatima. During the chief's absence, though Park was less molested than usual, he was also less regularly supplied with his scanty rations. For two successive days he received none at all, and had to endure the pangs of hunger as best he might. This he found painful enough at first, but soon discovered that temporary relief might be had by swallowing copious and repeated draughts of water.

Johnson—who meanwhile had been brought from Dina before he could leave for the coast—and Demba, not having the spirit of their master to bear them up in the midst of misfortune, sank into the deepest dejection, remaining for the most part prostrate on the sands in a sort of torpid slumber, from which they could scarcely be roused even when food arrived.

To the languor and debility brought on by semi-starvation was added on Park's part the affliction of sleeplessness; deep convulsive respirations shook him from head to foot; semi-blindness seized him, and with difficulty he fought a frequent tendency to faint.

But the cup of his misery was not yet full. The King of Bambarra, incensed at Ali's refusal to join him against Daisy, King of Kaarta, proclaimed war against him. This threw the country into confusion. The camp at Benaun was at once broken up, and a retreat further north commenced. On the first day a halt was made at a negro town called Farreni.

Again Park's rations were forgotten. Next day, foreseeing similar treatment, he proceeded himself to the head man of the town and begged some food. This was not only granted, but promised to be continued as long as he remained in the neighbourhood.

On the 3rd of May Ali's camp was reached, and found to be pitched in the midst of a thick wood. Here Park was presented to Fatima. This lady was singularly beautiful, according to the Ludamar Arab idea—that is to say, she was remarkably corpulent. "A woman of even moderate pretensions to appearance must be one who cannot walk without a slave under each arm to support her, and a perfect beauty is a load for a camel." To attain this pinnacle of perfection, the girls are gorged by their mothers with great quantities of kuskus and camel's milk, which must be taken no matter what the appetite may be. "I have seen a poor girl sit crying with the bowl at her lips for more than an hour, and her mother watching her all the while with a stick in her hand, and using it without mercy whenever she observed that her daughter was not swallowing."

At first Fatima affected to be shocked at Park's appearance, but showed that she had a woman's heart by presenting him with a bowl of milk. Later on she proved to be his best friend.

The heat had now become insufferable. Everything vegetable was scorched up, and the whole country presented a dreary expanse of sand dotted over with a few stunted trees and thorny acacia bushes. Water was almost unattainable, and night and day the wells were crowded with cattle lowing and fighting with each other to get at the troughs. The pangs of thirst rendered many of them furious and ungovernable, while the weak, unable to contend for a place, endeavoured to quench their thirst by licking up the liquid mud from the gutters—frequently with fatal consequences.

The suffering due to the scarcity of water extended to the people, and to no one more than the white captive among them. If his boy Demba attempted to get a supply of water, he was usually soundly thrashed for his presumption. This treatment became so intolerable in the end that Demba would rather have died than go near the wells. Park and his attendants were in this way reduced to begging from the negro slaves, but with indifferent success. Fatima, however, more than once relieved their necessities. Nevertheless, time after time, Park "passed the night in the situation of Tantalus. No sooner had I shut my eyes than fancy would convey me to the streams and rivers of my native land; then, as I wandered along the verdant brink, I surveyed the clear stream with transport, and hastened to swallow the delightful draught; but, alas! disappointment awakened me, and I found myself a lonely captive perishing of thirst amidst the wilds of Africa!"

One night, driven half wild by his tortures, he started off in search of relief. At every well he found struggling herdsmen, and from one and all he was driven away with outrageous abuse. At length at one he found only an old man and two boys, from whom he was on the point of receiving what he sought, when, discovering whom they were about to supply, they dashed the water into the trough, and told him to drink with the cattle. Too glad to get water in any way, "I thrust my head between two of the cows, and drank with great pleasure, until the water was nearly exhausted, and the cows began to contend with each other for the last mouthful."

Signs that the wet season was approaching began to show themselves towards the end of May in frequent changes of the wind, gathering clouds, and distant lightning. At the same time Park's fate was approaching a crisis, and he began to revolve schemes of escape. His hopes rose high when discovering that Ali was about to join some rebellious Kaartans in attacking Daisy, through the intervention of Fatima, he was permitted to accompany the expedition as far as Jarra. Once in Kaarta, he hoped that means would be found to escape from his barbarous captors.

Fatima next conferred a further favour on him by returning part of his clothes, of which he had been deprived since he fell into Ali's hands. Following these came his horse, now reduced, by hard work and starvation feeding, to skin and bone, but still fit for work.

On the 26th of May, Park set out with the Moors towards Jarra, accompanied by Johnson and Demba. At night they camped at a watering-place in the woods, but the accommodation being limited, Park was compelled to sleep in the open in the centre of the huts, where he could more easily be watched.

In the morning they had to face unprotected all the violence of a sandstorm, which raged with great fury the whole day. At times it was impossible to look up. The cattle, maddened by the driving sand, ran recklessly hither and thither, threatening to trample the prisoners to death.

Next day our traveller's rising hopes received a serious check. While preparing to depart a messenger arrived, who, seizing Demba, told him that henceforth Ali was to be his master, and that he must return at once to the camp they had left. With him were to go all his present master's effects, though "the old fool" Johnson might go on to Jarra.

Park was completely overwhelmed at the idea of his faithful boy being sent back to such a life of misery as would be his lot in the household of Ali. Unable to say a word to the messenger, he ran straight to the chief himself, and his indignation for once getting the better of him, he upbraided him in passionate language for the new injustice he was about to commit, compared to which all else was in his eyes as nothing.

To this generous but unwise outburst Ali made no reply, beyond ordering him, with haughty air and malignant smile, to mount his horse immediately or be sent back likewise. Terrible was the struggle in Park's inmost soul to refrain from ridding the world of such a monster, and giving vent to all the suppressed feelings of the last two months in one passionate outburst.

Happily he had not lost complete control over himself nor the ability to comprehend his situation, and he retired from the tent a prey to a hundred harassing emotions.

"Poor Demba was not less affected than myself. He had formed a strong attachment towards me, and had a cheerfulness of disposition which often beguiled the tedious hours of captivity." But part they must. "So having shaken hands with the unfortunate boy, and blended my tears with his, I saw him led off by three of Ali's slaves towards the camp at Bubaker."

On the 1st of June, Jarra was once more re-entered, and Park became again the guest of the slatee. Everything else now became subordinate for the time being to the one object of procuring the liberty of Demba. Before this duty even his own escape became of secondary importance. All his attempts were ineffectual, however. Ali could not be prevailed upon to sell or return his new-made slave, though he never ceased to hold out hopes that Demba might yet be let off for a consideration.

On the 8th, Ali with his horsemen returned to camp to celebrate a festival, Park, to his great joy, being left behind in the house of the slatee. Once more he began to think of his own safety, seeing that now it was proved beyond a doubt he could be of no use to Demba.

Meanwhile troubles began to gather rapidly round Jarra. Ali, after securing the price of his co-operation, treacherously left his allies to their fate. Daisy with his army was rapidly approaching the town, whose inhabitants could expect no mercy from their enraged king. Finding themselves left to their own resources, the latter made such preparation as was in their power to defend themselves, at the same time sending away their women and children, with such corn and cattle as they could take with them. Park prepared to depart along with these. He saw clearly that if he continued where he was he would run the risk of being involved in the general slaughter if Daisy were successful, or if the reverse, that he would sooner or later fall a victim to the Moors. And yet to go forward alone seemed terrible enough—for Johnson flatly refused to proceed—without means of protection or goods to purchase the necessaries of life, or an interpreter to make himself understood in the Bambarra language.

The one comparatively easy road was that to the coast, but "to return to England without accomplishing the object of my mission was worse than all."

The old spirit, never quite killed, was beginning to reassert itself, with the enjoyment of a certain measure of free will and liberty. Whatever was to be his fate, he should meet it, he determined, with his face towards the Niger.

On the night of the 26th, the women worked incessantly, preparing food and packing articles that were not absolutely necessary for the flight. Early in the morning they took the road for Bambarra.

The exodus was affecting in the extreme—the women and children weeping, the men sullen and dejected—all of them looking back with regret to the spot where they had passed their lives, and shuddering at the possible fate before them. Amid many heartrending scenes Park mounted his horse, and taking a large bag of corn before him, set forth with the flying multitude.

In this fashion he travelled onward for two days, accompanied so far by Johnson and the slatee. At Koiro a halt of two days had to be made to recruit his half-starved animal—an unfortunate delay, since it gave time for Ali's chief slave and four Moors to arrive in quest of their white prisoner. This new calamity had to be met with prompt action if Park was not to face an indefinite period of miserable captivity. At once he resolved to escape by flight—a "measure which I thought offered the only chance of saving my life and gaining the object of my mission."

Johnson was ready to applaud his master's resolution, but flatly refused to join him.

The Moors, thinking the white man safe, did not trouble themselves about him, and he was thus able to prepare a few articles to take with him. Two suits of clothes and a pair of boots were all he possessed. He had not now a single bead or other article of commercial value to purchase food for himself.

About daybreak the Moors were all asleep. Now was the time to make good his opportunity. Liberty and possible success were in the balance with renewed captivity and possible death. A cold sweat moistened his forehead as the importance of the step he was about to take was brought with twofold force to his consciousness. But to deliberate was to lose the only chance of escape. He must make one more bold attempt to regain liberty and reach the Niger. The thought was inspiration. He picked up his bundle, stepped stealthily over the sleeping negroes, and reached his horse. Johnson was bidden farewell, and once more begged to take particular care of the papers entrusted to him, and to inform his friends on the Gambia "that he had left me in good health, on my way to Bambarra."

A few years before, Major Houghton had sent an almost identical message to the same Gambian friends.

CHAPTER XI.
TO THE NIGER.

Once outside the village, it behoved Park to be on the alert, and get as quickly from the vicinity of the Moors as possible. With his horse reduced to skin and bone speed was out of the question, while the darkness and the nature of the country otherwise made progress slow. And yet how much was staked on every dragging mile—every moment might mean freedom or bondage, life or death to him. Half frantic at the thought of recapture, he imagined an enemy behind each bush, in every sound the tramp of pursuing horsemen.

It looked as if his worst apprehensions were about to be realised when unawares he stumbled upon a Moorish watering-place. Before he could retreat he was discovered by the shepherds. Immediately there was a howl of execration, and he was set upon with stones and curses, and driven forth as if he had been a prowling beast of prey.

Thankful to have escaped unhurt, Park, once rid of the fanatics, began to be more hopeful. He was not to get away so easily, however. Suddenly a shout rang behind bidding him halt. He hardly needed to look to know the nature of the danger that threatened. Three Moors on horseback were in full pursuit, ferociously brandishing their weapons, and screaming out threats as they bore down on him. Escape was impossible—his jaded steed was beyond all urging. With the dogged indifference of despair he turned and rode back prepared for the worst. Unmoved he looked at the upraised muskets of his pursuers— almost unheeding, so benumbed were his faculties, he heard that they were sent to bring him back to Ali. In reality, however, the Moors were robbers, and their object merely plunder.

On reaching a wood the wretches ordered their prisoner to untie his bundle. Great was their disgust to find nothing worth taking but a cloak. But to Park his cloak was the sole protection from the rains by day and the mosquitoes by night, and in vain he followed the robbers, trying to move their compassion, and earnestly begging them to return the garment. For sole reply, one of the band, annoyed at his persistence, presented a musket at him, while another struck his horse a brutal blow over the head. There was no resisting these hints, and once more possessed by the keen desire for life and liberty, Park parleyed no longer, but turned and rode off.

The moment he was out of sight he struck into the woods to avoid similar encounters. As he passed on, the sense of security growing ever stronger with the passing night, his sanguine temperament gradually resumed its sway. He felt as one recovered from a dangerous illness—he breathed freer, his limbs were as if released from cramping fetters, while the Niger magnet drew him on irresistibly as ever. Life became more desirable, earth and heaven more beautiful, and even the desert lost half its terrors. Beggary and the miseries of the rainy season grew less terrible to face with the growth of the hope that the guerdon of success was yet to be won.

But man cannot live on hope alone. However fair it might paint the vision of the future, it could not stifle the present demands of nature. Only too painfully Park awoke to the fact that starvation stared him in the face. He was destitute, and could not buy; unarmed, and therefore could not take; hunted, and therefore dared not beg. His every step was beset with innumerable dangers. His one chance lay in reaching a Bambarra village, where he would be among the negroes, and safe at least from the Moors.

To the pangs of hunger was speedily added the yet more painful agony of thirst. The sun overhead beat down upon him from heavens of lurid brilliancy. The scorching white sands, blinding to look upon, reflected back the heat as from the mouth of a furnace.

From the tree tops not a trace of human habitation was to be seen. Alone patches of thick scrub and hillocks of barren sand met the eye. In pushing on lay the only hope of escaping death. With his old undaunted spirit Park elected to push on—to struggle while his legs would carry him.

Towards four in the afternoon he came suddenly upon the dreaded yet welcome sight of a herd of goats. They were at once an indication of a great danger, and of possible food and water. His joy was great when after a cautious examination he discovered that the herd was tended only by two boys. With difficulty he approached them.

"Water! water!" he gasped. For answer the goatherds showed their empty water-skins, telling him at the same time that no water was to be found in the woods. Sick at heart and well-nigh exhausted, Park turned away to resume his weary tramp and almost hopeless quest.

Night was approaching, and already his limbs were failing him. His thirst had become intolerable, and his mouth was parched and inflamed. Sudden attacks of dimness at times came over his eyes, and more than once he almost fainted. Each moment it became increasingly clear that if he did not reach water before the dawn of another day he must inevitably perish. To relieve the pains in his throat and mouth he chewed the leaves of different shrubs, but only added to his agony.

In the evening he reached a ridge, and climbing a tree, gazed eagerly over the land—only a barren wilderness deserted by God and man spread out before him. "The same dismal uniformity of shrub and sand everywhere presented itself, and the horizon was as level and uninterrupted as that of the sea."

The sun sank, and with it went the fugitive's last hope. He was too weak to walk, and his horse, as much exhausted as himself, could not carry him. Even in his own extremity he had yet a kind thought for his faithful dumb companion, and that it might the better shift for itself he took off its bridle. Even as he did so a horrid sensation of sickness and giddiness seized him, and he fell on the sand, believing that his last hour had come.

In one swift flash of thought he saw the end of his weary struggle, and with it all his hopes of doing something worthy of remembrance. Then the shadow of death gathered over him, and he sank back unconscious.

But all was not yet over—for Park life had still somewhat in store of work and gladness. With the lowering of the temperature and the rising of the cool night breeze he awoke from his death-like swoon, and, gathering himself together, he resolved to make one more attempt to keep death at bay. With his old strength of will, though weak in limb, he staggered forward into the darkness of night, which seemed only too like the prospect before him. A few minutes more and a flash of lightning illumined the surrounding landscape. To him that flash was a promise of rain, and gave birth to a new hope that his agonies from thirst would soon be at an end. Soon flash followed flash, more and more dazzling, nearer and nearer. With a painful eagerness the exhausted wanderer watched the coming storm. He had no further occasion to struggle forward. He had but to sit still and wait. But what hopes and fears the while! Would it rain or not? Would the storm break on him, or career past on either side? Another hour and the answer came. On his ear fell the welcome sound of trees bending before the blast. His fevered face felt the first cool puffs of wind. A black column, dimly discerned in the darkness, and laden with moisture, as he thought, reared itself before him. It blotted out earth and sky, and tore onward borne on the wings of the wind. He rose to meet and welcome it. His parched mouth was opened to taste the heaven-sent rain. When, oh, misery! he found himself enveloped in a suffocating sandstorm. Stricken with unutterable disappointment, he sank to the ground behind a sheltering bush.

For above an hour the storm swept over him in choking whirlwinds. When it ceased, Park with undaunted spirit resumed his way in the darkness, though with ever intensifying thirst, ever lessening strength—perilously near his last struggle.

Again the lightning flashed across the sky. He hardly dared to hope, yet, nevertheless, he turned his burning face and stretched his shaking hands towards the advancing storm-clouds, that he might feel the first refreshing drops. This time there was no mistake, and tearing off his clothes, he spread them out to collect the heaven-sent rain, while all naked to the storm, amid the blinding glare of tropic lightning and the frightful crash of thunder, he sucked in the moisture by every pore of his body.

But he was only relieved of one series of pangs to be reminded that others lay behind—the miseries of starvation had still to be faced. There could be no rest, no sleep for him, till food as well as water was obtained. Accordingly he resumed his way, directing his footsteps by the compass, which the frequent flashes of lightning enabled him to consult. Soon these welcome gleams ceased, and then he had to stumble along as best he might. About two in the morning a light appeared. Thinking it might proceed from a negro town, he groped about in the darkness unsuccessfully trying to ascertain whether it was so or not, from corn-stacks or other signs of cultivation. Other lights now became visible, and he began to fear he had fallen upon a Moorish encampment.

Soon his worst doubts became certainties, and rather than fall into the hands of his late persecutors he elected to face death in the wilderness. As stealthily as possible, however, he tried to discover the water. In doing so a woman got a glimpse of him, and her scream brought up two men, who passed quite close to where he had crouched to hide himself. Clearly this was no place for him, and once more he plunged into the sheltering woods. He had not proceeded far when the loud croaking of frogs told him where to slake his thirst.

This narrow escape inspired Park to renewed exertions. At daylight he detected a pillar of smoke at a distance of twelve miles, and towards it he painfully plodded. After five hours of extreme toil the village from which the smoke arose was reached, and from a husbandman he heard that it was a Fulah village belonging to Ali. This was unpleasant news.

To enter might possibly mean return to captivity, yet possibly, too, he might be allowed to go unmolested. Meanwhile the immediate certainty was that he was dying of hunger, and that his position could hardly be made worse. Determined, therefore, to take his chance of the result, he rode into the village. On his applying at the head man's house, the door was slammed in his face, and his appeals for food were unheeded. Dejectedly he turned his horse's head, seeing nothing before him but death in the woods. As he was leaving the village he remarked some mean dwellings. Might he not make another trial. Hospitality he remembered did not always prefer the dwellings of the rich.

Prompted by the thought he advanced towards an old woman spinning cotton in front of her hut. By signs he indicated that he wanted food, leaving his haggard face and sunken eyes to tell the rest. Nor did he appeal in vain. The hut was opened to him, and such food as its owner could give was placed in his hands. The first pangs of hunger allayed, Park's next thought was for the four-footed sharer of his toils and agonies, and for it too a speedy supply of corn was forthcoming.

Meanwhile a dubious crowd gathered outside, and solemnly debated what they should do with the stranger who had thus appeared among them. Opinion was divided, however; and Park, seeing the danger of his position, thought it better to leave, however footsore and weary he might be. On seeing their unbidden guest prepare to depart, the villagers came to the conclusion that their wisest course was to do nothing.

Once clear of the town, and the boys and girls who followed him for some time, Park, who had not slept for more than two days and nights, sought the shade of a sheltering tree, and laid himself down to rest. Early in the afternoon he was awakened by two Fulahs, but without entering into conversation with them he continued his journey towards Bambarra and the Niger. It was not till midnight that finding a pool of rain water he again halted. Sleep, however, of which he stood terribly in need, was out of the question. The mosquitoes assailed him in maddening myriads, while the howling of wild beasts added to the terrors of his surroundings.

After a miserable night, the day was hailed with relief and delight. At midday another Fulah watering-place was reached, and here Park was hospitably received by a shepherd, who gave him boiled corn and dates for himself, and corn for his horse. Resuming his journey with fast returning hope and vigour, the resolute traveller pushed on, determined to journey all night.

At eight in the evening he heard wayfarers approaching, and had to hide himself in a thicket, and there hold his horse's nose to prevent him neighing. At midnight the joyful sound of frogs apprised him of the neighbourhood of water. Having quenched his thirst, he sought out an open space in the wood and lay down to sleep, happily unmolested till near morning, when some wild beasts compelled him to look after the safety of himself and his animal. Resuming his tramp, Park crossed the frontiers of Bambarra, and felt for the first time for many weary weeks in comparative safety and free from the horrid Moorish nightmare which had so long haunted him. At Wawra he was hospitably received by the chief of the village, and at last worn out with excessive fatigue and starvation, but rejoicing in the sweet new sense of security, was able to lay himself down and enjoy the luxury of a deep sound sleep.

To Park everything now seemed hopeful and encouraging. He was destitute and alone—a beggar in the heart of Africa; but now that he had safely escaped from the deserts of the north, and from the clutches of their fanatical and degraded Moorish inhabitants, his sanguine temperament made small account of his personal troubles. It was sufficient to know himself in a land of plenty, with villages at every mile, and among a people of kindly nature.

His hopes were not belied. Everywhere his reception was hospitable. The villagers gave of their food and shelter; the wayfarers their company, assistance, guidance, and protection. At most places he was not recognised as being a white man, but from his strange and destitute appearance was assumed to be a pilgrim from Mecca, and treated by the Faithful with the consideration such an one deserved. And thus the days passed on, ever bringing him nearer the goal of his hopes, ever adding to his assurance that the great prize for which men and nations had struggled for three centuries was to be his.

On the night of the 20th July, Park took up his quarters at a small village. Here he was told that he would see the Niger—or, as the natives called it, the Joliba or Great Waters—on the morrow.

The thought was intoxication, and between it and the myriad mosquitoes that preyed upon his unprotected body, sleep was out of the question. Before daylight he was up and doing, and had saddled his horse long ere the gates of the village were opened.

At length he got away. With eager eyes he looked towards the south—towards what for many terrible months had been his Kiblah—his Mecca. At last he was about to be rewarded for all the tortures of body and mind he had so heroically endured, so resolutely faced.

The road was crowded with natives hurrying towards the capital. Four large villages were passed, and then in the distance loomed up the smoke of Sego— Sego on the banks of the Niger! A little further and the joyful cry, "See the water!" announced to Park that the Niger was in sight. Ay, truly, there it was, sweeping along in a majestic stream towards the east, and glittering in the bright rays of the morning sun.

One long and ardent look, one sigh of supreme relief, and the pilgrim of geography hastened to the brink, and after drinking of the water, lifted up a fervent prayer to the Great Ruler of all things for having thus crowned his endeavours with success.

CHAPTER XII.
DOWN THE NIGER TO SILLA.

Thus was the River Niger for the first time reached by an European, and its eastward course determined. Park had left England inclined if anything to believe that it flowed west; but during his journey that opinion had gradually been undermined, and now with his own eyes he saw that its course was indeed towards the rising sun. There was no further question as to where it took its rise: its termination was now the great mystery which remained to be cleared up.

Sego, the capital of Bambarra, at which the white traveller had arrived, consisted of four distinct towns, two on the north bank of the Niger, and two on the south. Each was independently surrounded by high mud walls. Unlike the ordinary negro village, the houses were square with flat roofs, and built of mud. Some of them were two stories in height, and a few were whitewashed.

Besides these evidences of Arab influence, there were mosques in every quarter; and the whole town, with its thirty or forty thousand inhabitants, presented an air of civilisation and magnificence which Park was far from expecting. The river swarmed with large canoes, constantly crossing and recrossing; the streets were crowded with a busy population; and the whole surrounding country was in the highest state of cultivation.

Park speedily discovered that Mansong, king of Bambarra, lived on the south side of the river, and he prepared at once to cross and present himself at court. The crowded state of the ferry prevented him carrying out his intention immediately, as he had to wait his turn. In the interval the people gathered round him in silent wonder, full of speculation as to what could have brought the white man so far from the sea. With no small apprehension the weary traveller noticed among the crowd a numerous sprinkling of Moors. In each of the race he saw a malignant enemy who would stop at nothing to do him an ill turn, so indelible was the impression produced on him during his residence with Ali at Benaun.

An opportunity for crossing at last offered itself. Just as he was about to take advantage of it, a messenger arrived from the king to intimate that he could not possibly see his intending visitor until he knew what had brought him into the country. Meanwhile he was on no account to presume to cross the river without Mansong's permission, and must lodge for the night at a distant village which the messenger pointed out.

This reception was eminently discouraging. But Park was inured to disappointments, and happy in so far as he had at least seen and drunk of the waters of the Niger, he could bear with more equanimity such further reverses as might be in store for him. It required all his philosophy to sustain him, however, when on reaching the village he was refused admittance at every door. Every one looked upon him with astonishment and fear as a being of unknown species, whose power of physical or spiritual mischief was incalculable, and had better not be tried by closer contact than could be helped.

Thus shunned and boycotted as a human pariah, and not knowing where to go to seek shelter, Park sat down under a tree, which at least protected him from the overpowering glare of the sun. Hour after hour passed, and still no one offered him food or lodging. The day drew to a close. The wind rose, and clouds gathered threateningly in the sky. Everything portended a night of storm.

The sun fell, and still he sat unheeded. Darkness began to gather round him with tropical swiftness, and he lost all hope of moving the compassion of the natives by his forlorn and helpless condition. To escape death from lions and hyenas, he prepared to ensconce himself among the branches of the tree. Before doing so he proceeded to take off the bridle and saddle from his horse, that it might have greater freedom and ease in grazing. While thus engaged a woman returning from her work in the fields passed him. It required no words to tell her the stranger's plight. His dress and face spoke eloquently of weariness, destitution, hunger, and dejection. The negress stopped to ask his story. A few words told all that was necessary to move her woman's heart, and without further questioning she picked up his saddle and bridle and bade him follow her to her hut. There she lighted a lamp and spread out a mat for her guest.

In a short time a fine fish was broiling on the embers of the fire, while the various members of the family sat looking at the stranger in gaping wonder. A few minutes more and Park had satisfied his hunger and disposed himself to sleep. The women resumed their work of spinning wool, and while they worked they sang. To sweet and plaintive melody they wedded kindliest words, and their guest was the burden of their song:—

"The winds roared and the rains fell,

The poor white man sat under our tree;

He has no mother to bring him milk,

No wife to grind his corn."

And oft recurring came the chorus—

"Let us pity the white man,

No mother has he."[5]

Such, literally translated, were the words of the improvised song, and listening to them, sleep was driven from Park's eyes, as he turned and tossed a prey to the liveliest emotions of gratitude. Far into the night the women worked, and spinning ever sang—

"Let us pity the white man;

No mother has he;"

while outside the tornado spent its violence in blinding flashes and deafening peals of thunder, in raging blasts of wind and drenching showers of rain.

In the morning, as a token of gratitude, Park presented his kindly hostess with two of the four brass buttons remaining on his waistcoat, the sole articles he possessed having any value in native eyes.

During the day numerous rumours of the inimical machinations of the Moors came to Park's ears, but nothing definite concerning Mansong's decision as to his fate.

On the following morning, the 22nd, a messenger arrived to inquire what present the white man had brought to the king.

On the 23rd another messenger arrived, bearing the king's refusal to give Park an audience. It was accompanied by a present of five thousand cowries—the currency of the Sudan Basin—to enable him to purchase provisions, while indicating that his presence at Sego was undesirable, though he was at liberty to proceed farther down the Niger, or to return to the Gambia, as he pleased.

In Mansong's refusal to see him, Park could only see the "blind and inveterate malice of the Moorish inhabitants," though he could not but admit that the manner of his appearance among the people of Sego, and the to them incredible explanation of the object of his journey, warranted suspicion. To see the Joliba! Absurd! Were there then no rivers in the white man's own country that he should face such hardships and dangers to see ours? There must be something else behind. Send him away, but being destitute, let us supply his wants, so that the stigma of his death lie not at our doors. Such, it may be presumed, was Mansong's mode of reasoning, and such naturally the conclusion he arrived at.

Park was now called upon to make up his mind as to his future course. Would he go on or turn back? Surely he might return with all honour now that he had reached the Niger itself. Destitute as he was, what could he do? And yet it was hard to have to retrace his steps with such a glorious work before him. No, onward at least some distance he must go, to see and learn something more of the river's course and termination, perchance even to reach Timbuktu.

Park did not reach this conclusion without some misgiving, for he heard vague reports that the farther east he proceeded the more numerous became the Arab tribes, and that Timbuktu itself was in the hands of "that savage and merciless people." Whatever his horror of the Moors might be, however, he could not let his plans be stopped by "such vague and uncertain information, and determined to proceed."

BAMBARRA WOMEN POUNDING CORN.

Thus dauntlessly did our hero gather his rags about him, and with his bag of cowries proceed on the 24th on the exploration of the Niger River. On the first day he passed through a highly cultivated country, resembling the park scenery of England. The people were everywhere collecting the fruit of the Shea tree, from which the vegetable butter so named is produced. Park found the Shea butter whiter and firmer, and to his palate of a richer flavour, than the best butter he ever tasted made from cow's milk—a strange statement certainly, since to the palates of degenerate travellers and traders of the present day its taste is abominable. Even among the natives it is only used by the very poorest for cooking purposes, being considered infinitely inferior to palm oil.

In the evening Park reached Sansanding, a town of some two thousand inhabitants, largely resorted to by Moors from Biru engaged in exchanging salt and the commodities of the north for cotton cloth and gold dust. To slip as quietly into the town as possible, Park passed along the riverside, and by the natives was everywhere taken to be a Moor. At length a real Moor discovered the mistake, and by his exclamations brought a crowd of his countrymen about the stranger.

Amid the shouting and gesticulating mob Park contrived to reach the house of Counti Mamadi, the Duté of the place. The Moors, with their customary arrogance and assumption of superiority, pushed aside the negroes, and began to ask questions concerning Park's religion. Finding that he understood Arabic, they brought two men whom they called Jews, and who in dress and appearance resembled the Arabs, and were said to conform so far to Islam as to recite in public prayers from the Koran. The Moors insisted that the stranger should do the same as the Jews. He tried to put off the subject by declaring that he could not speak Arabic, when a sherif from Tawat started up and swore by the Prophet that if the Christian refused to go to the mosque, and there acknowledge the One God and His Prophet, he would have him carried thither.

Willing hands were ready to carry out this determination, but happily the Duté interfered, and declared the white stranger should not be ill treated while under his protection. This stopped immediate violence, but did not end the persecution. The crowd continued to swell, and grew ever more ungovernable. The clamour and excitement intensified every minute. Every coign of vantage was covered with multitudes eager to see the newcomer. That every one might be gratified he was compelled to ascend a high seat near the door of the mosque, where he had to remain till sunset, when he was permitted to descend and seek refuge in a neat little hut having a court in front of it. Even here, however, he found neither peace nor quiet. The Moors, though in the country only as traders, seemed to be allowed to do very much as they liked. They climbed over the court walls and invaded Park's privacy, desirous, as they said, of seeing him at his evening devotions, and also eating eggs. The latter operation Park was by no means loth to accomplish, though the intruders were disappointed on discovering that he only ate them cooked.

It was not until after midnight that the Arabs left the traveller alone. His host then asked him for a charm in writing, which was at once supplied in the form of the Lord's Prayer.

From Sansanding, Park proceeded to Sibila, and thence to Nyara, where he stayed on the 27th to wash his clothes and rest his horse.

At Nyami, a town inhabited chiefly by Fulahs, the head man refused to see Park, and sent his son to guide him to Madibu.

Between the two villages the travellers had to proceed with very great caution, as the district was notorious for its dangers from wild beasts. A giraffe was seen, and shortly afterwards, in crossing a broad open plain with scattered bushes, the guide who was ahead suddenly espied traces of a lion in the path, and called loudly to Park to ride off. His horse, however, was too exhausted for flight, and he continued to ride slowly on. He was just beginning to think that it had been a false alarm, when a cry from the guide made him look up in renewed trepidation. There was the lion lying near a bush, with his head couched between his fore-paws. To fly was impossible. Instinctively Park drew his feet from his stirrups, to be ready to slip off and leave the horse to bear the first onslaught if the lion should spring. With eyes riveted on the enemy he slowly advanced, expecting each moment that the lion would be upon him. The brute did not move, however, having probably just dined, and being in a peaceful mood in consequence. All the same Park was so held by a sort of wild fascination that he found it impossible to remove his gaze until he was a considerable distance out of danger.

To avoid any more such perils, Park took a circuitous route through some swampy ground, and at sunset safely entered Madibu. This village was perched on the banks of the Niger, of whose majestic stream it commanded a splendid view for many miles—a view further varied by several small green islands occupied by Fulah herds.

Here life was rendered almost unendurable by mosquitoes, which rose in such myriads from the swamps and creeks as to harass even the most thick-skinned and torpid of the natives. The nights were one continuous maddening torture, Park's rags affording him no protection from their attacks. Unable to sleep, he had to keep ceaselessly walking backwards and forwards, fanning himself with his hat to drive off his pertinacious tormentors. Nevertheless, by morning, his legs, arms, neck, and face were covered with blisters. No wonder, under such circumstances, that he grew feverish and uneasy, and threatened to become seriously ill. Perceiving this, the Duté of Madibu hurried him off, lest he should die on his hands.

Park's horse was as little able to carry him as he to walk. They had not struggled on many miles before the poor animal slipped and fell, and do what Park might, was not to be got up again. In vain he waited in the hope that after a rest the horse might come round. In the end there was nothing for it but to take off saddle and bridle, place a quantity of grass before him, and then leave him to his fate. At the sight of the poor brute lying panting on the ground his owner could not suppress a foreboding that he likewise before long would lie down and perish of hunger and fatigue. Oppressed with melancholy, many fears, and only too numerous physical ills, he staggered on till noon, when he reached the small fishing village of Kea.

The head man was sitting at the gate as he entered, and to him he told his story of destitution and sickness. But he spoke to one of surly countenance and crabbed heart, and his sole reply to the half dead stranger was to bid him begone from his door.

The guide remonstrated, and Park entreated, but all to no purpose. The Duté was inflexible.

At this juncture a fishing canoe arrived on its way to Silla, whereupon, to put an end to further parley, the Duté desired the owner to convey the stranger to that place. This, after some hesitation, the fisherman consented to do. Before setting forth Park asked his guide to see to his horse on the way back, and take care of him if he was still alive.

In the evening he reached Silla. Hoping that some one would take compassion on him, he seated himself beneath a tree, but though surrounded by wondering hundreds, no one offered him hospitality. Rain beginning to come on, the Duté was at length prevailed upon by Park's entreaties to let him sleep in one of his huts. The hut was damp, and a sharp attack of fever was the result. Let the traveller describe his situation at this juncture in his own words.

"Worn down by sickness, exhausted with hunger and fatigue, half naked, and without any article of value by which I might get provisions, clothes, or lodging, I began to reflect seriously on my situation.

"I was now convinced by painful experience that the obstacles to my further progress were insurmountable. The tropical rains were already set in with all their violence, the rice grounds and swamps were everywhere overflowed, and in a few days more travelling of every kind, unless by water, would be completely obstructed. The cowries which remained of the King of Bambarra's present were not sufficient to enable me to hire a canoe for any great distance, and I had but little hopes of subsisting by charity in a country where the Moors have such influence.

"But above all, I perceived that I was advancing more and more within the power of those merciless fanatics, and from my reception both at Sego and Sansanding I was apprehensive that in attempting to reach even Jenné (unless under the protection of some man of consequence amongst them, which I had no means of obtaining), I should sacrifice my life to no purpose, for my discoveries would perish with me.

"With this conviction on my mind, I hope my readers will acknowledge that I did right in going no farther. I had made every effort to execute my mission in its fullest extent which prudence could justify. Had there been the most distant prospect of a successful termination, neither the unavoidable hardships of the journey, nor the danger of a second captivity, should have forced me to desist. This, however, necessity compelled me to do; and whatever may be the opinion of my general readers on this point, it affords me inexpressible satisfaction that my honourable employers have been pleased since my return to express their full approbation of my conduct."

And who will not cordially coincide in their verdict? Never had a mission been more determinedly carried out, nor such inexhaustible patience and endurance shown in the face of every conceivable hardship, indignity, and danger—all of which were counted by the sufferer as naught compared with the inexpressible pleasure of achieving something of the task he had been despatched to accomplish.

When he thus made up his mind to return to the coast, Park had followed the Niger a distance of over eighty miles from Sego, finding that it still maintained its easterly course. In addition, he gathered from various traders the fact that it continued in the same direction for four days' journey more, when it expanded into a lake of considerable size, named Dibbie, or "The Dark Lake."

From Dibbie (Debo) the Niger was said to divide into two branches, enclosing a large tract of land called Jinbala, and uniting again after a north-easterly course near Kabra, the "port" of Timbuktu. From Jenné to the latter place the distance by land was twelve days' journey.

From Kabra, Park does not seem certain—at least he does not make it clear— what course the Niger took, though he correctly enough states that at the distance of eleven days' journey it passes to the south of Haussa (probably what is now known as Birni-n-Kebbi, a large town in Gandu, one of the Haussa States). Beyond this nothing further was known. It seems evident, however, that Park confounded the course of the Niger with that of its great eastern tributary the Benué, as had most of the geographers before him; and so was led astray from seeking for its natural termination in the Atlantic.

CHAPTER XIII.
THE RETURN THROUGH BAMBARRA.

Park's resolution to return to the coast was taken on the 29th July 1796. His hope of accomplishing this purpose in safety seemed almost as desperate as the task of going forward. Before him lay a journey on foot of eleven hundred miles in a straight line, to which must be added an additional five hundred for deviations and the windings of the road. He had thus before him nineteen hundred miles on foot through a barbarous country, where the stranger was considered fair prey, and the laws afforded him no protection from violence. He was without the wherewithal to buy food, and had only rags to shield him from the violence of the weather and the maddening onslaughts of mosquitoes. In addition he had to face all the horrors of the tropic winter, tornadoes of wind, rain, and thunder overhead, swamps and mire under foot, and flooded streams barring the way at every turn. The hardships were sufficient to have killed any man of less indomitable spirit and weaker frame. Even Park would probably have succumbed, but that he could not die while his discoveries remained uncommunicated to his employers and the public. Till then his work was only half done. With his death it would be wholly undone—all his toil and suffering in vain. To reach the coast was therefore now a point of as much importance as formerly it had been to see the Niger.

His mind once made up, Park acted with promptitude and resolution.

He arrived at Silla on the 29th July. The night sufficed to determine his course, and morning saw the commencement of his return journey. It behoved him indeed to waste no time. A few days more and the country would be impassable by land on account of the flooded rivers. Already it was so on the southern side of the Niger—a fact Park much regretted, as he had hoped to return by that way.

Crossing to Murzan by one canoe, he was there enabled to hire another to Kea. Here he was permitted to sleep in the hut of one of the head man's slaves, who, seeing him sick and destitute of clothes, compassionately covered him with a large cloth.

Next day, in proceeding to Madibu with the head man's brother, he had an opportunity of seeing a peculiar instance of the native respect for private property under some circumstances. A large pile of earthenware jars were lying on the bank of the river. They had been found there two years before, and as no one had ever claimed them, they were believed to belong to some supernatural power. People passing invariably threw a handful of grass upon them, which Park thinks was to protect them from the rain, but more likely was meant as a propitiatory gift to the spirit—the practice being common over all Central Africa.

Some time after passing the jars the fresh footprints of a lion were discovered. The travellers had accordingly to proceed with very great caution. Nearing a thick wood where the dangerous brute was supposed to have its lair, the guide insisted that Park should lead the way. Unarmed as he was, the latter naturally objected, and urged further that he did not know the road. High words followed, which ended in the desertion of the negro.

There was nothing for it now but to proceed alone, lion or no lion. With no small trepidation Park passed between the wood and the river, expecting every moment to be attacked. Happily he was left to pursue his way unmolested, and reached Madibu late in the afternoon. Here he was joined by the deserter. While in the act of remonstrating with him for his recent conduct, a horse commenced to neigh in a neighbouring hut. With a smile the head man asked Park if he knew who was speaking to him, and showed him the horse, which turned out to be no other than the traveller's own, very much improved by its rest.

Next day Park re-entered Nyami, and there was practically imprisoned by three days' continuous rain, the after results of which he had the most serious reasons to fear. Nor were his apprehensions belied. When he left Nyami the country was deluged, the fields knee deep in water for miles together, and the pathways undiscoverable. Where not actually submerged the land was one great quagmire, in which Park's horse stuck more than once, and had almost to be abandoned.

Next day the rain fell in torrents, detaining him again, and making travelling almost impossible. With difficulty he plunged and floundered a few miles through a swamp breast deep in water, and managed at length to reach a small Fulah village.

With tracks obliterated and the country thus flooded, it now became imperative that he should not travel alone. No guide, however, was to be found to show him the way and assist him at difficult places.

For some distance he accompanied a Moor and his wife who were proceeding to Sego with salt. They rode on bullocks, and proved to be as helpless as himself. At one place one of the bullocks suddenly fell into a hole in a morass, and sent both salt and wife into the water.

At sunset he reached Sibity, where an inhospitable reception awaited him. A damp old hut was all he could get in which to pass the night. Each moment he expected to see the rotten clay roof fall in—a common occurrence at the commencement of the rainy season. On all sides he heard the sound of similar catastrophes, and in the morning counted the wreck of fourteen dwellings.

Throughout the following day it continued to rain violently, making travelling out of the question.

On the 11th August, the head man compelled Park to move on. A new danger, it appeared, had fallen on his trouble-strewn way. It had got abroad that he was a spy, and not in favour with the king—a report sufficient to close each head man's door against him, and extinguish every hospitable feeling in the naturally kindly heart of the negro. He was now an object not merely to be treated with passive indifference, but actively shunned as a possible danger to whomsoever should have dealings with him.

With no small foreboding he re-entered Sansanding. Counti Mamadi, who formerly had protected him from the Moors, would now have nothing to do with him, and desired him to depart early in the morning. That the head man in thus acting did violence to his own natural kindliness was sufficiently shown by his coming privately to Park during the night and warning him of the dangerous situation he was in. Especially he advised him to avoid going near Sego.

This unpleasantly altered state of matters was further illustrated when arriving next day at Kabba, he was met outside the town by a party of negroes, who seized his horse's bridle, and in spite of his remonstrances, conducted him round the walls, and ordered him to continue his way lest worse should befall him. A few miles further on he reached a small village, but found no better reception. On his attempting to enter, the head man seized a stick and threatened to knock him down if he moved another step. There was nothing for it but to proceed to another village, where happily some women were moved to compassion by his destitute appearance, and contrived to get him a night's lodging.

On the 13th, he reached a small village close to Sego, where he endeavoured in vain to procure some provisions. He heard, moreover, that there were orders out to apprehend him, and it was clear that it would be highly dangerous for him to remain an hour where he was. He accordingly pushed on through high grassy and swampy ground till noon, when he stopped to consider what route he should now pursue. All seemed alike bad, but everything considered, he elected to proceed westward along the Niger, and ascertain if possible how far it was navigable in that direction.

For the next three days his journey was unattended with any worse hardship than having to live upon raw corn, lodging for the night having been obtained without much difficulty. It was different, however, on the evening of the 15th, when, on his arrival at the small village of Song, he was refused admittance within the gates. The numerous footprints which he had seen while on the march had made it abundantly clear that the country was infested with lions. The prospect of spending the night in the open without means of defence was therefore anything but pleasant; but it had to be faced. Hungry and weary himself, he could still think of his horse, and he set about gathering grass for him. With nightfall, no one having offered him food or shelter, he lay down under a tree close to the gate, but dared not allow himself to sleep. With leaden shoon the minutes passed. Every sound was a note of danger, and in a state of painful alertness the outcast wanderer peered into the blackness of night, ever expecting to see a creeping form, or the glitter of two fierce eyes.

At length, some time before midnight, a hollow roar suddenly resounded through the wood, apparently coming from no great distance. In the darkness he could see nothing, strain as he might. To sit thus defenceless awaiting his doom, yet not knowing when or whence it would come, was intolerable, and driven frantic at last by the horror of his situation, he rushed to the gate, and madly tugged at it with all the energy of one who struggles for dear life. In vain, his utmost efforts were as little able to move it as were his urgent appeals to touch the hearts of the natives.

Meanwhile the lion was all unseen prowling round the village, ever lessening its circle and drawing nearer its prey. At last a rustle among the grass warned Park of its whereabouts and dangerous proximity. A moment more and he would be in its fatal clutches. His sole chance now lay in reaching a neighbouring tree. With a rush he gained and climbed it, and then feeling comparatively safe among the sheltering branches, he prepared to pass the night there. A little later, however, the head man opened the gate and invited the stranger to come within the walls, as he was now satisfied that he was not a Moor, none of whom ever waited any time outside a village without cursing it and all it contained.

From Song the country began to rise into hills, and the summits of high mountains could be seen ahead. Even here, however, travelling continued to be a matter of toil and danger, all the hollows through which the road ran being transformed into nasty swamps. At one point Park and his horse fell headlong into an unseen pit, and were almost drowned before, covered with mud, they succeeded in emerging. One of the worst features of such occurrences was the danger he incurred of losing his notes, or finding them rendered useless—a misfortune which would have gone far to bring the results of his toil to naught.

After the above mishap, Park rode through Yamina, a half-ruined town covering as much space as Sansanding. Many Moors were sitting about, and everybody watched him passing with astonishment.

Next day the road quitted the Niger plain and skirted the side of a hill. From this higher elevation the whole country had the aspect of an extensive lake.

His next journey brought him to the Frina, a deep and rapid tributary of the Niger. He was preparing to swim across when he was stopped by a native, who warned him that both he and his horse would be devoured by crocodiles. On his hastily withdrawing from the water, the man, who had never seen a European before, and now saw one minus his clothes, put his hand to his mouth, as is the fashion among most negroes of expressing astonishment, and uttered a smothered, awe-stricken exclamation. He did not run away, however, and by his assistance the proper ferry was found, and Park safely landed on the opposite bank.

In the evening the traveller arrived at Taffara, where he met with a most inhospitable reception. This was partly due to the fact that a new head man was being elected. No one would take him in, and he was compelled to sit under the palaver tree supperless, and exposed to all the rude violence of a tornado. At midnight the negro who had shown Park the way—himself a stranger to the village—shared his supper with him.

On the following march Park was glad to appease his hunger with the husks of corn. At a village further on he found the head man of the place in a bad temper over the death of a slave boy, whose burial he was superintending. The process was sufficiently summary. A hole having been dug in the field, the corpse of the boy was dragged out by a leg and an arm and thrown with savage indifference into the grave. As there seemed to be no chance of procuring food, Park rode on to a place called Kulikorro, where his reception was more kindly. Here he found he could relieve his wants by writing saphias or charms for the simple natives. The charm being written on a board, the ink was then washed off and swallowed, so as to secure the full virtue of the writing. The practice is taken from the more ignorant of the Arabs, who think that by drinking the ink used in writing the name of Allah or prayers from the Koran they will derive a spiritual or material good.

Thanks to the demand for charms of this nature, Park was enabled to enjoy the first good meal and night's rest he had known for many days.

On the second day from Kulikorro he was directed on the wrong road, whereby he was brought late in the afternoon to a deep creek, which there was nothing for it but to swim, spite of the danger of being seized by crocodiles. This he did, holding the bridle of his horse in his teeth, and carrying his precious notes in the crown of his hat. An obstacle of this kind, however, was but a small matter to Park, who between rain and dew was now rarely dry, while the mud with which he was only too frequently bespattered made a swim both pleasant and necessary.

On this day's march the Niger was remarked to be flowing between rocky banks with great rapidity and noise, so that a European boat would have had some difficulty in crossing the stream.

Bammaku was reached in the evening of the 23rd August, and proved to be a disappointment in the matter of size, though its inhabitants were remarkably well off on account of its being a resting-place for the Arab salt merchants. The Moors here were unusually civil to the traveller, and sent him some rice and milk.

The information Park obtained at Bammaku as to his further route was anything but encouraging. The road was declared to be impassable. Moreover, the path crossed the Joliba at a point half a day's journey west of Bammaku, where no canoes were to be had large enough to carry his horse. With no money to support him, it was useless to think of remaining at Bammaku for some months. He therefore made up his mind to go on, and if his horse could not be got across the river, to abandon it and swim across alone.

BAMMAKU.

In the morning, however, he heard from his landlord of another and more northerly road, by way of a place called Sibidulu, where he might be enabled to continue his journey through Manding. An itinerant musician, going in the same direction, agreed to act as guide.

At first Park was conducted up a rocky glen, but had not gone many miles when his companion discovered that he had taken the wrong road, the right one being on the other side of the hill. Not seeing it to be his duty to repair his blunder as far as possible, the guide threw his drum over his shoulder and continued his way over the rocks, whither Park could not follow him on horseback, but had to return to the plain and find his way himself.

Happily he succeeded in striking a horse track, which proved to be the right road; and soon he had reached the summit of the hill, where an extensive landscape spread out before him. The plain at his feet was half submerged under the Niger waters, which at one place spread out like a lake, at another were gathered into a curving river, while far to the south-east, in the hazy sheen of distance, the summits of the Kong Mountains could be dimly descried.

Towards sunset the road descended into a delightful valley, leading to a romantically situated village named Kuma. Here Park for once met with a pleasant welcome. Corn and milk in abundance were placed ready for himself, and abundance of grass for his horse. A fire even was kindled in the hut set apart for him, while outside the natives crowded round him in naïve wonderment, asking him a thousand questions.

Fain would Park have lingered in this village to rest and recruit, but an eager longing possessed him to push on, lest the loss of a day should prove fatal to his further progress. Two shepherds proceeding in the same direction as himself agreed to accompany him. In some respects the road proved to be more difficult and dangerous than anything he had previously passed. At places the ascent was so sharp, and the declivities so great, that a single false step would have caused his horse to be dashed to pieces at the bottom of the precipices.

Finding that they were able to travel faster than their white companion, the shepherds after a time pushed on by themselves. Shortly afterwards, shouts and screams of distress apprised Park that something had gone wrong ahead. Riding slowly towards the place whence the alarm had seemed to proceed, and seeing no one, he began to call aloud, but without receiving any answer. By-and-by, however, he discovered one of the shepherds lying among the long grass near the road. At first his conclusion was that the man was dead, but on getting nearer him he found that he was still alive, and was told in a whisper that the other had been seized by a party of armed men.

On looking round, Park was alarmed to discover that he was himself in imminent danger. A party of six or seven men armed with muskets were watching him. Escape being impossible, he considered it his best course to ride towards them. As he approached he assumed an air of unconcern, and pretending to take them for elephant hunters, he asked if they had shot anything. For answer one of the party ordered him to dismount; then, as if thinking better of it, signed to him to go on. Nothing loth, Park rode forward, glad to be relieved from the fear of further ill-treatment.

His relief, however, was of short duration. A loud hullo brought him suddenly to a standstill. Looking round, he saw the robbers—for such they were— running towards him. Park stopped to await their coming. He was then told that they had been sent by the King of Fulahdu to bring him and all that belonged to him to his capital. Park, to avoid ill-treatment, unhesitatingly agreed to follow them, and in silence the party travelled across country for some time. A dark wood was at last reached. "This place will do," said one of the party, and almost simultaneously the unfortunate traveller was set upon, and his hat torn from his head. To lose his hat was like losing his life, for it contained all that made life dear to him for the time being. He betrayed no sign of trouble, however, but simply declared that he would go no further unless his hat was returned.

For answer one of the band drew a knife, and cut the last metal button from Park's waistcoat. The others then proceeded to search his pockets, which he permitted them to do without resistance. Finding little to satisfy their rapacity, they stripped him naked. His very boots, though so sadly dilapidated as to need a part of his bridle-rein to keep the soles on, were minutely examined. Yet even at this lowest depth of ignominy his paramount thought was his work. He could endure the loss of the last shred of clothing, but to be deprived of his notes and his compass was insupportable. Seeing the latter lying on the ground, he begged to have it returned to him. In a passion one of the robbers picked up his musket and cocked it, declaring that he would shoot him dead on the spot.

Humanity, however, was not quite suppressed in the hearts of these scoundrels, for after a moment's deliberation they returned him a shirt and a pair of trousers. As they were about to depart the one who had taken his hat jeeringly tossed it back to him. Never with more eagerness and delight did despairing mother gather to her bosom a long lost child, than did Park to his the battered remnant of a hat which contained his precious store of notes. With them there was still something worth struggling for, hopeless as his case might seem.

Never surely was man more tried. At every step he had met with new calamities, new obstacles, miseries, and dangers. Man and nature were alike in conspiracy against him. And now he had to add to his previous destitution semi-nakedness, and the loss of his horse. With hundreds of miles still before him, how could he hope to run the gauntlet of the fresh difficulties and dangers he would undoubtedly have to face? Yet even as he conjured up before his mind the perils ahead from wild beasts and evilly disposed men, from swamp and flood, from wind and rain, he began to take comfort as he recalled to mind his numerous past escapes, which were to him as proofs positive of a protecting Providence which never yet had failed him in his hour of need.

As his thoughts took a more hopeful turn, and his sanguine temperament and rooted faith in a God who overruled all things reasserted their influence, Park's gaze fell upon a tuft of moss. Irresistibly his mind was diverted from the horrors of his position to the beauty of the lowly plant before him. As he examined with admiration its delicate conformation, the thought occurred to him, "Can that Being who planted, watered, and brought to perfection in this obscure part of the world a thing which appears of so small importance, look with unconcern upon the situation and sufferings of creatures formed after His own image? Surely not!"

The next moment the old spirit came back to him. Not yet would he succumb. While there was life in him he would struggle, and while he could struggle there was hope. Starting up, he pushed forward once more, assured in his mind that relief was at hand. Nor was he disappointed. Near a small village he found the two shepherds, in whose company he once more proceeded, till at sunset they entered Sibidulu, his destination for the time being.

CHAPTER XIV.
REST AT KAMALIA.

Park had now entered the country of Manding. Sibidulu, from its position in a small valley surrounded by high rocky hills impassable to horsemen, had had the singular good fortune to escape being plundered during the numerous wars from time to time waging around it. To this happy immunity may possibly be ascribed the reception accorded to Park in his hour of need. As he entered the town the people gathered round and accompanied him in a pitying crowd to the head man of the village in order to hear his story.

While he related the circumstances of his ill treatment the native official listened with becoming gravity, and smoked his pipe the while. The narrative finished, the latter drew up the sleeve of his cloak with an indignant air, and laying aside his pipe, told the white man to sit down. "You shall have everything returned to you. I have sworn it!"

Turning to an attendant, he ordered him to bring the stranger a drink of water, and then proceed over the hills at dawn of day to inform the chief of Bammaku that the King of Bambarra's stranger had been robbed by the people of the King of Fulahdu.

The head man did not confine himself to words or to water. A hut was given to Park, and food to eat, though the crowd which gathered round to commiserate the white man's misfortunes could with comfort have been dispensed with.

The generosity of his reception was all the more admirable that at the time the people were suffering from semi-famine. Under these circumstances, after having waited two days in vain for the return of his horse and clothes, Park, afraid of becoming a burden to his kind host, asked permission to proceed to the next village. The head man showed no anxiety to hasten his guest's departure, but in the end told him to go to Wonda, and remain there till news was received of his missing possessions.

Accordingly on the 30th, he proceeded to the place indicated, a small town with a mosque, where his reception by the Mansa or chief was as hospitable as at Sibidulu.

The attacks of fever which had finally compelled Park to turn back at Silla now began to return with greater violence and frequency, and little wonder either that it should be so. His solitary shirt, worn to the thinness of muslin, afforded him neither protection from the sun by day nor from the dews and mosquitoes by night. As, also, it had become unpleasantly dirty, at Wonda he set about washing it, and had to sit naked in the shade till it dried. The result was a violent attack of fever which prostrated him for nine days.

All the while he had to do his best to conceal his illness, lest his host should find him too great a nuisance, and order him to move on. To this end he tried, like sick or wounded animals, to hide himself away out of sight, usually spending the whole day lying in the corn-field, thus undoubtedly aggravating his malady.

At this time the scarcity of food was so great that women brought their children to the head man to sell for forty days' provisions for themselves and the rest of their families.

At last messengers arrived from Sibidulu, bringing Park's horse and clothes. To his profound dismay and disappointment the compass—which next to his notes was his most valuable possession—was broken and useless. The loss was irreparable.

The horse proving to be a mere skeleton, he was handed over as a present to his kind landlord.

Though still ill with fever, and hardly able to totter along, the traveller now resumed his weary way.

On the two succeeding days starvation added to his weakness. On the third a negro trader gave him some food, and afterwards conducted him to his house at Kinyeto. Here, as if he had not yet sufficiently run the gamut of human suffering, he must needs endure the agonies of a sprained ankle, which swelled and inflamed so that he could not set his foot to the ground. The kindly trader, however, made him welcome to stay until quite recovered, but Park did not trespass on his hospitality longer than was absolutely necessary.

In three days he was sufficiently well to be able to limp along with the assistance of a staff, and in this fashion he contrived to hobble to Jerijang, whose chief—there being no king in Manding—was considered the most powerful in the country.

Dosita was the next village reached, and here rain without and delirium within compelled him to remain one day. Recovering slightly, he set out for Mansia. The road led over a high rocky hill, and almost proved too much for the exhausted wayfarer, who had to lie down at intervals to recover. Though only a very few miles distant, it was late in the afternoon before he reached the town. Here he was given a little corn to eat, and a hut to sleep in. Evidently, however, the head man thought Park richer than he looked, and during the night made two attempts to enter the hut, being each time frustrated by the traveller's vigilance. In the morning the latter thought it better to take French leave of such a host, and accordingly at daybreak set forth for Kamalia, a small town situated at the bottom of some rocky hills. This place he reached in the course of the afternoon.

At Kamalia, one Karfa Taura, brother of the hospitable negro trader of Kinyeto, extended a like welcome to the wayworn white man. By this time, so yellow was the latter's skin from his repeated fevers, and so poverty-stricken his appearance, that the trader was only convinced of his nationality when on showing him a white man's book in his possession, he found the traveller could read it. This was a Book of Common Prayer, of which Park obtained possession with no small surprise and delight.

Not too soon had some means of spiritual consolation come to him, for here he learned that the country before him—the Jallonka Wilderness, with its eight rapid rivers—was absolutely impassable for many months to come. Even then, when caravans found it difficult and dangerous, what would it be to a defenceless and destitute single man? With the knowledge that further advance at the present was hopeless, came the realisation of the fact that to utter exhaustion of outward resources was now to be added the complete loss of all inward force and strength. Exposure, hunger, toil, and fever had at last triumphed over Park's iron constitution, and laid him low. He might still will not to die, still hope that he would yet reach the coast, still keep up his determined and sanguine spirit; but meanwhile, what could he do when his physical powers had thus failed him?

But even in that moment, when he found himself overshadowed by despair and death, and at the extreme limit of all his earthly resources, he was once again to prove that a "Protecting Providence" watched over him. In his supreme need a kind host had been provided in the person of Karfa Taura to save him from death by fever and starvation, and not only to lodge and feed him, but at the proper time to conduct him to the Gambia, whither he was going with a slave caravan.

"Thus was I delivered by the friendly care of this benevolent negro from a situation truly deplorable. Distress and famine pressed hard upon me. I had before me the gloomy wilds of Jallonkadu, where the traveller sees no habitation for five successive days. I had almost marked out the place where I was doomed, as I thought, to perish, when this friendly negro stretched out his hospitable hand to my relief."

But neither food nor suitable shelter could stay the course of the fever. Each succeeding day saw Park weaker, each night more delirious, till at length he could not even crawl out of the hut. Six weary weeks he passed hovering between life and death—alone sustained by his intense religious beliefs and his eager hope of reaching the coast before he died. Little wonder surely that at times he spent "the lingering hours in a very gloomy and solitary manner," while the rains dashed down remorselessly on the hut wherein he lay in the damp stifling atmosphere and semi-darkness.

At length with the passing season the rains became less frequent, and the ground in consequence more dry. With improved conditions came improved health and stronger hope of life. At times the convalescent managed to crawl to his door to sniff the fresher and more wholesome air, to bathe in the bright light, and look upon the blue heavens. It was as if he had emerged from an open grave.

Soon from the door of his hut he could totter with his mat to the grateful shade of a tamarind tree, and there enjoy the refreshing smell of the growing corn, and the varied prospect of hill and valley, field and grove around him. At other times naïve converse with the simple natives, and half hours with his book of prayers, made glad the passing day.

Through it all Karfa Taura was ever the generous host and faithful friend, though many there were who vainly tried to turn him against his unknown guest.

Occasionally parties of slaves were conveyed through Kamalia. Once one of the unfortunate captives asked Park for food. The latter represented that he was himself a stranger and destitute. "I gave you food when you were hungry," was the reply; "have you forgot the man who brought you milk at Karankalla? But," added he with a sigh, "the irons were not then on my legs." Much touched, Park recalled the incident, and instantly begged some ground- nuts for him from Karfa.

With returning health of both body and mind, Park employed himself while wearily awaiting the completion of the slave caravan in a variety of inquiries regarding articles of commerce, trade routes, &c. Among other subjects he was much interested in the slave trade. He learned the various ways in which slaves were obtained—how the natives kidnapped from neighbouring villages and petty states, or warred with each other to keep up the traffic—how parents found a source of temporary relief in times of famine by selling their children, and kings a source of revenue by disposing of their subjects or those convicted of crimes, while people unable to meet their engagements in the ordinary way paid their debts by becoming the slaves of the creditors. Of the bloodshed and ruin resulting from the unholy traffic he had himself seen much, and now heard more, while remaining blind to Europe's share in encouraging this "great open sore" of Africa, that its merchants and planters might be enriched thereby. As for the unhappy victims of European commerce, they had a deeply rooted belief that they were to be devoured by white cannibals, and that the country across the sea was an enchanted land quite different from their own. Their usual question to Park was, "Have you really got such ground as this to set your feet upon?"

These ideas naturally caused the slaves to regard their fate at the coast with terror and horror, and to seek every opportunity of escaping.

Each day Park could see his future companions to the Gambia marched out, secured from flight by having the right leg of one attached by fetters to the left leg of another, with the additional precaution that every four men were fastened together by the necks with a strong rope. Some who were not amenable to this form of discipline had a cylinder of wood notched at each end fastened between the legs with iron bolts. At night additional fetters were put on the hands, and occasionally the prisoners were made further secure by having a light iron chain passed round their necks. Thus loaded with irons on neck, hand, and foot they were placed in batches and left to find sleep as best they could, guarded by Karfa Taura's domestic slaves.

One pleasant sight there was of which Park never wearied—the Mohammedan schoolmaster of Kamalia, and his school of seventeen boys and girls. To him "it was not so much a matter of wonder as a matter of regret to observe that while the superstition of Mohammed has in this manner scattered a few faint dreams of learning among these poor people, the precious light of Christianity is excluded. I could not but lament," he continues, "that although the coast of Africa had now been known and frequented for more than two hundred years, yet the negroes still remain entire strangers to the doctrines of our holy religion.... Perhaps a short and easy introduction to Christianity, such as is found in some of the catechisms for children, elegantly printed in Arabic, and distributed on different parts of the coast, might have a wonderful effect.... These reflections I have thus ventured to submit to my readers on this important subject, on perceiving the encouragement which was thus given to learning (such as it is) in many parts of Africa. I have observed that the pupils of Kamalia were most of them children of Pagans; their parents therefore could have had no predilection for the doctrines of Mohammed. Their aim was their children's improvement." So much indeed was education prized that the usual course was valued at the price of a prime slave.

By the beginning of the year 1797, everything was ready for departure, but on various trivial pretexts the leave-taking was put off from day to day till the approach of Rhamadan, when it was determined to wait till it was over before commencing their journey.

During the whole of the month of fast "the negroes behaved themselves with the greatest meekness and humility, forming a striking contrast to the savage intolerance and brutal bigotry which at this period characterise the Moors."

CHAPTER XV.
THE SLAVE ROUTE.

In the second week of April the Mohammedans of Kamalia were on the alert for the expected appearance of the new moon, which would terminate their month of fasting. On the evening of this joyful event it seemed for a time as if they were to be disappointed, and that yet another day would have to be added to their Rhamadan. Clouds veiled the sky. Only temporarily, however. The obscuring mists broke, and the delicate curved beauty of the new moon gleamed upon the upturned faces, and carried joy to every Mussulman heart. Shrill screams from the women and shouts from the men, hand clapping, drum beating, and musket firing gave voice to the general delight.

Orders were at once given by Karfa to prepare for the march, and on consultation the 19th of April was chosen for the day of departure. This was good news for Park, who, sick with hope long deferred, and "wearied with a constant state of alarm and anxiety, had developed a painful longing for the manifold blessings of civilisation." All the slatees had done their best to set Karfa against the white stranger, and the latter constantly feared that their evil machinations might prevail, and that he would be cast forth helpless and destitute among the dangerous wilds of Africa.

At last the wished-for day of departure arrived. The slatees assembled with their slaves before their leader Karfa's door. The bundles were finally roped, and the loads assigned to the men and women who were to carry them. When mustered, the caravan numbered thirty-five slaves, and thirty-eight free people and domestic slaves, a schoolmaster with eight pupils, and six singing men to lighten with song and antic the toils of the route, while at the same time making the presence of the caravan more welcome to the natives, and its reception more hospitable at their hands.

Amid much hand-shaking and various manifestations of fear, regret, and grief, the signal to start was given, and the caravan set out on its journey. At a rising some distance out of town a halt was called. All were ordered to seat themselves, the departing band of travellers with their faces towards the west, the townspeople who had so far accompanied them with theirs towards Kamalia and the east. The schoolmaster and two of the principal slatees, placing themselves between, raised a long and solemn prayer that their journey might be successful and safe under the protection of Allah. Afterwards the caravan was encircled three times, that a charm might be woven round the party, and their safety thus further ensured. The ceremony concluded, all sprang to their feet, and without further leave-taking the start was made towards the ocean.

At first the movements of many of the slaves were eloquent of the fetters they had worn for years. Their attempts at walking were marked by spasmodic contractions of the legs, and very soon two of them had to be released from the rope to allow them to go slower, so painful were their efforts to step out freely and briskly.

BAOBAB TREE.

In two marches Worumbang, the western frontier village of Manding, was reached without mishap. The party was now on the verge of the dreaded Jallonka Wilderness. Provisions had to be gathered for the passage of this trying region, and every one rested to prepare for the forced marches and hardships ahead.

On the morning of the 21st the outskirts of the wilderness were entered. On reaching the woods a halt was called, and a prayer offered up that Allah and his prophet might preserve them from robbers, keep them from hunger, and sustain them under fatigue. This ceremony over, it behoved every man to push forward with all his strength and will if Kinytakuro, the proposed destination of that day's march, was to be reached before dark. Every one, bond and free alike, knew the dangers before him, and ran rather than walked.

Soon the Niger basin was left, and the Kokoro, a tributary of the Senegal, was reached. At this time it was a mere rivulet, but there was ample evidence to show that during the rainy season it had risen twenty feet.

No halt was made throughout the day—nothing was heard but the order to push on. Well indeed was it for those who had the strength to do so. Some there were who could not. A woman and a girl began to lag behind. Threats and curses from time to time incited them to spasmodic efforts at exertion, but soon these failed in their effect, and fell on unheeding ears. The lash was next brought into play, and for a time gave the needed stimulus. Then it too failed. Savage hands grasped the unhappy victims of European commerce and dragged them forward, while others behind plied the whip with unabating ferocity. The limits of nature were reached at last, and both sank to the ground, not to be moved by any form of fiendish cruelty. Furious and disappointed, their master had at length to give in, and make up his mind to return home for the time being.

About sunset the town of Kinytakuro was reached, and the anxieties of the first day's march were over. The entry to the town was made with much ceremony and circumstance. The musicians led the way singing the praises of the villagers, their hospitality, and their friendship to the Mandingoes. After them followed some of the free men; then came the slaves, fastened in fours by a rope round the neck, with an armed man between each set. Behind the raw slaves came the domestic slaves, while the rear was brought up by the free women, the wives of the slatees, the scholars, &c. In this way the caravan marched to the palaver house, where the people gathered round to hear their story; after which lodgings and food were provided for the entire party.

At daybreak on the 23rd, the wilderness proper was entered. At ten o'clock the river Wonda, flowing to the Senegal, was crossed, and then strict commands were given that close order should be maintained, and every man travel in his proper station.

The guides and the young men led the way, the women and slaves occupied the centre, while the free men brought up the rear. The country through which they passed unmolested, though with hurried footsteps, was charming in the extreme, with its variety of hill and dale, of glade and wood, and meandering streams, to which partridges, guinea fowl, and deer gave an air of animation. On this day Park got his arms and neck painfully blistered by the burning sun, from which his scanty dress afforded him no protection.

At sunset a romantic stream called Comcissang was reached, and here the party halted for the night, thoroughly fatigued with their day's exertions, though no one was heard to complain. Large fires were kindled for cooking purposes, as well as to light up the camp and drive away wild beasts. Supper over, the slaves were put in irons to prevent their escaping, and then all disposed themselves to sleep; but between ants within the camp and wild beasts howling without the night's rest was sadly broken.

At daybreak morning prayers were said, after which a little gruel was drunk by the free men, the irons being thereafter once more taken off the slaves, and the march resumed.

The route now led over a wild and rocky country, where Park, with nothing better than sandals to protect his feet, got sadly bruised and cut. Fears began to oppress him that he would not be able to keep up with the caravan, and that he would be left behind to perish. The sight of others more exhausted than himself was, however, in some sort a relief from his apprehension. Neali, one of Karfa's female slaves, especially showed signs of giving in. She began to lag behind, complaining of pains in her legs, and her load had to be taken from her and given to another. About midday, while halting at a rivulet, an enormous swarm of bees, which had been disturbed by one of the men, set upon the caravan, and sent it flying in all directions. When the panic had subsided, it was discovered that Neali had been left behind. Before going back in search of her it was necessary to set fire to the grass to the east of the hive in order to clear away the bees with the smoke. The plan was effectual, and on returning to the rivulet, Neali was found half dead in the water, whither she had crept in the hope of escaping the onslaught of the bees. The stratagem had been of no avail, however, and the poor creature was almost stung to death.

It was the last drop in her cup of misery. Nothing else could touch her. Entreaties and threats were alike useless. Further forward she doggedly refused to go. Once more the efficacy of the whip was tried. Down came the brutal lash. The girl writhed in every muscle, but she neither screamed nor attempted to rise. Again the lash swung round her shrinking body, but with no more effect. Not until it had descended a third and a fourth time did her resolution give way. Then stung to superhuman effort by the fearful torture, she started up and staggered forward for some hours, till wild with agony she made a mad attempt to run away, but fell fainting among the grass. Her master's only remedy was the lash, and that he applied with renewed savagery. In vain—Neali was beyond its cruel compulsion. As a last resource the donkey which carried the dry provisions was brought, and the half dead slave placed on his back. But the girl's only wish was to die, nay, even now she seemed as one already dead.

Unable even if she had been willing to retain her seat, and the donkey at the same time emphatically objecting to his new load, that means of carriage had to be given up. The day's journey, however, was nearly over, and Neali being a valuable slave, the slatees could not bring themselves to abandon her.

Accordingly, they made a rude litter of bamboo canes, on which she was carried until the camping ground for the night was reached.

It now became evident that Neali was not the only slave for whom the journey was proving too much. The hard march with heavy loads under a broiling sun, without food, and with no better stimulant than blows and curses—with nothing to look forward to at night but additional chains, and in the future a horrible fate at the hands of white men across the seas—all this was beginning to have its natural effect. Sullen despair was in every feature—every gesture. Death, suicide, seemed preferable to such a chain of horrors.

The slatees were not slow to mark these ominous signs. At once fetters were applied—the more desperate of the slaves having even their hands chained; and thus bound they were left to rest as best they might.

Throughout the night Neali lay torpid and almost motionless, and morning found her with limbs so stiff and swollen that she could not stand, much less walk. The donkey was again brought into requisition, and to keep her on his back the girl's hands were tied round his neck, and her feet under his belly. Spite of these precautions, however, before long the donkey threw her, and bound as she was, she was nearly trampled to death before she could be released.

Meanwhile precious time was being wasted in a wilderness where every minute was of the utmost importance. To carry the girl in the fashion of the previous evening was out of the question, and the patience of every one was exhausted. "Cut her throat! cut her throat!" was the cry now raised by the slave dealers. Strange to say, Park did not seem to have anything to urge against this brutal suggestion—for Neali indeed the most merciful ending of her troubles— though being unwilling to see it put in force, he walked on ahead. A few minutes later one of Karfa's men came up to him carrying Neali's scanty cotton garment, which to Park was eloquent of the poor girl's fate. He could not bring himself to make inquiries then, but later on he learned that Neali had not had the good fortune to have her tortures ended at once by the knife. She was deserted, and a day of exposure, naked to the remorseless sun, without food or drink, had to drag slowly on before darkness drew a veil over the last horrible scene, in which she met death under the fangs of the wild beasts of the Jallonka Wilderness.

The fate of the slave girl had a wonderfully stimulating effect on the rest of the caravan; but the schoolmaster, in doubts as to how Allah would regard the incident, fasted the whole day. In deep silence the slaves travelled onward at a steady pace, each apprehensive that his too might be the fate of Neali. No one was more apprehensive than Park himself. Only by the most determined effort of will did he keep himself from succumbing on the march. Everything that could obstruct him in the least—even his spear—was thrown away, but still he could just barely struggle on. "The poor slaves, amidst their own infinitely greater sufferings, would commiserate mine, and frequently of their own accord bring water to quench my thirst, and at night collect branches and leaves to prepare me a bed in the wilderness."

On the morning of the 26th, two of the schoolmaster's pupils complained of pains in their legs, and one of the slaves walked lame, the soles of his feet being much blistered and inflamed. But there could be no halting for such trivial causes, and the caravan pushed onward with hot haste, eager to escape as soon as possible the hardships and dangers of the desert. In the middle of the day a rocky hill was reached, the crossing of which greatly aggravated the sores on the travellers' feet. In the afternoon evidences of a raiding party of horsemen were seen, and to hide their track the caravan had to disperse and travel wide apart for some distance.

Another day of toil ended the desert march. On the 27th, the village of Susita, in the district of Kullo, was entered. The rest of the road was comparatively safe. Next day the Bafing or Black River, the principal branch of the Senegal, was crossed by a bamboo bridge of singular construction. Trees tied end to end were made to support a roadway of bamboos—the centre of the bridge floating on the water, the ends resting on the banks. On the rising of the water during the rains this primitive bridge is carried away each year.

Though the caravan had now got into a well-populated district, their troubles were hardly over. They were refused admittance at village after village, and to complete their discomfiture, news came that two hundred Jallonkas had gathered to plunder them. This necessitated an alteration in their route, and a forced night march. After midnight a town was reached, but as a free man and three slaves were found to be missing, a halt was called, and while the caravan remained concealed in a cotton field, a search party returned to look for the runaways. In the morning the town was entered, and the day was passed in resting from their fatigues. Here, to the joy of all, the absentees turned up safely. One of the slaves had hurt his foot, and they had thus lagged behind and lost the caravan. The free man, foreseeing the danger of an outbreak, insisted on putting the slaves in irons. This they were inclined to resist, but a threat to stab them all had its due effect.

On the 3rd of May the caravan reached the schoolmaster's native village, Malacotta, where in consequence a hearty welcome awaited them. Three days were spent here recruiting the party. During that time Park learned the particulars of a remarkable story of Moslem zeal and Pagan chivalry and generosity, well worthy of being retold.

"The King of Futa Torra, inflamed with a zeal for propagating his religion, had sent an embassy to Damel, King of the Jaloffs.

"The ambassador was accompanied by two of the principal Mohammedans of the country, who each carried a knife fixed on the top of a long pole. 'With this knife,' said the ambassador, 'Abdul Kader will condescend to shave the head of Damel, if Damel will embrace the Mohammedan religion; and with this other knife Abdul Kader will cut the throat of Damel if Damel refuse to embrace it. Take your choice.'

"Damel replied that he had no choice to make. He neither chose to have his head shaved nor his throat cut; and with this answer the ambassador was civilly dismissed. War was accordingly declared, and the country of Damel invaded. The fortune of war, however, went against the earthly instrument of Allah, and his army was not only dispersed with great loss, but he himself taken prisoner. In this humiliating position Abdul Kader was brought in irons and thrown on the ground before Damel. Instead of setting his foot on the neck of his royal prisoner and stabbing him with his spear, as is the custom in such cases, Damel addressed him as follows—'Abdul Kader, answer me this question. If the chance of war had placed me in your situation, and you in mine, how would you have treated me?'

"'I would have thrust my spear into your heart,' answered the brave though fanatical prince; 'and I know that a similar fate awaits me.'

"'Not so,' said Damel. 'My spear is indeed red with the blood of your subjects killed in battle, and I could now give it a deeper stain by dipping it in your own; but this would not build up my towns, nor bring to life the thousands who fell in the woods. I will not therefore kill you in cold blood, but I will retain you as my slave until I perceive that your presence in your own kingdom will be no longer dangerous to your neighbours, and then I will consider of the proper way of disposing of you.' A decision which has been made the subject of the songs of the musicians, and a matter of applausive comment by all the tribes.

"Abdul Kader was accordingly retained, and worked as a slave for three months; at the end of which period Damel listened to the solicitations of the inhabitants of Futa Torra, and restored to them their king."

Of the truth of this story there seems to be no doubt.

CHAPTER XVI.
BACK TO THE GAMBIA AND HOME.

At Malacotta, Park could look forward with a considerable degree of confidence to his safe return to the coast. He was once more within the sphere of influence of coast trade, where the European was better known, and the hostile agency of the Moor was of small account. There were no more jungles to cross, and he was unaware of obstructing wars on the route. Through good and evil report Karfa had remained his staunch friend, and it was certain that now that his promised reward was coming nearer and nearer attainment, he would not alter in his honourable fidelity to his engagements. It was now only a question of so many more days' journey till the Gambia would be reached, and all Park's cares and troubles be at an end.

On the 7th of May the slave caravan left Malacotta, and resumed its journey to the coast. The Bali, a branch of the Senegal, was crossed, and Bintingala entered in the evening.

In the afternoon of the 12th the Falemé River was forded about 100 miles south of Park's fording point on his inland journey. At this place and time of year the river was only two feet deep, flowing over a bed of sand and gravel.

On the same day the caravan halted at the residence of a Mandingo merchant, who had his food served up in pewter dishes in the European fashion. Next morning they were joined by a Serawuli slave caravan. These traders had the reputation of being infinitely more cruel in their treatment of slaves than the Mandingoes. Park was soon to see a sample of their ways. The caravan was travelling with great speed through the dense woods, when one of the slaves began to show signs of exhaustion, and let his load fall from his head. A smart flogging proved a temporary stimulant to the unhappy victim, but hardly a mile was passed before nature once more asserted itself, and again the load fell. A double dose of the lash proved a second time effectual, and once more the slave struggled painfully forward. At last the limits of his powers were reached, and it became clear that flog as they might he would remain immovable.

The caravan could not wait till he recovered, and accordingly one of the Serawulis undertook to wait and bring him to camp in the cool of the evening. When the slave dealer did arrive in camp he came alone. No questions were asked, but every one knew that either the unfortunate man had been killed, or was left to be devoured by wild beasts.

Other examples of the slave dealers' methods were almost daily exhibited before Park's eyes. At one place a Mandingo, having a slave torn from a neighbouring district, agreed with Karfa to exchange him for another from a more distant country, to which he could not run away. The slave to be taken by Karfa was called on a trivial pretext to come into the house. The moment he entered the gate was shut, and he was told to sit down. At once he saw the danger of his situation—not only the more horrible fate of transportation across the seas, but the loss of all chance of escape to his native country. He would at least make one effort for liberty. With the wild leap of a hunted deer he cleared the fence of the court and bolted for the woods. But it was useless. His enemies were too many. A few minutes of wild flight, spurred on by wolfish cries, and then he was hunted down and brought back in irons to be handed over to Karfa.

At another place one of the male slaves in the caravan was found to be too exhausted to proceed further in spite of the usual physical stimulants. A townsman was found willing to exchange him for a young girl. No hint was given her of her approaching doom till the last moment. Along with her companions she had come to see the caravan depart, when all at once her master seized her by the hand and delivered her to the slave dealer. "Never was a face of serenity more suddenly changed into one of the deepest distress. The terror she manifested on having the load put upon her head and the rope round her neck, and the sorrow with which she bade adieu to her companions, were truly affecting."

Incidents like these were what chiefly characterised Park's journey to the Gambia. At times the curious as well as the horrible side of African life peeped out to entertain him, as, for instance, when one of the slatees, on returning for the first time to his native place after an absence of three years, was met at the threshold of his door by his bride-elect, who presented him with a calabash of water in which to wash his hands. This done, "the girl, with a tear of joy sparkling in her eye, drank the water," in token of her fidelity and attachment.

Another of the slatees turned out to be an African Enoch Arden. For eight long years he had stayed away from his wife, during which time she heard nothing from him. Concluding after three years that he was either dead or not likely to return, she seemingly without reluctance gave her heart and hand to another, by whom she had two children. The first husband now claimed her as his. The other objected on the ground that a three years' absence annulled a marriage. For four days a public palaver was held to settle this knotty point, ending in the decision that the husbands had equal rights, and that the wife had best settle the matter by making her own choice. The lady asked time to consider, but Park could perceive that not love but wealth would gain the day.

On the 20th of May the caravan entered the Tenda Wilderness, where for two days they traversed dense woods. With what pleasure must Park have noticed that the country shelved towards the south-west—that in fact he had entered the basin of the Gambia. At sunset of the first day a pool was reached after a very hot and trying march. To avoid the burning heats of the day a night march was determined on. At eleven o'clock the slaves were released from their irons and driven forward in close order, as much to prevent them escaping as to save them from wild beasts. In this fashion they travelled till daybreak, after a rest continuing the march to Tambakunda, the place almost reached by Jobson nearly 170 years before, and which he believed to be Timbuktu itself.

From Tambakunda the road led over a wild and rocky country, everywhere rising into hills, and abounding with monkeys and wild beasts. During the next two marches the reception everywhere met with by the caravan was far from being hospitable, and they were even in some danger of being plundered.

On the 30th of May the Nerico, a branch of the Gambia, was reached. As soon as it was crossed the singing men began to chant a song expressive of their delight at having got safe into the "land of the setting sun." Next day, to his infinite joy, Park found himself on the banks of the Gambia, at a point where it was navigable, though lower down there were shallows.

Three days later, Medina, the capital of Wulli, was reached, where Park had been so hospitably received seventeen months before. The caravan did not halt here; but Park, mindful of the old king's prayer on his behalf, sent word to him that his prayers had not been unavailing.

Next day Jindeh was reached, where the parting with Dr. Laidley had taken place. Here Karfa left his slaves till a better opportunity of selling them had arrived; but determined not to leave his white friend till the last, he accompanied him on his way to Pisania.

Park at this point remarks: "Although I was now approaching the end of my tedious and toilsome journey, and expected in another day to meet with countrymen and friends, I could not part for the last time with my unfortunate fellow-travellers, doomed as I knew most of them to be to a life of captivity and slavery in a foreign land, without great emotion.... We parted with reciprocal expressions of regret and benediction. My good wishes and prayers were all that I could bestow upon them, and it afforded me some consolation to be told that they were sensible I had no more to give."

On the 10th, Park once more shook hands with one of his countrymen. He found that it was universally believed that he had met the same fate as Major Houghton in Ludamar. He also learned with sincere sorrow that neither Johnson, who had deserted him, nor Demba, who had been enslaved by the Moors, had returned.

On the 12th, Dr. Laidley joined the long-lost traveller, and greeted him as one risen from the dead. Park was soon, under his hospitable hands, divested of his ragged Moorish garments. With them went the luxuriant beard which had been the delight and admiration of natives and Moors alike, among whom nothing is more envied, and he stood forth once more the handsome young Scotchman his portrait shows him to be.

Karfa was now paid off, the stipulated reward being doubled, and Dr. Laidley's interest also promised in getting his slaves disposed of to advantage.

Karfa was never tired expressing his wonderment at all he saw, though nothing surprised him more than the incomprehensible madness of a person in Park's condition in life leaving all and suffering so many hardships and dangers merely to see the river Niger. "I have preserved," says Park, "these little traits of character in this worthy negro, not only from regard to the man, but also because they appear to me to demonstrate that he possessed a mind above his condition, and to such of my readers as love to contemplate human nature in all its varieties, and to trace its progress from rudeness to refinement, I hope the account I have given of this poor African will not be unacceptable."

Looking back on his long and terrible journey, Park could afford to take a lenient view of all the people who had plundered, ill-used, or inhospitably treated him, except the Moors, of whom he carried a deep-rooted horror and hatred to his dying day. For the Mandingoes and kindred tribes he could ever find an excuse for all he suffered at their hands, and as a people he found them gentle, cheerful in their dispositions, kind-hearted, and simple, with a natural sense of justice which only very great temptation could overcome. He could not find words strong enough to describe the disinterested charity and tender solicitude shown by many of them, especially the women, whom he found to be universally kind and compassionate, sympathising with his sufferings, relieving his distresses, and contributing to his safety.

Reviewing what he had seen commercially, he found that slaves, gold, and ivory, beeswax and honey, hides, gums, and dye woods, constituted the whole catalogue of exportable commodities. Of other products, such as tobacco, indigo, and cotton, sufficient only was raised for native consumption. He concluded, nevertheless, that "it cannot, however, admit of a doubt that all the rich and valuable productions both of the East and West Indies might easily be naturalised and brought to the utmost perfection in the tropical parts of this immense continent. Nothing is wanting to this end but example to enlighten the minds of the natives, and instruction to enable them to direct their industry to proper objects. It was not possible for me to behold the wonderful fertility of the soil, the vast herds of cattle, proper both for food and labour, and a variety of other circumstances favourable to colonisation and agriculture, and reflect withal on the means which presented themselves of a vast inland navigation, without lamenting that a country so abundantly gifted and favoured by nature should remain in its present savage and neglected state. Much more did I lament that a people of manners and dispositions so gentle and benevolent should either be left as they now are, immersed in the gross and uncomfortable blindness of Pagan superstition, or permitted to become converts to a system of bigotry and fanaticism which, without enlightening the mind, often debases the heart." And yet which of the representatives of the two religions, Islam and Christianity, were doing the most good among the heathen according to Park's own showing—the Mohammedans, battling against the inrushing tide of rum and gin, encouraging education, and spreading a knowledge of Allah the One God; or the Christian merchants, fomenting and deepening all the horrors of native barbarism that their trade in slaves might be kept up, and adding to the degradation of the land by the drink and firearms they gave in exchange for its people?

As there was no ship in the river when Park arrived, he expected to have to wait for some months. In this, however, he was happily disappointed, for an American slave ship, the *Charlestown*, arrived on the 15th. Slaves were plentiful, and in a couple of days the cargo of human flesh and blood for the plantations of South Carolina was made up in exchange for rum and tobacco.

Though the route by America was excessively circuitous, it was such a chance as Park could not afford to neglect. Accordingly, on the 17th of June he bade farewell to all his English friends, and took passage in the American vessel.

He had now reason to suppose that all his cares, anxieties, and dangers were over, and nothing but rest and good treatment before him. Once more, however, he was dogged by his usual ill-luck. The passage down the river was tedious and fatiguing, the weather being exceedingly hot, moist, and unhealthy. The result was that before Goree was reached, four of the seamen, the surgeon, and three of the slaves had died of fever. At Goree, owing to the difficulty of obtaining provisions, the vessel was detained four weary months, so that it was the end of October before she eventually set sail for America.

The *Charlestown's* cargo consisted of 130 slaves, of whom twenty-five had been free Mohammedans, able to read and write a little Arabic. Some of the others had seen Park *en route*, and many had heard of him in their distant villages. But though he had not a word to say against the slave trade, Park had a feeling heart for the miseries of those whom, with his Calvinistic ideas, he believed predestined to a life of shame and suffering. Being able to speak to them in their native language, he did his best as a man and a doctor to comfort them. And in truth they had need of all the consolation he could bestow. The manner in which they were crowded, confined, and chained in the hold of the ship produced terrible sufferings, while the foul air, the wretched sanitary conditions, and the want of exercise brought on general sickness. "Besides the three who died on the Gambia, and six or eight at Goree, eleven perished at sea, and many of the survivors were reduced to a very weak and emaciated condition."

To make matters worse for all concerned, the *Charlestown* sprang a leak three weeks from Goree, and threatened to founder in mid-ocean. To avoid this, the ablest of the negroes were taken from their chains and kept at the pumps till they could be hounded on no longer, and sank down exhausted and half dead. In spite of everything, however, the leak continued to gain, and the misery of all on board was indescribable. As affording the only chance of safety, the *Charlestown* was turned from its course and steered for Antigua, which was reached thirty-five days out from Goree. But even in sight of harbour the ship narrowly escaped destruction by striking on a sunken rock.

Park remained at Antigua for two days, when on the 24th November he was taken up by a passing mail ship. After a short but tempestuous voyage he arrived at Falmouth on the 22nd December, having been absent from England two years and nine months.

CHAPTER XVII.
MUNGO PARK AT HOME.

Once landed at Falmouth, Park lost no time in proceeding to London. In those days there was no telegraph to apprise the world of his arrival, nor newspaper reporters to interview him, and give their readers a description of his appearance and a foretaste of his adventures.

He reached London before daybreak on the 25th December, and directed his steps to the house of his brother-in-law, Mr. Dickson. Not caring to disturb his relative at that early hour, he wandered about the streets for some time, till finding one of the gates to the British Museum Gardens open, he entered.

As it happened, Dickson had charge of these gardens, and on this particular morning had business which took him there unusually early. Conceive his amazement on coming face to face with what for a moment he almost took to be a vision or ghost of his young relative, long since believed to be dead. It did not take long to convince him, however, that here was no ghost, but the actual traveller himself, safe and well, his great mission carried through to a successful conclusion.

The interest, delight, and surprise of the Association, as well as of the public generally, were no less keen. For some time it had been looked on as a certainty that he had been murdered, and now the utmost curiosity prevailed to hear his adventures, and at last learn something authentic about the mysterious river of the negroes.

It looked indeed as if Park's own prediction to his brother before leaving for Africa, that he would "acquire a greater name than any ever did," was to be verified. In the absence of more definite news, the hand to hand reports which circulated only tended to exaggerate his feats and discoveries.

So eager became the demand for information that it was determined to issue a preliminary report of the principal geographical results of the expedition. This was written by Bryan Edwards, the Secretary of the Association, a gentleman of no inconsiderable literary attainments, and author of a "History of the British Colonies in the West Indies."

To the collaboration of Edwards was added that of Major Rennell, who worked out with very great care the traveller's routes, and the geography of the region generally. In addition, Rennell added a memoir on the upper course of the Niger beyond Park's furthest point, collating with his information that of the Arabian geographers.

But the public demanded something more than the dry bones of geography to satisfy their hungry appetite. They wanted also the flesh and blood of his narrative—how he lived and moved, what he felt and suffered, what dangers he faced, what hardships endured, the wonders he saw. Books of travel had not then deluged the market and saturated men's minds with details about the remotest corners of Inner Africa. It was practically virgin soil to the reader, who could in nowise guess beforehand what startling revelations were in store for him. Compared with the modern devourer of books of travel, his sensations would be as those of the first explorer of the Gambia to the subdued expectancy of our latest traveller.

To gratify this very natural curiosity Park now devoted himself. His materials, apart from his memory, were but scanty. They consisted, in fact, of short notes or memoranda, written on odds and ends of paper, which must often have been far from legible, considering how they were carried for months in the crown of a battered hat, exposed to damp and all manner of accidents.

In the task of authorship Park was no doubt materially aided by Mr. Edwards, with whom he lived on terms of great friendship. In one or two places the pen of Edwards is clearly traceable, but these are few and far between. Where he lent the most valuable assistance was in the pruning, rearrangement, and revision which the work of a novice in composition would almost necessarily require. In this respect, however, Park is not alone among travellers. Few indeed among them have had such a complete mastery of the pen and of the English language as to trust absolutely in their own literary powers and judgment, although, as in Park's case, the assistance required has seldom gone beyond guidance and revision.

Apart from his literary influence, it can hardly be doubted that Edwards very materially moulded Park's views on at least one important subject—the slave trade. At that time the question of abolition had become a burning one in the country, and Edwards was one of the warmest advocates of the old order of things. He would give Africa Light, but no Liberty. While actively employed in trying to open up the Dark Continent to European influence, he strenuously strove to ensure that that influence should remain of the most criminal and degrading nature.

Let the reader imagine what would have been the consequence to Africa if the advocates of slavery had had their way, and the exploration of the Continent had only been the forerunner of more widespread ramifications of the slave trade. However incredible it may appear, such might easily have been the case. People once accustomed to an evil soon forget that it is such, and begin to look upon it as one of the necessary and unavoidable ills of life. Take, for example, the survival of the African gin trade to this very day, increasing and flourishing long after its dissociation from its well-matched sister traffic in slaves, and everywhere dogging the explorer's footsteps. It is doubtful if even the slave trade has done more to brutalise and degrade the negro; and yet even in our time there is only a partial awakening to the frightful evils of the iniquitous traffic.

This culpable blindness or carelessness on our part is doubtless largely fostered by the comforting and comfortable belief that our missionaries are doing a great and noble work in Africa, and that mere contact with the European and European commerce must of necessity have an elevating effect upon the lower races. The truth is that for every negro nominally or genuinely brought under the influence of Christianity, ten thousand have been driven by drink to depths of moral and physical depravity unheard of among uncontaminated native tribes, and that so far contact with the European and his commerce has resulted not in elevation to the African, but in degradation of the most loathsome kind.

To what extent Park was really influenced in his opinions on the slave question by Edwards it would be difficult to say. It matters little, however, for whether he really believed in the righteousness of slavery or was merely reasoned into neutrality, his position was equally indefensible. Nay, more, if, as his friends say, he really believed that the trade was an unjust one, the position he assumed was nothing more nor less than criminal. These urge, as if it were an extenuating circumstance, that in private conversation he even expressed the greatest abhorrence of the traffic. This, it must be confessed, seems improbable. Such an attitude is utterly unlike what we should expect from a man of Park's marked individuality and strong earnest truthfulness. Moreover, it seems sufficiently clear that the public opinion of his day ascribed to him a belief in the righteousness of the principle of slavery, and if it was wrong, it seems strange that he took no means to correct it. But that it was not wrong seems evident from a speech delivered on the Abolition of the Slave Trade by George Hibbert in Parliament in 1803.

The following is an extract—valuable, too, as throwing light upon the share of Edwards in the writing of Park's book:—

"I have read and heard that we are to look to Park's facts and not to his opinions; and it has been insinuated that his editor, Mr. Edwards, had foisted those opinions (relating to the slave trade) into his book. It happened to me once to converse with Mr. Park at a meeting of the Linnean Society, when this very topic was started, and he assured me that, not being in the habit of literary composition, he was obliged to employ some one to put his manuscript into a form fit for the public eye, but that every sheet of the publication had undergone his strict revision, and that not only every fact but every sentiment was his own."

We must, therefore, till more convincing proof than hearsay evidence is forthcoming, believe that Mungo Park was a believer in the slave trade. Such a position we can understand and make all due allowance for as the result of the ideas of the time, and of those by whom he was immediately surrounded —to believe else were to place Park on a distinctly lower pedestal than that to which he is entitled by his many meritorious characteristics.

Shortly after the publication of the abstract of Park's narrative, he left London on a visit to his family at Foulshiels, where his mother still lived, though his father had been dead for some years. Here he remained the whole of the summer and autumn of 1798, working assiduously at the narrative of his travels. This was probably anything but an agreeable task to him after the eventful life he had led for three years, and unaccustomed as he was to literary work. But Park was not the man to shirk any work, however irksome, if it in any way appeared to him in the light of a duty. His mornings he devoted to writing, his evenings to strolls along the bank of his much-loved Yarrow, where, rarely troubled by native or by passing stranger, he could undisturbed recall the various events which marked his African wanderings, and on the dreamy rush of the mountain stream let his thoughts glide back to the majestic sweep of the Joliba moving eastward towards its unknown bourne. What hours he must have spent thus, seeking in his mind's eye to pierce the dark veil which so mysteriously shrouded the great African river beyond Timbuktu, and follow it to its union with the ocean, or its gradual disappearance in the Central Deserts.

At times restlessness and a feeling of revolt took possession of him, and then the only charm that could exorcise the demon of unrest within him or soothe his wild vague longings, was a long swift walk among the wild romantic scenery around. Up Yarrow's winding dale, on the bold front of Newark Hill, or the heathery summit of the Broomy Law, his was the keen pleasure of a soul that knows "a rapture on the lonely shore." The distant bleat of sheep, the plaintive call of the curlew, and the whirr of grouse, harmonised well with the mood possessing him, and touched his heart with the wild pathos of Nature. Happiest when alone, he found companions in all the sounds around him. The breeze, the rushing stream, the wild calls of bird and beast, all alike spoke to him, and adapted themselves to his every mood.

All this may be vaguely discerned by virtue of the gleams of light which have momentarily shot across the darkness of the past, and preserved a blurred though speaking print of the great traveller at home among his native hills.

But although thus isolated from the world at large, Park was not entirely cut off from communication with his fellow-men. His chief resort when in a mood for society was the house of his friend and master in medicine, Dr. Anderson, who still practised in Selkirk, within easy reach of Foulshiels. As one result of these frequent visits, the friendship of former days for Miss Anderson speedily developed into a warmer feeling, and summer saw them engaged.

Towards the latter part of 1798, Park returned to London to make the final arrangements for the publication of his narrative. Even then, however, much had to be done with the assistance of Edwards before the manuscript was finally ready for the press, and spring had come before the book saw the light.

It would be difficult to overestimate the enthusiasm with which it was received, or the interest in Park and Africa which it aroused. Two editions were sold off in rapid succession, and were followed by several others in the course of the following ten years.

Apart from its being almost the first of African books of travel, and from the absolute novelty of all it contained, the narrative was told with a charm and *naïveté* in themselves sufficient to captivate the most fastidious reader. Modesty and truthfulness peeped from every sentence. Its author claimed no praise, no admiration, beyond that due to him for having done his duty. He took to himself no credit for all the virtues he had shown. So afraid was he indeed that he might be charged with being the author of what are called "travellers' tales," that he deliberately suppressed several remarkable adventures. On this point he said to Sir Walter Scott, "that in all cases where he had information to communicate which he thought of importance to the public, he had stated the facts boldly, leaving it to his readers to give such credit to his statements as they might appear justly to deserve, but that he would not shock their credulity or render his travels more marvellous by introducing circumstances which, however true, were of little or no moment."

Happily his narrative required no aid from such suppressed adventures, however strange they might be, or however much we should have liked to know them. He had incident enough to make half-a-dozen of the spun out books of modern travel. Neither then nor since has any African explorer had such a romantic tale to tell, nor has any out of all the long list of adventurers who have followed told his tale so well. Some there have been who have flourished more theatrically across the African stage, and by virtue of striking dramatic effects, and a certain spice of bloodshed, have struck the imagination of those who are content with the superficial show of things, and are not too critical as to their significance. But for actual hardships undergone, for dangers faced, and difficulties overcome, together with an exhibition of the virtues which make a man great in the rude battle of life, Mungo Park stands without a rival. In one respect only—that of motive—does another surpass him. Here Livingstone stands head and shoulders above his predecessor, whose aspirations after personal name and fame, and apathetic attitude towards the anti-slavery movement, will ill bear comparison with the noble longings which inspired the great missionary to travel, that the negro heathen might be brought within the pale of Christian brotherhood, and stirred him to the consecration of his life in healing "the great open sore of the Universe."

Not that Park was altogether awanting in all that tends towards the spirit of self-sacrifice. On the contrary, throughout his whole narrative we fail to find the faintest trace of vulgar ambition or ignoble self-seeking. He deliberately suppressed incidents which would have added greatly to his fame, especially among those whose imagination is only appealed to by the marvellous. His whole nature shrank from notoriety. He was retired and reserved in manner, and instead of seeking to play the *rôle* of the "lion" in society, we find that he always looked forward to a time when, his labours ended, he should be able to seek the seclusion and retirement of the country—scarcely the goal this of a merely selfish ambition.

As little was he actuated by the desire of gain, as Ruskin would have us believe. Except perhaps in one conspicuous instance, African travel has never been known to lead to the attainment of riches, and certainly to Park money was never held out as an inducement. The spark that quickened his manhood to heroism, and fired him "to scorn delights and live laborious days," was the worthy ambition of a noble mind to work for the good of his country and the advancement of knowledge, rewarded solely by the approbation of his own conscience and the esteem of good men.

It is to be remembered that a hundred years ago Christian philanthropy had not become so cosmopolitan—so world-embracing—as to take within its sphere all who bear the name of man, without respect of race, religion, or degree of civilisation. From what we know of his intense religious convictions and kindly nature, Park, had he lived at the present day, would probably have been a missionary aflame for the cause of Christ and ready to lay down his life for it, or a traveller preaching a crusade, not only against the slave trade, which is so often ignorantly ascribed to the influence of Islam, but against the gin trade likewise, which with quite as much plausibility might be associated with Christianity.

At the period of the publication of Park's narrative the question of Abolition was in every man's mind. The horrors of the middle passage—the iniquities perpetrated in the plantations by men calling themselves Englishmen—were being painted in colours by no means too dark. Park's book came opportunely to add to the literature of the subject, and undoubtedly, in spite of the anti-abolition opinions he was believed to hold, the facts he disclosed regarding the horrors of the slave route added materially to the arguments of the Abolitionists. Coming, indeed, as was believed, from one of the opposite party, they were of all the more value, the natural assumption being that the worst aspects had been softened down and as good a case made out for slavery as was possible without direct violation of the truth. It was abundantly clear to all unprejudiced minds that the conditions under which the trade was carried on, and the evil results flowing from it as described by Park, were iniquitous and shameful in the extreme. To such Park's opinions were of small account compared with his facts, and we may safely conclude that these latter very materially contributed to the sweeping away of the vile traffic.

CHAPTER XVIII.
MUNGO PARK AT HOME—(Continued).

After the publication of his narrative there was nothing to detain Park longer in London, while there was much to attract him to Scotland. Accordingly he returned to Foulshiels in the summer of 1799.

On the 2nd of August of that year he was married to Miss Anderson. Of the personality of this lady we know little beyond the simple facts that she was tall and handsome, amiable in disposition, with no special mental endowments, and if anything somewhat frivolous and pleasure-loving— characteristics very unlike what we should have expected in the wife of such a man as Park.

In personal appearance the young explorer must have been quite a match for his wife. The portrait of him which has come down to us shows a head of noble proportions. The fine brow speaks of his mental powers; the prominent, finely chiselled nose, firm, well-shaped mouth, and powerful jaws, indicate the iron will and marked individuality which he showed himself to possess. No less striking and attractive are the eyes, which look forth so calmly, aglow with truthfulness, self-possession, and confidence. In person he was tall, reaching quite six feet, and exceedingly well proportioned. His whole appearance was prepossessing.

It is impossible to say what were Park's plans for his future life when he took to himself a wife. Probably they were but ill-defined even to himself. It may be safely concluded, however, that he had then no intention of returning to Africa. All the horrors of his recent experiences were still too strongly upon him to make the idea of a new journey welcome. Moreover, the after penalty of those months of starvation and atrocious fare had still to be paid by inveterate dyspepsia and its concomitant evils of gloom and despondency. While under its influence his sleep was much broken, and too often night was made one hideous nightmare by dreams of being back once more in captivity among the Moors of Ludamar, and subjected to the old tortures and indignities.

Probably, therefore, when he married, he did so in the belief that there would be no occasion for separation—no likelihood of his ever entering upon any engagements which should make him unable to fulfil his duty to his wife as a loving, ever-present protector and support.

At no time does Park ever seem to have been enamoured of his profession, and after the life he had recently led he felt a repugnance to settling down to its uncongenial routine.

For the moment, however, he did not feel called upon to come to an immediate decision as to his future work in life. The liberal remuneration which he had received from the African Association, together with the profits of his book, had placed him for the time being in easy circumstances. He could therefore afford to wait to see what might turn up. He had become well known. He had powerful friends. There was accordingly every likelihood that something congenial would be found for him. Meanwhile he resolved to settle down quietly at Foulshiels.

At this period his mother was still alive, and the farm was worked by one of his brothers. Most of the family had done well. One sister, as we have already seen, had married Mr. Dickson, who had risen both to moderate affluence and to considerable fame as a botanist. Another had found a husband in a well-to-do farmer in the neighbourhood. His brother Adam had gone through the same course as himself, and had become established as a doctor in Gravesend; while a second brother, Alexander, had been made under-sheriff for the county, the sheriff-principal being Sir Walter Scott.

Of this brother Scott himself gives us a sketch in his introduction to the "Lady of the Lake," when recalling his doubts of the poem's success:—

"I remember that about the same time a friend (Arch. Park) started in to 'heeze up my hope,' like the sportsman with his cutty gun in the old song. He was bred a farmer, but a man of powerful understanding, natural good taste, and warm poetical feeling, perfectly competent to supply the wants of an imperfect or irregular education. He was a passionate admirer of field sports, which we often pursued together." And then Scott goes on to tell how he was in the habit of reading the poem to him to experiment as to the effect produced on one who was "but too favourable a representative of readers at large." Archibald Park remained in Scott's employment for many years, and was frequently his companion in his mountain rides.

In 1799, the Government made certain proposals to Park relative to his going out in some official capacity to New South Wales. Of this, however, nothing came, though whether the fault lay with the Government or with the explorer is not known.

The natural consequences of idleness to a man of Park's personality and past life soon became apparent. With a wife of no particular depth of character and no special mental attainments, however attractive and amiable she might otherwise be, there could be but small absorption of his thoughts. With no other society, and no work to keep him occupied, there could be but one result

—restlessness and revolt against the position in which he found himself, and the gradual upgrowth of the old longings and ideas—the irrepressible fever of travel. Coincidently he began to forget the hardships and dangers he had experienced, and as they grew less and less vivid, and gradually dropped into the background of his memory, the fascination of discovery, of travel in strange lands and among strange peoples—the wish to settle the unsolved mystery of the Niger—began anew to assert their power and possess him with ever-growing force.

For the time the African Association was resting on their oars as far as prosecuting their work from West Africa was concerned, though in 1798 Horneman had been despatched to penetrate to the Sudan from Egypt.

No doubt this was partly due to the enormous difficulties and ever present dangers which Park had described, partly also perhaps on account of the war then being waged with France.

In 1800 Goree had been captured, an event which inspired Park to write (July 31, 1800) to Sir Joseph Banks, pointing out its importance in relation to renewed attempts to penetrate the interior of the Continent. After describing his views on the subject, he adds—"If such are the views of Government, I hope that my exertions in some station or other may be of use to my country."

In 1801 the negotiations with the Government relative to the New South Wales mission were resumed. A visit to London was found necessary for a satisfactory discussion of the matter, and accordingly we find Park in the metropolis in the early spring.

How deep and tender was his affection for his winsome wife is shown in a letter written to her during the visit—one of the few glimpses that have come down to us of the more private side of the explorer's character.

The letter is dated March 12th, 1801, and is as follows:—

"MY LOVELY AILIE,—Nothing gives me more pleasure than to write to you, and the reason why I delayed it a day last time was to get some money to send to you. You say you are wishing to spend a note upon yourself. My sweet Ailie, you may be sure I approve of it. What is mine is yours, and I receive much pleasure from your goodness in consulting me about such a trifle. I wish I had thousands to give you, but I know that my Ailie will be contented with what we have, and we shall live in the hope of seeing better days. I long very much to be with you, my love, and I was in great hopes of having things settled before now, but Sir Joseph (Banks) is ill, and I can do nothing till he recovers.

"I am happy to know you will go to New South Wales with me, my sweet wife. You are everything that I could desire; and wherever we go, you may be sure of one thing, that I shall always love you. Whenever I have fixed on this or any other situation I shall write to you. In the meantime, let nobody know till things are settled, as there is much between the cup and the lip.

"My lovely Ailie, you are constantly in my thoughts. I am tired of this place, but cannot lose the present opportunity of doing something for our advantage. When that is accomplished I shall not lose one moment. My darling, when we meet I shall be the happiest man on earth. Write soon, for I count the days till I hear from you, my lovely Ailie."

Again the negotiations with the Government fell through, and there was nothing for it but for Park to return once more to Foulshiels disappointed and discouraged, but possessed more than ever by the fever of unrest—more and more under the influence of the Niger magnet—against which the sole counteracting forces were love for his wife, the dread of being separated from her, and his duty as a husband.

It was in this not very suitable mood that he was forced to face the fact that he must no longer depend on the vague hope of finding a congenial opening, but must put his hand to something, however alien to his tastes and aspirations. For a time he thought of taking a farm, but at last reluctantly came to the conclusion that his best course would be to resume his profession as a doctor. An opening presented itself in the neighbouring town of Peebles, where he went to reside in the month of October, occupying a house at the head of the Brygate, while his surgery was a small projecting building—since demolished —east from the first Chambers' Institute. In a lane behind was his humble laboratory.

I had a letter from Adam on monday. last but
I suppose by this time he has sailed for India
my Comp.s to all friends and I remain
my lovely Allie yours ever

London
March 12
_1801_

Mungo Park.

P.S. write soon for I count the days untill
your answer comes

EXTRACT OF MUNGO PARK'S LETTER TO HIS WIFE.

Park threw himself into his work with characteristic energy and thoroughness, and speedily won for himself a fair share of the practice of the town and country. The profits, however, were of the poorest, and the work of the hardest—so much so, indeed, that he once said to Scott he "would rather brave Africa and all its horrors than wear out his life in long and toilsome rides over cold and lonely heaths and gloomy hills, assailed by the wintry tempest, for which the remuneration was hardly enough to keep soul and body together."

On the strength of this reported offhand remark, Ruskin, without troubling to inquire further into the history of the man, has formulated the following indictment. This "terrific" sentence, he says, "signifies, if you look into it, almost total absence of the instinct of personal duty—total absence of belief in the God who chose for him his cottage birthplace and set him his life task beside it; absolute want of interest in his profession, of sense for natural beauty, and of compassion for the noblest poor of his native land. And with these absences there is the clearest evidence of the fatalist of the vices, Avarice—in the exact form in which it was the ruin of Scott himself—the love of money for the sake of worldly position."

Never was more sweeping accusation founded on more slender data. Practically, Park is charged with absence of a belief in God, and of a sense of duty to his fellows, because he finds his profession toilsome and uncongenial.

The argument seems to be that the man is an atheist and a sinner against society who is not content to remain in the sphere in which he was born, and in which accordingly his life task is divinely set.

Were such a position tenable, it is difficult to see how any progress, either personal or social, would be possible. From it, in the present instance, would naturally follow that Park was as little to be justified in choosing to be a doctor rather than a peasant farmer, as in preferring to be an explorer rather than either.

What Ruskin takes exception to, however, is not Park's choosing a profession, but that the choice once made, he should seek to abandon it. But if it were permissible to him as a youth, ignorant alike of himself, the world, and the profession he was about to enter, to choose, surely it was equally permissible that as a man, with some knowledge of all three, he should withdraw in favour of the work to which he knew himself adapted. The instinct and capacities which fitted him for an explorer were as divinely implanted as his birthplace had been divinely appointed. Moreover, those "noblest poor of his native land," to whom Ruskin so pathetically refers, were not alone dependent on Park for medical aid—a circumstance which would have lent another colour to his final resolve to forsake them. Doctors there were in plenty, alike able and willing to serve them; but there was but one Mungo Park—but one man, as far as was known, who by his special gifts and wide experience was suited for the peculiar and arduous work of African exploration. Upon him then it devolved, with all the sacrednesss of a divinely appointed mission, as indeed he deemed it, and accepted it accordingly, to the exclusion of all narrower obligations.

There still remains the charge of Avarice, based on Park's simple statement that his "unceasing toil was hardly sufficient to keep soul and body together." Is then the physician less entitled than say the author to a just remuneration for his services, or does Ruskin share the not uncommon popular delusion that though butchers' and bakers' bills demand immediate attention, the payment of the doctor's is to be regarded as optional, or subject to the convenience of the patient. Neither supposition is to be entertained for a moment. Indeed the charge rests upon too flimsy a foundation ever to be taken seriously by any unprejudiced mind, and we can only regretfully wonder what could have induced Mr. Ruskin so far to forget the Justice and Charity he is so fond of preaching as to bring it forward.

Beyond the record of "unceasing toil" little is known of how Park spent the time he was resident in Peebles. The town itself is described as being in those days "quiet as the grave"—a reputation it still maintains, judging from the innuendo in the ironical phrase, "Peebles for pleasure!"

To Park, however, the absence of the brighter aspect of life was a small matter. Society had but little attraction for him, and his was the severe Scottish nature which avoided as almost sinful anything bordering upon frivolous pleasure. From all lionising and the silly questioning of the ignorant and the impertinently curious he had a natural shrinking, though at any time delighted to talk of his travels and of matters African with the intelligent and the well-informed. Quiet and seclusion were, however, more to his mind, and were to be enjoyed to the full in the peaceful little town. Such society as he wanted he had in his own domestic circle, beyond which he was happy in the intimacy which sprang up between him and two distinguished residents— Colonel John Murray of Kringaltie and Dr. Adam Ferguson, formerly Professor of Moral Philosophy in Edinburgh, and author of several well- known works. Toilsome and monotonous as was his professional life, it was not without its brighter and more humorous side, as witness the following story told by Dr. Anderson, the nephew of Park's wife:—

"One wild night in winter Park lost his way, till discovering a light, he directed his horse towards it, and found himself before a shepherd's cottage. It so happened that the Doctor arrived there in the nick of time, for the shepherd's wife was on the point of confinement. He waited till all was safely over, and next morning the shepherd escorted him to where he could see the distant road. Park, noticing his conductor lag behind, asked him the reason, on which the simple or humorous man replied, ''Deed, sir, my wife said she was sure you must be an angel, and I think sae tae; so I am just keepin' ahint to be sure I'll see you flee up.'"

As time went on, Park's longing to return to Africa grew ever more intense, nourished as it was by hopes from time to time held out to him. Barely, for instance, had he settled down to life in Peebles, when he received a letter from Sir Joseph Banks, acquainting him that in consequence of the Peace (then recently signed with France), the Association intended to revive their project of sending a mission to Africa in order to penetrate to and navigate the Niger. If Government took up the matter, Park would certainly be recommended as the person proper to be employed for carrying it into execution. As with previous projects, however, nothing came of it for the time being, though it continued to be talked about more or less during the next two years.

In the autumn of 1803 he was desired by the Colonial Office to repair without delay to London. This summons he promptly obeyed. On his arrival he had an interview with the Earl of Buckingham, the Secretary for the Colonies, who informed him that the Government had resolved on fitting out an expedition to Africa, of which he was to have the command, if he was willing to take it. It was exactly what he wanted—exactly what he had been impatiently awaiting for three years; but nevertheless he asked for a short time to think the matter over and consult his friends. The favour was granted, and he returned to Scotland. The consultations referred to being for the most part a mere formality, in a few days his acceptance was forwarded to London, whither he followed immediately after arranging his affairs and taking leave of his family.

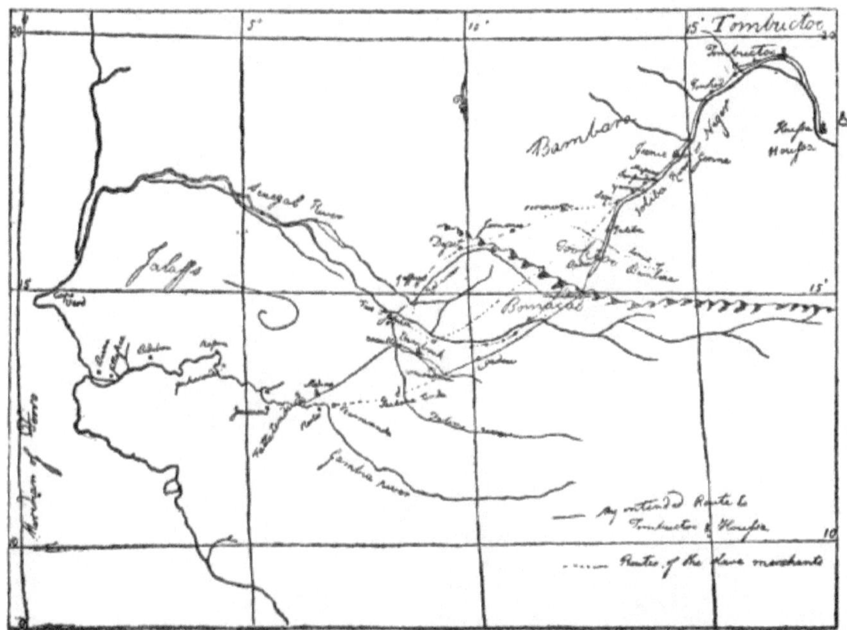

REDUCED FAC-SIMILE OF MUNGO PARK'S AUTOGRAPH MAP.

CHAPTER XIX.
PREPARING FOR A NEW EXPEDITION.

In this as in his earlier expedition, Park was dogged by his usual ill-luck.

Disappointment met him at the very outset.

He had left Scotland in the belief that almost every arrangement had been made, and that a very short time would suffice to complete the necessary preparations.

He arrived in London only to hear that the departure of the expedition had been postponed till the end of February 1804. With what patience he possessed he waited. The allotted time went by. Once more everything was ready. Part of the troops destined for the service were actually on board ship, when orders came countermanding the expedition, pending the decision of Lord Camden, the new Colonial Secretary, as to whether it should go at all or not.

Park was naturally bitterly disappointed at thus being thrown again on the seas of uncertainty. The expedition might now never set out, and the task of solving the great African problem would be reserved for another.

Meanwhile the date of departure was provisionally put off till September, and till then he was recommended to return to Scotland and occupy the interval in perfecting himself in taking astronomical observations and in learning Arabic —acquirements which would be of the utmost importance to him afterwards.

A suitable teacher of Arabic was found in one Sidi Ambak Bubi, a native of Mogador, and then residing in London. Accompanied by the Moor, Park returned to Peebles in March. Here he remained till May, when he finally quitted that town and took up his residence at Foulshiels while awaiting the decision of the Colonial Office.

It was at this time that the great traveller came in contact with his still greater countryman and neighbour, Sir Walter Scott, then living at Ashesteil, and separated from Foulshiels only by the sharp ridge of hills which divides the Yarrow from the Tweed.

Between two such men—the one absorbed in a career of prospective action in a new continent, the other revelling in a romantic world of retrospective thought—it might be supposed there was little in common.

In reality there was much. Scott, though he delighted to sing of the past and conjure up its knightly deeds, had a soul capable of appreciating all forms of glorious and adventurous enterprise, whether seen in the prosaic lights of the passing moment, or invested with the romantic vagueness and fascinating glamour which the shades of time gather around bygone days. To such an one Park was a man after his own heart. Had but his deeds been surrounded with the pomp and circumstance which glorified those of the knights of old, Scott might have sung them in a similar heroic strain. Mayhap the day will come when another Scott will arise to do for Park and his successors what Sir Walter and others have done for the heroic figures of our nation's history.

On the other hand, Park, imbued as he likewise was with the romantic instinct, could not fail to be attracted by Scott's peculiar genius. Moreover, both were Scotchmen, both Borderers, and both alike were passionate lovers of the minstrelsy, tales, traditions, and ballads of their native country. The ballads especially were dear to Park, and he tells how, in his last expedition, one of his followers used "to beguile the watches of the night with the songs of our dear native land."

But whatever were the links which drew these two famous men together, they were sufficient speedily to develop a very warm and cordial friendship, and visits were frequently interchanged across the heathery hills which separated them. On one of these occasions Scott discovered Park sitting alone beside the noisy Yarrow, employed in the apparently idle and boyish amusement of throwing stones into the river and anxiously watching the bubbles as they rose to the surface. On being asked what interest he found in such a pastime, Park replied that he was thus in the habit of ascertaining the depth of rivers in Africa before venturing to cross them—the time taken by the bubbles to rise being an indication of the depth.

Early in September came the long expected summons to repair to London, and Park lost no time in settling his affairs preparatory to leaving home. Among others, he paid a farewell visit to Sir Walter Scott at Ashesteil, where he spent the night. Next morning his host accompanied him on his way to Foulshiels. The path lay up the Glenkinnen to Williamhope, whence it continued over the ridge and passed between the Brown Knowe and the humpy elevation of the Broomy Law. As they passed from the birchen slopes of Glenkinnen into the heather and grass-clad zones above, Park talked much of his plans of exploration, and the results that would accrue to science and commerce should he prove successful.

Under other conditions the panorama which slowly unfolds itself with the ascent of the hill would have been sufficient to draw even Park's thoughts from Africa and the Niger. The various glens and valleys of the Tweed, the Gala, the Yarrow, and the Ettrick divide the land into a picturesque succession of winding ridges, isolated hills, and rounded mountain tops, where wood, heather, and grass give variety of colour to the higher levels, while below waving crops and busy harvest-fields, ruined castle and noble mansion, humble cottage and straggling village, with glancing bits of stream and river, flocks of sheep and scattered herds of cattle, combine to produce the softer effects of "cultivated nature."

But on this day of leave-taking a leaden-coloured mist hung over hill and valley, hiding their every feature. Only now and again did the breeze lift a corner of the enshrouding veil and give a momentary glimpse, vague and fleeting, of glen and hill-top. As they talked of the coming journey Scott seemed to see in the vaguely defined landscape an emblem of his friend's prospects, where all was problematic, uncertain—the path beset with unknown dangers and pitfalls, nothing sure save the presence of surrounding perils which might neither be foreseen nor prepared for. In this ignorance as regards the exact nature of the dangers to be faced lies one of the chief difficulties and terrors of travel in unexplored savage lands. All the traveller does know is that dangers in various forms will most assuredly confront him, and he must depend upon his presence of mind and readiness of resource at the moment to avoid or repel them.

But Park was not to be debarred from his enterprise by any thought of the difficulties in the way. To all that Scott could urge he had his answer. The idea of solving the question of the Niger's termination was one which possessed him to the exclusion of all thoughts of self. As well have asked him to renounce his belief in the existence of God as expect him to give up his cherished scheme.

At last the glen of the Yarrow lay before them. At the bottom could be hazily defined the "birchen bower," from which the stately tower of Newark and the humble cottage of Foulshiels alike looked forth on the beautiful murmurous stream.

Here they must say good-bye. A ditch divided the road from the moor, and in crossing it Park's horse stumbled and nearly fell. "I am afraid, Mungo," said Scott, "that is a bad omen." "Freits" (*i.e.*, omens) "follow those who look to them," was the prompt reply; and without another word Park rode away and disappeared in the mist.

It now only remained to Park to take farewell of his wife. Brave as he was, the ordeal was more than he dared face. Not that she had raised any objections to his going, or put any barriers in the way. Seeing how much her husband's heart was in it, and not perhaps without some natural womanly pride in being the wife of a hero rather than of a nobody, she seems to have accepted as a matter of course his determination to avail himself of the chance of further distinction presented by the proposed expedition. Still, the moment of actual parting, with the prospect of at best a long period of separation, would be agony. Even better than his wife Park knew how many chances there were that the separation might be final—that wife and children, of whom there were now three, might never see him again. Sanguine as he was of success, there were moments when he could not but admit that the coming enterprise looked very like a forlorn hope—moments, too, when it became difficult for him to discern whether his duty to humanity or to his family had the stronger claim upon him.

It was under the influence of some such feeling of despondency that he finally resolved to spare both himself and his wife the anguish of a parting scene, and betaking himself to Edinburgh on the plea of business, thence wrote to her his last farewell.

On his arrival in London in September 1804, Park presented a written statement to the Colonial Office embodying his views as to the commercial and geographical results likely to accrue from the intended expedition, at the same time pointing out the best means to accomplish the work as regards men and goods. In this memorandum he pointed out the course he proposed to pursue. Passing through Bondu, Kajaaga, Fuladu, and Bambarra to Sego, he would construct a boat and proceed by way of Jenné and Kabara (the port of Timbuktu) through the kingdoms of Haussa, Nyffé (now called Nupé), and Kashna, &c., to the kingdom of Wangara. If the river ended here, he pointed out, his chief difficulty would begin. To return by the Niger, to cross the desert to Tripoli or Egypt, or to pass eastward to the Nile and Abyssinia, he considered equally difficult. The most feasible course seemed that towards the Bight of Benin. If, however, the Niger was, as he confidently believed, in reality the Congo, he would follow it to its termination. After pointing out the grounds for his belief, Park concluded with the opinion that when "your Lordship shall have duly weighed the above reasons, you will be induced to conclude that my hopes of returning by the Congo are not altogether fanciful, and that the expedition, though attended with extreme danger, promises to be productive of the utmost advantage to Great Britain. Considered in a commercial point of view, it is second only to the discovery of the Cape of Good Hope, and in a geographical point of view is certainly the greatest discovery that remains to be made in the world"—a very strong statement of the case, it must be admitted, though undoubtedly if the Niger and the Congo had proved to be one, it could scarcely have been said to be too strong.

Park had been converted to this view of the identity of the two great rivers by one George Maxwell, a West African trader, who had seen much of the Congo near its mouth, and had published a chart embodying the results of his observations. When closely examined, the arguments in its favour were of small value, and practically arose out of the fact that there was a large river with a southerly trend whose termination was unknown, while further south there was a second, the Congo, whose origin was equally a mystery. Prolong these in the necessary direction and the result is identity, and the mystery of both is settled.

Meanwhile Major Rennell stuck to his view with all the pertinacity of the arm-chair geographer, and the man of one idea. For him the Niger ended in the desert wastes of Wangara and Ghana. Unfortunately for his theory the Major was unconsciously confounding two Wangaras separated from each other by fifteen hundred miles and more, and likewise the old Empire of Ghana on the middle course of the Niger with Kano at the eastern extremity of the Haussa States. A similar confusion also appears in Park's memorandum, where he speaks of the continuation of the river after Nupé to Kashna (Katsina) and the kingdom of Wangara.

Strange indeed it seems to us now that no geographer even at this time ever suggested that the outlet of the Niger might be in the Bight of Benin, among the numerous creeks that penetrate the low swampy mangrove ground which here subtends the Bight. Looking at the map, the suggestion seems to us to come naturally, yet Park had to carry the course of the river away south to the Congo; Rennell turned it west, and ended it where our maps are now occupied by Lake Chad, while there were not wanting others, like Jackson, who persisted in joining it to the Nile, "en abusant, pour ainsi dire, du vaste carrière que l'intérieur de l'Afrique y laissait prendre," as D'Anville had said of earlier geographers.

Whatever we may now think of Park's theories as to the termination of the Niger, they did not appear in any way absurd in his own time. The wildest conjecture was permissible as regards a vast river flowing by an uncertain course through a continent still blank on our maps. Accordingly his memorandum was received favourably by Lord Camden, and the despatch of the expedition to carry out the traveller's ideas was determined on.

A liberal compensation was to be given to Park on his return, and it was also stipulated that in the event of his death, or of his not being heard of within a given period, a certain sum should be paid by Government as a provision for his wife and family.

Meanwhile Rennell, in the most friendly fashion, not only argued against Park's views as to the Niger termination, but earnestly advised him to relinquish his dangerous project. With as little effect in the one case as in the other, however. The explorer's determination, like his opinions, was not to be shaken. Sir Joseph Banks took up a more philosophic position. He admitted the hazardous nature of the enterprise; but since the work was not to be accomplished without risk of life, he could not attempt to dissuade Park from it, he being the man most likely to carry it through with least danger of a fatal issue.

Gradually the affairs of the expedition began to take shape. Dr. Alexander Anderson, Park's young brother-in-law, was selected as his second in command, and Mr. George Scott, a fellow-dalesman, was added to the party as draughtsman. A few boat-builders and artificers were also to accompany the party from England, for the purpose of constructing the boat intended for the navigation of the Niger when it was reached. Soldiers to assist and protect the expedition were to be selected at Goree, where a garrison of the African corps was stationed.

It was now a matter of paramount importance that the expedition should leave England at once if it was to take advantage of the dry season. But official red-tape was as difficult to galvanise into activity and life as African apathy, and in spite of his utmost endeavours to push matters on, delay succeeded upon delay, and Park saw the good season gradually dwindling away, leaving him to the maddening contemplation of all the additional difficulties and dangers engendered by the rains. Two whole months were thus lost; and when he at last received his official instructions, he knew that the Government, by its continued procrastination, had done much if not everything to ensure a disastrous termination to the expedition.

In the instructions supplied to him Park's mission was defined as being to discover whether and to what extent commercial intercourse could be established in the interior of Africa for the mutual benefit of the natives and of His Majesty's subjects. He was directed to proceed up the Gambia, and thence to the banks of the Niger by way of the Senegal. The special object of his journey was to determine the course of the Niger, and to establish communication with all the different nations on its banks. He was at liberty to pursue any return route which he might find most suitable, either by turning west to the Atlantic, or by marching upon Cairo.

To carry out this great mission effectively, a captain's commission was bestowed on him, and that of a lieutenant on Anderson. European soldiers to the number of forty-five, and as many natives as he might deem necessary, were to be selected at Goree, and a sufficient number of donkeys at St. Jago. He was further empowered to draw for any sum he might want not exceeding £5000.

CHAPTER XX.
PARK'S SECOND RETURN TO THE GAMBIA.

On the 31st January 1805, Park, with his companions and four or five artificers, sailed from Portsmouth in the *Crescent* transport for St. Jago, Cape Verde Islands.

In crossing the Bay of Biscay they were considerably detained by storms and contrary winds, so that it took five weeks to reach their primary destination. From St. Jago, where forty-four donkeys were purchased, they proceeded to Goree, arriving at that station on the 21st of March. Here the idea of an expedition to the Niger was received with such enthusiasm by officers and men alike that the entire garrison was ready to join—the officers for the adventure and honour of the thing, the men for the increased pay and promised discharge on their return.

One officer, Lieutenant Martyn, was selected, and with him thirty-five privates and two seamen.

Park's idea of taking with him a considerable number of European artisans and soldiers must be considered one of the greatest blunders he ever made. A moment's thought should surely have told him that he ran a terrible risk of speedily losing the greater number by death, and that through sickness the majority of those who kept alive would be more a hindrance than a help to him. He should have known that these ignorant men were not as he himself seemed to be—rendered disease and privation proof by the determination to achieve a certain great object. Against all forms of death, save death by violence, his *will* was to him a magic mail. With his men it was different. Ignorant of what was before them—incapable of comprehending it even had it been told—they only saw in the enterprise a certain freedom from irksome garrison restrictions and military discipline, increased pay, and the prospect of early discharge. To all else they were blind.

Brought face to face with hourly dangers, privations, and incessant toil, they quickly realised their mistake. Everything was forgotten save the present physical suffering. Sick and dispirited, what was the question of the Niger's course to them? A mere name, without power to fire their imagination or inspire their enthusiasm. How insignificant, too, appeared the material recompense. Thus with nothing to buoy them up, nothing to lure them on and keep them from magnifying and dwelling on their troubles, there could be nothing but apathy—with apathy, despondency, and finally death. This has been the history, more or less, of nearly all African expeditions in which ignorant European men have been employed, tempted to join merely for pay or other considerations of a personal character. In proportion as the members of an expedition have been inspired by its ultimate objects, they have lived to see it through, because in that proportion they have given less attention to their hardships and sicknesses. The less they have thought of themselves, and the more their minds have been centred on their work, the better have been their chances of pulling through.

But though all the whites of the Goree garrison were willing to accompany Park, not one of the negroes of the place could be induced to join, and he therefore had to depend on getting such natives as he wanted on the Gambia. He left Goree on the 6th of April, and reached Kayi, on the Gambia, a few days later.

The prospect now before him was anything but pleasant. The rainy season, which he had such good grounds to fear, was rapidly approaching. There were but two alternatives—either to wait till the next dry season before starting, or go on and face the worst—the fevers, the rains, the marshes, the flooded rivers, and all the other accompaniments of the wet season. These must undoubtedly produce much sickness, probably many deaths, innumerable exasperating delays, and other troubles—must increase, in fact, by a hundredfold the perils and trials of the expedition. On the other hand, to wait would mean a delay of seven months—seven months of inaction, of intolerable fretting at the very threshold of the enterprise. The idea was out of the question. Besides, men, animals, and goods were ready for the road, and the Government expected them to proceed forthwith. A delay of the kind had not been foreseen, and had not been provided for in Park's instructions. Of the two evils, therefore, he chose the one which was most in harmony with his own eager spirit, determining to risk all and start forthwith. Having once made up his mind, he put aside all fears and apprehensions, and would allow nothing to damp his sanguine hopes. In this spirit he wrote to Dickson:
—"Everything at present looks as favourable as I could wish, and if all things go well this day six weeks I expect to drink all your healths in the water of the Niger. The soldiers are in good health and spirits. They are the most *dashing* men I ever saw, and if they preserve their health we may keep ourselves perfectly secure from any hostile attempt on the part of the natives. I have little doubt but that I shall be able, with presents and fair words, to pass through the country to the Niger, and if once we are afloat the day is won."

We can easily believe that Park in this letter does not give a faithful indication of his real position at the moment of writing. He may have expressed his hopes truly enough, but he carefully avoids showing the fears which went side by side with them. What exact significance the term "dashing," as applied to his soldiers, bears in relation to their qualities as members of an African expedition, might be a matter of discussion; but while we have every reason to believe they were the best the garrison could supply, it must also be remembered that the African corps was the residuum of the British army at a time when it was the chief resort of the rascaldom of the country. A residence, however short, in a West African garrison, could have improved neither their physique, their morals, nor their discipline, and certainly was not calculated to fit them for one of the most dangerous and trying enterprises any man could enter upon, and requiring moral and physical qualities which only the very few possess.

To his error in taking with him such a large party of Europeans, Park added an even worse mistake, and one for which less excuse can be found. Nowhere in his diary do we find a single reference to his having any native followers to do the common drudgery of the camp and the road. This was a want of foresight which appears almost incredible in one who knew what was before him, and the results which followed when all the men fell sick were disastrous beyond description.

Thus, then, to the extreme perils and hardships which attend an African expedition at all times, Park added a start at the worst possible time of the year, and with the worst possible selection of men. What came of it the following pages will show.

On the 27th of April 1805, all was ready for the march. The initial point was Kayi, on the river Gambia, a few miles below Pisania, the place from which Park started on his first expedition. How different were his preparations for this new attempt. In the former he had left for the interior attended by a man and a boy—a single donkey carrying all the goods and stores he required. This time he was provided with forty-four Europeans, and a large quantity of baggage of all kinds, transported by as many donkeys as there were men. As already said, we find no allusion in his letters or journals to his having any native attendants, though possibly there might have been one or two as personal servants. Isaaco, a Mandingo priest and merchant, had been engaged to act as guide, and he it seems was accompanied by several of his own people.

Under cover of a salute from the *Crescent* and other vessels gathered on the river, the caravan filed out of Kayi, and took the road for the interior—each man, according to his temperament, aspirations, and education, filled with varied emotions of hope and fear, at once attracted and repelled by the vague unknown which lay before him.

The troubles and worries attendant on leading a large caravan in Africa became only too soon apparent. The day was extremely hot. Under the influence of the overpowering temperature the overloaded donkeys lay down and refused to proceed, while others, resenting the imposition of any burden, did what they could to kick themselves free, thus giving an infinite amount of trouble to their drivers.

The men themselves, fresh from the relaxing life and coarse debaucheries of a West African garrison, soon began to give in as well as their donkeys, so that before long the caravan, from being a continuous line, was broken into detached groups and isolated individuals resting here, struggling on there. Finally the party got completely divided, some under Lieutenant Martyn taking one way, and the rest with Park another. Towards evening they again became united, and reached a suitable camping ground thoroughly fatigued by their first march. Next day Pisania was reached, and here a halt became necessary to make some final preparations and purchase eight more donkeys.

On the 4th of May the journey was resumed. The caravan was divided into six messes, each with its due proportion of animals marked for easy identification. Scott and one of Isaaco's men led the way, Martyn took charge of the centre body, while Anderson and Park brought up the rear. Even with the additional beasts of burden there was a repetition of the troubles which marked the first march—troubles which became each day more harassing with the failing strength of the donkeys and the sickness which after a time developed among their drivers. The leaders were each provided with horses for riding, but in a very short time they had to take to their feet, that their animals might be utilised for the transport of loads belonging to broken-down donkeys. A few days more and this likewise proved insufficient, and both new donkeys and new drivers had to be hired.

By the fourth day from Pisania two soldiers were attacked by dysentery, and a further addition to the strength of the caravan was found necessary. In a week the expedition reached Medina, the capital of Wuli, without special mishap, but with ever growing worries for its leader.

The keen eye to business so characteristic of negro races was well shown by the women of Bambaku, who, on hearing of the coming of the white men, drew all the water out of the wells in the hope of forcing the strangers to buy it at a high price in beads and other gauds dear to the negro heart. In this, however, they were outwitted by the soldiers, and they had the inexpressible mortification of seeing twenty-four hours' labour utterly lost, and the beads as unattainable as ever.

Meanwhile the report of the passage of a rich caravan conducted by many Europeans spread like wildfire, gaining in exaggeration with every mile, and putting all the robber bands and chiefs on the alert. Preceded by such rumours it became necessary to travel with great circumspection, and in constant readiness for an attack. No one was allowed to lay aside his gun. By way of invoking the aid of a higher power than that of man, Isaaco, on entering the reputedly dangerous woods of Simbani, laid a black ram across the road, and after reciting a long prayer, cut its throat as a sacrifice. These woods were alive with hundreds of antelopes. The Gambia, where it traversed them, was a hundred yards wide, and showed a perceptible tide. On the sands were great numbers of alligators, while the pools teemed with hippos. Viewed from an eminence, the country towards the west appeared abundantly rich and enchanting, the course of the Gambia being traceable by its fringing lines of dark green trees winding in serpentine curves seaward.

At a place called Faraba, while unloading the animals preparatory to camping, one of the soldiers fell down in an epileptic fit, and expired in an hour. Here water was only to be got by digging. During the night, as they were in the wilderness, and liable to attack, double sentries were posted round the camp, and every man slept with his loaded musket beside him.

Next morning the Neaulico stream, then nearly dry, was passed, and on that and a succeeding night they camped in the woods, the second occasion being at the river Nerico.

On the 18th the caravan entered Jallacotta, the first town of Tenda.

Two days later they met with an insolent reception from the chief of the independent village of Bady, who refused the caravan-tax sent him, and threatened war if his exorbitant demands were not satisfied. Park tried personally to arrange the dispute, but only met with threats. The soldiers were at once ordered to be in readiness for whatever might happen, while the chief was told that nothing more would be given him, and that if he would not allow their peaceable passage through his district, another would be found. After many angry words Park prepared to carry his resolution into effect, but before the necessary preparations were completed, Isaaco's horse was seized by the Bady people. On the owner going to demand its restitution, he himself was laid hold of, deprived of his gun and sword, and then tied to a tree and flogged. At the same time his boy was put in irons.

It was now dark, but prompt action was necessary. Accordingly Park, with a detachment of soldiers, entered the village to seize the robbers of the horse, intending to hold them as hostages for the safe delivery of the guide. This attempt naturally led to much uproar, ending finally in blows, and the driving of all the chief's people out of the village. Isaaco, however, was nowhere to be found, and Park was somewhat puzzled to know what to do. It would of course have been easy to burn down the village, but this would have entailed death and ruin on many innocent persons, possibly without producing the desired effect. Under the circumstances it was deemed advisable to wait till daylight before making an attack. This course proved to be both wise and humane, for in the morning Isaaco was liberated and his horse restored, so that eventually all ended amicably.

On the 24th of May much lightning was seen to the south-east—ominous premonition of the approaching rains. Of the party Park and Isaaco alone could realise what those electric flashes betokened to the fortunes of the expedition.

Their way for the next three days lay through the Tenda Wilderness—with all the hard marches, short rations, and scant supplies of water which an uninhabited district at the end of the dry season implies, and which were hardly to be compensated by the exceeding picturesqueness of the scenery.

At the second camp in the wilderness an extraordinary mishap befell them. A hive of bees was disturbed by one of the men, with the result that they swarmed out in angry myriads to attack the intruders. They set upon man and beast alike, and in a twinkling had routed every two-legged and four-footed thing in the camp. The men threw down weapons—everything—and fled in dismay, along with frantic braying donkeys. The horses similarly broke loose, and galloped to the woods in a panic. Meanwhile the fires which had been kindled, being thus left unattended, speedily began to spread to the surrounding dry grass and bamboos. When Park and his companions had time to look round, they discovered to their dismay that the whole camp was on fire, and menaced by absolute and irretrievable ruin.

Forgetful of all else before such an appalling danger to the expedition, those who had suffered least from the furious bees rushed back to save what they could. Happily not too late. Before the goods were reached by the fire, Park and some of the men were ready to receive the enemy, and eventually succeeded in extinguishing it.

The impending conflagration over, the horses and donkeys were with difficulty collected from the woods, many of them terribly stung and swollen about the head. Three animals, besides Isaaco's horse, disappeared altogether. One donkey died that evening, another next morning, and a third had to be abandoned, so vicious and deadly had been the bees' onslaught.

Many curious superstitions were noticed by Park *en route* through Wuli and Tenda. At one place death was believed to be the portion of any one who slept under a particular tree; at another, the fish in the river must not be caught, else the water would dry up entirely; while at a third, any traveller who would assure himself of a safe journey, must lift and turn round a particular stone.

At Julifunda the chief made exorbitant demands on the caravan, threatening to attack them in the woods if these were not complied with. Park's resolute attitude, however, combined with an addition to his first present, brought the quarrel to an amicable conclusion, and he was permitted to continue his route unmolested.

The expedition had now reached the eastern confines of the Gambia basin, and writing home to his wife, Park reviewed his situation as follows:—

"We are half through our journey (*i.e.* to the Niger) without the smallest accident or unpleasant circumstance. We all of us keep our health, and are on the most friendly terms with the natives…. By the 27th of June we expect to have finished all our travels by land, and when we have once got afloat on the river, we shall conclude that we are embarking for England. I have never had the smallest sickness, and Alexander (Mrs. Park's brother) is quite free from all his complaints…. We carry our own victuals with us, and live very well—in fact we have only had a very pleasant journey; and yet this is what we thought would be the worst part of it."

In looking back undoubtedly Park had every reason to be satisfied with his journey so far. His men seemed to have worked heartily enough—at least we find no indications in his journal of insubordination, grumbling, or bad conduct. But then he never was in the habit of putting the least stress on his troubles. It was of more importance to him to be able to say that he had advanced a day's march nearer the Niger than that he had been subjected to a week's maddening worry. All vexations and discomforts he treated like the suppressed adventures of his former narrative, of which he said that as they were only of importance to himself, he would not weary the reader with a recital of them.

MUNGO PARK'S ENCAMPMENT.

It is only too probable that he had much trouble with his men, and certainly between the lines we gather that he had an immense amount of work to perform—looking after his caravan on the road, buying food, and holding innumerable palavers, &c., in camp. Even the nights he could not call his own, for observations for latitude and longitude must be taken at all hours— notes written out, and the observations calculated. He had to be at once overseer, buyer of food, interpreter, surveyor, doctor, and general inspirer of the whole party. But he was equal to everything that could be put on his shoulders. Within him he had a sustaining force such as was known to none of those about him, and which gave him a giant's strength and the spirit of the gods.

CHAPTER XXI.
STILL STRUGGLING TOWARDS THE GREAT RIVER.

Park in his letter home was careful only to look backward: it is now our business to accompany him forward, and see what happened as he passed across the Senegal basin on his way to the Niger.

On the 7th of June he crossed the Samaku, which flows north to join the Falemé, and in fear of an attack, travelled rapidly through an uninhabited district by a forced march. Here two of the donkeys had to be abandoned, and there being no guiding pathway, as darkness came on, muskets were frequently fired to prevent the men losing each other.

Early next day the Falemé was seen in the distance. The carpenter, who had become very ill, could not sit upright on a donkey, and time after time threw himself off, declaring that he would rather die. Latterly it took two men to hold him in his seat by force, and at the Falemé, which was crossed in the course of the day, he had to be left behind in charge of a soldier. He died a few hours after.

That night a heavy tornado burst upon the caravan. Five soldiers who had not been under proper shelter, and got a wetting, became ill in consequence.

It could no longer be ignored that the rains were at last upon them, and that just when they were in the network of streams into which the Senegal and the Niger divide in their uppermost reaches. One terrible necessity of their situation was, that sick or not sick, there could be no halting to allow of possible recovery. They must push forward towards their goal, though the route should be marked by the dead bodies of their comrades. The longer the delay, the more difficult would the march become, from flooded rivers, more incessant rains, and the increasing swampiness of the country.

Up to this time Park had followed his former return route. He now determined to strike a line further north in order to avoid the Jallonka Wilderness, of whose horrors he had such a lively recollection. The new route was hard and rocky, and very fatiguing to the donkeys. As the day went on many of the sick became hopelessly unfit to drive their animals. One of them Park mounted on his own horse while he himself assumed the part of donkey driver. Even then four of the donkeys had to be left in the woods, and he himself did not reach camp till long after dark. Before the tents could be pitched a tornado came down upon them and drenched them to the skin. The ground was speedily covered to a depth of three inches, and in this uncomfortable plight—fireless, tentless, dripping—they had to pass the night. A second tornado about two in the morning completed their discomfiture.

This night, in Park's own words, was "the beginning of sorrows…. Now that the rain had set in, I trembled to think that we were only half way through our journey. The rain had not commenced three minutes before many of the soldiers were affected with vomiting, others fell asleep, and seemed as if half intoxicated. I felt a strong inclination to sleep during the storm, and as soon as it was over I fell asleep on the wet ground, although I used every exertion to keep myself awake. The soldiers likewise fell asleep on the wet bundles."

The immediate result of that night was the addition of twelve men to the sick list. Next day all the horses and spare donkeys were requisitioned to carry such as were unable to walk. The road proved to be a difficult one along the base of the Konkadu mountains, whose precipices overhung the line of march in threatening masses.

Barely had camp been reached when once more a tornado burst in all its fury, but thanks to the proximity of a village, with less disastrous results than on the previous evening.

The storm past, Park proceeded to examine some gold diggings; after which, accompanied by Scott, he set off to the top of the Konkadu hills, finding them cultivated to the highest elevations. There also he found villages romantically situated in delightful glens, with water and grass in abundance throughout the year; and there, "while the thunder rolls in awful grandeur over their heads, they can look from their tremendous precipices over all that wild and woody plain which extends from the Falemé to the Bafing or Black River."

To struggle forward handicapped with incapable men and driverless donkeys was now hard work. Half the caravan were sick, or too weak to exert themselves with effect. The result was never-ending confusion and delay. Unable to hold together, men and donkeys alike went astray, keeping Park, who could not be in a dozen places at once, in a state of continual watchfulness and motion, doing his best to bring up the incapables, and "coaxing" them to further exertions each time they insisted on lying down, indifferent alike to robbers, lions, or the fevers of night.

In spite of his iron constitution and sanguine heroic spirit Park himself was not altogether invulnerable, and he too became fevered at times—only, however, to show himself superior to suffering by virtue of his marvellous will and the exigencies of his situation. Conscious that the whole fate of the expedition depended upon his keeping well, he dared not give way. He was a second self to every one—without him all were absolutely helpless.

On leaving Fankia on the 15th of June, most of the men were ill, some of them even delirious. In this condition the caravan had to commence the ascent of the Tambaura mountains. The road was excessively steep—the donkeys terribly overloaded under their double burden of sick men and goods. Owing to the nature of the ground, each animal would have required at least one separate driver to guide and assist, but in the present case this was impossible. The result was a scene of dreadful confusion and disaster. Loaded donkeys were constantly tumbling over the rocks or falling exhausted on the pathway, while sick men, indifferent to their fate, threw themselves down, declaring they could go no further. The natives, discovering the predicament of the caravan, crept down among the rocks and stole what they could when a favourable opportunity offered.

At length, by means of superhuman exertions, Park succeeded in bringing all safely out of the perilous pass to a village, where he had the inexpressible pleasure of meeting the Mohammedan schoolmaster who had been so kind to him at Kamalia, and while travelling with Karfa. As an earnest of his gratitude for past favours, Park gave him a handsome present of cloth, beads, and amber, with which the good old man was delighted. The God-fearing Scotchman did not neglect to add an Arabic New Testament to his other gifts.

The history of the expedition was now one of growing trouble, sickness, and disorganisation. Tornadoes were almost of daily occurrence, and the country and the streams became more and more difficult to traverse.

Up to the 17th of June two men had died, and on that date two more were left behind at the point of death. The three days following Park himself was sick, as were now more than half his men, though still they struggled on. To add to the dangers of their situation, they were utterly unable to keep proper watch over their goods either by day or night—a fact the natives speedily learned, and constantly dogged their footsteps, intent on plunder.

At one village the inhabitants turned out *en masse*, prepared to find the white man's caravan so reduced by sickness as to fall an easy prize. As a preliminary to further depredations one of the villagers seized the bridle of the sergeant's horse and tried to lead it and its apparently helpless owner inside the village walls. The presentation of the rider's pistol made him think better of it. At the same time others made as if they would drive away the donkeys. They had reckoned without their host, however. Galvanised into new life, the soldiers promptly loaded their muskets and fixed their bayonets, at sight of which warlike preparations the natives were not slow to quit their prey and retire to a safer distance.

ROCK SCENERY OF THE UPPER SENEGAL.

Having driven their animals across a torrent, the soldiers left certain of their number to guard them, and returned to the village, ready to give its inhabitants a lesson in courtesy and hospitality. At this moment Park arrived on the scene. Ever anxious to avoid bloodshed, he called a palaver, and speedily convinced the chief how insane it would be for him or his people to molest him. At the same time, desirous of leaving a favourable impression behind, in case any sick men might have to repass this way, Park gave the chief a present, with the remark that it was to show he did not come to make war, though if he were attacked he would fight to the last.

Beyond this point the country became picturesque beyond words, resembling in its physical features all sorts of architectural forms, ruined castles, spires, pyramids. One rocky hill looked so like a ruined Gothic abbey that the whole party had to approach close to it to satisfy themselves that its various features were not really what they seemed. Beyond this *lusus naturæ* a compact mass of red granite stood up bare and gaunt, absolutely destitute of a relieving blade of grass. Here and there were villages clustering in the curved niches of giant precipices, alike secured from tropic blasts and the devastating attacks of men. Everything was rugged and grand—the sterner features only enhanced by the interchange of beautiful fertile hollows and silvery streams winding through the green fields and darker forest tracts.

Similar scenes characterised the whole journey through Konkadu, and the caravan at length reached the borders of Wuladu at the Bafing. The crossing of this river in small rickety canoes was not accomplished without a sad fatality, one of them capsizing with three soldiers, of whom one was drowned.

The people of Wuladu had a notorious reputation as thieves, the justice of which was speedily illustrated by their various more or less successful attempts to lift from the strangers whatever they saw, thus keeping the latter continually on the alert.

After crossing the Bafing, many of the sick who had struggled on bravely so far began to lose all spirit. An unconquerable lassitude at times seized them, and no matter what the danger of the situation, their only desire was to lie down and be left to die. To escape the cajolery and coercion to which they were subjected, they frequently left the track, and gave their leader no end of worry and trouble hunting them up after camp was reached. In this way several men disappeared altogether, bringing up the total losses on the 29th June to nine.

Besides its human cormorants, Wuladu proved to be infested with various beasts of prey, whereby further anxiety and watchfulness were entailed on the harassed and despondent little band, weak, and growing every day weaker.

Anderson and Scott, on whom Park so much depended to encourage and push on his followers, besides themselves doing the work of three or four, now became incapacitated, while as far as we can gather from the journal, Lieutenant Martyn never seems to have been of any use. Everything, accordingly, devolved on the leader himself, who, ailing as he was, had to put forth superhuman exertions—driving refractory and exhausted donkeys, lifting the fallen, and reloading such as had kicked off or dropped their burdens—at every step spurring on the sick and despondent to strive towards their destination, and not allow themselves to be murdered by natives, devoured by wild beasts, or overcome by the deadly malaria of the jungles. In camp he had as little rest as on the road. No one else was fit to do anything— or being fit, was not willing—so that he had to be man-of-all-work to nearly forty men. The night brought neither oblivion nor relaxation—only new anxieties and new duties. Sleep he could only get in short snatches—between whiles taking his astronomical observations, and making the round of the camp to stir up indifferent and sickly sentinels. Not unfrequently he had to mount guard himself throughout the whole night to save the donkeys from being killed or stampeded by the wild beasts which kept constantly prowling about. The stormier the night, the greater necessity was there for him to be up and doing, no matter what the cost to himself personally.

On the 4th of July the Furkomo River, another important tributary of the Senegal, was reached. The number of deaths now amounted to eleven, most of them having occurred within the last fortnight.

In crossing the Furkomo or Bakhoy, Isaaco had a narrow escape from a crocodile. When near the middle of the river, he was seized by the left thigh and pulled under water. With wonderful presence of mind he thrust his finger into the reptile's eye, with the result that it let go its hold. Ere he could regain the shore, however, the crocodile returned to the attack, and seized him by the other thigh. Again he thrust his finger into its eye, with a similar happy result, and before it could come at him again, bleeding and lacerated, he reached land. That night, though it threatened rain, every one was so sick and exhausted— even Park being unable to stand upright—that it was only with the utmost difficulty that the tents were put up and the loads placed inside. Isaaco's wounds made travelling impossible for him, and as the caravan was largely dependent on his services, a three days' halt was decided on.

With the guide's partial recovery the march was continued to Keminum, the neighbourhood of which they reached with apprehension. The town was fortified in a remarkably strong fashion. There was first a ditch 8 feet deep, backed by a wall as many feet high. Inside was a second wall 10 feet in height, within which was a third of 16 feet.

The chief and his thirty sons were neither more nor less than an organised band of robbers who terrorised over the whole district. Ample evidence of the manner of his rule was afforded by the heap of human bones outside the walls, where he executed such prisoners as were not made slaves of. During the night all the energies of the caravan were employed in seeking to protect themselves from the incessant attempts of the natives to steal; but so helpless were most of the men that they allowed themselves to be deprived of great- coats, muskets, pistols, almost without resistance.

The morning brought no reprieve. The chief's sons, not satisfied with their share of the present and the plunder, did their best to secure some valuable souvenirs of the white man. This one of them first tried to do wholesale by simply lifting a load from a donkey, but the culprit was chased and had to drop his plunder. The confusion produced by this incident gave another thief a chance to bolt with a musket.

Innumerable exasperating attempts of a similar nature kept Park in constant alarm lest some of the soldiers should use their weapons and precipitate a fight. Accordingly, his chief anxiety became to get away as quickly as possible. Riding a little way out of the village to see the nature of the road ahead, one of the chief's sons distracted his attention while he halted, whereupon the other suddenly snatched away the traveller's loosely held musket. At once Park gave chase with brandished sword. Anderson, seeing what had occurred, rushed to his assistance with upraised gun; but observing who was the offender, he hesitated to fire, with the result that the thief escaped safely to the rocks. Meanwhile the brother had leisurely helped himself to whatever loose property he found on Park's horse.

Orders were now given to shoot the first person found stealing. But the princes were not easily frightened, and during a tornado that burst overhead, one of them got off with a musket and a couple of pistols. An attempt was next made to drive off the donkeys, but fortunately was frustrated. By way of example, a native detected in stealing was promptly fired at. On the march being resumed, every foot of the road was dogged by the plundering wretches, who scented their prey in every man who lagged behind, and every donkey that fell or strayed from the path.

It was dark before a camping place was reached, and the night was passed in much misery, man and beast lying on the wet ground without shelter, exposed to the excessively heavy dews.

The march through Wuladu was simply a daily repetition of the experiences at Keminum. Thieves hung on the skirts of the caravan like hyenas on the track of blood, never quitting them by night or by day. All stragglers, human or animal, they made their prey, and by their attempted depredations kept the unhappy travellers in constant alarm. Each morning and evening had its tale of loss. Everything, however, was tolerated, that bloodshed might be avoided —a forbearance only looked upon as weakness and cowardice by the natives, who were encouraged accordingly to continue their marauding with increased audacity. Park was at length driven to stronger measures, and on one occasion pursued a robber on horseback, and after hunting him down, shot him through the leg. This example had a most salutary effect for a time, though that day's tale of spoliation alone included the more or less complete stripping of four sick men, and a donkey loaded with the muskets, &c., of the other invalids.

Let us quote a characteristic day's proceedings from Park's own journal:—

"*July 19th.*—Having purchased an ass in lieu of the one stolen, we left Nummabu, which is a walled village, and proceeded onwards. Had two tornadoes. The last, about eleven o'clock, wetted us much, and made the road slippery. Two asses unable to go on. Put their loads on the horses and left them. Mr. Scott's horse unable to walk. Left it to our guide. At noon came to the ruins of a town. Found two more of the asses unable to carry their loads. Hired people to carry the loads, and a boy to drive the asses. Passed the ruins of another town at half-past twelve, where I found two of the sick who had laid themselves down under a tree and refused to rise. They were afterwards stripped by the negroes, and came naked to our tents next morning. Shortly after this came to an ass lying on the road unable to proceed with its load. Put part of the load on my horse, which was already heavily loaded. Took a knapsack on my back. The soldier carried the remainder, and drove the ass before him. We arrived at the Ba Winbina at half-past one o'clock." Here follows a description of how a bridge was built, which, though instructive in the extreme, is too long for insertion. "Our people being all sickly, I hired the negroes to carry over all the baggage, and swim over the asses. Our baggage was laid on the rocks on the east side of the river, but such was our weakly state that we were unable to carry it up the bank. Francis Beedle, one of the soldiers, was evidently dying of the fever, and having in vain attempted, with the assistance of one of his messmates, to carry him over, I was forced to leave him on the west bank, thinking it very probable that he would die in the course of the night."

Day after day the same disheartening tale had to be told. Now a man is found expiring, and no time can be lost waiting for his death. Anon another left for dead is galvanised into life by the appearance of wolves ready to make a meal of him. On the 27th July one man had to be left in camp at the point of death —four more dropped down on the road and refused to proceed, wishing only to die. Park himself was "very sick and faint, having to drive my horse loaded with rice and an ass with the pit saw. Came to an eminence from which I had a view of some very distant mountains to the east half south. The certainty that the Niger washes the southern base of these mountains made me forget my fever, and I thought of nothing all the way but how to climb over their blue summits." But to his men the sight gave neither health nor inspiration, and but for the fact that to go back was as difficult as to push forward, they would speedily have shown in what direction their desires tended.

What the inmost thoughts of the intrepid explorer were at this time we would give much to know. In his journal he nowhere lifts the veil. Throughout there is only the bare statement of fact that to-day so-and-so has died—yesterday such another had to be left to his fate: here a donkey was plundered—there an astronomical observation taken. The one thing that can touch his feelings is the sight of the blue summits of distant hills whose bases are washed by the waters of the Niger.

CHAPTER XXII.
TO THE NIGER.

Writing home on the 29th of May, Park, calculating from his rate of progress so far, predicted that he would reach the Niger on the 27th of June. It was now the 27th of July, and he was still in the heart of Wuladu, and quite a hundred miles in a straight line from Bammaku, his primary destination.

Meanwhile every one of the donkeys he had originally started with had died or been stolen, and great inroads had been made on his stores in replacing them, not to speak of the loss entailed by plunder and other unforeseen causes. Twenty of his men had died or been murdered, and all of them were more or less unfit for work. Nevertheless his hopes were as unquenchable as ever, and he buoyed himself up with the belief that if he could reach the Niger with a certain proportion of his caravan, the success of his mission would be assured, as the rest of the wet season might be passed in comparative comfort while making preparations for navigating the river. Once launched on its broad bosom, there would be no more transport difficulties, and but little work for his men, so that everything might be expected to end happily and successfully.

Looking forward thus hopefully, Park turned S.W. from Bangassi, the chief town of Wuladu, and set his face towards Bammaku. But however sanguine he might be, he could not improve the conditions of his march. The rains were now at their very worst. They fell no longer in passing tornadoes, but in an incessant drenching downpour. Every stream was swollen to the dimensions of a river— every plain became a lake or swamp through which the luckless travellers had to slip and plunge as best they might. The very pathways developed into rushing torrents. Subjected to such conditions of travel, disease demanded its daily quota of victims, while reducing the strength of all to the vanishing point. The men speedily became unable to load their animals
—could hardly even drive them along. Nearly the whole work of the caravan fell upon its indomitable leader, who even on the road would sometimes have as many as thirteen fallen donkeys to raise up and reload.

On the 7th of August matters became so bad that he found it necessary to halt for two days—a delay which to him was almost maddening.

At the Ba Wulima, Park found Anderson lying under a bush apparently dying, and had to carry him over on his back. To assist in the transport of loads, &c., he had to cross the river sixteen times, with the water reaching to his waist. In spite of his exertions, however, several soldiers with their donkeys had to be left behind.

In two days four men had been lost—the slow agony of death from fever being undoubtedly in each case accelerated by the daggers of robber negroes or the fell fangs of wolves and other wild beasts.

On the day after leaving the Ba Wulima, Park was the only European able to do any work, and but for the assistance of Isaaco and his men, the caravan would have been compelled to remain in camp. The day's march was a trying one. Anderson seemed at the point of death, and it was with difficulty that his brother-in-law succeeded in holding him on a horse. Every hour threatened to be his last, and only by frequent rests could he be got forward in short stages. While thus employed supporting and cheering his well-loved friend on the way towards camp, Park was suddenly confounded by coming face to face with three large lions making rapidly towards them. Intent first of all on saving Anderson, with splendid courage he ran forward to meet them half way, and so as to reserve himself a second chance if his musket should miss fire, he aimed as soon as the lions were within easy shot, and fired at the middle one of the three. This reception brought the enemy to a standstill, and after seemingly taking counsel of each other, they turned tail and bounded away. One, however, quickly stopped, and turned round as if meditating another attack, but thinking better of it, again resumed its flight, and left the travellers to continue their way, though not without the strongest suspicions that they were still being tracked, and might be pounced upon in the fast gathering darkness. Before camp was reached the path taken by the caravan was lost, and in the darkness Park and his companion wandered into a gully, where the road became so dangerous that at length they dared not move further from fear of being killed by falling over a precipice. Accordingly they were compelled to make the best of their position, and wait till morning tentless and foodless. Fortunately they were able to raise a fire, near which, while Anderson lay wrapt in a cloak, Park kept watch all night, to drive off lions and wolves. In the morning it was discovered that half the caravan had passed the night in scattered parties in much the same manner as their leader. Happily there were no casualties.

At a place called Dumbila, Park had the pleasure of meeting his old friend and protector, Karfa Taura. Here Anderson became too ill to be moved, Scott had disappeared, and only one man was able to drive a donkey. At night rain descended in drenching torrents, and the men took refuge in the village, leaving their leader alone to watch that the donkeys did not stray into the neighbouring corn-fields, and to defend them and their loads alike from the attacks of wild beasts and from the bands of marauding natives. But no matter how heavy the burdens, not a grumble escaped the hero who had to bear them all—not a hint that he felt himself badly treated by his men and their officers.

On the 19th of August, Park, with the helpless, shattered remnant of his caravan, ascended the mountain ridge which forms the watershed between the Senegal and the Niger. Pushing on eagerly to the summit of the hill, the toil and careworn traveller's eyes were gladdened by the spectacle of the "Niger rolling its immense stream along the plain."

"After the fatiguing march which we had just experienced, the sight of this river was no doubt pleasant, as it promised an end to, or at least an alleviation of, our toils. But when I reflected that three-fourths of the soldiers had died on the march, and that in addition to our weakly state we had no carpenters to build the boats in which we proposed to prosecute our discoveries, the prospect appeared somewhat gloomy. It, however, afforded me peculiar pleasure when I reflected that in conducting a party of Europeans with immense baggage through an extent of more than five hundred miles, I had always been able to preserve the most friendly terms with thenatives."

The latter sentence is well worthy of note as illustrative of Park's methods of travel at a time when the sanctity of human life, whether black or white, was not quite so much thought of as at present.

In speaking of the distance traversed as five hundred miles, it must be remembered that what is meant is the distance in a straight line expressed in geographical miles. The actual number of English miles travelled over would be in reality little short of a thousand.

Notwithstanding his frightful experiences, Park considered that his "journey plainly demonstrates—first, that with common prudence any quantity of merchandise may be transported from the Gambia to the Niger without danger of being robbed by the natives; second, that if this journey be performed in the dry season, one may calculate on losing not more than three, or at most four men, out of fifty."

We would naturally have expected him to add as a third conclusion, that under no circumstance should Europeans be employed in such a caravan except as conductors, or it might be as guards. That conclusion, however, he apparently did not reach—indeed, we look in vain throughout his journal for any indication that he was at all aware of the frightful nature of his blunder in starting only with Europeans.

And yet before him was the tangible fact, that of thirty-four soldiers and four carpenters who left the Gambia with him, only seven entered Bammaku, while Isaaco and his attendants were all alive and hearty, though much of the white men's work had fallen upon them in addition to their own.

Three days after their arrival at Bammaku the travellers continued their way. Martyn, with the men and the donkeys, proceeded by land, while Park, Anderson, and the goods glided down the river in canoes, at the rate of five knots an hour, without the necessity of paddling. At their starting point the river was a mile broad; but further down, where it passes through a range of hills and forms rapids, it attains twice that breadth. Here the great mass of water is gathered into three principal channels, along which it rushes with much noise, and a speed which made Park sigh as the frail canoes containing all his precious stores sped into the sweeping tide, and seemed threatened with momentary destruction.

Two such rapids and three smaller ones were safely passed during the afternoon. At one place an elephant was seen standing on an island, so near that if Park had not been too ill, he would have had a shot at it.

At several points the canoes ran considerable danger of being upset by hippos. At night the party landed, and after a supper of rice and fresh-water turtle, spent a night exposed to the violence of a tropic storm.

At Marrabu, where they arrived on the second day, a halt was called, while Isaaco was despatched to Sego with a message and a present for Mansong, king of Bambarra, whose good offices were likely to prove invaluable, ruling as he did over the whole country from Bammaku to Timbuktu. While awaiting his messenger's return, Park, who had been suffering from dysentery ever since his arrival on the river, and found himself failing fast under its deadly attacks, dosed himself with calomel till it affected his throat to such a degree that he could neither speak nor sleep for six days. The experiment was successful, however, as regards stopping the progress of the disease, and his health speedily began to improve.

The interval of waiting to which he was now subjected was a time of extreme anxiety. The check which all the physical difficulties of the march and the death of three-fourths of his men had failed to give him might be effected by the will of Mansong. On the decision of the negro ruler depended Park's further movements. A Yes might assure the complete realisation of all his dearest hopes—a No would be their death-knell.

Each day brought its crop of unfavourable rumours. Among others came the report that Mansong had killed Isaaco with his own hands, and intended to finish off the white men in a similar summary fashion. Happily this and kindred stories proved to be pure inventions, and after a fortnight's delay a messenger arrived to conduct Park to Sego, bringing with him an encouraging account of Mansong's disposition towards him.

The drastic methods of the emissaries of negro kings were well illustrated by the following incident. A native refusing to give up a canoe for the messenger's use, the latter not only seized the canoe in question, but cut the owner across the forehead with his sword, broke the brother's head with a paddle, and finally made a slave of the son. Before such deeds criticism was dumb.

And now all seemed about to go well with the expedition. Cradled on the majestic bosom of the great river, with toils and worry over, its leader could afford to allow himself to be lulled into a sweet dreamland, in which he saw himself gliding peacefully towards the Congo and the Atlantic. Of goods he had still sufficient for his object—of men, too, there were enough; and with mind thus comparatively at ease, he could give himself up to the enjoyment of the beautiful views of "this immense river—sometimes as smooth as a mirror, at others ruffled by a gentle breeze, but at all times sweeping along at the rate of six or seven miles an hour."

In two days Yamina was reached, and a third brought the party to Sami, where once more they halted while the messenger went forward to inform Mansong of their proximity, and ask instructions concerning them. Two days later Isaaco joined them from Sego. He reported that Mansong's position was very neutral. The king showed impatience when the subject of the white men was broached, though he had said that they were at liberty to pass down the river. In addition he gave Isaaco to understand that he wanted no direct dealings with Park.

On the following day a king's messenger arrived to receive Mansong's present from Park's own hands, as well as to hear the object of his visit. In his speech the traveller told how he was the same poor white man who, after being plundered by the Moors, was so hospitably received by their king, whose generous conduct had made his name much respected in the country of the Europeans. He then proceeded to point out what a trading people his (the traveller's) were, and how all the articles of value that reached the country of Mansong were made by them, being afterwards brought by Moors and others by long and expensive routes, which made everything extremely dear. That these European goods might be brought cheaper to Bambarra for the mutual benefit of whites and blacks, his king had sent him to see if a short and easy route could not be found by way of the Niger. If such was discovered, then the white men's vessels would come direct all the way from Europe and supply them with abundance of all their good things at cheap prices.

In reply to this speech the emissary said that the white man's journey was a good one, and prayed that God might prosper him in it. Mansong would protect him. The sight of the presents added to the friendly feelings thus expressed.

To dash Park's joy at the favourable aspect of affairs two more soldiers died —one of fever, the other of dysentery—leaving him with only four men, besides Anderson and Martyn.

In a couple of days the king sent a further message intimating that the white strangers would be protected, and that wherever his power and influence extended the road would be open to them. If they went East, no man would harm them till beyond Timbuktu. Westward, the name of Mansong's stranger would be a safe password through the land to the Atlantic itself. If they wished to sail down the river, they were at liberty to build boats at any town they pleased.

As Mansong had never once expressed a wish to see him, and seemingly had some superstitious fear of the possible consequence, Park fixed upon Sansandig as the best place to prepare for his new adventure. Here, too, he would have more quiet, and would be more exempt from begging, than within the daily range of the king's officials.

In his passage from Sami to Sansandig, Park was attacked by a violent fever, which rendered him temporarily delirious. According to the sufferer, the heat was so terrific as to have been equal to the roasting of a sirloin, and there was neither covering to ward it off nor slightest puff of wind to temper it.

On reaching his destination the traveller was received by his old friend Kunti Mamadi, who placed the necessary huts at his disposal. On the following day two more of his men expired, and it began to look as if at the very moment when success seemed assured he was to be doomed to lose all. So frightfully were they all reduced at this time, and so little able to look after each other, that, unmolested, hyenas entered the dead men's hut, dragged one of them out, and devoured him.

From Park's journal we get an interesting glimpse of Sansandig, with its 11,000 inhabitants and its mosques, of which two were by "no means inelegant." But, as in all African towns, it was the market-place which was the centre of life and interest. From morning till night the square was crowded with busy groups of people gathered round the various mat-covered stalls which formed the shops, each containing its own speciality—beads in every gorgeous hue to catch the eye of the ornament-loving sex, antimony to darken and beautify the tips of the ladies' eyelids, rings and bracelets to attract wandering male glances to female feet and hands. In more substantial houses were scarlet cloths, silks, amber, and other valuable commodities which had found their way across the desert from Morocco or Tripoli—over roads marked out by the skeletons of slaves and camels who had sunk down to perish under the frightful hardships of the route. Vegetables, meat, salt, &c., each had their own stalls—beer, too, in large quantities, near a booth where leather work found its purchasers.

Such was the everyday state of the square; but the scene was still more animated and interesting on the occasion of the Tuesday weekly market. On that day enormous crowds of people gathered from the whole surrounding country to buy and sell wholesale, and many were the delightful glimpses of native life and character continually presenting themselves to the eyes of the observant traveller. He even found a means whereby to turn the market to his own advantage.

Mansong being slow in carrying out his promise to supply canoes to be turned into boats, Park opened a shop himself for the purpose of exchanging some of his articles for cowries, by which he hoped to purchase the necessary means of transport. He made such a tempting display that he had at once a great run of business, and became the envy of all the merchants of the place. In one day he secured 25,000 cowries.

While thus peacefully employed, every effort was being made on the part of the Moors and native merchants in order to set Mansong against the white man, and get him killed, or sent back by the way he had come. They even did not hesitate to say that his object was to kill the king and his sons by means of charms. Mansong, however, was not to be prevailed on by such instigations, though his behaviour showed some belief in the reported magical powers.

After much delay, Park succeeded in obtaining two canoes, to join which together he and Bolton, the sole remaining capable man, now set themselves with great vigour. The rotten parts were replaced, the holes were repaired, and after eighteen days' hard labour the united canoes were launched and christened His Majesty's schooner *Joliba*, the length being forty feet, and the breadth six. Being flat-bottomed, it drew only one foot of water.

While Park was thus toiling with feverish energy to complete his preparations, Martyn seems to have been taking life very easily. From a letter written from Sansandig to a friend at Goree we get an idea of the sort of man he was, and how much he assisted in the work of the expedition. "Whitebread's beer," says the Lieutenant, "is nothing to what we get at this place, as I feel by my head this morning, having been drinking all night with a Moor, and ended by giving him an excellent thrashing." Could the contrast possibly be greater between Park and this man—the one possessed with a consuming desire to accomplish a work seemingly beyond mortal power, slaving with the strength of half-a-dozen ordinary men, uncrushed by a myriad misfortunes, his hero's spirit equal to every difficulty and danger; the other spending his time in drunken orgies, seemingly as careless of his life as indifferent to the great mission that was partly his.

The last and worst stroke of evil fortune that could befall Park came upon him in the form of his brother-in-law Anderson's death, which occurred on the 28th October. He had been Park's special support in all his trials, ever the one to whom he could open his heart, or from whom he could seek advice and encouragement. His thoughts and feelings on the occasion, Park, with characteristic reserve, does not put on paper, though he cannot help observing "that no event which took place during the journey ever threw the smallest gloom on my mind till I laid Mr. Anderson in the grave. I then felt myself as if left a second time lonely and friendless amidst the wilds of Africa."

CHAPTER XXIII.
THE LAST OF PARK.

By the middle of November the last preparations for the great voyage on the Niger were completed. Isaaco had been paid off, and one Amadi Fatuma, a native of Karson, and a great traveller, hired in his place to guide the party to Kashna, which Park still believed to be on the river. To Isaaco, Park's precious journal was entrusted for conveyance home.

On the 17th November, dating from "On board of H.M. schooner *Joliba*, at anchor off Sansandig," Park wrote to Lord Camden. After some remarks on his situation, he continues—

"From this account I am afraid that your Lordship will be apt to consider matters as in a very hopeless state, but I assure you I am far from desponding. With the assistance of one of the soldiers I have changed a large canoe into a tolerably good schooner, on board of which I shall set sail to the east, with the fixed resolution to discover the termination of the Niger or perish in the attempt. I have heard nothing I can depend on respecting the remote course of this mighty stream, but I am more and more inclined to think that it can end nowhere but in the sea.

"My dear friend Mr. Anderson, and likewise Mr. Scott, are both dead; but though all the Europeans who are with me should die, and though I were myself half dead, I would still persevere, and if I could not succeed in the object of my journey, I would at least die on the Niger. If I succeed in the object of my journey, I expect to be in England in the month of May or June, by way of the West Indies."

On the 19th he wrote to his wife—

" ... I am afraid that, impressed with a woman's fears and the anxieties of a wife, you may be led to consider my situation as a great deal worse than it is.... The rains are completely over, and the healthy season has commenced, so that there is no danger of sickness, and I have still a sufficient force to protect me from any insult in sailing down the river to the sea.

"We have already embarked all our things, and shall sail the moment I have finished this letter. I do not intend to stop nor land anywhere till we reach the coast, which I suppose will be some time in the end of January.... I think it not unlikely but that I shall be in England before you receive this.... We this morning have done with all intercourse with the natives. The sails are now being hoisted for our departure to the coast."

These letters are full of brave words, yet they do not express one iota more than what Park was capable of. They breathe his remarkable personality in every line. They show the heroic spirit that does not know the word impossible, that does not know when it is beaten—that having once set itself a task, is incapable of turning back. They speak eloquently of a stubborn resolution which only death itself can render powerless, and such a resolution as the world has rarely seen.

It is almost impossible to realise the position of our hero at the moment when he prepared to embark on one of the most perilous and uncertain voyages history records. In some aspects it deserves to rank with the voyage of Columbus across the Atlantic. The bourne was equally uncertain, the distance not so very much less, the perils quite as great. It might even be said that compared with that of Park, the enterprise of Columbus was most hopeful. Columbus, too, had always the option of turning back. For Park there was no such door of escape. Success or death was his only choice, and even success might mean captivity or worse, the best geographer of the time holding that the Niger termination was not in the ocean, but in the heart of the continent. If he proved right, how many were the chances against Park's ever finding his way out again.

It is to be remembered, in addition, that this voyage of from 2000 to 3000 miles—supposing the Niger to be the same as the Congo—was not embarked upon in the heyday of the party's hopes, but after an unparalleled series of misfortunes and a frightful tale of death.

For sole means of carrying out this wonderful enterprise Park had nothing better than an unwieldy half-rotten canoe, and a crew consisting of an officer wholly unsuited to the work, three European privates, of whom one was mad and the others sick, and lastly, Amadi Fatuma, the guide, and three slaves— nine men in all.

With this "sufficient force to protect me from insult," the canoe had to be navigated without a pilot for hundreds of miles along a river studded at parts with dangerous rocks, and everywhere infested by equally dangerous hippos —a river whose banks were occupied for much of the way by fanatical Moors and Tuaregs, while beyond were unknown tribes of cannibal savages and other bloodthirsty natives.

But nothing could daunt the intrepid explorer—nothing make him waver in his "fixed resolution to discover the termination of the Niger or die in the attempt."

Thus spiritually armed and inspired, and thus materially supported, with the writing of his last words to the world, the sails of the *Joliba* were unfurled to the wind, and like Ulysses of old, Park pushed off from land bent on some work of noble note. And though made "weak by time and fate," still "strong in will, to strive, to seek, to find, and not to yield" till death itself should close his toilsome struggle, or Ocean once more happily receive him on its broad bosom, and bear him to the "Happy Isles" and the blessed guerdon of his accomplished work.

The die was cast, and down the great river he glided towards the untravelled countries of the east and south—towards the heart of savage Africa, and the deep darkness of the Unexplored.

His journals and letters in the hands of the faithful Isaaco safely reached the coast and afterwards Europe, thrilling all true-born men and women with the unparalleled tale of travel they so simply yet graphically unfolded. All waited with eager impatience for the reappearance of the hero. Speculation was rife as to his point of exit, or whether he would ever be heard of more.

May of 1806 passed into June without bringing further news. The year 1806 gave place to 1807, and then fears as to the ultimate fate of the expedition began to find expression. To strengthen these, rumours from West Africa reached home that native traders from the interior reported a disastrous close to the enterprise. With each succeeding month these reports grew in number and consistency, till Government could no longer ignore them, and determined to send a reliable native to the Niger to make special inquiries.

For this task Isaaco was engaged, and in January 1810 he left Senegal. In October of the same year he reached Sansandig, where he was so fortunate as to find Amadi Fatuma, the guide Park had taken with him down the Niger.

On seeing Isaaco, Amadi broke into tears and lamentations, crying out, "They are all dead, they are lost for ever!" His story was soon told. The substance of it was as follows:—

On leaving Sansandig, Park, in pursuance of his plan not to hold communication with the people on land, so as if possible to avoid attack or detention, pursued his course down the middle of the stream. At Silla another slave was added to the party, and at Jenné a present was sent to the head man, though no landing was made at either place.

On reaching the point where the Niger divides to form the island of Jinbala, they were attacked by three canoes armed with pikes and bows and arrows, which were repulsed by force on the failure of more peaceful methods.

At a place called Rakhara a similar attempt was made to stop the progress of the *Joliba*, and a third near Timbuktu. On each occasion the natives were driven back with the loss of many killed and wounded.

On passing Timbuktu, the country of Gurma and the lands of the Tuaregs lay before them. In this part of the river a determined attempt to dispute their passage was made by seven canoes; but the natives having no guns, were easily repulsed by the crew of the *Joliba*, which, though reduced to eight in number, were well supplied with muskets, constantly kept ready for action. Here another soldier died. Further on the *Joliba* was attacked by sixty canoes, but without serious result.

If the guide is to be trusted, Martyn seems to have enjoyed this part of the work to the full—so much so, indeed, that once, after a good deal of bloodshed, Amadi seized the Lieutenant's hand and begged him to desist, there being no further necessity for fighting. So enraged was Martyn, that the humane interference would have cost Amadi his life, but for Park's intervention.

Some distance beyond the scene of this battle the *Joliba* struck on the rocks, and during the confusion which ensued a hippo nearly completed their discomfiture by rushing at the boat, which it would have destroyed or upset, but for the timely firing of the men's guns. With great difficulty the canoe was got off without having suffered any material damage.

The party had now reached the centre of the ancient empire of Songhay, and everything was going as well as could be expected. They had still sufficient provisions to make landing unnecessary.

At a place called Kaffo three more canoes had to be driven back, and further on the guide, on landing to buy some milk, was seized by the natives. Park, seeing this, promptly laid hold of two canoes which had come alongside, and let their owners understand that unless his man was released he would kill them all and carry off their canoes. This threat had the required result, the guide being released, and amicable relations resumed.

Beyond the point where this incident happened, the river became difficult to navigate. It was broken up by islands and rocks into three narrow passages. The place is probably that marked in Barth's map, some seventy miles south of Gargo, the former capital of Songhay. The first passage tried was found to be guarded by armed men, "which," says the guide, "caused great uneasiness to us, especially to me, and I seriously promised never to pass there again without making considerable charitable donations to the poor." On trying a second channel the party was not molested.

A few days later they reached the Haussa country, probably near the Gulbi-n-Gindi, which comes from Kebbi, the western of the then independent states. Here, according to Amadi, his agreement ended, though, according to Park's letters, he was to have gone as far as Kashna. Before separating from his guide Park wrote down the names of the necessaries of life and some useful phrases in the dialects of the remaining countries through which he had to pass. This task occupied two days, during which the *Joliba* remained at anchor, but without landing any of her crew.

Though thus losing his interpreter, and adding in consequence to the dangers of the voyage by having no one through whom to communicate when necessary with the natives, Park had every reason to be hopeful. He had now sailed over a thousand miles down the river without any serious mishap, though the way had lain through the country of the Moors, and their equally fanatical co-religionists the Tuaregs. Ahead lay the land of the negroes, among whom, all things considered, he had ever found a kindly welcome and hospitable treatment. Especially encouraging was the fact that the Niger was flowing due south—consequently towards the Atlantic, and not to the inland swamps of Rennell's theories.

There was therefore no great reason to consider the want of an interpreter as an important drawback, and consequently no attempt was made to induce Amadi to go further than Yauri, the next district to the south of the Gulbi-n-Gindi. Here Amadi went ashore, and after exchanging presents on the part of Park with the king, Al Hadj, or the "Pilgrim," bought more provisions, to enable the white men to continue their way without landing. This, though probably a necessary business, was destined to prove fatal to the prospects of the expedition. The cupidity of the natives was aroused by the wealth which the strangers were believed to have with them—a sample of which was afforded by the presents sent to the king.

Immediately to the south of Yauri, the low, flat valley of the Niger contracts to a glen or gorge, where the subtending sandstone hills pass into abrupt and precipitous masses of hard metamorphic rock, and break up the channel of the river by dangerous rocks and islands occupied by villages. Thus narrowed and divided the waters of the river sweep onward in three branches—one of them easy to navigate; the others difficult at flood time, and almost impossible when the river is low.

During the delay at Yauri the news of the strangers' coming either spread in the ordinary way to Bussa, or was conveyed by special messenger, and preparations were made to stop them.

THE BUSSA RAPIDS.

Unconscious of the dangers ahead, Park left Yauri and continued his way south. Having no one acquainted with the river in his canoe, he unluckily struck upon the worst of the three channels, and rushed to his doom. Once in the sweep of the current to turn back was impossible. To land was equally out of the question even had it been possible, for to right and left the rocks and islands were crowded with natives in war array bent on stopping the intruders. The energy and attention of the handful of travellers was divided between the double danger—the rapids and rocks around and ahead of them, and the weapons hurtling through the air. Two of the slaves were speedily killed; for the rest there was no other course but to keep onward, alternately firing and paddling, ever hoping to make good their escape. A little more and they would be out of danger. Before they were aware, however, the *Joliba* rushed into the grip of a hidden cleft rock and there stuck fast. With desperate energy each man seized his paddle, and mindful only of the supreme peril of the moment, plied it with the strength of one who works for dear life. In vain—the *Joliba* would not yield to their frantic efforts. With delighted yells the natives gathered on the neighbouring rocks, and sure of their prey, plied their weapons with renewed zeal.

The last resource was to lighten the canoe, and everything of weight was accordingly thrown into the river. That too proved useless, and now Park and his little band of followers knew they had reached the culminating point of their misfortunes. For a time they fought on as if determined to sell their lives dearly, but at length desisted, struck with the futility of their efforts. Their goods were gone—their number was reduced to four. To continue fighting was only further to enrage their enemies. What were the feelings of the hero at this supreme moment of disaster—what his last determination, who shall say?

Amadi tells us that in the end Park took hold of one white man and Martyn of the other, and thus united they all four jumped into the river, whether to die together, or with the intention of mutually assisting each other, will never be known. The latter supposition is the more probable, for with Park while there was life there was hope. In any case the result was the same. The Niger claimed him as its own, and since to unlock its secrets was not to be his, what more fitting for him than death beneath its rushing waters.

Of the party only one slave remained alive. Of the contents of the canoe the sole articles left were a sword-belt, which the King of Yauri utilised as a horse-girth, and some books, one of which has reached England.

The guide did not escape scathless any more than the other members of the expedition. Scarcely had he taken leave of Park, when he was seized and loaded with chains, remaining in imprisonment for some months. His first business on obtaining his freedom was to find out the sole survivor of the expedition, and learn from him the manner of its leader's death. Having satisfied himself as far as might be on this point, he returned home to Sansandig, from which rumour gradually carried his sad tale to the coast, and resulted in the mission of Isaaco.

To obtain the sword-belt, and otherwise substantiate Amadi's story, Isaaco despatched a Fulah to Yauri. The Fulah succeeded in stealing the belt, and gathered confirmation of the tale of disaster, whereupon Isaaco set out for the coast with the melancholy tidings and solitary relic.

With the many the tragic story obtained immediate credence. A few there were, however, who refused to give up hope, though that hope was but the offspring of their love and ardent wishes. Among these was Mrs. Park, who to her dying day, thirty years after the above events, clung to the belief that her husband was yet alive, and would some day be found.

The Government, not unmindful of their duty to the family of such a heroic servant, granted Mrs. Park a small pension, which she continued to receive till her death in 1840.

Her children as they grew up speedily showed that they inherited much of the spirit of their father. Mungo, the eldest, obtained a commission in the Indian army. But he had not his father's constitution, and he died ten days after landing at Bombay. His younger brother, Archibald, was more fortunate in the same field of honour, and rose to the rank of Colonel.

But it was the second son, Thomas, who seemed most largely to have inherited the adventurous nature of his father. He, like his mother, never lost belief in the idea that his father was somewhere a prisoner in the heart of Africa. Thither, in the ardent, impulsive days of youth, his thoughts perpetually turned, till the desire of ascertaining the truth possessed him as strongly as the solution of the mystery of the Niger had formerly possessed Park himself. But by this time the Parks were alone in their belief, and unsupported, the impetuous young fellow was next to helpless. In secret, however, he continued to scheme and plan all the more, ever with the one object in view.

At length in the year 1827 he embarked on board a vessel bound for the South Seas. In some way or other he contrived to leave the ship and reach the Gold Coast, determined now to carry out by himself his long cherished desire to discover his father's fate.

The following letter, dated Accra, 1827, tells all we know of his plans:—

"My dearest Mother,—I was in hopes I should have been back before you were aware of my absence. I went off—now that the murder is out— entirely from fear of hurting your feelings. I did not write to you lest you should not be satisfied. Depend upon it, my dearest mother, I shall return safe. You know what a curious fellow I am, therefore don't be afraid for me. Besides, it was my duty—my filial duty—to go, and I shall yet raise the name of Park. You ought rather to rejoice that I took it into my head. Give my kindest love to my sister. Tell her I think the boat would do very well for the Niger. I shall be back in three years at the most— perhaps in one. God bless you, my dearest mother, and believe me to be, your most affectionate and dutiful son,

Thomas Park."

Thereafter an ominous silence followed. Like the elder Park, the hot-headed young fellow, whom we cannot help loving for his folly—knowing as we do its mainspring—disappeared from sight in the Dark Continent, whence only vague rumours ever came back, sorrow-laden, telling of a speedy and bloody close to his wild yet heroic mission.

And so fatally ended the connection of the Park family with the exploration of the River Niger, and thus closed the first great chapter in the history of the opening up of Inner Africa.

CHAPTER XXIV.
THE FULAH REVOLUTION.

Simultaneously with the commencement of Park's work of exploration, an event of almost equal moment in the history of the Niger basin had begun to germinate. This was the phenomenal rise to a position of immense political and religious importance of the Fulahs—a people known among the Haussa as Fillani, and in Bornu as Fillatah.

As Park was the forerunner of Christian enterprise, so Othman dan Fodiyo, a simple Fulah Malaam or teacher, in raising the banner of Islam, marked the revival of the political and religious spirit of Mohammedanism in the Central and Western Sudan.

We have seen how the huge empire of Songhay crumbled into pieces before the musketeers of a Moorish sultan—how with its political influence went its civilising influence, and whole kingdoms and provinces fell back into the old idolatry and barbarism.

Similarly and almost contemporaneously, Bornu, largely though not so entirely, lost its old military power and progressive force. The Haussa States, left to themselves, showed a like degenerative tendency, and largely lapsed into the old heathen ways.

But in all the mass of idolatry was a leaven of quickening influence, which prevented it from becoming altogether dead and sodden. From Lake Chad to the Atlantic there was scattered one remarkable race who forgot not God, neither lapsed into the abominations of the infidel. Though without political status, and holding no better position than that of semi-serfs—being, moreover, spread broadcast in small groups as shepherds—they yet had in them a bond of union and an inspiring force which supported them in all their trials, and kept them from racial annihilation.

GROUP OF FULAHS.

That race was the Fulah, and their bond of union was the religion of Islam.

Where they came from is unknown. Everything relating to them is a matter of conjecture, though in the Sudanese chronicles we find various allusions to them extending back several centuries.

Their well-chiselled features, straight wiry hair, and copper-coloured skin, all distinctly mark them off as not African, and point towards the East as the cradle of their race. Still more, their well-developed skulls and high intellectual average place them on an altogether higher level in the scale of humanity than any of the negro or Bantu races among whom they settled.

At some remote period, we may safely conjecture, they immigrated from the East, and gradually moved westward—not as warrior-conquerors, but as peace-loving shepherds, whose knowledge of cattle, &c., made them welcome additions to every country they reached. Nomadic in habit, and depending for subsistence on their flocks and herds, it was impossible for them to settle in large numbers in any one place—the country being already occupied by the negro inhabitants. Accordingly it was ever necessary for them to move westward, leaving behind them only such numbers as could conveniently get a living.

By the fourteenth or fifteenth century the Fulahs had reached the watersheds of the Niger and the Gambia. Here the migratory tide was stopped by physical and other causes. The country beyond proved to be less adapted for pastoral pursuits, and possibly was already thickly populated.

There being no further outlet westward, the newcomers naturally accumulated as does the dammed back stream. They increased in numbers, and correspondingly in power, till they became of no small importance, and founded for themselves a kingdom which has been already mentioned under the name of Fulahdu.

When Islam crossed the desert and found its way in the ninth and tenth centuries into the Sudan, the Fulahs were the very first to become converts to the new religion. Their temperament, their higher intellectual development, made them more quickly susceptible to the new influences, and hence it was that while as yet the great mass of the aborigines were still infidel, the Fulahs with one voice were proclaiming their belief in Allah and His Prophet. Persecution, as in the case of other religions, had only the result of burning the tenets of Islam deeper into their souls, causing their faith to shine with a clearer and more spiritual light to the edification and instruction of the surrounding idolaters. In the Western Sudan, where they enjoyed, or came to enjoy, an independent existence, Islam spread among the Fulahs with special rapidity; and with the fall of Songhay and the crippling of the influence of Timbuktu, they became the chief propagators of Mohammedanism and the great encouragers of learning by means of mosques and schools—rarely by the power of fire and the sword. Not only did they and their co-religionists of neighbouring tribes, the Mandingoes and the Jolofs, thus spread a knowledge of the One God—they at the same time did an equally noble work in arraying themselves against the rapidly advancing flood of gin which Christian Europe was pouring into their country. With that traffic they would have nothing to do, and unlike so many of our Christian merchants, no consideration of profit would tempt them to a compromise between their conscience and the lust for gain.

Meanwhile the Fulahs of the kingdoms of the interior had much to do to hold their own among their Pagan masters. Their position was most galling to a race which knew themselves infinitely superior to those whom they were obliged to own as masters—more bitter still that they, the inheritors of the promises, should be ruled by idolaters and men whose portion was Gehenna. Broken up as they were into little groups scattered over an enormous area, what could they do? The answer to that question was speedily forthcoming. They had, as we have shown, the necessary bond of union and the inspiring spiritual force to make them fight as one man for a common end. They only needed the leader to utilise this force and bring it into action. Such a man is never wanting when the times demand him, and he in this case was forthcoming in the person of Othman, the Imam or religious sheik of the Fulah of Gober, the northern of the Haussa States.

Under the influence of this sheik the Fulah of that region were roused to a state of religious fervour such as they had never known before. His fiery eloquence touched their excitable and imaginative nature as he brought home to them the shame of their semi-enslaved position. The fires of discontent were thus set smouldering, and required but a little more fanning to cause them to blaze into the flames of rebellion.

Meanwhile their Haussa ruler, Bawa, was not blind to the dangerous ferment existing among them, and fearing the results, summoned Othman to his presence, and severely reprimanded him. This was sufficient for the proud and enthusiastic "Believer." He left Bawa's presence only to raise the standard of revolt—the sacred banner of Islam. The effect was electric. In response to his summons the Fulah at once gathered around him in an enthusiastic army.

But they were mostly shepherds—men of peace, unaccustomed to the use of arms; and they could not be at once transformed into successful warriors. Consequently at first they met with discomfiture and defeat in every encounter. Had they been fighting for themselves the movement would undoubtedly have collapsed at the first rude shock of arms. But happily for them they had a higher interest at heart. They fought for God and His Prophet, whose instruments they believed themselves to be. In such a warfare there could be no doubt in their minds as to whose would ultimately be the victory. With ever-growing zeal they returned to the charge, stimulated in their glorious crusade by their leader Othman's religious songs and fiery words, which told them that theirs was a cause for which it was much to live and fight, but even more to die, if it should be God's will.

Thus led and encouraged, the Fulah grew in experience of battle and the use of arms. The hordes of shepherds were gradually beaten into a disciplined army of warriors, and from defeat rose to victory.

Thus it was that Othman and his ever-victorious army burst forth from Gober on their irresistible career, filling the wild wastes of Central African heathendom with their cry of "None but the One God," till the whole of the Western and Central Sudan, from Lake Chad to the Atlantic, acknowledged more or less temporarily the political supremacy of the Fulah. Yet it was no mere temporal power that Othman and his people sought to establish—theirs was a conquest for God. They acted but as His agents. Before them fetishism and all its degrading rites disappeared. No longer did the natives bow down to stocks and stones, but to Allah, the One God. Once more, as in the palmy days of Songhay and Bornu, schools and mosques sprang up throughout the land, and the Greatness, the Compassionateness, and the All-embracing Mercy of the Ruler of the Universe were taught to natives released from the foul blight of idolatry in its worst form.

In this work of releasing the Faithful from their bondage to heathen taskmasters, and bringing new light in a forcible fashion to the barbarous and breechless natives, the Fulah did not stop till from every village of the Central Sudan there was heard in the grey dawn of the tropic morning the stentorian voice of the negro Mueddin, announcing that prayer was better than sleep— bringing from out the faintly illumined houses the devout Moslems to humble their faces in the dust, and acknowledge their utter faith in and dependence on Allah.

No less thoroughly was the material welfare of the people cared for. "The laws of the Koran were in his (Othman's) time strictly put in force, not only among the Fillahtah (Fulah), but the negroes and the Arabs; and the whole country, when not in a state of war, was so well regulated, that it was a common saying that a woman might travel with a casket of gold upon her head from one end of the Fillahtah dominions to the other." So wrote Clapperton a few years after the death of Othman, as eye-witness of the wonderful revolution effected by the Fulah.

Unhappily the religious fervour of the remarkable leader speedily developed into religious mania, and ended in his death in 1817.

On the death of Othman, the huge empire he had raised was divided between his sons Bello and Abd Allahi. To the former was given Sokoto and all the east and south, while to the latter fell the western provinces along the Niger, with Gandu as capital. The countries to the west of the Niger, including Massina, became independent under Ahmed Lebbo, one of Othman's lieutenants, who conquered that region immediately before the death of Othman.

CHAPTER XXV.
NEW ENTERPRISES AND NEW THEORIES.

As we have seen, Park's second expedition was fruitful in nothing but disaster, and the legacy of experience that helps others to success.

The journal Isaaco brought back from the Niger did not add anything to our knowledge of the river, and so little did Amadi Fatuma's narrative supplement it as to the results of the voyage down the stream to Bussa, that in the map attached to the published journal and biographical notice in 1816, Park's furthest point is placed only some eighty miles to the E.S.E. of Timbuktu, instead of nearly 700 miles in a straight line S.E.

There was one geographer, however, more far-seeing than the others, who, though at the time unheeded, struck upon the real solution of the problem of the Niger's termination. This was M. Richard, a German, who published his views on the subject in the "Ephemerides Geographique" as far back as 1808. These, briefly stated, were as follows. The Niger, after reaching Wangara, takes a direction towards the south, and being joined by other rivers from that part of Africa, makes a great turn thence towards the south-west, pursuing its course till it approaches the north-eastern extremity of the Gulf of Guinea, where it divides and discharges itself by different channels into the Atlantic, after having formed an immense delta, of which the Rio del Rey constitutes the eastern, and the Rio Formosa or Benin the western branch.

Never was a better instance of a mental discovery of a geographical fact. Richard's hypothesis is a graphic description of the actual geography of the middle and lower Niger. This of course was not to be recognised by the world, before whose eyes the Kong Mountains ever loomed up as an impassable barrier running across the suggested line of drainage. Till these could be removed, turned aside, or broken up, no geographer was prepared to allow that the Niger could possibly discharge itself into the Gulf of Guinea.

Mungo Park had left one legacy of theory behind him, viz., that the Niger and the Congo were one. What was known of his last voyage in nowise helped to disabuse men of that idea—on the contrary, it obtained more widely than ever.

To set at rest once for all this important question, the Government, undeterred by the disastrous termination of the last expedition, determined to fit out another on an even larger scale, and in spite of the dire fate which had befallen Park and his companions, there were not wanting plenty of ardent spirits to risk all the dangers of a similar enterprise.

To ensure success the expedition was divided into two parts—one to follow Park's route more or less closely and descend the Niger; the other to ascend the Congo, haply to meet half way, if the fates were propitious.

Captain Tuckey was the leader of the Congo section; and along with him went a botanist, a geologist, a naturalist, a comparative anatomist, a gentleman volunteer, and fifty of a crew.

The party left England on the 16th February 1816, and reached the mouth of the Congo in five months and a half. The impression they received on entering the river was one of disappointment, the river appearing as one of second class magnitude instead of the gigantic stream they had been taught to expect.

In vain, too, did they look for traces of the great kingdoms described by the early Portuguese explorers, or of the churches and cities founded by the Europeans in the early days of Portuguese national and Christian enterprise. For the most part they were met only by the dark depths of malarious mangrove swamps, and the profound stillness and impenetrable vegetation of the tropical forest, though here and there in the clearings were miserable villages, inhabited by idle, good-humoured natives, with a decided appetite for ardent spirits— seemingly the only legacy permanently left behind by the Europeans.

Pushing up the river, they at length reached the first cataracts of the Congo, which, instead of proving to be another Niagara, seemed to their jaundiced eyes "a comparative brook bubbling over its stony bed"—a description, needless to say, not confirmed by subsequent expeditions.

Unable to proceed further in their boats, Tuckey and his companions continued the exploration by land, and in spite of the extreme difficulties they had to encounter in cutting their way through pathless forests without a guide, they surmounted the first stretch of falls, and reached a point where the river widened and presented no difficulties to navigation. Unhappily, however, the old story of disease commenced. Three of the principal men had successively to return to the ship; and finally Tuckey and his companion Smith, the botanist, abandoned their projects, seeing their further progress hopeless in face of so many difficulties and their own helpless condition under the paralysing influence of disease. They reached the ship to find their three companions dead. Smith was the next victim. Finally, overcome by depression and mental anxiety, Captain Tuckey died also. How many sailors succumbed we are not told.

Meanwhile no better luck fell to the lot of the other section of the expedition.

On the 14th December, this party, consisting of 100 men and 200 animals, under the command of Major Peddie, landed at the mouth of the Rio Nunez, nearly midway between the Gambia and Sierra Leone. Major Peddie's intention was to pass across the narrow part between the Ocean and the Niger. Hardly had he landed, however, before the fell demon of disease, which in its foul lair keeps watch and ward over the fair expanse of Inner Africa, laid its invisible hand upon him, and ere the march was begun he found a grave in the land he had come to explore.

Under Captain Campbell the expedition experienced only a succession of disasters. The donkeys rapidly perished under the hands of men unaccustomed to look after them. Food was only to be obtained with the utmost difficulty, and at ruinous prices.

Arrived near the frontiers of the Fulah country, they were detained for four months owing to the suspicions entertained towards them by the king and his people.

Everything they had began to melt away at an alarming rate. Soon not a beast of burden was left, and when, seeing advance hopeless, they turned seawards, their retreat became one continued story of plunder. Kumner, the naturalist, died *en route*, and Campbell only reached Kakunda to add his name to the list of victims to African exploration. The final stroke was given to the unlucky fortunes of this evidently ill-conducted enterprise by the death of Lieutenant Stoker, a young naval officer who assumed command, and was about to make a new attempt to penetrate the country.

Clearly African exploration was no light matter, requiring the making of wills and the setting of earthly affairs in order for such as put their hand to the work. Yet strangely enough there was no halting—no dearth of volunteers. When one died, another was ready to take his place.

> "Each stepping where his comrade stood
>
> The instant that he fell."

In this spirit Captain Gray, a survivor of Peddie's party, made an attempt to follow Park's track, but got no further than Bondou, from which, after being detained for nearly a year, he managed to return to the coast.

But what all these various disastrous attempts were unable to achieve was meanwhile being once more accomplished by a stay-at-home geographer, James M'Queen. The circumstances under which he was attracted to the subject are in harmony with the romantic character of African history. A copy of the narrative of Park's first expedition found its way into the hands of M'Queen while resident in the Island of Grenada, West Indies. Among the negroes under his charge were several Mandingoes from the banks of the Niger. One Haussa negro he came in contact with had actually rowed Park across the Niger.

Already imbued with pronounced geographical tastes, M'Queen's imagination was at once taken captive by the mystery of the Great River. With all the enthusiasm of an ardent temperament, he devoted himself to the solution of the question as thoroughly as Park himself, though in a very different manner. While, one after another, explorers toiled and struggled, sickened and died, with but small result to science, he set about collecting information from all the negroes and freemen he met who had come from or even set foot in West Africa. More especially did he study all the available materials supplied by Arabs who had travelled and traded in the Sudan, or by Europeans and natives who, bent on commerce or discovery, had penetrated to the interior from the West Coast.

With extraordinary genius and industry, and admirable clear-sightedness and judgment, he set in their true light and pieced together the various items thus collected relating to the course of the Niger, till he succeeded in mapping out for himself the broad geographical features of the whole region through which it runs. As far back as 1816 the first sketch of his views was given to the world in a small treatise, in which he pointed out, as had Richard before him, that the Niger certainly entered the ocean in the Bight of Benin. The treatise fell unheeded, however—at least by the world at large; but undiscouraged, M'Queen continued his researches for five years more, and in 1821 produced a book, "Containing a Particular Account of the Course and Termination of the Great River Niger in the Atlantic Ocean."

In this interesting work M'Queen reviews all the various theories respecting the Niger. He demolishes Rennell's opinion that it disappeared in some central wastes of sand, or becomes evaporated in a series of swamps under the burning heats of a tropical sun. The view that it flows east and joins the Nile met a similar fate before his army of facts. The obstructing Kong barrier was cleft asunder with a Titan's strength, and made to separate instead of join the Congo and the Niger.

But the writer was not merely destructive. He could build as well. With the very weapons with which he pulled down the theories of the past, he set about constructing a theory of his own. Laying together fact upon fact, gathered from every available source, he traced the course of the Niger in a southerly direction. Bussa, from being left near Timbuktu, he transported several hundred miles further south. From the kingdom of Bornu and adjacent states he gathered together the various drainage streams, and ran them into a common channel—the Gir or Nile of the Sudan; but instead of directing it to the true Nile, as had formerly been the case when it was believed to be the Niger itself, he gave it a westerly course south of the Haussa States and Nyffé (Nupé) to its junction with the Kwora or Main Niger. Here the Arab writers and traders failed him, though leaving him without a doubt as to the ultimate destination of the Central Sudanese waters.

For the termination, however, he had to seek information from the Atlantic side. Everything pointed to the Bight of Benin as the only possible place of discharge of such a huge river. Here was found an unknown extent of low flat country and fetid mangrove swamp, pierced by many-branched anastomosing creeks. From Calabar to Benin canoes could pass in all directions by means of these creeks, and it was known that they extended far into the interior. Though subject to the ebb and flow of the tide, there was no question as to the volume of fresh water which moved seaward, bearing floating islands on its discoloured floods.

Supported by a convincing array of facts such as these, M'Queen could come to no other conclusion but that "in the Bights of Benin and Biafra, therefore, is the great outlet of the Niger, bearing along in his majestic stream all the waters of Central Africa from 10° west longitude to 28° east longitude, and from the Tropic of Cancer to the shores of Benin."

Never was a piece of arm-chair geography worked out more admirably. In its broad outlines it was perfectly correct. To M'Queen it was as much a certainty as if he had actually explored and mapped it on the spot.

Imbued with this faith, he proceeded to point out the importance of the Niger to the commerce of England and the future of Africa. With Fernando Po and the Niger in the hands of his countrymen, he saw Britain mistress of the fate of the continent. Bussa was to be the inner key of the situation. "Therefore," he says, "on this commanding spot let the British standard be firmly planted, and no power on earth could tear it up.... Firmly planted in Central Africa, the British flag would become the rallying point of all that is honourable, useful, beneficial, just, and good. Under the mighty shade thereof the nations would seek security, comfort, and repose. Allies Great Britain would find in abundance. They would flock to her settlement, if it had the power and the means to protect them. The resources of Africa, and the energies of Africa, under a wise and vigorous policy, may be made to subdue and control Africa. Let Britain only form such a settlement, and give it that countenance, support, and protection which the wisdom and energy of British councils can give, and which the power and resources of the British empire can so well maintain, and Central Africa to future ages will remain a grateful and obedient dependency of this empire. The latter will become the centre of all the wealth, and the focus of all the industry, of the former. Thus the Niger, like the

Ganges, would acknowledge Great Britain as its protector, our king as its lord.... A city built there under the protecting wings of Great Britain, and extended, enriched, and embellished by the industry, skill, and spirit of her sons, would ere long become the capital of Africa. Fifty millions of people, yea, even a greater number, would be dependent on it."

These are brave words, truly, about what after all was merely a "mental discovery," and taken alone, they might only evoke a smile, if we did not know that they are those of a man of no ordinary genius and power of insight. Looking back seventy years after he wrote, we can see how truly prophetic he was in most that he wrote, and that he was no more the blatant patriot than the geographical dreamer. His genius for looking ahead was as great as for looking around. Take, for instance, his warning of the danger of a French advance from the Senegal to the Niger, and its far-reaching consequence, if carried out, to our commercial and political position in West Central Africa. He it was who foresaw nearly seventy years before its accomplishment the necessity of a Chartered Company to take full advantage of our (then prospective) position on the Niger, and the results that would ensue without such a method of developing the resources of that region. Of these matters, however, we shall treat in their proper place. Enough for the moment if we show how thoroughly M'Queen had made himself master of the geographical problems then before the public, as well as of the political and commercial situation that was to follow the opening up of the Niger to European intercourse. Only now, after more than half a century of gross and irreparable mismanagement in West Africa, we are waking up to the wisdom of his views, and striving in some measure to carry them into effect.

CHAPTER XXVI.
THE TERMINATION OF THE NIGER.

Unhappily for the stay-at-home geographer, no matter how skilfully he may set forth the discoveries made in his study, his triumph can only come after they have been demonstrated by actual travel, and even then the credit that falls to his share is small. The case of M'Queen is one in point. We have no evidence that his theory regarding the Niger's termination made any special impression upon the general opinion of the time. Unfortunately for him, too, his views were published immediately after several disastrous attempts from the West Coast to settle the question he had so ably worked out, so that Government and people alike were disposed to fight shy of the fatal region.

Yet with every succeeding failure the attraction of the mysterious river seemed ever to become greater, and a stubborn determination was evinced to break through the deadly belt which hedged in the countries of the interior. Conquered and rebuffed in one direction, there was nothing for it but to try another, and once more the Arab caravan route from Tripoli to the Sudan was thought of. As has been elsewhere shown, attempts in this direction had already been made by other travellers, and all had alike failed. Of these Horneman alone had penetrated beyond the northern borderland of the desert, only, however, to disappear for ever. In every other case these expeditions had failed at the outset through fatal fevers and Oriental obstructiveness—what, then, had the traveller to expect, who, surmounting these initial dangers, found himself face to face with the terrors of the great Sahara, where nature in its fiercest aspects reigned supreme, and man was represented only by wild roving tribes savage as their environment.

Nevertheless men there were ready and eager to try this route, as had been others before them to brave the dangers of the West Coast.

CAPTAIN CLAPPERTON.

In 1820 Britain held an exceptionably favourable position in the councils of the Court of Tripoli, while at the same time the Basha, thanks to his guns, exercised a very marked influence over all the Arab, Berber, and Tibbu tribes lying between his country and the far-distant regions of the Sudan. Hence any one starting under the protection of the Basha had a fair guarantee of success, provided he could withstand the possible onslaughts of disease, and the terrible privations incidental to desert marches.

Encouraged by this favourable state of matters, the British Government determined to make another attempt to explore by the Arab route the regions which they had so signally failed to reach from the Atlantic.

Lieutenant Clapperton—like Park, a Scottish borderer—Dr. Oudney, and Major Denham, were selected for the task, and the 18th November 1821 saw them landed in Tripoli. Little time was lost in making their preparations and in setting forth for Murzuk in Fezzan, where they were to make their final arrangements before plunging into the dread Sahara. Here, though received kindly enough by the Sultan, they were threatened with the system of Oriental delays which had proved fatal to previous travellers. This, however, they were not the men to brook, and Major Denham promptly returned to Tripoli to lay a complaint before the Basha. As promptly he started for England on getting nothing but promises. This was sufficient to throw the Basha and his Court into consternation, and vessel after vessel was despatched to bring back the indignant traveller. They succeeded in catching him up at Marseilles, and induced him to return. On his arrival in Tripoli he was informed that already his escort awaited him at Sokna, on the borders of the Tripolitan desert.

Murzuk was triumphantly re-entered on the 30th October 1822. Clapperton and Oudney were found much reduced by the fevers, which were here so prevalent that even amongst the natives anything like a healthy-looking person was a rarity. To get away from this dangerously unhealthy place, Bu Khalum, the leader of the caravan, exerted himself with most unoriental and praiseworthy energy, though the task of gathering together the various elements of such a company as his was no small matter.

When ready, the party consisted of four Europeans, and servants to the number of ten, an Arab escort of 210, gathered from the most obedient tribes under the rule of Tripoli, and a number of merchants and freed slaves, who brought up the roll to about 300.

It was the 29th November before the whole party was ready for the road. The Europeans were in no very promising plight. They were all more or less down with fever, and Oudney and Hillman, a carpenter, were in a specially hopeless condition, considering what was before them. Nevertheless each one was eager and determined to go on, always hoping in the future, as is the manner of enthusiasts.

Almost with the disappearance of the walls, mosques, and date-trees of Murzuk in their rear, the desert rose up grim and terrible before them. The second day saw them among wild wastes of burning billowy sands, where was seen no living thing, nor other sound heard than the melancholy sweep of the wind over the endless tracts of sand. For some days, however, watering- places were not unfrequent, while here and there small oases gave a temporary relief to the monotonous landscape, and afforded a scanty subsistence to Tibbu or Berber inhabitants, who preferred to face the terror of the wilderness rather than live under the harsh rule of Arab masters. With the continued advance southward the wells grew more scarce, and it became a matter of congratulation when the day's march ended beside one. With the wells went the date-trees and the cultivated oases, the prowling beast and the wandering native—only a great yellow expanse perpetually unrolled its vastness and monotony beneath the brazen canopy of a cloudless sky.

Into this realm of Desolation and Death the caravan now passed, their route marked out by the skeletons of human beings, ominously indicative of the dangers ahead and the horrors of the slave trade. As many as 107 such skeletons were counted by the wayside in a single march, and 100 were found around one well. At some places the numbers were beyond calculation. For days together now there was nothing but desert—hummocky mounds, painful stone-strewn stretches of barrenness, and shattered ribs of rock, grim, gaunt, and terrible. The wind came like blasts from a furnace, and from the cloudless sky the sun poured down its burning rays in a painful flood. Under the influences of heat, thirst, and fatigue, no word was spoken—even the camels uttered not a groan, as if conscious of the dire alternative to not pushing on. At times the horses' hoofs crunched through the bones of human beings who had perished on the march. Night only brought relief from the hardships of the route. Then came the clear soothing darkness lit by a myriad stars, the cool refreshing breezes, and the soft couch of sand, so inexpressibly welcome to the weary, parched, and blinded wayfarers.

Thus the year passed away, and 1823 was ushered in, bringing promise of a successful issue to the enterprise. The explorers had now reached a scantily populated Tibbu country, where, in equal danger from drought, famine, sandstorms, and the murderous raids and plundering onslaughts of Berber tribes and passing caravans, men somehow contrived to wring from the flinty, almost arid, bosom of mother earth the wherewithal to keep body and soul together.

On leaving Bilma, the chief centre of this district, another desert tract had to be crossed, necessitating long and harassing marches, under the hardships of which as many as twenty camels would sink down exhausted in a single day. This dread region was at length also safely traversed, and infinite was the relief and thankfulness of all when towards the end of January the approach to more fertile tracts was indicated by the appearance of clumps of grass, and further on of a few scattered and stunted trees. This miserable and dingy vegetation looked delightful and refreshing to travellers who for over two weary months had been in a land of death and desolation. Tibbu inhabitants, with their flocks and herds, reappeared with the vegetation, and fresh meat and camel's milk were to be had in abundance.

The caravan had this time reached no mere oasis. With each day's march south the country improved in appearance, till the party found themselves in charming valleys shaded by leafy trees, festooned with creeping vines of the Colocynth, while underneath the sheltering canopy the ground was aglow with many-hued and brilliantly-coloured flowers. Nor was there lack of animal life to give animation and variety to the scene. Hundreds of twittering birds fluttered from tree to tree, careless of the vultures and kites which gracefully circled far up in the heavens. From a distance shy gazelles watched the newcomers with their beautiful eyes wide-stretched, but ready, if alarmed, to bound away at a moment's notice to their forest haunts. The very sky reflected the softer conditions of nature, and showed a brighter blue cloud- speckled; and the natives in their smiling faces and hospitality harmonised with the happier conditions under which they lived, though from time to time the ruthless acts of the Arab caravan sent them flying in terror.

There was no mistaking the fact that the Sudan—the country known by hearsay for over four centuries, but which so far had baffled all attempts to explore it— had at last been reached. On the 4th February 1823 the travellers' eyes were greeted with a sight "so gratifying and inspiring that it would be difficult for language to convey an idea of its force. The great lake Chad, glowing with the golden rays of the sun in its strength, appeared within a mile of the spot on which we stood. My heart bounded within me at the prospect, for I believed this lake to be the key to the great object of our search (presumably the Niger), and I could not refrain from silently imploring Heaven's continued protection, which had enabled us to proceed so far in health and strength even to the accomplishment of our task."

Nine days later the river Yeou was discovered flowing from the west. The name given to it by the Arabs unlocked the secrets of many geographical misconceptions. But that it was neither the true Nile nor the Niger was soon made patent—for, on the one hand, its course ended in the Chad; and, on the other, its size, and the reports of the natives, made it clear that it drained only the eastern Haussa States.

February 17 was a momentous date in the history of the expedition, for on that day they reached Kuka, the capital of Bornu.

Their entry was made in great state, worthy the traditions of a powerful semi-civilised Sultan. Several thousand well equipped and marvellously caparisoned horsemen awaited the strangers outside the town, and on seeing them, charged as if with the intention of annihilating the little band. Suddenly, while at full gallop, they pulled up right in the faces of the newcomers, almost smothering them with clouds of dust, and putting them in some danger from the crowding of horses and clashing of spears.

The Sultan's negroes, as they were called, were specially conspicuous, "habited in coats of mail composed of iron chain, which covered them from the throat to the knees, dividing behind and coming on each side of the horse. Some of them had helmets, or rather skull caps, of the same metal, with china pieces all sufficiently strong to ward off the shock of a spear. Their horses' heads were also defended by plates of iron, brass, and silver."

It would be difficult to give the faintest idea of the strange sights and scenes which now opened up before our travellers in the centre of the ancient empire of Bornu. Nothing more remarkable had ever been seen by any European explorer—at least in Africa. From the Sultan and his much-robed courtiers down to the scantily-draped country people, all were alike interesting. The teeming life in all its varied forms—Arab, Berber, Fulah, and negro of twenty different tribes—made up a picture of strange attractiveness. Not less interesting were the curious customs, the industries, the mixture of a considerable degree of civilisation and religious elevation with the lowest depths of barbarism and degrading superstition. These were the more marked, inasmuch as when the English travellers saw Bornu and its remarkable court, it was just re-emerging from a temporary eclipse of its national glory. Only a short time before it had thrown off the temporary domination of the Fulahs, to whom it had succumbed in their first irresistible onrush.

The reception of Clapperton and Denham was exceedingly promising, and a bright career of discovery seemingly lay open to them.

Matters assumed a worse aspect, however, when differences of opinion arose among the Arabs of the caravan. They had been despatched as an escort to the travellers, it is true, but they were not placed directly under their command. To do absolutely nothing but look after the safety of the Europeans was as alien to their conception of duty as the idea of travelling all the way to Bornu without turning the journey to profitable account. The majority of them not being merchants, and therefore not supplied with goods for barter, had only their weapons to depend upon to recoup them for their trouble. A slave raid was therefore determined on, in spite of the opposition and remonstrances of Bu Khalum and the Europeans. As the Arabs were not to be turned aside from their project, the leader reluctantly agreed to go with them, and Denham, finding himself helpless, resolved to join the party likewise in order to extend his knowledge of the region.

The mountains of Mandara, to the south of Bornu, were chosen as the most suitable spot for a slave hunt, and thither the raiders proceeded, accompanied by a considerable contingent of the Bornu army.

Leaving Kuka in the middle of April, they reached Mandara towards the end of the month, without any misadventure. Here they found themselves surrounded with mountain scenery, which could scarcely be exceeded for beauty and richness. On all sides interminable chains of hill closed in the view in rugged magnificence and picturesque grandeur. Here, too, nature revelled in its most luxuriant forms among giant trees almost masked under the wealth of creepers which wound around the trunks and branches, or hung in graceful festoons swaying responsive to the passing breeze. Native villages were everywhere to be seen perched airily, like eagles' nests, far up on the rocks and mountain tops, or nestling in the valleys, hidden like the wild deer's lair in the depths of the forest. Such was the lovely district into which the Arabs had come to bring death, ruin, and slavery. But for once they had miscalculated their powers, or depended too much on the co-operation of the Bornu contingent. At the first attack the invaders drove the natives before them, but soon they were outnumbered. Bu Khalum was severely wounded along with the leader of the Bornuese, and Denham received a wound in the face. Beaten on all sides, the only safety of the survivors lay in flight.

A frightful scene ensued. Denham passed through a series of the most marvellous escapes, but at last, unhorsed and unarmed, was seized and stripped, receiving several wounds from spear thrusts in the process. Seeing nothing but a cruel death before him, he resolved to make one more effort to escape, and putting the thought into action, he slipped below a horse, and started for the woods, pursued by two Fulah. Reaching the shelter of the trees, hope revived on his seeing a ravine opening in front of him, and offering a further chance of life. As he was on the point of letting himself down the cliff into the stream, a puff-adder raised its head to strike. He recoiled horror-stricken, and fell headlong into the ravine, his fall fortunately made harmless by a deep pool of water, where, recovering his presence of mind, three strokes of his arms sent him to the opposite side, and placed him in comparative safety among the dense vegetation.

Shortly after, he met the remnants of the defeated party, and six days later they re-entered Kuka, after enduring great hardships.

For the next few months little of importance was done to elucidate the geography of the Chad Region. An expedition westward to Manga was accomplished with less disastrous results than that to the Mandara mountains; and then the rainy season set in, threatening for a time to end the days of the European travellers by the fevers which accompanied it. With the return of the dry season came renewed health and renewed determination to add further to their discoveries.

On the 14th December, Clapperton and Oudney set forth to visit Kano and the Haussa States in the company of a trading caravan.

Two days later a Mr. Toole arrived at Kuka with fresh supplies for the expedition, at a moment when they were much needed.

In the beginning of the year 1824 Denham and Toole started for the district of Logun with the object of visiting the Shari River. The project was safely accomplished, and they found a majestic river 400 yards broad, flowing from the south and south-west into the Chad.

The difficulty of obtaining correct geographical information from the natives was well illustrated in their case, it being clear that they confounded with the Shari a great river (the Benué) they heard of as flowing *from* the south and south-west of Mandara, whereas in reality the latter flows *to* the west. It is extremely probable, however, that some sort of connection exists between them in the wet season.

At Logun Mr. Toole died.

Meanwhile Clapperton and Oudney were travelling towards Kano, and giving shape and form to the confused and conflicting accounts over which geographers had quarrelled for a couple of centuries. Unfortunately on this journey, Oudney, who had never enjoyed good health from the day he left Tripoli, gradually became worse, and died on the 12th January 1824. Left to himself, Clapperton passed on to Kano, which he found to be a town of 30,000 to 40,000 inhabitants, and chiefly important as a trading and industrial centre, it being famed as such from the most remote times.

VIEW IN SOKOTO.

On the 16th of March he reached Sokoto, the capital of the new Fulah Empire, and there was hospitably received by Bello, son and successor of the founder. From Sokoto he hoped to make his way to Yauri and Nupé, to clear up as far as possible the question of the course of the Niger. At first everything looked favourable for his plans, but gradually his hopes vanished, as every one set about dissuading him from attempting the journey.

At last the Sultan himself withdrew his promise of protection, on the plea of excessive danger to his guest. In the face of such a decided veto it was useless to attempt to proceed, though for several weary weeks Clapperton waited on in the hope that something would turn up which would open a way for him. No change for the better occurred, however, and at length he took leave of Sultan Bello, and returned to Bornu.

On September 3rd a caravan having been got together, the homeward journey was commenced.

In the course of the next four months the Sahara was safely recrossed, and Tripoli re-entered on the 26th January, the travellers having been absent nearly three years on their arduous undertaking.

This must be considered the most successful African expedition up to that period—successful alike in its scientific results and in the extent of country explored for the first time. Once for all it settled the question as to the direction in which the mouth of the Niger must be looked for. Certainly it neither flowed east, nor did it end in any known desert or lake. Yet curiously enough, to judge from the travellers' maps, they were still some way behind M'Queen in their knowledge of the general geography of the great eastern tributary of the Niger. Through a misunderstanding on Clapperton's part as to the direction of the Benué, the River Shari was represented as draining its waters from the west instead of from the south and east. But perhaps the most valuable result of the expedition was, that for the first time form and coherence were given to the geography of the Arab writers and traders, and exact information collected regarding the remarkable kingdoms forming the Central Sudan.

CHAPTER XXVII.
THE TERMINATION OF THE NIGER— (Continued).

Among the many valuable results arising from Clapperton and Denham's expedition, not the least important was the great encouragement it gave to renewed enterprise. With the successes of these two explorers the tide of evil fortune seemed to have turned, and they had shown that death or failure did not necessarily meet whomsoever had the temerity to seek to unlock the secrets of Ethiopia.

Clapperton, moreover, had brought back with him from Sokoto the most friendly messages from Bello, the Sultan, expressive of his desire for direct intercourse with the British, and pointing out how that intercourse might best be established by way of the Niger and the West Coast, to which, he asserted, his dominions extended. To take advantage of this more hopeful state of affairs, the British Government organised another expedition, once more with the object of settling the vexed question of the Niger termination, and at the same time opening up a way to the rich provinces of Sokoto, Bornu, &c.

Clapperton was again selected as leader, and with him were associated Captain Pearce and Surgeon Morrison.

The Gulf of Benin was chosen as the landing point, the reason being that there they hoped to find the entrance to the river and follow it to Bussa. On their arrival, however, it was deemed advisable not to lose time and health among the interminable creeks and fatal mangrove swamps known to distinguish the probable delta of the Niger. It was known that Haussa caravans were in the habit of annually descending overland to the coast at Badagry, a point a few miles to the west of what is now known as Lagos. With much wisdom and common sense Clapperton and his companions therefore elected to penetrate to the Niger by this route, and after completing their business with Sokoto, to descend the river in canoes.

On the 7th December 1825 the party left the coast. Hardly, however, had they got beyond earshot of the Atlantic rollers, when it seemed as if the fate which had befallen so many earlier ventures was about to overtake Clapperton's also. Through imprudently sleeping in the open air, they were all attacked by fever. Undismayed and unsubdued, they nevertheless pushed on, staggering forward as best they might. But there were limits to their defiance of disease. Morrison gave in first, and turning to retrace his way to the coast, died on the road. Captain Pearce was the next victim, and he, like the soldier who falls in battle with his face to the foe, dropped on the road, struggling onward to the last.

Though now deprived of both his friends, Clapperton was not yet absolutely alone. He had with him an English servant named Richard Lander, who, with a spirit worthy of such a master, faced all the perils and hardships of the route. Happily, however, by the end of the month the deadly coast belt was safely passed, and healthier lands lay before them. They entered the populous country of Yoruba, with its teeming population, its well cultivated fields, enormous towns, and general air of prosperity. Through Yoruba they passed in a semi-triumphal procession, with no greater trouble to face than the anxiety of the king to keep the white men in his own capital, or the siren wiles of the widow Zuma, who, with her colossal charms, sought to woo them from the path of danger and toil to the flower-strewn haunts of love and ease. Heedless alike, however, of kingly favours and full-fed charms—the widow being fat and twenty—Clapperton held on his way, as also did Lander, who was as little to be seduced from his master's side as his master from the path of duty.

Clapperton had hoped to reach the Niger at Nupé, but news of war and bloodshed in that region caused him to deviate from his intended route and strike the great river somewhat higher up. As the fates would have it, he reached the Niger at the very point where Park had ended at once his voyage and his career. Clapperton's reception seemed to belie the story of Amadi Fatuma as to the manner of Park's death, but a little investigation proved beyond a doubt the truth of its chief particulars. The natives had attacked him under a misconception as to his nationality, and every one spoke with regret of the unhappy catastrophe. The place was pointed out where the boat and crew were lost.

At this point the river is divided into three channels, none more than twenty yards broad when the water is low. The left branch is the only safe one for canoes, the other two being broken up by rocks into dangerous whirlpools and rapids. Bussa itself stands on an island about three miles long by one and a half broad.

From Bussa, Clapperton passed through Nupé and across the Haussa States to Kano. Thence he proceeded to join Bello at Sokoto. He arrived, however, at an unfortunate time. Civil war and rebellion were rife on all hands, and it seemed as if the great Fulah Empire was about to fall to pieces as quickly as it had been built up. Bello, in consequence, was in a fit state to listen to all sorts of insinuations as to the causes which brought the Europeans into his country, and the results that were likely to follow. Accordingly, Clapperton's reception was anything but friendly, and under the worries consequent on his treatment, and the fevers by which he was attacked, he at length succumbed on the 13th April 1827.

Of the members of the expedition there now remained only Richard Lander, who had attached himself to Clapperton with such remarkable fidelity. Three courses were open to him—to return to England by way of the desert and Tripoli, to go back by the way he had come, or thirdly, to attempt to carry out his late master's intention of tracing the Niger to its mouth. Lander was a man of no ordinary intelligence and character, notwithstanding his subordinate position in life, and as if Clapperton's mantle had fallen on him, he elected to do what he could to complete the unfinished work.

With this object in view he returned to Kano from Sokoto, and thence started south to reach the Niger, being under the belief that the great river in that direction was the object of his search—while in reality it was another.

In this, however, he failed. He had almost reached the great town of Yakoba, when his progress was stopped, and he was compelled to return to Kano. Thence he made his way back as he had come through Yoruba to Badagry, which he reached on the 21st November 1827.

The unhappy issue of Clapperton's second expedition somewhat chilled African enterprise for the time being. Our knowledge of the course and termination of the Niger was left exactly where it had been before—though it was made more and more clear that from Bussa it flowed south to Benin. Still the river seemed to lie under some charm fatal to whomsoever should brave it and seek to lift the veil.

The Government began to lose hope, or to conclude that the deadly nature of the climate rendered the discovery of the mouth of the Niger one only of geographical importance. But though they wavered and felt disposed to give up the task, there were still plenty of volunteers eager to make one more attempt.

No matter what the dangers were, Africa had a strange power of fascination which irresistibly drew men under its influence; not those merely who had never set foot on its deadly shore, and who consequently could not fully realise all that travel in Africa meant, but men who had seen their companions die beside them on the road, struck down by disease or the weapon of the savage, and who had themselves known what it was to be at death's door. It is a species of mesmeric influence this of African travel, irresistibly compelling him who has once come beneath its spell to return again and again, even though at last it be to his death.

Lander was no exception to the rule. He went out to Africa knowing nothing, and probably caring less, for the objects of his master's expedition. But he was of the right sort to come beneath the fatal charm; and with the death of his master he felt himself consecrated to the work of exploration. In this spirit he returned to England with Clapperton's journal, only to offer himself for one more effort to complete the task the death of the writer had left unfinished. Such an offer the Government could not very well refuse, though the terms promised by them showed that they had but little faith in a favourable outcome.

RICHARD LANDER.

But Lander was no longer the servant. African travel had ennobled him and placed him in the roll of her knight-errantry. He knew no sordid motives, asked no pay or other remuneration. Success should be his only reward. His enthusiasm infected his brother John with a like spirit, and caused him to throw in his fortunes with him.

The 22nd March 1830 saw the gallant fellows landed at Badagry. They followed practically the same route as Clapperton's expedition to Eyeo, from which they were compelled to take a circuitous northerly course to the Niger at Bussa, which they reached in three months from the coast.

After having paid a visit to the King of Yauri some distance up the river, preparations were commenced for the voyage down to the ocean. With difficulty two canoes were obtained, but at length, on the 20th September, everything was ready for departure. Before pushing clear of the land, the Landers "humbly thanked the Almighty for past deliverances, and fervently prayed that He would always be with us and crown our enterprise with success." Having thus placed themselves under Divine protection, the word was given to push off, and away the canoes glided towards their uncertain bourne.

The first part of the voyage lay through a narrow valley bounded by metamorphic hills, through which the river wound its way in broad curving reaches, broken up at times by inhabited islands, which rose precipitously from the dark waters, and gave variety to the scene. Majestic trees lined the banks, and lent their own peculiar charm to the panoramic landscape, while village and cultivated field spoke of industrious inhabitants. From the latter they had nothing to fear—on the contrary, the travellers were everywhere received hospitably, and sent on their way with prayers for their safety and food for their wants. A more instant danger lay in the numerous rocks which thrust their crests above the water, or more treacherously lay hid beneath, requiring constant watchfulness.

Soon this rocky section was passed, and the district of Nupé entered.

Here the river, emerging from the metamorphic hills, turns eastward and widens, flowing through a broad valley whose precipitous sides form the escarpments of a low sandstone plateau-land. This section is scantily inhabited and sparsely wooded, on account of the fact that while the river is in flood, the great plains which form the bottom of the valley are submerged, and the river assumes the aspect of a lake.

Sixty miles further down is a picturesque range of mountains—now called Rennell's—shortly after passing which comes the town of Egga. From thence the broad valley begins to narrow, and the river to wind in sharp curves through the low sandstone gorges, till, turning sharply to the south, it enters a lake-like expanse, where the Landers found that a large tributary from the east, which they conjectured to be the Tchadda or Benué, joined the main stream. This was the river which Clapperton had confounded with the Shari, though M'Queen had worked out its true relationship to the Niger system.

Immediately beyond the point of junction, the Niger leaves the sandstone plateau and passes through a series of bold picturesque mountains by a narrow gorge, guarded on either side by isolated peaks and table-topped mountains, which frown over the waters in defiant, barren ruggedness. As if to stop all ingress or egress, small islands and hidden rocks rise in mid- stream, round which the swift currents of the contracted river angrily sweep and swirl.

This natural gateway passed, the river expands again into majestic reaches, sunning its full bosom under the tropic sun, unbroken by rock or island. The mountains fall into gentle undulations, and these again into a limitless, flat expanse, but little raised above the level of the river. With every mile the vegetation grows more and more luxuriant, more and more prodigal, till the primeval forest lies before the traveller in all its height and depth and solemnity. Never before had the brothers Lander seen such trees, such a profusion of shrubs, such a tangle of varied creepers.

Here and there villages, charmingly adorned with nodding palms, peeped cosily from their bosky corners in the dark protecting forest. Near the houses stood or lolled groups of scantily clothed natives, passing the lazy hours away in dreamy idleness, as became the lords of creation. Children, naked as the day they were born, gambolled in the river like frogs; and women, ever at work, busied themselves with domestic cares. At some places battle had been given to the rank luxuriance of nature, and small clearings made in the forest for the raising of yams, beans, or sugar-canes.

Not least inviting in the scene was the Niger itself. Now it spread before the voyagers like a beautiful lake, ringed with fringing festooned trees, and flashing brilliantly under the rays of the tropic sun. Again, far ahead, the forest frame opened and displayed the serpentine course of the silvery river, edged with yellow banks of sand. Canoes were seen gliding swiftly down stream, or with more laborious paddling were forced upward against the current. On the banks left by the falling waters, crocodiles disposed their repulsive length like rotting logs of wood, while in the deeper pools the hippos snorted defiance. Waterfowl in great numbers skimmed along the surface of the water, fished in the shallows, or rested on *terra firma*.

The scene was arcadian and fascinating seen from the river. A closer acquaintance did not enhance its attractiveness. The voyagers were now among a people far different from those above the confluence of the Niger and the Benué (Tchadda). Here were only Pagan savages, steeped in the lowest barbarism, and ruled by the grossest superstition. Murder and plunder were in congenial union with fetishism and cannibalism, and hospitality was unknown. Only by force could Lander get his men to venture into this dangerous region. That their fears were not mere fancies was speedily proved on the very first occasion of landing, and again later on they only escaped utter destruction, to fall into semi-captivity to a party of men in large canoes who were up river ready to trade with the strong, and to attack and plunder the weak.

The travellers now found themselves among people who came from near the sea, and who had not only heard of, but had actually traded with Europeans. It was therefore in no despondent mood that they submitted to their fate, and proceeded on their way, the captives of the Ibo.

Soon it was clear that the delta of the river had been reached. From being a united volume of water it began to break up into numerous branches, running in all directions. At the apex of the delta the land was dry, and clad with palm oil groves and silk cotton trees. Gradually, however, these disappeared, and as the dry land gave place to hybrid swamp, the mangrove asserted its ownership. Nature then showed as repulsive an aspect as is to be met with in any other region on the face of the globe—what was swamp when the tide was out resembling a submerged forest when the tide was in, and both then and at all other times, reeking with pestilential vapours from the slimy mud oozing from between the octopus-like roots of the mangrove.

AKASSA.

In passing through this foul region the travellers had little reason to wonder that no one had ever ventured to explore the labyrinthine creeks and river branches which penetrated the mangrove in all directions, but seemed to lead to nowhere in particular.

On the 24th November 1830 the dull thunder of the Atlantic rollers breaking on the shore came like sweetest music to the travellers' ears, growling a gruff but hearty welcome, and soon the sea itself lay before them—its cool healthy breezes fanning them with delicious touch, its gleaming limitless expanse fair as a glimpse of heaven.

The Niger mystery was solved at last, and the river portals thrown wide open to the world, never again to be closed.

CHAPTER XXVIII.
FILLING UP THE DETAILS.

While Clapperton and Lander were thus bringing the work of Park to a successful conclusion, and proving the accuracy of M'Queen's geography of the Niger basin, there were others at work in the region which the labours and death of their great pioneer had made classic ground. Major Laing, in the course of a Government mission, had travelled from Sierra Leone to Falaba, in the country of Sulima, and ascertained that the Niger took its rise in the Highlands of Kurauka, some 70 miles south-west of Falaba, and not more than 150 miles east of Sierra Leone. The river itself he was prevented from reaching, but none the less did he come under the irresistible influence of its fascination.

More than ever had Timbuktu and the Niger become names to conjure with, as well as to infect men with a species of reckless self-sacrifice that no amount of past experience, prudence, or common sense could dispel. As in the case of Lander, and others of his predecessors, having once tasted the bitter-sweet of African exploration, there could be no rest for Major Laing until he had gathered again the magic fruit. Accordingly, after an interval of three years, he once more set forth, determined to carry his cherished dreams into realisation.

Timbuktu and the Upper Niger were the goals of his journey. Like Denham and Clapperton, he took Tripoli as his starting-point. Thence he passed south-west to Ghadamis and the oasis of Twat. Between the latter and Timbuktu lay the wild wastes of the Sahara—never trodden by man without extreme risk of encounter with plunder and bloodshed-loving nomads, and death from thirst or privation. Even these factors of an African journey had their wild attraction for men of Laing's temperament, adding a *sauce piquante*, as it were, to the otherwise monotonous march and daily routine of worry and privation. To such, too, the frowning immensity of the Sahara—the frightful desolation which marks its every feature—and the flaming sun and lurid heavens that hang above it, have elements which strike them with the profoundest feelings of awe, and leave an indelible impress on their minds.

For sixteen days after leaving Twat, Laing underwent all these sensations in their most striking form; and that his experiences of desert travel might be complete, he was attacked at night by a party of Tuareg marauders, and left for dead, with no less than twenty-four wounds. Thanks, however, to the secret elixir of heroic minds and the soundness of his constitution, he miraculously recovered, and undismayed, continued his way to Timbuktu, which was reached on the 18th August 1826.

Laing was the first European who had ever entered that historic city, which for four centuries had been the loadstone of kings, merchants, and savants. He arrived in an unhappy hour. Only a short time before the first waves of the approaching tide of Fulah influence had entered the region of the Upper Niger. Already Timbuktu had felt its strange power, though resenting the political position usurped by the ministers of the new revival.

For a month Laing was allowed to remain unmolested. Then he was ordered to leave the city of the Faithful. There was no resisting the mandate, and he passed forth on the 22nd September, only to be foully murdered two days later by the people who had undertaken to escort him across the desert. With him unfortunately perished the records of his observations and inquiries.

Two years later, Caillé, a somewhat illiterate, though persevering and intrepid Frenchman, entered the city from which Laing had been driven forth. Years before, this young explorer, in his far-off French home, had heard the echoes of African enterprise. Inflamed with the romantic story, he had seen by the blank maps of the continent how much there was to be done, and what fame there was to be acquired by him who could make his mark on those still virgin sheets. To be an African traveller became thenceforth the object of his life. For years he dreamed of and prepared himself for the work. But it was one thing to dream of—one thing even to reach the threshold of new lands—and quite another to penetrate them, as he soon found. Time after time his hopes, when almost at the point of realisation, were rudely dashed to the ground; but uncrushed, he waited his time and opportunity, though without private means, and conscious that the ears of the wealthy and the powerful were deaf to his schemes and representations.

But while Caillé dreamed and petitioned he also worked. As a subordinate official under the Government of Sierra Leone, he was enabled by dint of economy and industry to save the sum of £80. To him this slender sum appeared the "open sesame" of fame and fortune. It was the instrument whereby he should open the oyster shell, and gain the priceless pearl within.

On the 19th April 1827, Caillé left Kakundy, on the River Nunez, and midway between Sierra Leone and the Gambia, in the company of a small caravan of Mandingoes. Travelling east, he crossed the country of Futa Jallon, through which northward ran the upper tributaries of the Senegal, and eastward those of the Niger. The latter river was reached at Kurusa, in the district of Kankan, and was found to be even there a fine stream from eight to ten feet deep.

Having crossed the Niger, he continued east to the country of Wasulu, a well cultivated and thickly inhabited region. Thence he travelled north-east, till at length he again reached the banks of the Niger, a short distance to the west of Jenné. This town he was the first European to enter, though Park had seen it on his last journey.

From Jenné, Caillé sailed down the Niger in a rudely built vessel of considerable dimensions to Kabara, the port of Timbuktu, whence he proceeded on horseback to the city itself.

The aspect of Timbuktu in nowise realised the glowing anticipations of the traveller. Instead of the wealthy and powerful city, touched with the glamour of the shining orient, which he had been taught to expect, there lay before him only a collection of miserable mud buildings, among which rose several mosques, looking imposing only in comparison with the rude huts around them. To the north-east and south spread the immensity of the great desert as one vast plain of burning, repellent sands, over which the silence of death brooded, except where pariah dogs or loathsome vultures feasted on the carrion or offal thrown out of the town. Such was the place in which Commerce had established her Central African emporium, and gathered together the trading veins and arteries which ramified more or less throughout the whole of North-eastern Africa. Here, too, amid these dreary wastes, Moslem learning had made her seat; and here the religion of Islam had found an abiding centre from which to radiate its influence into the most barbarous depths of negro Africa.

Seen thus in relation to its surroundings, its position, and its functions, the mud huts and rudely built mosques which compose it acquire a tinge of the sublime, and strike the imagination more even than the stupendous wonders of a London or a Paris.

For a fortnight Caillé—secure in his disguise—remained in Timbuktu, after which he set forth with a caravan to cross the desert to Morocco. Along no other part of the Sahara does the desert appear in such a terror-striking aspect. Through one tract the caravan had to travel with all possible expedition for ten days, not a drop of water being obtainable. The privations endured were indescribable, men and animals alike being reduced to the direst extremity before water was reached and their tortures assuaged. Further north similar experiences awaited them, till the caravan arrived at the River Dra. Thence the march was performed with comparative comfort by way of Tafilet and the Atlas to Fez and Tangier, where Caillé arrived on the 18th August 1828.

TIMBUKTU.

With Lander's descent of the Niger from Bussa to the sea, the course of Niger enterprise received a new development and impetus. The glowing accounts brought back by its explorers of the rich lands and powerful civilised kingdoms through which it flowed found eager hearers in England; and now that an entrance had been found by which the heart of these promising regions could be reached, such hearers were not slow to act and test in a practical fashion the commercial value of the great waterway.

In this new movement Macgregor Laird, of Liverpool, was the leading spirit. Under his instructions two steamers were specially constructed for the work. Laird himself took command, and with him were associated Lander, and Lieutenant Allen of the navy, with Dr. Briggs and Mr. Oldfield as medical attendants.

Hardly had the party entered the Nun branch of the river, in August 1832, when the malaria commenced its ravages, causing the death of a captain and two seamen. The first business of the expedition was to find a suitable navigable channel among the many bewildering branches, creeks, and backwaters which spread a labyrinthine network over the delta, whose mangrove swamps were "uninviting when descried, repulsive when approached, dangerous when examined, and horrible and loathsome when their qualities and their inhabitants were known." Here the air reeked with the essence of poisonous odours—damp, clammy, and deadly; and the nights were made hideous by the never-ceasing attacks of clouds of mosquitoes and sandflies.

VIEW OF THE NIGER ABOVE LOKOJA.

For six weeks Laird was engaged in his exploration of the delta, with the result that eighteen men succumbed to fever. For a time the expedition threatened to end in the death of the entire party, hardly one escaping the dire effects of the malaria. But Laird and his companions were men not easily discouraged or defeated, and at length they got away from the deadly area, and reached the undivided river and healthier upper regions. It was like an escape from a loathsome purgatory to an earthly paradise, when the party sailed into the open reaches of the noble stream, barred in by tropic forest and swept by cooling breezes. Viewed commercially,however, the prospect proved somewhat unsatisfactory, and did not correspond with the glowing hopes with which the party had left England. There was no thought, however, of giving way to the first feeling of disappointment, and in the belief that matters would improve once beyond the barbarous zone, they continued their way up the river. Unfortunately, they had chosen the wrong time of the year to make the ascent. Already the river was falling. More than once the larger of the two steamers grounded on sand-banks, and finally had to be laid up till the rising of the waters should set in once more. Attempts to reach Rabba signally failed, though Laird ascended the Benué some distance in a boat.

In the following season Oldfield and Lander were more successful. The Benué was ascended to a distance of 104 miles before they were compelled to return from want of supplies. On the Main Niger they were also more fortunate than in the previous year. Rabba was safely reached, and found to contain a population little short of 40,000, being at that time the capital of Nupé.

Beyond Rabba it was found impossible to proceed, and it was deemed advisable to return to the coast, to recruit and prepare for another attempt to establish a trade in the river.

This new venture, however, ended in disaster. On the way back Lander was shot, and was only kept alive till Fernando Po was reached. With him ended for the time being Macgregor Laird's enterprise. Though carried out with splendid persistence and self-sacrifice, its results were sadly negative, while out of the forty-nine Europeans who had been engaged in it only nine survived the fevers.

For several years nothing more was done to turn what was only too well named "the white man's grave" to further account. In 1840, however, Governor Beecroft ascended the river to within thirty miles of Bussa, and got back without much loss of life, though adding but little to our knowledge of the geography of the region.

Meanwhile philanthropists were as much interested in the opening up of the Niger basin to European influence as was the commercial world. Laird's expedition, though having trade as its primary object, "hoped also to aid in suppressing the slave trade, in introducing true religion, civilisation, and humanising influences among natives whose barbarism had hitherto been only heightened by European connection."

These unselfish aims were further emphasised in 1841, when the Government, still undaunted by the fatal character of the work, sent out three steamers with the object of making treaties with the Niger chiefs for the suppression of the slave trade. A model farm was to be established at the confluence of the Benué and the main river, to teach the natives better methods of agriculture, and generally the foundations were to be laid of the great British Empire of which M'Queen had dreamed. Thus, in some small way, expiation was to be made for the sins of earlier generations. Everything that science and forethought could suggest was done to make this expedition a success, but unhappily no way had yet been found to ward off the insidious attacks of malaria, or counteract the effects of the fever germs once they had gained a footing in the system. The result was death and disaster. No higher point than Egga was reached, and that only by one steamer. Out of one hundred and forty-five men, forty-eight died within the two months the vessels were in the river.

The project of turning the Niger to profitable account, in the face of such frightful mortality and deadly climatic conditions, seemed now to be utterly hopeless. From Major Houghton downwards, death by violence, privation, or disease had been the fate of whoever had attempted to open it up to European influence. No other river had such a romantic history of heroic self-sacrifice —none such a martyr roll—none such a record of heroism and precious blood apparently uselessly thrown away.

Was it really all in vain? Was neither the European nor the native to derive any benefit from the exploration of this silvery streak through the beautiful West Coast Highlands, the densely populated plains of Sego and Massina, the depopulated half desert wilderness of Songhay and Gandu, the forest depths of Igara and Ado, and the mangrove swamps around the Bight of Benin. Were Park, Clapperton, Lander, and all the other explorers of the Niger basin, only to be remembered in future ages for the heroic virtues they had shown, and not as the pioneers of a new era of hope to the African—the founders of a great national enterprise, bright with promise alike to Britain and to Africa?

The thought of such an ending was not to be entertained without reluctance, yet it seemed inevitable. Savage opposition and ordinary physical difficulties might in time be overcome, but who could fight against the disease which lurked unseen in the fœtid depths of mangrove forests, and filled the air with its poisonous germs? Who could avoid the incurable blight of its deadly breath?

Already such questions had been asked, when the failure of Tuckey's expedition gave pause for a time to Niger exploration, till Clapperton and Denham, attacking the region from the rear, had made the despondent once more hopeful. Strangely enough, the recurrence of the same crisis brought with it a similar cure.

In 1849 an expedition set forth from Tripoli, under Government auspices this time, commanded by Richardson, and Drs. Barth and Overweg.

The frontiers of Bornu were safely reached, and here the party divided— never to meet again. Richardson and Overweg went the way of Toole and Oudney, and only Barth was left to carry out the objects of the expedition. Right worthily he performed his task. Never before had such a rich harvest of geographical, historical, ethnographical, and philological facts been gathered in the African field of research.

From Kanem to Timbuktu, from Tripoli to Adamawa, he laid the land under contribution. Vain would it be in the restricted space of these pages to follow him in his wonderful travels. It may be noted, however, that while travelling south-west from Kuka in Bornu to the Fulah province of Adamawa, he reached on the 18th June 1851 the river Benué, at its junction with the Faro, and 415 geographical miles in a direct line from its confluence with the Niger. Not since leaving Europe had he seen so large and imposing a river. Even at this distant point the Benué, or "Mother of Waters," is half a mile broad, and runs with a swift current to the west. It was said to rise nine days' journey to the south-east, while the Faro came from a mountain seven days' journey distant.

Only second in importance to his discovery of the Benué so far to the east of the Niger, was his exploration of the great bend of the Niger itself.

Travelling from Bornu, he passed west through Sokoto and Gandu to the Niger at Say, some distance above the point where the Gulbi-n-Gindi from

Sokoto joins the main river.

From Say he travelled in a north-easterly direction across the great bend, among wild Tuareg tribes, and the romantic mountains of Hombori, to Timbuktu. Thence he once more returned to the safer Haussa States along the river banks, whereon no European eye save Park's had ever before rested. Here he was in the centre of the once wonderful Songhay Empire, of which the sole relics left after the destructive blows of Moor, Tuareg, and Fulah, were a few miserable villages, whose inhabitants eked out a wretched existence, equally ground down by drought and the ravages of human marauders.

One result of Barth's discovery of the Benué so near Lake Chad was the despatch of another expedition, to determine if possible the navigability of the river, a point which previous attempts had failed to settle satisfactorily.

Macgregor Laird was again the leading spirit in this new enterprise, and anything that past experience could suggest was taken advantage of to ensure a successful trip. Dr. Baikie, R.N., and D. J. May, R.N., went as surveying officers and leaders, several other gentlemen being associated with them. This in some respects was the most successful of the Government surveying expeditions, for it not only explored and surveyed the Benué for a distance of 340 miles, but returned without any special loss of life.

With this trip practically closed our Government's participation in the work of opening up the Niger. Thenceforth it contented itself with sending from time to time a gunboat into the river on some punitive mission, but no special attempts were made to further enlighten the world as to its geography and resources. Henceforth all such work was left to private enterprise, Government remaining aloof, disposed neither to encourage nor discourage, but clearly satisfied that nothing of importance could be made of a partially navigable river, flowing through a country of seemingly no great commercial capabilities, and with a climate which made colonisation out of the question, and even a residence, however short, almost impossible to the average European.

CHAPTER XXIX.
THE FRENCH ADVANCE TO THE NIGER.

With the practical withdrawal of our Government from Niger enterprise, M'Queen's magnificent dream of British Empire in the heart of Africa seemingly vanished for ever. A new school of politicians appeared in our national councils who had so little read the secrets of our country's greatness, that their cry was for no more foreign expansion—no more colonial responsibilities.

The influence of the retrograde movement soon began to tell on the fortunes of West Africa. Already its natural development had been retarded by a deadly climate, a scarcity of valuable products, and the barbarity and laziness of its inhabitants. To these were now added Government neglect and mismanagement. Administrators and governors were told to restrict their operations to the narrowest limits. Merchants were either debarred access to the interior, or informed that they would advance at their own risk, and with no hope of Government support. Geographical enterprise shared in the general blight. The work of exploring a region which had become classic through the travels and martyred lives of so many of Britain's most worthy sons was stopped.

Needless to say, such a policy led to disgraceful results. British influence was confined to the coast region, there to eke out a miserable political and commercial existence among its deadly swamps; our governors were given the old woman's task of administering ludicrously unsuitable laws, or palavering over petty disputes with still more petty tribal chiefs; our merchants, thanks to the conditions under which they were placed, became degraded into barterers of gin, rum, tobacco, gunpowder, and guns, the best Europe had to give in return for Africa's oils, gold, and ivory. But while we were thus degenerating into an invertebrate abortion of British colonial genius, fit occupant of slimy swamps and fever-breeding jungles, a continental rival was preparing to step into our shoes, and reap the reward of our former labours.

Almost coincidently with the practical throwing up of our work on the Lower Niger, the French began to bestir themselves on the Senegal, and cast longing eyes towards Bambarra and the Upper Niger. They too began to dream of Central African Empire—as once M'Queen had done—and to see far off in the future their flag supreme from the Mediterranean coast line of Algiers to the shores of the Atlantic. The key of the situation they clearly saw lay in the

Niger. Once established there, with the necessary openings to the west, they would have command of the whole of the Western Sudan, and possibly also of the Central Region.

With patient foresight they began to send explorers along the line of proposed conquest, carrying with them ready-made treaties, French flags, and blank maps. Already French influence had made itself felt far up the river, and forts had been established in the very earliest days of their rule. Such of the latter as had fallen into ruins or had been deserted were once more occupied and repaired, and new advance posts were pushed further into the heart of the country.

Soon they had firmly established themselves as high up the Senegal as the point where Park in his first expedition had crossed it on his way to Kaarta. This was the limit of the river's navigability in the wet season. But no consideration of natural difficulties gave limit to their dream of power.

In 1863, two officers, E. Mage and Dr. Quintin, prospected a way to the Niger across the intervening highlands lying between the two rivers. French arms were not slow to follow where French explorers led, and speedy preparations were made to complete the base of operations for the final advance to their promised land.

Meanwhile our representatives on the coast, stewing in their miserable, disease-stricken belt, were not blind to the progress being made by our enterprising neighbours, nor unaware of their vast designs of conquest and commercial monopoly, and the probable result to England's political and commercial position in these regions. In vain they drew the attention of the Home Government to the situation, and asked for power to act before it was too late. They were but as voices crying in the wilderness, to which as little heed was paid as gives the Bedouin to the desert mirage. More than that, the coast authorities were told to let the French go where they liked, and not to throw any obstacles in their way.

The French were not slow to take advantage of the field thus left open to them. By 1880 their line of forts on the Senegal was completed, and everything ready for their next move. For this enterprise Captain Gallieni was appointed leader, and at the head of a small army of drilled troops, and a considerable train of donkeys, native drivers, native servants, &c., he started in 1880 on his mission of planting the French flag on the Upper Niger, where, from our geographical position and priority of exploration, the Union Jack alone should have floated.

As far as the confluence of the Bakhoy and the Bafing, the march of Gallieni was attended by nothing worse than the usual amount of worry and trouble incident to the passage of a small army through a barbarous or semi-barbarous country. Beyond, however, lay the unoccupied and but partially explored country between the Senegal and the Niger. Here the special trials and cares of the expedition commenced. Food was often obtained with difficulty. Their advance was naturally viewed with suspicion by the natives, and much care and tact was required to prevent friction. In spite of all obstructions, however, they gradually pushed south towards their goal, leaving French flags in the hands of the chiefs, and bearing with them treaties placing the latter and their people under the protection of France.

Before the Niger was reached the expedition came near being destroyed by a determined attack made on it by a people called Beleris. The Beleris were successfully repulsed, however, and two days later Bammaku on the Niger was reached, where already the tricolour was found floating—an advance section of the party having succeeded in concluding the customary treaty. By what means the treaty was obtained we are not told, though we do learn that Gallieni's reception was cold and inhospitable.

It now only remained to get to Sego, to see the Suzerain of the Upper Niger chiefs and kings, and conclude a treaty with him. For this purpose Gallieni crossed the Niger and travelled along the south side of the river. On his arrival in the neighbourhood of the capital, he was stopped, and ordered to remain where he was, till his business was settled. Many weary weeks and months were passed in the attempt to get Amadu, the Sultan of Sego, to sign a treaty, placing his country under a French protectorate. In the end the necessary signature was obtained, and from that moment French rule—on paper—was supreme from the sources of the Niger to Timbuktu.

France, however, was by no means inclined to be satisfied with a merely mental recognition of her authority. With splendid energy and perseverance she pushed forward her forts into the valley of the Bakhoy—the watershed of the two rivers; and finally built herself an abiding habitation on the Niger itself. At the same time a railway was commenced, having for its object the connection of the highest navigable point of the Senegal with Bammaku. At the same time a gunboat was carried over in sections, and put together on the river, as a further symbol of French authority, and a potent instrument to spread its influence.

To further secure their prize from the possible results of the awakening of the British Government, France set about isolating the River Gambia by a cordon of treaties, leaving the waterway British, but making all else French. To make her position yet more strong, all the countries towards the upper tributaries and sources of the Niger were placed under French protection, and almost the entire coast line from the Gambia south to Sierra Leone was taken possession of. And through it all our Government peacefully slept on, having left orders not to be awakened; or it woke up only to blink approval, delighted to be rid of the whole troublesome business.

Sixty years before M'Queen had written—"France is already established on the Senegal, and commands that river, and if the supineness and carelessness of Great Britain allow that powerful, enterprising, and ambitious rival to step before us and fix herself securely on the Niger, then it is evident that with such a settlement in addition to her command of the Senegal, France will command all Northern Africa. The consequences cannot fail to be fatal to the best interests of this country, and by means surer than even by war and conquest, tend ultimately to bring ruin on our best tropical colonial establishment."

What M'Queen had feared, had now come to pass, as regards the political aspect of the action of the French in the Niger kingdoms. It still remains to be seen what is to be the commercial outcome of their African dream.

CHAPTER XXX.
THE ROYAL NIGER COMPANY.

It has ever been a good thing for British commercial enterprise that its agents have never had to rely on their Government to pioneer new trade routes, and secure for them unexploited territory. Our merchants have required nothing but a free hand to cut out their own paths, and that the fruits of their labours should not be taken from them by the political action of other nationalities. What has been accomplished on these terms let half our colonies say.

The above rule, though general, has not been invariably applied, as witness the case of West Africa, already described, in which, as the result of Government restriction and interference, the harvest of British labour has passed into French hands, and commercial enterprise has become crushed and degraded along with the regions in which it has been carried on.

Happily for our position in West Central Africa, the Niger basin never fell under these blighting influences. When our Government withdrew from that region it withdrew completely, otherwise there would have been yet another chapter of lamentable mal-administration and gross betrayal of a nation's trust to add to the annals of West African history.

The Niger was thus left free to be made the most of by the operations of private enterprise.

For a few years after Baikie's expedition nothing more was done to establish a trade in the river. Not that the task was abandoned as hopeless. On the contrary, new plans were germinating and steadily taking shape and form preparatory to renewed attempts under more hopeful conditions.

By this time people had begun to realise more thoroughly the nature of a tropical life, and knew better how to fight the insidious and dangerous influences of excessive heat and moisture, and the germs of disease they fostered. By substituting quinine for the lancet in the treatment of fever, that hitherto deadly disease had been robbed of half its terrors.

Once more Macgregor Laird—a name that must be bracketed with those of Park, M'Queen, and Lander—was the leader in the new movement. Undaunted by past losses and failures—on the contrary, shown by their teaching how victory was to be achieved—he again entered the Niger in 1852
—this time not to leave it till he had laid the permanent foundations of British commercial influence.

In this new enterprise the pioneer did not restrict himself to mere voyages up the river and passing calls at the chief marketing centres. He established stations at various points, in the form of movable hulks moored in the river, which had the double advantage of being capable of removal bodily, and of providing a certain measure of security from hostile attack. At the same time, profiting by past experience of the deadly nature of the climate, the number of European agents was reduced to a minimum, and educated coast natives were employed instead.

Palm oil, ivory, and Benni-seed were the sole products exported—cotton goods, metals of various kinds, beads and salt, being the chief articles given in exchange. Nearer the coast, gin, rum, gunpowder, and guns were largely in demand, as a result of the old shameful days of slave dealing. A profitable trade was soon established, and before many years Macgregor Laird had to compete with new firms who sought to share the profits.

But though the Europeans thus increased in numbers, their position continued to be extremely precarious. The cannibal tribes of the delta were not slow to recognise that their monopoly of the trade of the upper river was being completely abolished, and they sought to bar the way by incessant attacks on the steamers and stations of the various traders. These having conflicting interests, could not be made to combine for common action against the common enemy. From time to time a gunboat paid a hurried punitive visit, but produced no permanent impression upon the refractory inhabitants.

The result of this divided action on the part of the traders, and the growing power and truculence of the native tribes, was extremely disastrous for Macgregor Laird, who eventually was forced to retire from the river.

Along with the growing dangers to the various houses engaged in the Niger trade, new troubles began to loom up before them, retarding the proper and healthy commercial development of the region, and threatening all in a common ruin. At first the field to be exploited was so large that the traders came but little into conflict. Gradually, however, with the entrance of new firms, and the planting of new stations, they began to encroach on each other's districts. The result was soon seen in the keen competition which ensued. The price of native produce began to go up, till it threatened to rise above its value. To keep the trade going profitably the agents were forced to become more and more unscrupulous as to the nature of the articles of import
—more and more regardless of the claims of their commercial competitors. Each sought to drive the other out, and the natives, not slow to see the advantages to themselves, did their best to encourage the strife. Under such conditions all legitimate progress was rendered impossible. At any given point the inhabitants were in a position to say, Thus far shalt thou go and no further, or could clear the merchants out if they thought fit. Enterprise

requiring considerable outlay was out of the question when the fruits were probably to be reaped only by rivals. The trade, from being restricted to useful articles, was rapidly degenerating, so as largely to include vile spirits and weapons of destruction. Gradually the conditions of competition were making a wholesome trade an impossibility, and the natives, instead of being bettered spiritually and materially by European intercourse, were being driven down into deeper depths of barbarism. A state of things which our prophet M'Queen had foretold in these memorable words—"If this erroneous policy is pursued, then to the latest period of time the central and southern parts of that vast continent are doomed to remain in the same deplorable state of ignorance, degradation, and misery which has been their lot during the lapse of three hundred years."

This was a consummation of their labours which the merchants could not contemplate with equanimity. That they were honourable men we have no reason to doubt. True, they went to the Niger in order to make money, but they had no thought of growing wealthy on the ruin and degradation of the people among whom they traded. They had become the victims of the circumstances under which their business was carried on, whereby they were driven irresistibly and even unwittingly into the deplorable situation in which they at length found themselves. In a manner they were more to be pitied than blamed, for they had conjured up a Frankenstein that threatened to be their ruin. To one and all it was alike clear that as long as open unregulated competition lasted, the character of the trade could not be altered—must indeed go from bad to worse—their profits become less and less, and their footing in the country more precarious, subject as it was to the whims, enmities, extortions, and restrictions of the barbarous tribes, armed by the traders themselves with guns which on occasion were turned against the vendors.

A turning point in the commercial history of the Niger had been reached, and everything now depended on the course pursued whether the next departure would be for the weal or for the woe of all concerned.

Happily the right man was forthcoming at this critical juncture, when the necessity of a change was evident to all. Clear-headed, far-seeing business men were in the trade—the peers among British merchants wherever engaged; but something more was wanted in him who should extricate his fellows from the difficult situation in which they had placed themselves. Some one was needed who, with business instincts and knowledge, should combine the *savoir faire* and knowledge of the world of the diplomatist. Such an one was Sir George T. Goldie—then Mr. G. Goldie Taubman—a name which, like that of Macgregor Laird, must ever rank in the galaxy of great names associated with the annals of Niger enterprise.

At the time Sir George Goldie joined the Central African Company of London, the only other houses in the river were Messrs. Miller & Co., Glasgow, the West African Company of Manchester, and Mr James Pinnock of Liverpool. Trade was carried on as far north as Egga, though commercially the Benué still remained a closed river. A visit to the seat of operations was sufficient to make Sir George aware of the exact situation, and the absolute necessity of a change, if a legitimate and at the same time profitable trade were to be continued. The other firms were already impressed with the same opinion, and the result of a little laying of heads together was the amalgamation of all the firms into the United African Company in the year 1879.

The happy results of this policy were soon made apparent in improved profits. The expense of management was enormously reduced. Where formerly there had been floating hulks, permanent stations were built on land, and at the same time the number was increased. The Company thus found itself on an altogether new footing with the natives, who could now be treated with on equal terms. The trade grew by leaps and bounds, and bade fair to become of national importance.

Naturally such prosperity could not continue without attracting the envious attention of other nations, and more especially of the French, who, having succeeded far beyond their wildest expectations in reaping the harvest sown by the English in the Upper Niger basin, hoped by a little judicious manipulation to be able to do the same along the lower course of the river, and so carry out their dream of an almost exclusive African Empire stretching from Benin to the Mediterranean.

Under the patronage, more or less open, of Gambetta—certainly instigated and encouraged by him—the first feelers were thrown out in the establishment of two commercial associations—the Compagnie Française de l'Afrique Equatoriale of Paris, with a capital of £160,000; and the Compagnie du Senegal et de la Côte Occidentale d'Afrique of Marseilles, with a subscribed capital of £600,000.

Happily for British enterprise in the Niger basin our interests were watched over by argus eyes, else the course of events would have taken a different turn, French commerce bringing everywhere with it the French flag and administrative system, to the eventual strangling of any trade of ours.

The United African Company, till then private, was promptly thrown open to the public, and the capital raised to a million sterling. Thus provided with "the sinews of war," the Company proceeded to give battle to the foreign interlopers, and speedily swept them out of the entire region. None the less, however, did the French contrive to do incalculable harm during their brief inglorious career, under which the gin trade flourished, and further anarchy was spread among the savage tribes, as usual ever ready to take full advantage of division and enmity among the European traders.

With the annihilation of the French Companies our merchants once more reigned supreme, and all immediate danger of French political and commercial aggression was completely quashed.

The footing, however, which the former had even temporarily been able to effect, had shown the precarious position of the British Company's hold on the country, unsupported as they were by Government backing. They were still open to renewed attempts at aggression—still liable to have the fruits of their labour and enterprise wrested from them. Under such conditions there could be no real attempts to develop the resources of the country, or introduce new civilising institutions among the natives, to effect which ends it was perfectly clear that two things were necessary—first, that the Niger basin below Timbuktu should be declared British, as a guarantee against all further foreign intrusion; and second, that a Royal Charter should be obtained, under the authority of which the Company would be enabled to proceed with the work of development and progress.

The necessity of this latter step had already been foreseen by M'Queen long before the Lower Niger had been explored, except in M'Queen's own mind. With an insight truly prophetic, he pointed out that if ever Great Britain's mission in the Niger was to be achieved, it could only be by means of a Chartered Company. While deprecating a prolonged term of privilege, he argues that its duration ought not to be narrowed too much, otherwise that circumstance would tend to discourage the merchant, and prevent him from laying out money at the first outset, or embarking in the trade with that vigour which alone could render it productive and successful.

In answer to the argument against exclusive privilege, he shows that this exclusive privilege is for a trade yet to be formed, and that the commercial conditions of a civilised and an uncivilised country are totally different. In the latter "everything is to do. Regular commerce is to be created. Society is almost altogether to be formed. Security and civilisation, law, order, and religion are each and all yet to be introduced. Unity of action and design, therefore, become absolutely necessary to accomplish all these desirable objects—conflicting interests amidst such a disjointed population must and will indefinitely retard it. A charter is clearly and indispensably necessary in order to conduct mercantile affairs to a prosperous issue—in order to regulate the supply, to explore the country and find out the proper markets, to negotiate as an irresistible and stable power with the native princes, to purchase lands, to protect trade, to punish aggression, to rear up gradually an empire in Africa such as had been done in India, against which no native power shall be able to raise its head. Then and not till then the trade may be thrown open.... Without such regulations for a time there is too good reason to dread that our connection with Africa will never be more than the transient visitations of insulated merchants," &c. &c. In these and other remarkable words M'Queen graphically sketches the history of the sixty years of British intercourse with the Niger subsequent to the time at which he wrote. Only after such a lapse of time, and through a long series of mistakes and the rude buffeting of facts, were our eyes opened to the necessity of taking his advice.

Even then, however, the National African Company might have petitioned the Government in vain to make the Niger secure from foreign aggression, or to put them on the only possible footing to exploit and develop a savage country lying under the blight of a deadly climate, but for the sudden awaking of Europe to the supposed-to-be vast latent possibilities of the African continent. A magnificent bubble was puffed up into view, dazzling all eyes with its iridescent hues, and inflaming all minds with its promise of wealth and power. European commerce was to be regenerated—the pressure on the population was to be relieved—nations were to rise in power and importance. El Dorado and Second India were terms too weak to express the possibilities of the future when Africa was under discussion.

Under the electric glow of the new craze deserts were made to bloom like Eden, swamps became veritable arcadias, the wilderness was repeopled, and peace and a demand for European goods were discovered to be the prevailing characteristics of the natives. The result was the scramble for Africa, in which the chief nations of Europe made themselves ridiculous by the indecent haste with which they rushed to raise their respective flags. Our own Government was the last to feel the quickening influences, and then only awoke under the pressure of public opinion, and after much that should have been ours had been lost.

But for the National African Company the Niger would probably now have fallen a prey to France or Germany, but with admirable forethought they had strengthened their position and secured their rights by treaties with every native tribe from the mouth of the Niger to the Benué. By virtue of persistent nagging at the Foreign Office, these treaties were recognised by Government, and a protectorate proclaimed over the region thus acquired.

Then came the Berlin Conference in the winter of 1884, in which the free navigation of the Niger was established, but the administration of the river from Timbuktu to the sea was left in the hands of the British.

This was much; but more remained to be done. The Niger and Benué above their confluence still lay open to political and commercial aggression, which might be fatal to the best interests of this country as well as to the Company which had already done so much.

Thanks to the persistent efforts of one Herr Flegel, the Germans were not slow to recognise this fact. This indefatigable trader and explorer commenced his career as a clerk in a trading house in Lagos. Filled with an ambition to explore and extend German influence, he contrived to ascend the Niger in British mission steamers and trading vessels, spying out the land wherever he went, and ever on the outlook how the British bread he ate might be turned to German account. With much daring and industry, and assisted by German funds, he added much on subsequent trips to our knowledge of some parts of the Niger and Benué.

The result of his inquiries and exploration was to fire the German Colonial Society with the hope of establishing their national influence in the regions beyond the British Protectorate.

Happily the National African Company were as usual wideawake, and soon became aware of the new danger which threatened them. Immediately they set about preparing to forestall any action on the part of the Germans. Already in their self-imposed task of securing Britain's rights in the Niger they had used up all the profits of their trade, but they had no thought of shrinking from the work. To have the Germans in the Niger would mean irreparable ruin to legitimate commerce, and the flooding of the whole land with the styx- like flood of gin which would inevitably flow in a devastating flood from Hamburg. At this supreme moment it became necessary once for all to secure the Niger basin to Britain. The Company did the writer of these lines the honour of inviting him to take up the task. Accordingly, in February 1885, I found myself once more steaming towards the tropics, while as yet my friends for the most part imagined me recruiting in the Mediterranean from the effects of my recent expedition to Masai-land.

CHAPTER XXXI.
THE ROYAL NIGER COMPANY—(Continued).

On the 16th March 1885 we entered the Nun mouth of the River Niger.

Heavy leaden clouds hung overhead, from which rain fell in a steady downpour, and lightning flashed at rapid intervals. From time to time thunder crashed deafeningly about us, or more distantly blended with the monotonous impressive roar of the Atlantic breakers. A steaming atmosphere threw its depressing shroud over the scene, suggesting fever germs, and all manner of liver and stomachic complaints. On all sides stretched a discoloured reach of water, reflecting the leaden tints overhead, and running into the mist-veiled mangrove that ringed the horizon.

As we stood on the deck of the S.S. *Apobo*, under a dripping awning, we could not but be infected by the melancholy of the scene, and might doubtless have exclaimed in Roman heroics, "We who come to die salute thee," but that we had to pack our traps and prepare for landing.

A few more miles of steaming into this "white man's grave," and our thoughts were diverted from the melancholy of our immediate prospect by a new and more interesting feature. There ahead of us, on the left, where creek and mangrove met, a leviathian-like object stretched its weird length far into the water, and laved its hundred limbs in the placid depths. This was the iron pier of Akassa, the then chief trading centre and depôt of the National African Company.

Soon we were enabled to distinguish the beach strewn with the relics of the ships and barges of other days, and with the boats and canoes still in use. Higher up lay piles of stores and palm-oil casks, while behind rose a series of roomy warehouses built of corrugated iron. Further seaward stood the quarters of the Company's agents—the whole cosily ensconced in the arms of the mangrove forest, which in the distance looked fascinating, but on closer acquaintance proved to be a fever-breeding quagmire.

Such was Akassa, where throbbed with undying energy the busy current of British commercial life.

With our arrival in the river my days of ease were over, and prompt action and stern work became the order of the day. No one knew where Flegel was, or where he might turn up. With his minute knowledge of the river, he was a rival not to be despised. It behoved me, therefore, to waste no time, and accordingly, having collected such stores as were necessary, I started on my voyage in the steam launch *Français* two days after reaching Akassa.

For the first hour we steamed up the rapidly narrowing creek till we found ourselves confronted by a dense barrier of mangrove. For an instant we seemed to be insanely heading to wreck and disaster, when all at once the wall of vegetation presented a narrow opening, and we were engulfed in its leafy depths. Could this be the Niger—the mighty river which drained the quarter of a continent—only a stream thirty yards in breadth, and some five in depth, lazily flowing seaward? That stream was formed of Niger water, but it was not the Niger.

Up this insignificant winding waterway our course now lay. First there was mangrove and nothing else simulating the appearance of dry land, alternately exposed as pestilential mud or covered by water, according to the state of the tide. After a time land appeared on the level of the highest tides—the swamp vegetation began to exhibit a less vigorous growth, and was intermingled with other trees and bushes. Each mile made the transformation more marked. The land rose higher and higher; the mangrove trees grew more stunted and fewer in number; terrene plants took their place, and grew in size, in beauty, and in majesty, till the ideal tropical forest spread its romantic depths before our admiring eyes.

Coincidently other developments of the panorama were taking place. The river gathered together its various branches and increased in breadth and depth, till in its full majestic unity it sunned its broad bosom in the tropic glare—a magnificent stream from a mile to a mile and a half broad.

With the gathering together of the various branches and the improvement in the physical conditions, evidences of human occupation began to show themselves.

For the first eight hours not the faintest trace of man had been discernible. Then appeared a deserted fishing weir, next an old plantation, by-and-by a new clearing, and immediately after a canoe propelled by two women, which was seen creeping slowly along under the river's banks.

At last, towards sunset, a couple of villages were sighted, and thenceforward man proclaimed his sway over the land, giving animation to the scene, with now and then a picturesque effect.

As we continued our course our eyes were greeted by the sight of much that Lander and his successors had only dreamed of as the possible to be. Already trade had laid a prosaic hand on the great highway of Tale and Travel—the river sacred to romance, whose "golden sands," by the alchemy of its touch, are now transmuted to a golden freight of palm oil.

The surging screws, the puff of steam and clang of machinery, break the impressive stillness of the forest, and fill the tropic air with their unhallowed echoes, driving the hippo from his favourite pool, the crocodile from the yellow sand-bank. Amid such sounds, the shrill scream of the parrot, and the indignant chatter of the monkey, strike upon the ear with a strange sense of incongruity.

Here and there the graceless front of a trading station, with its whitewashed corrugated iron walls and roof of European design, glares forth unblushingly from its bosky niche of palm and silk cotton tree. Thence issues the matter of fact trader—no longer in the picturesque disarray of the "palm oil ruffian," but resplendent in the dazzling glory of a well-starched shirt and snow white duck trousers—who strolls down to the landing-place through a garden aglow with sunflowers and walks shaded by a canopy of trailing vines and other creepers.

TRADERS' HOUSE, ABUTSHI.

The natives around the station share in the unromantic changes. They still carry about with them an air of picturesque sansculottic barbarity, but jarring elements have been superadded. The negro has degenerated into that hybrid creature the "nigger," bids you "good morning" as he asks for a pipe of tobacco or a nip of gin, or calls your attention to his lawn-tennis hat—the latest fashion, and almost his sole dress.

The only circumstance which serves to maintain an air of romance about him is the knowledge we possess that he still loves his neighbour to the extent of becoming at times literally one flesh with him.

Everywhere there is evidence that the trader is in possession. The missionary has accompanied him, eager in the cause of Christ and humanity. Not unfrequently the sweet tones of the church bell may be heard ringing silver clear from the cathedral gloom of the forest. They call, alas! to those who will not hear, though doubtless to the yearning ear of faith those sweetly solemn sounds shape themselves into a prophecy of the coming good destined to re-echo some day through every forest depth and wide waste of jungle.

Meanwhile, whatever be the future of Christianity in these lands, one thing becomes abundantly clear to us as we continue our ascent of the river, namely, that it is not the only religious force which is penetrating the sodden mass of Niger heathenism. Islam, with untiring missionary enterprise, has entered the field and thrown down the gauntlet to the older religion for the possession of the natives. Unhappily so far, as compared with the advancing tide of Mohammedanism, the progress of the Christian faith is practically at a standstill. Half way between the Delta and Lokoja the pioneer Moslem outposts are found wielding a marked and yearly increasing influence on the ideas and habits of the natives. With each mile nearer the Sudan that influence becomes more and more discernible, till before we have reached the confines of Gandu we have altogether left behind the congenial trinity—fetishism, cannibalism, and the gin bottle—and find the erewhile unwashed barbarian in a measure clothed and in his right mind, instinct with religious activity and enthusiasm, and wonderfully far advanced in the arts and industries. Here it is clear that we are in the presence of no assumed veneer, no mere formality, no extraneous influences to bolster up a savage people to the semblance of higher things, but face to face with a force which has taken deep root in the lives of the inhabitants and altogether transformed them.

On nearing Lokoja we bade adieu to the reeking plains and dense forest region, and entered a picturesque section of lofty table-topped and peaked mountains, delighting the eye by their varied shape and rugged aspect—here stern and threatening with bare precipices; there basking under the tropic sun in smiling slopes, beautified and shaded by groups of trees; at other places swelling upwards and towering into fantastic peaks. But however delightful to us as passengers and spectators, this part of the journey was anything but pleasant to our skipper, whose whole thoughts were absorbed by the hidden rocks in the river-bed and the fierce currents which swirled around them.

The passage, however, was safely accomplished on the evening of the 25th, and we anchored off Lokoja just as the last glints of sunshine passed from the hill-tops, and gave place to the sepia shades of evening.

In continuing our journey it now behoved us to proceed with more circumspection. We had reached the southern confines of Gandu, the western half of the great Fillani (Fulah) Empire. At this time Maliké, Emir of Nupé, held a complete monopoly of the trade between the Company and the rest of Gandu. We were only too well aware that any attempt to break through this monopoly would be strenuously resisted by him, and that therefore if he scented the object of our expedition to his liege lord at Gandu, we might bid adieu to all hopes of advancing inland. As our presence could not be kept secret from him, we thought it well to send him a letter merely to intimate that we were passing.

On the 28th we left Lokoja and pushed on to Rabba, at work now in dead earnest, making up loads in the small hold of the launch, where we were nearly roasted alive. At various stations porters were shipped secretly and stowed away in barges, everything being made ready for a surprise-march the moment we landed.

On the 8th April we reached Rabba, from which our land march was to commence. Maliké was still expecting a visit from us at Bida, when we were actually landing a hundred miles to the west with a hundred and twenty men, two educated negro traders, one Arab interpreter, and two Europeans besides myself. So completely had all our plans been laid that we started on the following day, leaving the chiefs and headmen dumfounded and perplexed, not knowing what to do without instructions from the capital.

Our first feelings of joy on leaving Rabba behind were speedily damped when one of my European companions got his leg broken, and had to be promptly returned to the launch. Soon a shoal of troubles and worries descended on us. The headmen of the various districts began to throw every possible obstacle in our way, refusing us guides, porters, and food. The men, unaccustomed to scanty fare and the steady grind of a caravan march, mutinied, and tried to force us to turn back. They threatened to murder us, and more than once presented their rifles at us by way of intimidation. One man tried to stab me, and was only secured after a terrific struggle, the porters passively looking on. Yet it was a matter of life and death to us that we should press forward in spite of all opposition—a few days might mean ruin to the expedition, by giving the emir's messenger time to come up with us. The thought inspiredus to redouble our exertions. We fought like men at bay, though we were but two against a hundred and twenty; and happily by dint of machiavellian strategy and diplomacy, with not a little determined flourishing of revolvers, we came out of the battle triumphant—safe beyond the clutches of Maliké, and complete masters of the situation.

HAUSSA HUT.

It is quite beyond the scope of this chapter to tell how we continued our way through Nupé to Kontakora, and thence by way of Yauri, the Niger, and Gulbi-n-Gindi to Jega, Sokoto, and Wurnu, where the Sultan of Sokoto had established his court.

Here we were in a region teeming with varied interest, having reached the religious, political, and commercial centre of the Western and Central Sudan. We could hardly believe our senses, and realise that we were in the heart of Africa, among a people popularly called negroes. Rather did it seem to us as if, worn out by the tiresome miles and the monotonous jogging of our horses, we had fallen asleep, and in a dream imagined ourselves in some part of Moorish Africa. A blazing sun beat down with terrific effect upon a parched land, in which here and there appeared green oases of acacia, baobab and *doum* palm, in which nestled villages and towns half hid by the grateful shadow of the foliage.

On all hands, as we pushed along, we were reminded of Mohammedan customs, of eastern amplitude of dress, if not of gorgeousness of colour. Everything bore the impress of Moorish ideas and North African civilisation. In the early dewy mornings, in the sultry heats of noontide, at the close of the tropic day, we could hear the sacred call to prayer. By the wayside, far from mosque and town, were to be seen spots marked off by stones, which with silent eloquence invited the dusty and footsore traveller to stay his weary march and wean his thoughts for a moment from his worldly affairs.

The types of men, the fashions in dress, were of the most varied character.

Specially interesting were those mysterious people the Fillani, or Fulah, numbers of whom passed us from time to time. Simple herdsmen, semi-nomadic in habit, and semi-serfs in position at the beginning of this century— warriors and Mohammedan propagandists a few years later—they are now the rulers of a hundred races between the Atlantic and Bornu. Portentously picturesque, with their voluminous garments, their massive turbans, and *litham*-veiled faces, they pranced along on gorgeously caparisoned horses with the dignified bearing of the Moor.

PORTRAIT OF THE SULTAN OF SOKOTO'S BROTHER.

More numerous were the Haussa, the most intelligent and industrious of black races.

Very different from this interesting people were the Tuareg visitors from the plateau lands of Asben, who stalked past us in artistically ragged dresses, with eyes which seemed to glow in the shadow of their face cloth and overhanging turban with the fiercest of human passions.

On the 24th May the goal of our expedition was reached, and the object of our mission attained a very few days after. No time was then lost in proceeding to Gandu, where similar success met our efforts; and then with treaties written in Arabic, sealed with the seals of the two Sultans, and signed by their respective wazirs, practically placing their two empires under a British Protectorate, and giving all commercial privileges to the National African Company, we commenced, with no small elation, our return home.

The one unpleasant occurrence which marked our journey coastwards was the stealing of my journals and personal effects, though happily the precious treaties remained safe. Rabba was duly reached, and thence we continued our way down the river in canoes to Lokoja. On the way the German expedition, which had meanwhile been set afoot with a view to forestalling other nations in the regions we had just quitted, was met moving up the river, all unconscious of the fact that not a yard of ground from Timbuktu to Akassa, or from Bornu to Yoruba, had been left on which to plant the flag of the Fatherland.

Within seven months after leaving Liverpool I was back home again, my work successfully accomplished in a much shorter time than at the outset I had dared to hope.

Next year our Government, now awake to the errors of the past, and recognising the incontestable claims and magnificent patriotic enterprise of the National African Company, granted it a Royal Charter, and the right to the title of Royal Niger Company, which it now bears.

The Right Honourable Lord Aberdare was its first Governor, and Sir George Goldie—to whose diplomatic genius and untiring industry this country as well as the Company owes so much—was the Deputy-Chairman. Around these gathered as counsellors and advisers many who had been among the pioneers of British trade and influence on the Niger, and had assisted in preparing the way for the magnificent national undertaking they have lived to see inaugurated. Among these are the Messrs. Miller, Mr. Edgar, and Mr. Croft, whose names cannot but find an honourable place in the annals of the Company.

Of the career, bright with promise, upon which the Company has thus entered, it is unnecessary to speak at length. Already good results are flowing from the new administration. The gin traffic has been taken in hand, suppressed where possible, and restricted elsewhere by enormous duties. Arms and gunpowder are also no longer sold wholesale to the savage natives. The resources of the country are being tested and developed as they never were before, and with the most gratifying results.

HAUSSA VILLAGE.

In closing this record of Niger exploration we cannot do better than quote the prophetic words of M'Queen—applicable still, though later than they might have been in approaching fulfilment. He it was who first conclusively demonstrated the course and termination of the great river. His was the first warning of the certainty of the French advance; his the clear vision which foresaw the necessity of a Chartered Company. Let him, then, speak for the future, foretelling what is to come, as he foretold what is now past, in the concluding words of his Commercial Survey of the Region.

"I have thus, though feebly, I confess, in comparison to the magnitude of the subject brought forward, completed the object which I had in view, namely, to call the attention of the British Government, and the power and energies of our people, to an honour of the first rank, and at the same time endeavoured to rouse the resource and enterprise of our merchants to engage in a trade of the first magnitude. By means of the Niger and its tributary streams, it is quite evident that the whole trade of Central Africa may be rendered exclusively and permanently our own.... To support and carry into execution the measures necessary to accomplish this undertaking is worthy of the ministry of Great Britain, and worthy of the first country of the world. It will confer immortal honour on our native land, lasting glory on the name and reign of George the Fourth, bring immense and permanent advantages to Britain, and bestow incalculable blessings and benefits on Africa. Agriculture, manufactures, and commerce, learning and religion, will spread rapidly and widely over a country abounding in the richest productions whether on the surface of the earth or below it, but at present a country overspread with the most abject servitude, and sunk in the deepest ignorance, superstition, and barbarity. Every obstacle will vanish before judicious and patient exertions. The glory of our Creator, the good of mankind, the prosperity of our country, the interest of the present and the welfare of future generations—glory, honour, interest call us, and united point out the sure path to gain the important end. Let but the noble Union Ensign wave over and be planted by the stream of the mighty Niger, and the deepest wounds of Africa are healed."

INDEX.

Adamawa, 13.

Africa, early exploration of, 2, 16.

—— English in, 24, 26, 29, 46-245, 255, 257, 265, 276, 289, 299, 308, 293-332.

—— French in, 29, 291, 302-306, 313.

—— Germans in, 317.

—— Portuguese in, 20.

African Association, the, 31, 41, 45, 176, 178, 184.

—— Company, the, 28.

Agades, 17.

Ahmed Baba of Timbuktu, 11.

Akassa, 320.

Ali of Bornu, 13.

—— of Ludamar, 83, 93.

Amadi Fatuma, Park's guide, 233, 237, 238, 239, 243.

Anderson, Dr. Alexander, Park's brother-in-law, 194, 214, 217, 222, 232.

Arabs, 7, 16, 272.

Arab conquests, 6.

—— explorers, 16.

—— historians, 16.

Armour, Sudanese, 270.

Askia, 10.

—— Ishak, 11.

Badagry, 278, 281, 283.

Bady, 203.

Bafing R., 151, 210, 213.

Baikie, Dr., 299, 308.

Bakhoy or Furkomo, 215.

Bambaku, 202.

Bambarra, district of, 72, 76, 105, 226.

—— king of, 108.

Bambuk, 29, 34.

Bammaku, 128, 226.

Bangassi, 220.

Banks, Sir Joseph, 41, 45, 184, 194.

Barth, 8-12, 239, 297.

—— quoted, 9, 10, 12.

Bathurst, 46.

Bawa, king of Haussa, 250.

Beecroft, Governor, 296.

Bees, caravan attacked by, 147, 205.

Bello, Sultan of Sokoto, 252, 275, 277.

Benaum, Moorish camp at, 82.

—— Park's reception at, 83.

Benin, Bight of, 193, 260.

Benué or Tchadda, 119, 274, 286, 295, 298, 316.

Berbers, 8, 268.

Berlin Conference, 316.

Bintingala, 154.

Birni-n-Kebbi, 119.

Birthplace of Park, 36.

Biru, 15, 113.

Bombyx or silk-cotton tree, 46.

Bondou, district of, 58, 59, 258.

Bornu, district of, 9, 12, 246, 270.

—— historians of, 13.

—— kings of, 13.

—— rise to political importance, 13.

Bridge, a primitive, 151.

Bushreens, 51.

Bussa, 240, 261, 279, 283.

Caillé, 290-292.

Campbell, Captain, expedition of, 257.

Captivity of Park. *See* Park.

Caravan, a day with, 218.

—— an early, 56.

—— Park's, 201.

—— a slave, 143-158.

Catherine, the, voyage of, 24.

Chad, Lake, 9, 193, 269.

Chandos, Duke of, 28.

Charlestown, the, 161.

Charms, 127.

Charter for Royal Niger Company, 330.

Chivalry, Pagan, an example of, 152.

Christianity in Africa, 6, 161, 323.

Clapperton, Lieutenant, 265-275.

Commerce, articles of, 160, 308, 309.

—— on the Gambia, 48.

—— on the Niger, 309.

Companies, chartered, 262, 314.

—— commercial, enterprise of, 294-332.

Company, the African, 28.

Congo River, the, 192, 256.

—— cataracts of, 256.

Conversion, a Mohammedan mode of, 70.

Counti Mamadi, 113, 123.

Cowries, <u>111</u>, <u>231</u>.

Customs, Negro, <u>56</u>, <u>58</u>, <u>77</u>.

Daisy, king of Kaarta, <u>89</u>, <u>94</u>.

Dalli, <u>81</u>.

De Barros, <u>21</u>.

Debo (Dibbie) Lake, <u>118</u>.

Demba, Park's servant, <u>54</u>, <u>68</u>, <u>79</u>, <u>80</u>, <u>82</u>, <u>89</u>, <u>92</u>, <u>159</u>.

Denham, Major, <u>265</u>, <u>273</u>.

Dibalami Dunama Selmami, king of Bornu, <u>13</u>.

Dina, <u>79</u>, <u>82</u>.

Discovery. *See* <u>Exploration, African</u>.

Dunama ben Humé, king of Bornu, <u>12</u>.

Duté, <u>113</u>.

East India Company, <u>42</u>.

Ebn Batuta, <u>16</u>.

—— Khaldun, <u>8</u>, <u>16</u>.

—— Said, <u>13</u>, <u>16</u>.

Edris Alawoma, <u>13</u>.

—— king of Bornu, <u>13</u>.

Education, Mohammedan, <u>141</u>, <u>249</u>.

Edwards, Mr. Bryan, <u>165</u>, <u>166</u>, <u>171</u>.

Effects of European intercourse, <u>50</u>.

Egga, <u>284</u>, <u>296</u>.

Egypt, <u>15</u>.

El Bekri, <u>16</u>.

—— Edrisi, <u>16</u>.

Endeavour, the, voyage of, <u>46</u>.

English. *See* <u>Africa, English in</u>.

Explorers. *See* <u>Exploration</u>.

Exploration, African, under—
  The Nasamones, 4.
  Ebn Batuta, 16.
  Leo Africanus, 16.
  Gilianez, 21.
  Nuno Tristan, 21.
  Fernandez, 21.
  Lancelot, 21.
  Richard Thompson, 24.
  Richard Jobson, 26.
  Bartholomew Stibbs, 29.
  Ledyard, 32.
  Lucas, 32.
  Horneman, 33.
  Houghton, 33.
  Park, 46-242.
  Tuckey, 255.
  Peddie, 257.
  Campbell, 257.
  Gray, 258.
  Denham and Clapperton, 265-275.
  Clapperton and Lander, 276-281.
  The Brothers Lander, 282-287.
  Laing, 288-290.
  Caillé, 290-292.
  Barth, 297.
  Baikie, 308.
  Commercial companies, 294-332.

Factories, 48.

Falemé River, 34, 61, 154, 208, 210.

Falika, 59, 60.

Family, the, of Park, 177.

Fatticonda, 60, 62.

Fernandez, 21.

Fetters of slaves, 140.

Fevers, African, and Europeans, 208-211, 212, 214, 219, 256.

Flegel, 317.

Formosa River, 255.

Fortifications, Negro, 216.

Foulshiels, 37, 169, 187.

French. *See* Africa, French in.

—— African Companies, 29, 313.

Fulahs, Fulatah, or Fillani, the, 14, 59, 246-253, 328.

—— characteristics of, 248.

—— conquest of Sudan by, 251.

—— history of, 248.

—— nomadic habits, 248.

—— pastoral life, 248.

Fulahdu, 248.

Fuludu Mountains, 73.

Furkomo River. *See* Bakhoy.

Futa Jallon, district of, 291.

—— Larra, 70.

—— Torra, 152.

Gallieni, Captain, 304-306.

Gambia, commerce on, 48.

—— exploration of, 21, 24, 26, 29, 157, 158, 198, 203.

Gandu, 119, 253, 329.

Ghana or Ghanata, 8, 10, 17, 192.

Gilianez, 21.

Gin trade, the, 50, 161, 167, 249.

Gober, 17, 250.

Gogo, 12, 16.

Gold, 29.

Goree, 161, 178, 196.

Government, British, the, and the Niger, 296, 299, 301.

Gray, Captain, expedition of, 258.

Guinea, Gulf of, 255.

Gulbi-n-Gindi River, 239, 327.

Gum, 29.

Gurma, 237.

Hadj Mohammed Askia, 10.

Hanno, expedition of, 2.

Haussa States, 119, 193, 239, 246.

Hawkins, 23.

Heat, tropic, 230.

Herodotus, 3, 4.

Hibbert, Mr. George, 168.

Historians, African, 3, 8, 11, 13, 16, 21.

Horneman, 32, 178.

Hospitality, Negro, 68, 109.

Houghton, Major, 33.

Ibo, the, 286.

Inauguration of modern exploration, 31.

Intercourse, European, effects of, 50.

Isaaco, Park's guide, 200, 203, 215, 226, 233, 237, 243.

—— attacked by a crocodile, 215.

Islam. *See* Mohammedanism.

Jalonka Wilderness, the, 137, 145-151.

Jarra or Yarra, 75, 77, 91.

Jenné or Jinni, 12, 119, 237, 291.

Jillifri, 46.

Jinbala, Island of, 119, 237.

Joag, 65.

Jobson, Richard, 26, 157.

Johnson, Park's servant, 54, 66, 79, 89, 94, 159.

Joliba. *See* Niger.

Joloffs or Jaloffs, the, 65, 152, 249.

Jonkakonda, 46.

Journals, Park's, 236, 254.

Kaarta, district of, 72, 76.

—— capital of, 74.

—— Park's reception at, 74.

Kabara or Kabra, 16, 119, 291.

Kajaaga, district of, 65.

Kakundy, 291.

Kamalia, 137.

Kankan, 291.

Kano, 17, 193, 275, 280.

—— Clapperton and Oudney's expedition to, 274.

Karfa Taura, 137, 143, 155, 158, 159, 224.

Kashna or Katsena, 17, 191, 193, 233.

Kasson, district of, 68.

Kayi, 69, 198, 200.

Kokoro River, 145.

Kong Mountains, 129, 255.

Konkadu Mountains, 210.

Kugha, 18.

Kuka, 18, 270.

Kullo, district of, 151.

Kuranka, Highlands of, 288.

Kurusa, 291.

Kwora or Main Niger, 260.

Laidley, Dr., 34, 47, 54, 158, 159.

Laing, Major, 288.

Lancelot, 21.

Lander, Richard, 278, 280.

Ledyard, 32.

Leo Africanus, 16.

Logun, district of, 274.

Lotophagi, 77.

Lucas, 32.

Ludamar, district of, 75.

—— Park's sojourn in, 78-96.

Macgregor Laird, 293, 299, 308.

Mage, E., 303.

Makrizi, 16.

Malacotta, 152.

Mandara Mountains, 272.

Manding, district of, 134.

—— famine in, 135.

Mandingoes, 55, 160, 249.

Manga, Denham's expedition to, 273.

Mangrove swamps, 46, 256, 286.

Mansong, king of Bambarra, 108, 111, 226.

March, a desert, 267.

Market-place, an African, 230.

Martyn, Lieutenant, 196, 214, 232, 238, 242.

Medina, 33, 56, 158, 202.

Melli, kingdom of, 10, 11.

Modibu, 115, 122.

Mohammedanism. 6, 8, 51, 70, 141, 161, 246, 249, 292, 323.

—— influence of, <u>9</u>, <u>51</u>, <u>141</u>, <u>161</u>, <u>247</u>, <u>292</u>.

—— propagation of, <u>8</u>, <u>70</u>, <u>141</u>.

—— spread of, <u>6</u>, <u>249</u>, <u>323</u>.

Moorish conquests, <u>11</u>.

—— idea of beauty, <u>89</u>.

Moors, <u>78-96</u>, <u>160</u>, <u>231</u>, <u>239</u>.

Morocco, <u>11</u>, <u>12</u>, <u>15</u>, <u>16</u>.

Mortality from fever, <u>208</u>, <u>212</u>, <u>221</u>, <u>225</u>, <u>229</u>.

Mosi, <u>10</u>.

M'Queen, James, <u>17</u>, <u>258</u>, <u>314</u>.

—— quoted, 306, 310, 315, 331.

—— theory of Niger geography, 259.

—— views on commercial importance of Niger, 261.

Mulai Hamed, 11.

Mumbo Jumbo, 57.

Murzuk in Fezzan, 265.

Nasamones, the, expedition of, 4.

National African Co. *See* United African Co.

Necho, expedition, of 2.

Negro, the, and European intercourse, 50.

Nereko River, 61, 158, 203.

New South Wales, Park's proposed mission to, 177.

Niger or Joliba, the, 106, 128, 145, 224, 226, 228, 232.

—— ancient knowledge of, 3.

—— commercial development under—
   Macgregor Laird, 294, 299, 308, 309.
   Oldfield and Lander, 293, 295.
   Beecroft, 295.
   British Government, 296, 299.
   The French, 302-306, 312.
   The Germans, 317.
   The Royal Niger Co., 307-332.

—— course of, 118, 254, 283, 291.

—— delta of, 255, 286, 293.

—— exploration of. *See* Exploration, African.

—— importance of, to Britain. *See* M'Queen.

—— Park reaches, 106.

—— source of, 288.

—— supposed identity with Congo, 192, 255, 260.

—— —— Nile, 4, 260.

—— —— termination in interior, 192.

—— termination of, 192, 193, 233, 235, 254, 261, 264-287.

Nile, 4, 17, 260.

Nun River, 293, 319.

Nunez River, 257, 291.

Nupé, kingdom of, 191, 193, 280, 284, 327.

Othman dan Fodiyo, 246-252.

—— conquest of Sudan by, 251.

Oudney, Dr., 265, 275.

Overweg, 298.

Park, Mungo, early life, 36-43.

—— choice of a profession, 40.

—— religious convictions, 43.

—— voyage to Sumatra, 44.

—— connection with African Association, 45.

—— first African expedition, 46.

—— views on the slave trade, 49, 168.

—— captivity among the Moors, 85.

—— his escape, 90.

—— reaches the Niger, 106.

—— journey to Silla, 107.

—— return to coast, 122.

—— fever at Kamalia, 137.

—— reaches the Gambia, 158.

—— sails for England, 161.

—— reception in England, 165.

—— publication of journals, 166, 171.

—— marriage, 175.

—— proposed mission to New South Wales, 179.

—— practises medicine in Peebles, 180.

—— second journey, 196.

—— proposed route, 191, 195.

—— preparations, 186-195.

—— voyage down Niger, 235.

—— death, 242, 279.

—— family of, 244.

Park. Thomas, son of the explorer, 244.

Peddie, Major, 257.

Peebles, Park's life in, 180-184.

Pisania, 47, 200.

Pliny, 3.

Portuguese. *See* Africa, Portuguese in.

Products, African commercial, 160.

Protectorate British, proclamation of, 316, 329.

Ptolemy, 3.

Quintin, Dr., 303.

Rabba, 295.

Railway between Senegal and Bammaku, 305.

Rapids, 241, 256.

Reception, a Sudanese, 270.

Relics of Park, 243.

Rennell, Major, 165, 192.

Rennell's Mountains, 284.

Rey, Rio del, 255.

Rhamadan, the month of fasting, 86, 141.

Richard, M., and the Niger termination, 254.

Richardson, 297, 298.

Robbers, Park among, 130, 203, 216, 218.

Royal Niger Company, 307-332.

—— prospects of Niger basin under, 330.

Ruskin's charges against Park, 181.

Sahara, 11, 15, 33, 265, 267, 289, 292.

Samaku River, 208.

Sansandig, 113, 123, 229, 230, 237, 243.

Saphias. See Charms.

Scenery, African, 27, 46, 55, 65, 69, 203, 210, 213, 240, 272, 283, 320, 321.

School, a Mohammedan, 141.

Scott, Mr. George, 194, 214.

—— Sir Walter's, friendship with Park, 187.

"Scramble for Africa," the, 316.

Sego, 106, 107, 226.

—— Park's reception at, 108.

Senegal, the, 21, 29, 69, 145.

—— exploration of, 29.

—— the French on, 302.

Senegambia, 9, 21.

Serawulies, the, 65, 155.

Shari River, 274.

Shea butter, 112.

Sibidulu, 129, 134.

Sieur Brue, 29, 69.

—— Denham and Toole's expedition to, 274.

Silla, 117, 237.

Slave caravan, departure of a, 144.

—— raid, a, 272.

—— route, horrors of, 49, 143-153.

—— ship, a, 162.

—— trade, <u>23</u>, <u>48</u>, <u>147-149</u>, <u>155</u>, <u>156</u>.

—— Park's views on, <u>49</u>, <u>168</u>, <u>174</u>.

Slaves, how obtained, <u>136</u>, <u>140</u>.

Sokoto, <u>10</u>, <u>253</u>, <u>275</u>, <u>327</u>.

Sonakies, <u>51</u>.

Song of the Negro women, <u>110</u>.

Songhay, kingdom of, <u>9</u>, <u>10</u>, <u>246</u>, <u>299</u>.

—— kings of, <u>10</u>.

—— historians of, <u>11</u>.

Stibbs, Bartholomew, <u>29</u>.

St. Joseph, Fort, <u>29</u>, <u>69</u>.

St. Louis, Fort, <u>29</u>.

Strabo, <u>3</u>.

Sudan, the, <u>8</u>, <u>14</u>, <u>269</u>.

—— Christianity in, <u>6</u>.

—— Denham's expedition to, <u>266</u>.

—— early exploration of, <u>2</u>.

—— early trade with, <u>15</u>.

—— Fulah conquest of, <u>251</u>.

—— historians of, <u>3</u>, <u>8</u>, <u>11</u>, <u>13</u>, <u>16</u>.

—— Mohammedan conquest of, <u>6</u>, <u>9</u>, <u>246</u>, <u>254</u>.

—— Moorish conquest of, <u>11</u>.

Superstitions, Negro, <u>56</u>, <u>58</u>, <u>68</u>, <u>73</u>, <u>121</u>, <u>202</u>, <u>205</u>, <u>231</u>.

Tambaura Mountains, <u>211</u>.

Tchadda. *See* <u>Benué</u>.

Tenda, <u>29</u>, <u>203</u>.

—— wilderness, <u>157</u>, <u>204</u>.

Thompson, Richard, <u>24</u>.

Thomson, Joseph, <u>318-329</u>.

Tibbu tribes, 267.

Timbuktu, 8, 15, 16, 48, 119, 237, 288, 291.

—— first entered by a European, 289.

Tombaconda or Tombakunda, 157.

Toole, 274.

Treaties, commercial, with Sokoto and Gandu, 329.

Tripoli, 13, 15, 265, 275, 289.

Tuaregs, 15, 237, 239, 289, 328.

Tuckey, Captain, on the Congo, 255.

Twat or Tuat, oasis of, 10, 12, 16, 289.

United African Company, the, 312, 315, 316, 317.

Voyage of the *Catherine*, 24.

—— *Endeavour*, 46.

—— *Joliba*, 235.

Wadan, 13.

Walata, 15, 16.

Wali, district of, 33, 56, 158, 202.

Wangara, 191, 192, 254.

Wawra, 105.

Wonda, 135.

—— River, 146.

Wuladu, 213, 217.

Wuli, district of, 33, 56, 158, 202.

Wulima River, 222.

Wurnu, 327.

Yakoba, 280.

Yamina, 126, 228.

Yarra. *See* Jarra.

Yauri River, <u>240</u>, <u>327</u>.

Yeou River, <u>270</u>.

Yoruba, <u>279</u>.

Zeghaza, <u>12</u>.

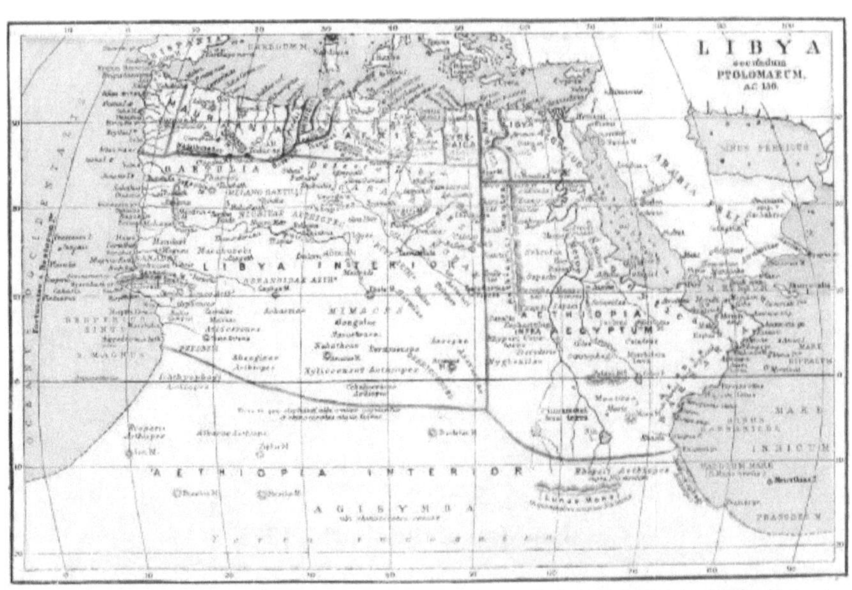

EDRISI'S AFRICA 1154

Catalan Map of the World, 1375.

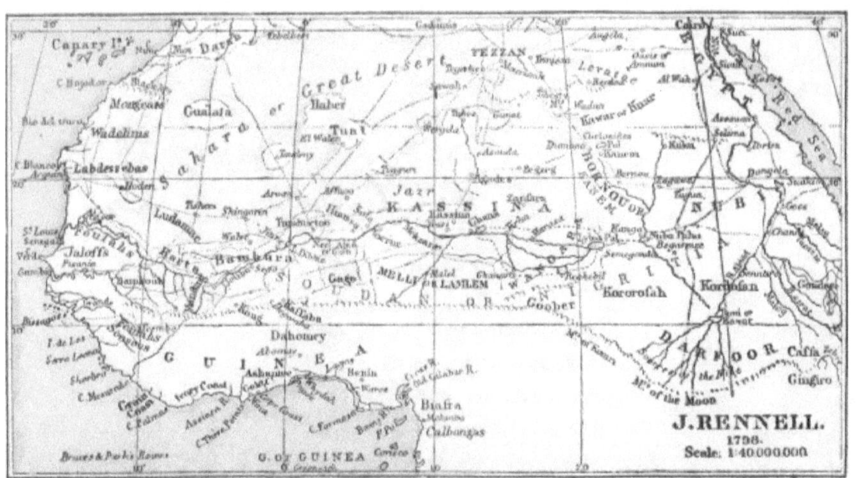

FOOTNOTES:

[1] Barth's Travels, vols. ii. and iv., Appendices V. and IX.

[2] Barth's Travels, vol. iv. p. 415.

[3] Barth's Travels, vol. iv., Appendix IX., p. 624.

[4] A Geographical and Commercial View of Northern and Central Africa.

[5] The following is the Duchess of Devonshire's version of the above incident:—

"The loud wind roared, the rain fell fast,
The white man yielded to the blast;
He sat him down beneath a tree,
For weary, sad, and faint was he,
And ah, no wife, no mother's care
For him the milk or corn prepare.

CHORUS.

The white man shall our pity share;
Alas, no wife or mother's care
For him the milk or corn prepare.
The storm is o'er, the tempest past,
And mercy's voice has hushed the blast,
The wind is heard in whispers low,
The white man far away must go,
But ever in his heart must bear
Remembrance of the negro's care.

CHORUS.

Go, white man, go—but with thee bear
The negro's wish, the negro's prayer,
Remembrance of the negro's care."